FINDING HYDRANGEAS

Finding Hydrangeas

TOM SMYLY

LUMINARE PRESS

WWW.LUMINAREPRESS.COM

Finding Hydrangeas
Copyright © 2021 by Tom Smyly

This is mostly a work of fiction, but like a lot of fiction, it contains the
experiences of the author. That being said, any similarities of persons or
events, past or present, is probably coincidental.

Printed in the United States of America

Luminare Press
442 Charnelton St.
Eugene, OR 97401
www.luminarepress.com

LCCN: 2021922523
ISBN: 978-1-64388-852-1

For Jennifer.
Who always knew that I could.

For Janet.
Who I could not have done it without.

Throughout history the hydrangea has held a place of significance, especially in Japan, where it's believed the flower originated. According to Japanese legend, the hydrangea became associated with heartfelt emotion and gratitude. The flower is often identified with apology.

The name hydrangea comes from the Greek words hydros, meaning water, and angos, meaning jar. This is fitting because these plants need a lot of water. However, one must be careful, for over watering can kill them.

In many cultures, hydrangeas represent gratitude, grace and beauty. They also radiate abundance because of the lavish number of flowers and their often large round shape. Their colors symbolize love, harmony, peace and gratitude.

The hydrangea can teach us that where we grow matters, as their colors will change - pink, blue, purple, white - depending on the acidity of the soil in which they grow.

"The burden of regret is that, unless we come to understand the value of the choices we made in the past, we may fail to see the gifts they have brought us.

The blessing of regret is clear—it brings us, if we are willing to face it head on, to the point of being present to this new time of life in an entirely new way. It urges us on to continue becoming."

JOAN CHITTISTER, *The Gift of Years*

OCTOBER 22

DEATH RUNS DEEP IN MY FAMILY.

My mother could never say the word cancer without putting the word goddamn in front of it. Both of my parents lost both of their parents when I was young. So I knew these grandparents just barely. I liked them, but they seemed old, older than their years. And a little odd, if memory serves me correctly. My mom's mom, Gigi, used to send me monogrammed handkerchiefs for Christmas. And Pawpaw, my dad's dad, once sent me a cheese cutting board for my birthday. I was four. So they were a little peculiar. One died because of a heart attack, another to a stroke. But then the other two to cancer, colon and pancreatic. Goddamn cancer.

I had an uncle die in Viet Nam, Uncle Ernie. He died when his jeep rolled over when he was returning from a strip club in Saigon. Not that it should matter, but that "strip club" qualifier always seemed to follow whenever his name came up at family gatherings. "Ernie died in that horrible, unjust war that we were lied into," someone would say. And then someone else would say, "God damn Johnson." Then there would be a "God damn Nixon." And then someone else would always say, "Oh, please. He was on his way to look at naked women," or "he was going to see some boobies," or something along those lines. But Uncle Ernie's name is still on the memorial wall in Washington DC. So there's that.

I had a second cousin die in what really should be hilarious circumstances, but I guess no one really dies hilariously. Apparently he was asleep in a hide-a-bed couch when it malfunctioned and folded in upon him and he suffocated. Cousin Archie, short for Archibald, would never be able to live that down if he had, you know, actually lived. My dad never tired of telling the story of Archie, complete with snickers and snorts. Dad was a family practice doctor and death was always a little matter of fact to him. He never seemed to be able to finish the story of Archie's demise without cracking himself up so much that everyone around him would be laughing at the way he was laughing. And my mom, Anna Lee, would simply roll her eyes. "That's just bad karma, Daniel." We never had any hide-a-bed couches around my house. And I would have to say those kinds of couches give me the willies. Isn't that weird? One time while in college I stayed with a friend. He pulled out the couch, making it into a bed, but as soon as he went into his bedroom, I grabbed the blanket and pillow and spread them on the floor. I told him it was because of my bad back, but it was really because of Cousin Archie.

There was an Uncle Julius who everyone thinks died, but family members always used air quotes while saying "died." It seems that his car was found at the bottom of a cliff that protruded into the Pacific Ocean off the Oregon Coast. They never found a body, and it was generally surmised that he was washed out to sea, shark food. The insurance company eventually settled the death claim and so it was. But apparently he was in debt "up to his conniving eyeballs" it was said with more air quotes. It certainly seems that my family loves air quotes. But Uncle Julius liked the ladies and seemed to owe a lot of people a lot of money. So rumors abound.

There was a great aunt, Esther, who died when she was heating up a lava lamp on the stove, who knows why, and it ruptured and caught the house on fire. Another cousin, Steven, choked to death on a tater tot. And still another cousin, Lance, was murdered when a jealous husband caught him in bed with his wife. The jealous husband's wife, not Lance's wife Maureen. As a side note, Maureen eventually remarried Mr. Appliance, a local washing machine and refrigerator repairman, and was often featured in his TV commercials. So I guess that made her Mrs. Appliance.

Then there is my dad's cousin Jake, who according to Dad, was his best friend. He died while cross country skiing up around Jackson Hole, Wyoming when an avalanche buried him. He was only nineteen years old. So when I was born, my dad was insistent that I be named after this favorite cousin. So, Jake I am.

Of course there have been other, more normal deaths here and there, like in most families I suppose. But the circumstances have always seemed, if not exactly interesting, at least more unusual in my family. Maybe that's why I often wander around cemeteries, as I am doing now.

I think about all of the lives lived by the residents of this cemetery. Were their hopes and dreams realized? Were their lives littered with regrets? Were they missed by those they left behind? I don't worry about them haunting anyone, but I am interested in what haunts them.

I remember a teaching that I learned long ago. Death is not to be feared by those who have lived wisely. How does one know if they are living wisely? Maybe if you don't fear death.

I like older cemeteries with aged headstones, beaten and weathered by wind and rain and dirt. The one that I am in currently doesn't seem really old, at least not the centuries old graveyards that I am often drawn to. I'm not finding any markers that are particularly old. Most of the headstones lay flat into the ground, especially the more recent ones, making it easier to mow I suppose. They seem to be weathering more rapidly than the upright ones.

I'm taking a break from reading the names of the deceased, which is what I like to do when wandering around grave sites. I'm sitting, leaning against a tree, listening to my breathing, mixed in with birds chirping and the sound of kids playing soccer in the distance in a field across from the cemetery grounds. I take a few more minutes to listen to these different noises. I try and separate each of them out for just a few seconds at a time and just focus on a single sound.

Next to me is my dog, Orson, an old yellow lab and an old friend. Every once in awhile, a scent will alert his nose that something interesting is near and he will raise his head and take in these many different smells. Mostly, he seems to realize the reverence of the place where we are and acts appropriately solemn, laying with his muzzle upon his paws that are stretched out in front of him.

I'm feeling peaceful.

I am not looking for a particular name on any of these headstones, and I've been walking up one row and then coming back down another. I read each name off each headstone that I come across. I find it respectful to do so as I feel a little weird walking across their remains. I say their names aloud, an acknowledgment and apology for disturbing them. I have heard that a person dies twice. The first time is when they stop breathing. The second time is when someone speaks their name for the last time.

So I sit here, a man in his sixties, a collection of all the past experiences that have brought me to this particular spot, under a tree in a large cemetery in the rolling brown hills north of Los Angeles. Houses dot the rolling hills for as far as I can gaze. The cemetery is an oasis, a large green patch dropped upon the browned grasses of the hills that surround it.

I don't know why I'm beginning my story here. This place is more of the end than the beginning. And as I tell you my story, I'm expecting you to judge me. Perhaps harshly. No, definitely harshly. But no more harshly than I judge myself.

I'm still trying to figure this whole forgiveness thing out. It's hard to keep track of all of one's failures. My regrets seep through my skin like mud through soggy shoes. I suppose you make peace with your failings. Eventually.

You do not need to remind me of my failures. I have not forgotten them.

Previous

I GREW UP IN SOUTHERN CALIFORNIA. MY FAMILY LIVED fairly simply in a ranch style house in the San Fernando Valley. My dad, Daniel, was a family practice physician, back in the day when doctors were often in practice by themselves. My mom was mostly a stay at home mom, though she was also a registered nurse who worked two days a week for a local orthopedic surgeon. It was definitely a middle class life.

I would have to describe my father as mostly a nerd. He was quiet, a good listener, and mostly he stayed out of my business as I was growing into a teenager, a fact that later in life I grew to appreciate more and more. He worked long hours and then was on call one day a week. The pager/beeper that he wore attached to his belt loop is a memory that has never left me and the tone of it quietly droning from his belt is music from the soundtrack of my childhood. He was a gentle and kind man, who loved his wife and kids, and generally tried to be a good citizen. He was ahead of his time when it came to diet and healthy eating, and he was even a jogger, though seeing him running through the neighborhood while wearing Hush Puppy shoes and jeans was quite embarrassing. But he was oblivious to my embarrassment, and would exchange greetings with all those he met on his jogs around the neighborhood.

I always heard my father referred to as either Doctor Campton or Daniel. I never heard anyone, be they friends or family, refer to him as Dan or Danny. He was always Daniel. He had black glasses that seemed too big for his head and the button down shirts that he always wore added to the whole nerd persona.

My mother, Anna Lee, ran the house, made the meals, washed the clothes, and did the general house cleaning. She did it all in such an effortless way that she was definitely taken for granted by the rest of the family. And she did all this while working two days a week for her "pin" money, as she called it. Mom was part of the PTA, always brought treats to school events and volunteered for the many things that simply had to be done. She was a doer, not one given to relaxing, and always seemed to be busy with a project or two.

My mom would be considered a natural beauty in her day, blonde hair of medium length and blue eyed, short and limber. She eschewed make up, dabbing some on for special occasions, but mostly just letting her natural beauty come through.

I didn't think so at the time, but as I look back I would describe my parents as cute together. One thing I remember is that when mom would cook, she would always stick a spoonful of what she was making in front of dad's face and say, "Help me out, Daniel. What else does it need?" And dad would dutifully take a bite and say, "Salt." It was always salt. This is also part of the soundtrack of my childhood.

Though my parents weren't outwardly affectionate, I remember that sometimes I would see dad blow mom a kiss from across the room which she would catch and place next to her heart. Whenever I recall that image, it makes me smile. I never heard them argue. I'm sure that they did, but they didn't do it in front of their children.

Then there was my younger sister, Jenna, who was two years younger than me. We were close when we were kids, her joining me in games of cowboys and indians, imitating many of my western heroes. And I would join her in her tea parties. We grew apart in my teenage ears as she became the annoying younger sister, often showing up, trying to embarrass me in front of my friends. But we became closer as we both grew into adulthood. She was cute and thin, taking after her mother, and she was a soccer player, though the opportunities were more limited for her because of the times, what with opportunities for female athletes few and far between in the 1970s. I've thought that if she had been born in a different era she would have been a college soccer player, her competitiveness driving her. She also played tennis and was pretty good at that. And she was wicked smart. I got decent grades, but hers were always much more stellar.

We lived in a house across the street from a park, with swings and teeter totters and lots of other metal playground gear for kids to maim themselves on. It had a few basketball courts and a football/baseball/soccer field, depending on who was using it and what ball they were using. I spent many an evening shooting hoops on the basketball courts, often joined by others in the neighborhood. The clang of the basketball going through the chain nets is another sound of my youth. If I close my eyes I can still hear it.

It was at that very soccer field when I first met Otter. It was September and I was beginning 10th grade, which was the first year of high school here in Southern California. I was fifteen years old and I was determined to make the high school soccer team. I bribed Jenna with a promise to take her turn at kitchen clean up if she would come play goalie while I tried to kick the soccer ball by her. Jenna was 13 but, as I said, she was very athletic. She was also very competitive so she was good practice fodder. School had been going for a couple of days and I wanted to get in some practice. Tryouts were the next day.

While kicking the ball towards the goal, with Jenna playing goalie, I noticed a tall, skinny kid watching us from several yards away. He was nondescript, average looking, with straight blond hair that dropped down over his collar and fell across his eyes. He would constantly shake his head to flip the blond hair back. I felt that I had seen him before, and then I remembered that he was in my beginning Algebra class. I couldn't recall his name, just that he was in the class.

I had my bag of soccer balls with me and I would kick one towards the goal and my missed shots would clang against the back fence. When all the balls ended up against the fence, Jenna and I would gather them up and I would take them back onto the field and start kicking them at the goal again.

Eventually the skinny kid walked over to the back fence behind the goal and he would toss back the missed shots that clanged against the fence. This was quite helpful as now we did not need to stop and gather all the wayward shots and I nodded thanks every time he grabbed a ball and rolled it back to me. He seemed satisfied to participate in that way. This went on for several minutes, me kicking the ball towards the goal and either I scored into the net, or Jenna blocked it, or it rolled to the fence to be returned by the skinny kid with the shaggy blonde hair.

After a few more minutes, skinny kid asked if he could be goalie for awhile. Jenna said that was fine with her as she was getting pretty bored and somewhat annoyed at chasing my shots. So I started to shoot the soccer balls towards the goal as the skinny kid played goalie.

I thought I should take it easy on the new guy so the first couple of balls I kicked at half speed. He easily caught them and rolled them back to me with a sort of smirk. So I kicked it harder. And then harder still. And even though I was trying as hard as I could, I could not get any ball by him. No matter how hard I kicked or tried to curve the ball, the skinny boy either easily knocked the ball away or simply caught it and rolled it back to me. I tried kick after kick, but he returned them all. It was almost as if he knew what direction the ball was going to go before I kicked it. So it continued, me kicking, him catching, then flipping the blond hair out of his eyes before rolling the ball back.

Finally I had enough. "Wow. You're really good at this. Do you play soccer?"

"Nope." That's all he said.

I waited for more of a response, but none came. "I'm hoping to make the soccer team." Still no response. "Aren't you in my math class?"

He looked at me and started walking towards where I was standing. His gait seemed a little strange, then I realized that it was more of a shuffle, his feet barely leaving the ground between steps. He got closer, stopped and said, "I think so. Mrs. Parker's class. You sit towards the front?"

"Yeah. And you're towards the back." I waited for him to agree or say something. Silence. I then noticed his eyes, blue and almost probing in their intensity. "Well, you're a damn good goalie."

He ignored my compliment. "Is that your sister?"

"Yeah."

"Well, she sucks at goalie." Jenna didn't hear this as she had already started walking home.

"I'm Jake," I said. More silence. "You?"

"Otter." I waited for some explanation for the name, but he had already begun gathering up the stray soccer balls.

"Otter? Is that a nickname?"

"Nope." It was becoming clear that Otter wasn't much of a talker.

"Do you live close by?" Otter nodded his head at a group of duplexes across the soccer field on the other side of the fence.

"Otter is a different name."

"It's Mark Otter. But no one calls me Mark." And that was true. In all the years that I knew him, my parents were the only people I ever remember calling him Mark. Maybe a teacher or two. I think even his mother called him Otter.

"Well, anyway, thanks for the help. You should try out for the soccer team. You're really good."

Otter handed me a couple of the soccer balls which I stuffed into the ball bag. "I don't really like sports," he said. "Besides, I do martial arts after school."

I had gathered up all the balls and I prepared to walk back across the field towards my house. "Martial arts is cool," I said. Otter walked a few steps with me in the direction I was going. "Do you walk to school? Want to walk together?" I asked.

"Sure. Where do you live?"

I pointed to a house across the field. "The one with the ivy growing along the side. 7:30?"

"Yep, see you then. Don't let your meatloaf." And he peeled off and began walking towards the duplexes where he lived.

And that's how I met Mark Otter.

HURRICANE LAMP
by Mark Otter

There is a lamp that gives light,
protected light.
A light surrounded by glass,
a glass blockage
To protect it from sudden gusts of wind.
A Hurricane Lamp.

No matter how hard the wind blows,
It cannot affect the light.
The light that is protected.

I wish I had the ability
to protect myself from sudden gusts of wind.
To put myself inside the Hurricane Lamp.

But I'm just in the hurricane.

Tom Smyly

OCTOBER 6

AUTUMN EVENINGS ARE PARTICULARLY BEAUTIFUL IN Montana. I love sitting outside on my back deck, watching the sun play peek-a-boo in the Madison Mountain Range, casting long shadows along my property, making it appear later in the day than it is. I live alongside Highway 191, south of Four Corners and north of Big Sky, on the Gallatin River in southwest Montana.

My partner of over thirty years, Susan, pokes her head out the back door and implores me to come inside, that it's time for bed, and I tell her I'll be in soon. But falling asleep worries me.

The last five nights I have been having the same dream. It's the dream I would have every few months, maybe three or four times a year, but now it is occurring nightly. I lay awake in bed, afraid of sleep, afraid to dream.

In the dream, I am alone in the desert, no food, no water, no shelter. Many paths surround me, maybe seven or eight of them, trails worn into the landscape. I close my eyes, and do some kind of eeny, meeny, miney, mo and take one of the paths. I hike along it without finding food or water, for which I grow increasingly desperate, and I am totally alone. And the sun is at its hottest, beating down upon me and I'm sweating profusely. I'm thirsty. I'm hungry. I don't know where I'm going.

After hiking for what seems like miles, I arrive at an obstacle, maybe the trail ends at a mountain, or a large boulder blocks the trail, or a stream flows too rapidly to cross. Many times it's a cliff that would require me to hike down in order to continue. Sometimes I'm just too hot or too tired to go on. So instead of climbing the mountain, or climbing over the boulder, or fording the stream, or ignoring the discomfort, whatever the obstacle may be, I turn around and hike all the way back to the beginning.

When I get back to the beginning, I eeny, meeny, miney, mo and choose another trail and set off again, only to have the same set of obstacles confront me. And then it's back to the start once more. Sometimes I will take three or four paths during a dream only to end up with the same result.

After the dream I awake in a sweat, as if I had actually been exerting myself physically instead of just lying in bed. Susan often shakes me as I wake her with my tossing and turning, sometimes kicking her as I shift uncomfortably and uncontrollably under the covers. Exhaustion and a sour stomach tend to accompany the awakening. For the past several years I have been having this dream, not often, but often enough to have the threat of it nick at me every night when I go to bed. It's very specific, rarely deviating from dream to dream. The same desert, the same wagon spokes of trails leading away from me, and the same conclusion each time I take one of the trails. And I awake in a sweat, almost panting and gasping for air from the exertion. And now I've had the same dream for five nights in a row.

I eventually get up from my seat on the deck and get ready for bed. Susan is already there, reading, and I pick up a book and read in bed next to her. She quickly falls asleep and I continue reading, afraid to turn off the lights, wondering if the same trip into the desert awaits me.

Eventually I do turn off the light and stare at the dark room until I nod off. And then I see the shapes of the desert, with its red rocks and brown sagebrush. My shoes are covered with sand and the dust fills my nose, making it difficult to breathe. Ahead of me are the labyrinth of trails, going off in different directions, confusing me as I follow with my eyes each one as it winds through the desert. I still don't know which one to take, and I trudge off into what seems like an abyss, kicking up more dirt and dust as I walk along.

I hike and I hike and I hike, and eventually I come to a cliff. I look over the edge and I cannot see a way to continue hiking the trail, down the side of the mountain. So I turn around and trudge back to the beginning. But this time, as I near the starting point, I see a figure sitting on one of the red rocks. I can't quite make out who it is and I squint my eyes through the dust.

"I knew you'd be back here soon," the figure tells me as I near. And I recognize that it's Otter, and a rush of emotions run through me. Fear. Excitement. Wonder. Dread. I haven't seen Otter in over forty years.

This is a new occurrence. Otter has never appeared in these dreams. He looked like he did when we first met, long hair that often fell across his face and into his eyes, necessitating a flip of his head, something I had seen when we first met as tenth graders so long ago. In the dream I ask him why his hair is long. "Because I don't have to cut it, dumb ass," was his reply. And this night in the dream he simply said, "Dude, what's taking you so damn long? I'm waiting."

"Is it you I am supposed to see?" I sputter. "I didn't know."

"What do you mean?" Then he mocked me, repeating "I didn't know" in a cartoonish voice.

I feel embarrassed. "I'm trying. But there are things that get in the way."

Otter is exasperated. "Just walk around or climb over what's in your path. Why do you go all the way back to the start when you don't have to?" I feel shamed and tell him that it's harder than it looks. "No. You're making it hard." Then he says "Hey, I know it's not easy. But you can do this." He stands up. "Follow me." With that he is off, taking one of the trails.

I follow after him, but try as I might, I can not catch up to him, even though I holler at him, begging him to go slower and wait for me. But to no avail, he doesn't listen to my pleadings and stays far ahead. Every once in awhile, he turns and looks back towards me, motioning for me to hurry up with an impatient wave of his hand and then he starts walking again. He doesn't seem to be walking with a hurried gait, just that shuffle of his. But I cannot keep his pace.

Then all of a sudden, it was like all of the other dreams. I come upon a stream blocking the path and I freeze for a minute, looking up the trail towards Otter who is now on the other side. I contemplate turning around and going back to the start. I see Otter waiting, standing impatiently on the trail on the other side of the stream, waving at me. Then he wades through the water back towards where I am standing until he is just a few yards away. "Just walk through it, it's not deep," he says quietly, with no emotion to his voice. Then he turns and wades back across the stream and up the trail. This time, instead of turning back, I walk through the water, feeling it rush around my legs and he is right, it isn't deep. The water is cold, but refreshing, and I keep my eye on Otter the whole time. Once I cross the river, I start back on the path, walking towards Otter, seeing him in the distance, but still never able to catch him.

Soon I come to a large boulder blocking my path. Otter is waiting on top of the rock and he instructs me where to place my hands so I can more easily scale the boulder. I climb over the rock and we continue along the trail, me lagging behind and him waiting every few minutes for me to catch up.

Finally, I am getting exhausted. "Where are we going?" I holler up the trail in frustration.

Otter, far ahead, "You know where."

"I don't," I gasp, out of breath from the exertion. "I really don't." I hear panic rising in my voice. I don't know where we are or where we are going.

"Then I guess you'll find out." With that comment, he smiles and sort of chuckles. "I need you to hurry. You need to get this done." And he was off again.

All of a sudden, I awake from the dream, covered in sweat, the sheets and the pillow drenched in wet. I lie in bed shaking from the vividness of the dream.

I know that I should have done something more when I heard about Otter's death. And it should not have taken me over forty years to know that. But it did. And now Otter was telling me it was time to bear witness to his life.

So much life has gone by, meandering at times, speeding at others, and here I am forty years later wondering what I should have done, if there was something that could have been done. Was my wondering a form of anguish? Misgivings? Sorrow? Or just regret? Simple regret?

What if I had done something different, if anybody had done something different, would the result have been altered? Or are we foreordained to travel along some path, ending in a destination of circumstance, led there by unalterable choices, our own as well as others?

Have you ever reflected on the unfairness of death? When I reflect on Otter's death, and I reflect on his death often, I wonder about the unfairness of life. And I wonder not at the unfairness of dying but at the unfairness of living.

I've heard it said that destinies change from catching or missing a bus. I wonder how my life has changed by knowing Otter. And how his life was changed by knowing me. And if his path could have been my path if circumstances were different.

Everything that has a beginning has an ending. That is simply a truth. It becomes necessary to make peace with that.

I think about the Christmas movie *It's a Wonderful Life*. In it, George Bailey is shown what the world would have looked like had he never lived. He discovers how everyone he knew would have had a much different life. George's life had made a difference in that it enriched hundreds of lives.

But what if you got to see life as if you had never lived and everyone was better off? What if seeing that life without you had made life better for others?

I have been thinking about this movie frequently as of late. I'm not sure why and I have tried to find the reason for that being so.

I shared these dreams with Susan. And I also shared this longing to find meaning in these dreams. I told her of the last dream, the dream where I saw Otter at the starting point. I told her this while she was repotting some plants from starters she had lovingly raised. She would move plants around the house and the yard as she felt they needed a different view of the world at times. She would hum tunes to the plants, singing softly to them as she relocated them around our property. Things like this endeared her to me and I thought about how deeply in love with her I was.

I had talked with Susan in the past about the desire to travel to where I grew up, that I needed to try and piece some things together. This was something that I had talked about doing before, plans that I had made but never followed up on. She always listened with attention. I'm always surprised at her patience with me. As I shared the details of the latest dream with her, it was becoming clear to me that I needed to find some peace.

"What are you seeking?" she asked. She brushed a stray hair off her face, streaking her cheek with some of the potting dirt. There was no gall to her question, just a sincerity to know. There was no fake in her fire. There never had been.

"I'm not sure. Forgiveness, maybe. A reason why things turned out the way they did." I truly did not know why I felt compelled to do this. Maybe that was the reason, to find out why. I thought of Otter telling me that he guessed I would just find out. And that I needed to hurry. I need to get this done.

I began to consider what I would require for my trip, food, maps, other things I needed to get at the store. Maybe I would set out in a week or so, as soon as I got an itinerary together. My mind was racing, and I noticed that I was babbling about the minutiae of trip planning.

Susan listened quietly, attentively. And in her soft quiet way she said, "You're on a quest." She gently patted down the soil around another of her plants. "Quests can't be organized or prepared. There are no road maps. Just leave and follow your truth. You'll know where to go and more importantly, how to get there."

And I felt nothing but gratitude to the universe for allowing me to find this wonderful, spiritual person almost thirty years earlier. She loves me and supports me and mostly understands me. She encouraged me to do whatever I felt I needed to do. Susan was always an independent soul with a lovely heart, a far better heart than I deserved. We have lived together in this small cabin along the Gallatin River not far from Bozeman, where we both worked, she as a physical therapist and me as a researcher at Montana State University. It is a calm and lovely life, a life of simplicity and fulfillment. I always felt as if I knew Susan long before we met, that perhaps our bodies may have met for the first time, but that our hearts had connected somewhere before.

I went over and kissed her on the forehead and wiped the streak of dirt off her cheek. "You're right, as usual. I think I need to leave tomorrow." She smiled that crooked smile of hers.

I don't know what souls are made of, but hers and mine, they are the same.

. . .

One day a young Buddhist on his journey home came to the banks of a wide river. Staring hopelessly at the great obstacle in front of him, he pondered for hours on just how to cross such a wide barrier.

Just as he was about to give up his pursuit and discontinue his journey he saw a great teacher on the other side of the river. The young Buddhist yells over to the teacher, "Oh wise one, can you tell me how to get to the other side of this river"?

The teacher ponders for a moment, looks up and down the river and yells back, "My son, you are on the other side".

I HAD FORGOTTEN THAT OTTER AND I HAD AGREED TO walk to school together, but when I left my house the morning after meeting on the playground, there he was. So we walked to school together, a walk of about twenty minutes. We talked about our classes, which ones we liked, which ones we didn't. We had common ground around several rock bands, though his tastes ran a little louder than mine. We talked about a couple of cute girls in our classes, the quickest way to get to the lunch line, where our lockers were, and how we both didn't like the mandatory PE classes.

I told him about my dad being a family practice doctor and my mom a part time nurse. He said he lived with his dad and mom. They had just moved to Southern California three weeks earlier from North Carolina. His dad worked the swing shift at an auto parts manufacturing plant. I asked about his mom and he said she was an aide at a nursing home. No brothers. No sisters. But it was the way he said it, a way that communicated that there would not be any more information forthcoming about the subject of his family. It wasn't like he was trying to keep anything a secret, it just seemed like he was uncomfortable talking about his family.

As we walked through the neighborhoods close to the school, we came upon a house that was ringed with bushes of colorful flowers. Even though it was the beginning of September, their colors were still brilliant, and this house had several of these bushes across the front windows and they continued down the driveway and along the sidewalk. The area was filled with blues and pinks and purples. Otter was clearly interested in these flowers and he stopped and touched some of them, putting his face close to several as we made our way past the house and continued towards school.

"You really like flowers, huh?"

"Not really," Otter replied. "Just these." He continued his shuffle down the sidewalk.

"What kind of flowers are they?" I asked.

"Hydrangeas. My martial arts instructor puts some of the petals in his tea. He says it gives him peace."

I didn't know what to say to that. "Cool" was all that came out.

Otter seemed to think that I thought it might be somewhat strange to like this one particular variety of flower. "I like the thought of flowers giving peace. I think that's what flowers do."

When we got to school, we went our separate ways, but I saw him in my Algebra class and we nodded to each other. I did see him at lunch off in the distance, standing by himself, but not really seeming to be alone. It's hard to explain, he just seemed at ease.

We had not made any agreement about walking together the next morning, but he was standing at the end of the driveway when I walked out the door. So we started going to school together most mornings. I liked his company. He was funny, always making witty observations, especially about people that we saw on our walk. One time there was an old man standing in a driveway across the street, picking up his morning newspaper and Otter made up a story about how the old man had a secret camera in his newspaper, that he was actually a Russian spy. He would tell me that this poor Russian had Tourette's Syndrome.

I fell for the bait. "How do you know that?"

"Because his name is Yukanol Fukov." He would do this in a Russian accent. And then he would laugh. He had this great laugh, one that would startle those around him. Just a loud "Ha!" He liked to make people laugh. And he liked telling jokes and doing funny accents.

He was also smart. In algebra class, he never participated unless he had to, but when called upon by Mrs. Parker he was prepared and always had the correct answer. On some of our walks to school, I would ask him what answer he got on an assignment I was struggling with and he would dig out his homework which was usually wadded up inside his algebra book and we would compare answers.

After a couple of weeks of walking together, when we parted to go to our separate classes in the morning, I told him to meet me at the cafeteria for lunch, which he did. I had a few friends that I would hang out with, and Otter joined us, though he would rarely participate in the conversation. He was mostly quiet, especially in groups. Every once in awhile he would offer a remark, usually sarcastic. Or he would say something in an accent of some sort.

We started hanging out a lot together, either at school or over at my house. While at my house we liked to listen to music in my room, though my tastes were more aligned to folk, Simon and Garfunkel, John Denver, Joni Mitchell, and similar. And Otter's was more rock, more Led Zepplin, more Rolling Stones, more Allman Brothers.

We spent many afternoons listening to my poor quality record player, spinning our records and playing disc jockey. That was our big goal in life, to become disc jockeys and get on the radio. We even called the Columbia School of Broadcasting, their ads inundating us on the local AM radio stations. I called and asked to be sent, (risk free!) the information needed to enroll and start my career as a disc jockey. I was told that I was too young. So Otter called, and he used a deep voice trying to sound older, and he was told the same thing. Then Otter would call, trying different accents, Russian, Japanese, French, but they still would not send us the information that we needed to start our journey to DJ stardom. After about 10 calls we gave up. Soon we found out, to our surprise, these were long distance calls. When my parents got the phone bill and saw all the toll calls to the Columbia School of Broadcasting, well, let's just say Dad was not too pleased. I had to wash both of the family cars every weekend for a month, but Otter came over and helped out and we had fun doing that. I'm sure the car wash job wasn't the best, but it made Dad feel like he had meted out punishment, so everyone was happy. Needless to say, we weren't able to sign up for broadcasting school.

I liked sports and would sometimes watch college football on Saturday afternoons, or join friends in playing football at the park across the street. And I liked basketball. But my real love was baseball and the Los Angeles Dodgers. Many a night would find me lying in bed with my small transistor radio next to my head, straining to hear the voice of Vin Scully as he did the play by play, all the while trying to keep the volume down so as not to get the knock on the door and told to turn it off and go to sleep. I would tell Otter what had happened to the Dodgers the next day, but he was not interested in team sports. Or any sports it seemed. He did like being active and doing active stuff, but he would never join in the group games, like the football games in the park. But sometimes just he and I would go over to the park and shoot hoops. Otter wasn't very good, and would shoot awkwardly, sort of a one handed throw towards the basket. But we still had fun, playing one on one, counting down for last second shots, things like that.

We also liked to wander around the local city library, me reading books on sports and Otter reading martial arts magazines, and we would check out the high school girls that might be there at the same time. We would often sit at a table reading the latest Mad Magazine, snickering and snorting, which got us dirty looks from other library goers. Otter would keep me snickering as he would make up stories about other patrons with his over-the-top accents. This got us threatened with banishment more than once. We were connected by our similar funny bones.

As the school year progressed, we spent more and more time together, and while we often spent time at my house, we never went to his. I was never invited. Otter rarely talked about his home life, but every once in awhile he would mention his dad, and it would not be in a positive light. It sounded like his dad was strict and domineering. And even though we hung out quite a bit together, I had not met either of his parents. Otter met my family, often joining us for dinner at my house, usually after we had been hanging out listening to music and playing ping pong in the garage. My mom would ask if he would like to stay for dinner. He would then call his parents and ask if he could stay. Otter would always turn his back to the rest of us when he made that phone call and he would speak quietly when talking to his parents, almost as if he didn't want anyone to hear the conversation. Then he would say that he could stay, but that he needed to get home right after dinner.

One Sunday I asked him to meet me across the street at the soccer field and play goalie. I had made the soccer team and I wanted to practice my shots on goal. So we met that afternoon by the soccer net at the park.

Just like the first time that we met on the soccer field, when he took the place of Jenna as my practice partner, I could not get any shot past him. He moved with such ease, almost predicting where the ball would go before I even knew where I was kicking it. I can't explain it. He didn't seem very athletic, but he moved with an almost leisurely pace to get to any shot that I kicked towards him. It was like he simply glided to the ball. Soon he began to tease me a bit, a little ribbing because I could not get a kick by him no matter how I tried. This only frustrated me more and my kicks began going wild, often missing the net entirely. This meant that we had to collect the balls more often, something we were both tiring of quickly.

After gathering the balls up one more time, he came out to where I was kicking. "You try too hard," he said while placing a ball on the ground. "You think about everything but the ball. You look at me, where I am standing, where the net is, the direction of the wind, everything but the ball."

I looked at him like he had two heads. "What?" I pretty much scoffed. "What the hell does that even mean?"

Otter pointed to the ball. "Don't look at anything else. Just the ball." He backed away a couple of feet. "Now I want you to kick the ball into the upper right corner of the net."

I looked at the corner of the goal and he lightly smacked the back of my head. "Don't look at the goal, you know where that is, but look at the ball."

"I need to see where the goal is," I said with some exasperation.

"The goal doesn't move. It stays in the same place. Only the ball moves." I stared down at the ball. "Now while looking at the ball, see it going into the right corner of the net." He pointed at the ball. "See nothing else besides the ball, but see in your mind where you want it to go."

He stepped back another foot or so. "Okay, now see the ball going where you want it to go and just kick it to that spot."

I stayed focused on the ball and after a second or so, I could see in my mind the ball going exactly where I wanted it to go. I got into kicking position, approached the ball, and sent it towards the net, all without looking at anything else except the ball. After kicking it I looked up to see the ball curving into a perfect arc into the upper right corner of the net.

I was speechless for a second. "Easy peasy," Otter said. "We practice this kind of stuff in Tae Kwon Do. See what you want to do before you even try to do it." He walked over to the net. "See the target before you throw the punch." He tossed a ball towards where I stood. "Now try and get them by me."

For the next twenty minutes I kicked the ball towards the goal, guarded by Otter. Before approaching the ball, I would see it going where I wanted it to go and almost every time that's what the ball did. Otter still blocked some of the shots, but I was finally able to get several by him. It felt like such a victory.

Then something strange happened. I was feeling pretty elated and after one shot that went by a diving Otter, I ran up to him to do a little trash talking of my own. But as he stood up, he froze, his gaze going across the soccer turf and towards the fence that surrounded the field. Seeing this abrupt change in his demeanor, I stopped in front of him and turned to follow his gaze. A couple hundred yards away was a man standing on the other side of the fence. He wasn't doing anything, simply standing with his hands in his pockets. I turned back to Otter and then back to the man, who after a couple of seconds, left and walked across the street towards the duplexes where Otter said he lived. I looked back towards Otter, who simply said "I got to go," and he broke into a sprint towards where the man had been standing. I wanted to say something, ask about the man who seemed to send him into another zone, but Otter was quickly gone.

I stayed on the field for another couple of minutes, watching as Otter sprinted to the fence and instead of going further down the field to a gate, he climbed to the top of the chain link fence and jumped down to the other side. He then ran across the street and towards the duplexes where he disappeared from my view. I stayed frozen in the same spot. I was confused. I kicked another ball towards the net, but my attention and focus were no longer on soccer. I wondered what had just happened. I gathered up the soccer balls, put them back into the ball bag and headed home.

SWIMMING ALONE
Mark Otter

I step into the water along the edge of the sand.
It's moving slowly.
But I can see as I get further from the shore,
no... I can feel as I get further
from the shore,
the current picks up.

I've always been told not to swim alone.
Take a Swim Buddy.
But I have to get to the other side.
Or do I?
I fight the current.
The current fights me.
And I can't win.

There is no Swim Buddy.
Should I not swim without a Swim Buddy?
But what could he have done?
Two people getting washed away with the current.

No.
It's best to swim alone.
Limits the damage.

OCTOBER 7

AFTER TALKING WITH SUSAN, I SPEND THE REST OF THE afternoon making simple preparations for travel. I have a 2010 Toyota Tacoma pickup truck that I had out-fitted with a canopy some years earlier and I rolled out a memory foam mattress onto the bed of the truck. I packed a cooler with water and fruit and other perishables, mostly for breakfasts and snacks. I would eat the rest of my meals along the road so I wouldn't have to bother with too much cooking. Then I added a small suitcase, some toiletries, a couple of books, and some maps, trying to travel as lightly as possible.

My traveling companion would be my yellow lab, Orson, an older gentleman of a dog who is always ready for an adventure. A bin of food, a couple of rolls of poop collecting bags, a jaunty neckerchief, and a container of treats sufficed for his packing.

Orson was a kind of rescue dog, discovered by Susan while on a hike in the woods one day. She was hiking with a friend when they came upon a rancher who lived on one of the many ranches in the area. He was leading this hand-some yellow lab by a rope that was tied loosely around the dog's neck. They struck up a conversation and when Susan found out that the rancher was going to put the dog down, possibly with the rifle that he was carrying, she was aghast. Even though it was explained to her that was what was done on farms and ranches with too many animals, Susan immediately told the rancher that she would take the dog and find it a home, to which the rancher agreed and handed this friendly dog over to her. I've often wondered if this was simply how the rancher got rid of too many dogs or cats, not by shooting them, but by "happening" upon a hiker or two and telling them that story.

I had never owned a dog, we did not have one while growing up, but I have always liked them. Susan and I would have the occasional discussion about getting one. It just never seemed to materialize. So when she brought home this eight month old puppy, it was still with the intention of finding him a home.

But we, and by we I mean mostly me, fell in love. We named him Orson, after the great film maker Orson Welles, since we were studying old movies at the time, and it seemed to fit him. Soon he was my constant companion, going pretty much everywhere I went, even occasionally coming with me to my job on campus. When I did field work, he was always along, windows of my pickup rolled down, his head sticking out so his nose could take in the many smells. As cliche as it sounds, he was my best friend.

Though a Labrador Retriever through and through, he was missing some of the common traits of labs. He would often turn up his nose to certain types of food, especially if it didn't meet his qualifications, preferring specific brands of kibble with water added and a sloppy gravy made. I always imagined that if he were human, he would be wearing a cardigan sweater with leather patches on the elbows, possibly a pipe sticking out of one side of his mouth. There was an aristocratic side to this pooch, and he always seemed to carry himself with an air of dignity. He would be the perfect traveling companion.

I was pretty limited in what I could carry, space-wise. I placed all of the food, sleeping bag, flashlights, extra batteries, in the bed of the truck. As the truck had a full size cab, I put my toiletries and extra clothes in a small backpack which would go on the front passenger seat. Orson could spread out on the back seats, giving him room to stretch out. I also packed a small backpacking stove, mostly to warm water for tea or coffee and the occasional instant oatmeal. I planned to pick up what I needed daily so as to keep the supplies down given the limited space.

The last thing I packed was what Susan and I referred to as The Repository. It was an old coffee can, the kind that once housed Folgers or some other supermarket brand. The wrapper had long since been discarded and it had a rubber band around it lengthwise so the plastic lid would not come off and allow the contents to scatter. I took it out of its resting place in the corner of our bedroom closet and wedged it behind the back seat of the pickup so that it could ride upright, but also so that I could get to it easily when needed. I was ready to go.

I had not thought about The Repository for a couple of years, though I knew where it was. I handled it with reverence, closing my eyes and saying a couple of Buddhist prayers as I placed it into the truck. I had thought about obtaining a fancier holder for the contents, but that desire went away and I felt that the old coffee can was perfect. And it was.

Susan prepared a farewell dinner with vegetables collected from her mindfully cared for garden. It was the first week of October so we were getting to the last of the summer vegetables. After dinner we sat out on the deck and watched the Montana sun slowly sink behind the mountains, turning the evening cooler, and we both put on warmer sweatshirts.

We didn't say much as we sat on the deck. There wasn't much need for conversation. Orson joined us, lying sprawled out on the redwood, almost like a rug. I talked to Susan about my sort-of planned route and she simply smiled and took my hand and gave it a squeeze and assured me that all would be fine back here at the house. She arose and went inside, leaving me alone for a few minutes, and I began to have some self doubts. These were the doubts that always befriended me whenever I thought about making this trip that I had planned and replanned so many times over the years. Susan came back out with a cup of warm tea, her own blend that she had made. She seemed to sense my self doubts as she ran her hand across the back of my neck. "You've wanted to do this for awhile," she leaned down and whispered into my ear. "Now is a good time."

She had listened to me muse about this trip for years, thus she knew that when the time was right, I would go. I told her that I would probably be gone for three weeks, give or take a day, and she encouraged me to not worry about placing a time limit on my pursuit. This was her way, to live fully in the present. She encouraged me to do the same.

As we prepared for bed, we could hear a thunderstorm echoing in the distance. We crawled beneath the covers, spooning up next to each other and Susan soon fell asleep. I had a harder time finding slumber, but I was content to lay in bed next to her, thinking about the past and the upcoming journey I was embarking upon.

It was well after midnight when I saw the first lightning through the bedroom window, casting shadows
along the walls as it moved from one side of the room to
the other, lighting up the dark. The thunder came next,
several seconds later, a low rumbling sound as it rattled
around the mountains. The rain began shortly after that,
a steady pitter-patter, and then lightning flashed again,
followed even more closely by thunder, louder this time.
I imagined the heavens were giving a benediction to my
journey.

I love all of these sounds and I tried to pick each one of
them out and hear them all separately. Each sound has an
energy, something to say to me, and I longed to hear the
message in every raindrop that splashed against the roof
and window frame. And I counted my blessings along with
the raindrops.

I slid closer to Susan in the bed we shared, she seemingly unstirred by the lightning and the thunder. I watched
her breasts rise and lower with her breath, her lips slightly
parted, and I moved closer so that I could feel that gentle
breath on my face.

And I thought that there were only two wants in my life;
to love this woman and for her to love me, too.

I lay there in that spot for several more seconds, listening to the rain against the roof. The lightning exploded
across the room once more, followed immediately by the
crash of thunder, and this stirred Susan just a bit and I slid
closer to her and her eyes opened into mine, those eyes that
said so much. We looked into each other's eyes for several
seconds, resting our heads against the pillows. And as her
eyes started to close, I kissed her forehead and let her know
that I loved her.

The next morning I arose early, kissed Susan one last time and told her to stay in bed and go back to sleep. I made a quick breakfast of yogurt and fruit, let Orson outside to take care of his business, and put the remaining gear into the truck. I then helped Orson into the back seat, since he was a little too old to be able to jump up there himself, and I started the engine. I looked back at the porch and Susan was standing there in her robe, and as our eyes met, she pressed her hand to her lips. I did the same to mine, and pulled the truck out of the drive onto the highway.

• • •

A Buddhist teacher was traveling with his students and they soon found themselves as honored guests in an extremely poor area of the country. They were invited to a big feast where they were served pork, which was forbidden in their religious practice. The students watched in shock as the teacher calmly ate of the generous gift. "Teacher," they said, "Is not the meat of the pig forbidden by our order?"

The teacher continued with his meal, clearly savoring every bite, and he ignored the students' pleading. When he finished, he turned to the students. "Can you not see that this was a great gift given at much sacrifice by the residents of this village? It was a gift given of humbleness and generosity. Who am I to refuse such a gracious gift?"

"Besides," he continued. "It is not what goes into your mouth that defiles you, but what comes out."

After the Sunday soccer field episode, when I walked out of the house the next morning to head to school, there was Otter, waiting at the end of my driveway like always.

I wanted to ask him about the previous day's experience, who the man was, and why he looked so panicked when he saw him. But I didn't want to come out and ask, and Otter wasn't the kind to volunteer much information, so I started out just chatting, mostly about the Dodger game of the night before.

Otter listened, but didn't say much. Finally I said, "You sure left in a hurry on yesterday."

"Yeah. I had to get home." That was all Otter had to say. We kept walking.

I changed the subject back to the Dodger game. "Man, that Steve Garvey can pound the ball. Another homer last night."

"Uh huh," was the reply.

Finally. "What was up with running away so fast yesterday?" I decided to just come out and ask. "I mean, you looked panicked. I've never seen you run so fast."

"Oh, I was supposed to do something and I didn't do it very good, so my dad was pissed."

"What were you supposed to do?"

Otter stopped walking and looked at me intently, as if he were deciding if this information was something he should reveal. There was no emotion in his stare, no anger or calm, just an intense look in his eyes.

"I was supposed to have the ironing done before he left for work." Otter said this simply, matter of factly, as if this was a totally normal routine. "My dad said that it wasn't up to his standards."

That wasn't a response I expected. I was bewildered on two counts. One, that someone would get pissed if shirts weren't ironed correctly. I wasn't even sure what a correct way to iron shirts would be. And two, why would an adult want Otter to iron his shirts? "Is ironing your usual job?" The question came out meekly.

"One of them," Otter replied. "Don't your parents have jobs that you're supposed to do?"

"Well, yeah, of course."

We started walking again. "What are your jobs?" he asked.

I thought for a second. "I have to clear the table and put dirty dishes in the dishwasher. Then put them away when they're clean."

"Okay. One of my jobs is to do my dad's ironing."

"And that's what you forgot to do?" I treaded lightly. We were friends, but it was a new friendship and I wanted to be careful, but I was curious. I had never heard of a kid who was responsible for the family's ironing.

If Otter was annoyed, he didn't show it. "No. I didn't forget. I did the ironing. It just wasn't done good enough."

"So he was pissed at that?"

"Yep," and we continued our walk along the sidewalk.

"So.....," there was a long pause before I continued, "what happens then?" We were nearing the school. "Do you get grounded? Does something get taken away?"

Otter stopped and gave me that look again, the one with no emotion, seemingly trying to decide if he should reveal anything further. Then he rolled up his left shirt sleeve to reveal a large bruise, the size of a tennis ball. It was a deep purplish color, covering most of his upper shoulder. I was speechless at the size of it, and knew that it had to have hurt. And that it must still be hurting.

"How'd that happen?" I felt that my voice rose about two octaves in order to get that question aloud and I'm sure I sounded just like a little boy.

Otter continued to look at me, but this time with more of a 'Really? You really need to ask that question' look. The silence seemed to last forever, me waiting for an answer, Otter just looking at me.

"Your dad did that?" I finally broke the silence. My voice was still high.

"Yep." Otter's voice had the same emotion as if he were responding to me asking if he had cereal for breakfast. "Three slugs on the arm for not doing my best."

We walked along in silence for awhile. I was having a hard time wrapping my head around what I had just heard. Otter's dad hit him three times, hard, on his arm? For not ironing the shirts good enough? This was foreign to me. I couldn't ever imagine my dad getting upset for the ironing not being done a certain way, much less hitting me. Finally I asked softly, "Does that happen often?"

"When I don't get things done as they should or if I don't get things done on time or if I forget to do something. It could be a lot of things." We continued walking towards school. I was definitely disturbed at hearing and seeing what the results of not having ironed a shirt wrinkle free brought to my friend's life. If Otter was disturbed, he didn't show it.

He had told the whole story matter of factly. The rest of the walk was done in silence.

I think Otter was beginning to feel a little uncomfortable in the silence, maybe feeling that he had revealed too much. "It really isn't a big deal," he said. We continued on in quiet.

Otter broke the quiet again as we neared the entrance to the school. "What does your dad do when he gets pissed?" I stopped and thought for a minute. The question seemed to be asked with an implication that all parents would respond in similar ways. I told Otter that my dad didn't really get pissed much and that I was pretty sure he wouldn't punch me in the arm if he did. That made Otter go "Hmmmm," and then, "even if he was really pissed?"

I just shook my head. "I don't think my dad would ever hit me, no matter how mad he was."

Otter stood there for a few more seconds, trying to process the information that I had just given him. "Okay. See you at lunch." And he was off down the corridor towards his first period class.

I stood at the school gate and watched him saunter down the path towards the classrooms. I was still trying to wrap my head around the size of the bruises on Otter's arm, even more confused, even alarmed, that they were given to him by his father. This was certainly a shocking thing to learn about Otter.

I turned and walked the opposite way and headed to my first period class.

CHOICE
by Mark Otter

Choice.
Some are chance.
    Heads or tails
    Red or black
    Paper, rock, scissors.

Some are consequential.
    Who to take to the prom
    Who to go into business with
    Who to marry

Sometimes they determine where to go
    Left or right
    Up or down
    East or west

But then there's
    Rod or Belt

Which punishment do you take?
    Rod or belt?

Does it matter?

Fuck it.
Do your worst.

Tom Smyly

OCTOBER 8

THE SUN WAS STILL CLIMBING OVER THE MOUNTAINS AS I started on my journey, casting the road in shadows as I drove along the highway as it followed the Gallatin river towards Bozeman. I needed to stop at my office and clear my upcoming absence. I had long stopped teaching in the Fish and Wildlife Biology department and was now exclusively a researcher. I was currently involved in studying the migratory patterns of the big horn sheep that lived in and around the national parks. It was mostly administrative at this point in my career, supervising several graduate students in their research. It was a job that I loved, especially in my partial retirement and I just needed to clear some time, which I did.

Though it was surely a cliche, I had decided to simply follow my heart on this trip. I suppose that was the challenge, to know where my heart was leading. I knew that I needed to eventually end up in Southern California where I needed to reconnect...no...maybe confront, some long ago memories. But I wanted to see other places, make some other stops first. During my sleeplessness of last night, I decided to make my first stop Whitefish, Montana, a favorite stomping ground of my younger days. It would be a good location to drop some of the contents of The Repository.

I told myself that spreading the contents of The Repository was the principal purpose of this trip. But if I analyzed myself, I would have to admit that the purpose was murky. I just knew that I needed to travel to times past. If getting rid of the contents of The Repository gave me an excuse for these eclectic plans, so be it.

I had fallen in love with the mountains of Montana while traveling after college. It was really love at first sight and that love affair has never diminished. Montana is appropriately named Big Sky Country and I love how the mountains connect with the sky for an endless horizon. It never fails to move me with its beauty.

I recalled a lesson from my early Buddhist training. A master had preached for many years that life was just an illusion. Then his son died and the master spent weeks in mourning, weeping for his loss. His students came to him and asked why he could weep when he had told them so many times that life was merely an illusion?

"Yes," said the master, wiping away the tears as they continued down his face. "But he was such a beautiful illusion."

Everything may be temporary in life, but what a beautiful thing, these majestic mountains. After traveling to other parts of the country, or even the world, I knew I was home when I saw these mountains.

I headed north out of Bozeman, taking a circuitous route towards my destination of Whitefish. I passed by the town of Ringling, named after John Ringling of Ringling Brothers Circus fame. That was because the railroad went through this small Montana town. I had hoped to refill my coffee mug, but nothing was open, so I continued onward towards White Sulphur Springs. There I stopped for coffee at a local stand outside the hotel that housed the springs.

While getting coffee and a breakfast sandwich composed of bacon and eggs, I contemplated going for a soak at the sulphur springs inside the hotel grounds but passed in order to continue along the highway that followed a small meandering stream.

I found a spot along the stream to park and finish my sandwich. I got Orson out to stretch his legs and then we sat on a rock and enjoyed each other's company. Morning was coming to a close and the October sun was high in the sky. I flipped the lid off of my coffee cup and felt the steam from it against my face. I love the color of coffee when just the right amount of cream is added. And I felt appreciation for a life that allows me to add just the right amount of cream to my coffee and even purchase a bacon and egg sandwich. I wondered if life had a message for me in all of this.

Then life let me take Orson for a walk along the banks of this gentle stream, the sound of the water cascading down and over rocks and logs, musically making its way downstream. I gazed along the flowing waters where whole generations of biological processes were taking place along the banks and under the water. Reeds poked out of the stream along the shoreline, reflecting both the water and the sunlight, swaying slowly in the light breeze, telling the story of a natural world that keeps turning no matter the color of my coffee or how many breakfast sandwiches I may choose or not choose to eat. A heron passed slowly by and settled close to the shore on the other side, standing so still that it seemed to be made of something other than flesh and bone and sinew. I stared at this beautiful bird as it stood motionless, silently staring at the moving water. And the question that the river and the reeds and the heron seem to ask - am I too preoccupied to appreciate this moment?

There is movement beneath the water as it laps up gently to the shore. Is there a lesson to take away?

Then life suggests that I remember the years I ran around, the years I developed a lifestyle a little too consumed by what others' thought, advocated a carelessness, owned a chilly heart. Regrets can easily come to me in these moments and I try and let them travel by me and leave along the water. I sit still and become generally surprised at how quiet I've become. The quiet allows me to sink into the sounds and truly pick out the individual rhythms of this stream.

I shared the last of the sandwich with Orson who thanked me with a wag of his tail. Then I got back into the truck and contemplated all of this. Loves lost, hearts given, and both found again. And regrets...regretted I suppose. I think this is life's way of letting me know that I am simply lucky, maybe a little smart, maybe a little brave, but really just lucky. Because I was born at a good time. Because I was able to listen when people spoke to me. Because I stopped when I should have, and then started up again.

I often reflect upon my blessings as well as my misfortunes. In an honest counting, it isn't even close - blessings are much more plentiful.

I started my truck and pulled it onto the highway and began climbing through the mountains. The sun rose higher and higher in the sky. I reached for my sunglasses and rolled down the windows of the pickup truck. Both Orson and I enjoyed the smells of the day as they wafted around us.

. . .

Once upon a time, in ancient China, there was a teacher widely regarded for his wisdom. One day, he was passing through a village when it began raining. While seeking shelter, he saw an old woman, weeping and wailing in the middle of town. Many of the village people passed her by, paying no attention to her loud sobs.

The teacher inquired about the lady to others of the village and he was told that this woman was constantly weeping and crying and that she was referred to as the "Sad Lady" because of her prolonged weeping.

Filled with compassion, the teacher approached the Sad Lady and asked her why she was crying and so sad. "Master," she said, "I have an older son who owns a fan shop. So when it rains, no one will come and buy his fans and I fear he will fail and he and his family will be placed into ruin."

"But weather never lasts, " said the teacher. "For soon the sun will come out and it will be hot once more."

This news made the woman wail even louder. "I have a younger son who sells umbrellas. So when the weather is nice, no one will visit his shop and then he and his family will be ruined. This makes me even sadder."

"I see," said the teacher. "Will you take me to this umbrella shop? I would like to see it."

The teacher and the Sad Lady proceeded to the

son's umbrella shop and it continued to rain heavily. The son was very busy selling umbrellas to travelers, as many had been caught unawares by the storm. The son was so busy that he could hardly look up, so many were the customers. Slowly a smile came across the Sad Lady's face as she saw the many travelers purchasing umbrellas from her son.

Soon the rain stopped and the teacher asked to see the other son's fan store. The weather grew quite hot and by the time they arrived at the son's fan store, business was brisk from the many customers who now needed fans to cool themselves from the hot and muggy weather.

The teacher turned to the Sad Lady and said, "When it was raining, your older son had little business, but your younger son's business was thriving. And now that it is sunny, no one is interested in buying umbrellas, but now they want fans. So, you see, no matter what the weather is, just think about the son who is doing well and you will no longer feel sad."

The Sad Lady took the teacher's instructions to heart and simply changed her thinking. Soon she went from someone who was always crying to someone who was constantly happy, always smiling and laughing. And the people of the village began calling her the "Happy Lady."

Previous ————————————————————————

MY TENTH GRADE YEAR CONTINUED TO RUN TOWARDS summer vacation, as did my friendship with Otter. But, as time went by, I began to notice some subtle changes in his behavior. One was that he didn't seem to be as prepared for Algebra, often not having the homework completed and not being prepared in class. This seemed to be what was happening in other classes as well, his being unprepared and he even told me that he wasn't getting good grades anymore.

It did cross my mind a time or two of what may be happening in the Otter household. I saw what happened if he didn't do the best job of ironing a couple of dress shirts. I wondered what might happen if his class work was held to the same fatherly standard.

I also noticed some physical changes. There were times he seemed tired, like he had not had enough sleep the night before. He even fell asleep in Mrs. Parker's algebra class, his head resting on his elbow. The student at the desk next to his dropped a book on the floor and the loud crash startled Otter, making him give a little yelp, which then resulted in the class having a good giggle at him. I asked him why he was so tired and he said that he had stayed up too late reading.

There were some other physical things I noticed. One time he came to school with a bruise under his eye. I asked him about it and he said it happened in Tae Kwon Do.

Another time there were red marks across his back. He said that he fell against the railing on his front porch. I thought at the time that he was telling the truth. The explanations that he offered seemed plausible.

I suppose I didn't think about it too much.

I did mention to my mom and dad about the time that Otter showed me his bruised arm. This was met with mostly furrowed brows and not much else. My dad seemed to think it wasn't that big a deal, but it was always hard to get a read on my dad's thoughts. My mom was a little more concerned, but even she thought it wasn't out of the ordinary for parents to "punish" their children, and while this may have gone too far, she thought it best to just pay attention to see if it was a frequent occurrence.

One time during family dinner, my mom asked about Otter, asking if he talked about anything else regarding his parents, especially his dad. I replied that Otter and I never really talked about our home lives. And then my dad said, "Let it go, Anna Lee. I'm sure Jake will tell us if there is something to be told." But that rarely deterred my mom from asking about Otter's home life. The truth was, I just didn't know much about his home life and he never volunteered much information. The fact was that even though we had almost gone through a school year of being friends, I still had never been invited over to his house.

My mom asked about what Otter was bringing for lunch at school, and I said I didn't really know. All I knew was that he never had money to buy a school hot lunch so I just assumed that he brought a lunch from home. At my mom's suggestion, I began paying attention to what Otter was bringing for lunch, if anything. I noticed that if he had something it was usually just a piece of fruit, an apple or banana, that he took out of a paper sack from his locker. I told this to my mom and she decided that she would make an extra sandwich for my lunch and I could offer it to Otter. I thought that was a good idea, though I was unsure how he would react.

The next day I offered my extra sandwich to Otter, saying that I was way too full to eat two sandwiches. He thanked me and wolfed the sandwich down in just a couple of bites. I told this to Mom, and she began making an extra sandwich and putting it in my lunch sack, which I would offer Otter. I began offering him this extra sandwich on a daily basis, even giving him an extra bag of chips. I always told him it was because I was full or that my mom was extra ditzy that morning when she made me and my sister lunches. If he suspected that I was making it up, he never let on. He always thanked me and ate whatever I had that was "extra."

One morning as the school year was winding down, I went outside to walk to school, expecting to see Otter in his usual position at the end of the driveway. And he was there, but I almost didn't recognize him. His long straight blond hair was no longer and in it's place was a crew cut, hair barely half an inch on the top of his head. All I could say was "Wow." And then, "What happened?"

"My fucking dad." Otter said that hard, an anger simmering just behind his teeth as the words came out.

I didn't say anything. I didn't know what to say. He continued to tell me that his dad was angry at his grades and that his English teacher had called to say that Otter was behind in the class and did he need any extra help? Then, according to Otter, his dad yelled and raged and produced some hair clippers and shaved his head almost down to the scalp. He said that he did it to "motivate" him to do better in school. Otter, who was usually pretty laid back, seemed to be seething, his anger barely contained.

I understood. And that's all I could tell him. This was the 1970's and longer hair was certainly the more accepted style. Otter was surely going to stand out, and for all the wrong reasons.

After a few days, he seemed to calm down a bit, even making fun of himself and being self deprecating about his new hair style. If he got much teasing at school, it didn't seem too bad and Otter seemed to mostly laugh it off.

One day Otter and I were walking home from school, talking about stupid things I'm sure, when a dark sedan slowed down beside us and then pulled over. Otter froze as the driver reached across to the passenger side and rolled down the window. "Mark, I need you at home," came words from a man inside the auto. "Get in the car." There was no anger or sense of urgency in his request. Just a matter of fact statement, get in the car. And I realized that this was the first time that I had ever seen Otter's dad up close.

"Yes sir, " Otter replied and he opened the passenger door and started to get in.

"Who's your friend?" the man asked.

"Oh, this is Jake. I told you about him."

The man hunched down to look through the passenger window. "Hello," he said.

"Nice to meet you, sir," I replied, using all of the manners that I could muster.

"Mark says you may be interested in joining us at our church someday." Though this was news to me, I tried not to register any surprise, trying to make sure I was covering for anything that Otter may have told his father.

"Yes sir. Possibly." I tried to keep it as vague as I could.

"Well, we would love to have you join us some Sunday. Right, Mark?" And he looked over at Otter in the passenger seat, who merely smiled weakly and nodded his head. "What about this Sunday? You would love our church youth program."

I tried to casually play it off. "I have to check with my parents. I think we may be going to the beach this weekend."

Otter's dad leaned across Otter to better shout out the passenger window. "Well, I know you'd love it. Let's get you to church to learn about our Jehovah. And give Him praise." Then he leaned back across to the driver's seat and off they drove.

I walked the rest of the way home, reflecting on how Otter went from telling me jokes while shuffling along the sidewalk to his total change in personality when the car pulled up. I can't say that his dad was imposing, or angry, or even had a mean face. But there was something about him that just made me feel uneasy.

I remember my dad talking about his patients and how he often knew how they were feeling by just seeing their face. "It's something in their countenance," he would say. "You just know." That was it. There was something in Otter's dad's countenance.

The next morning when I walked out my door to head for school, there was Otter, looking the same as always, except for maybe the shorter hair. I asked if everything was okay.

Otter knew what I was referencing. "Yep. He just needed someone to hold the ladder and a flashlight. He was cleaning something out of the attic." Otter said this with an almost audible sigh, like he was as relieved as I was that this was all. He didn't say anything about the church attendance request, and I didn't either.

And now I had met Mr. William Otter.

COLLATERAL DAMAGE
By Mark Otter

War.
It kills soldiers
but it also kills those who are not involved.
They call it Collateral Damage.

It makes the people who wage war feel better
to give the killing and maiming a name.

Collateral Damage.

But people are just as maimed,
just as dead.

Does it make those who are collateral damage
feel any less maimed,
less dead?

No.

The people I see every day.
Collateral Damage.

OCTOBER 8-9

ORSON AND I SPENT THE REMAINDER OF THE DAY MEAN-dering our way from White Sulphur Springs through the Lewis and Clark National Forest, stopping in Great Falls for some tea and dog treats, and then on into Whitefish. We found a local bar which had outdoor seating, and I enjoyed a dinner of fish and chips, the fish a delicious fresh trout, I'm sure pulled recently out of one of the many nearby streams. Afterwards, Orson and I loaded back into the pickup and drove towards Glacier National Park, found a parking area to camp in, and settled in for the night.

It had been a good first day and I meditated for a bit and thought about what I wanted to do the next day. Though there were several other campers, mostly in tents all around Orson and I, it was very quiet. As the night got darker, I pulled a book out of my backpack and read for awhile. I had recently begun rereading The Way of the Peaceful Warrior by Dan Millman, which is a favorite book of mine. It tells the story of a chance meeting between a service station attendant and a young, upcoming gymnast. This service station attendant and becomes a father figure to this young gymnast and teaches him how to become a "Peaceful War-rior." I wanted to reread certain passages that talked about the journey being the way to happiness and not necessarily the arrival at the destination. I flipped through a few more pages before turning off the overhead light. I popped the back end of the camper shell open and helped Orson down, and we took a brief walk around where we were camped. Orson enjoyed all of the smells that were unique to this area of Montana.

I marveled at the thousands and thousands of stars that dotted the sky. I tried to identify some familiar constellations, but the vast number of stars made it almost impossible. I reveled in the smallness of my being.

My sleep was a little restless, I wasn't used to sleeping alone, except for Orson, of course. And I wasn't used to sleeping in the back of the camper, though Susan and I had done so on several camping trips. My sleep was littered with dreams, some vivid, some not, but none that I could particularly remember when I awoke.

I do remember awaking with a start, thinking that I had heard something outside my window, and I pulled back the curtains and peered out into the darkness, made even darker by the many trees that shaded the campground. Orson, obviously perturbed at being awakened, stood up and shook his body, no easy feat in the small area. As he settled back down, I scratched him behind his ears and he emitted a low rumble of a growl, showing his pleasure. I fluffed my pillow and tried to fall back asleep.

The next morning broke brightly through the small windows of my truck cab. I stiffly got out of bed and gave Orson a quick walk, had a breakfast of beef jerky, fruit, and tea, and then we walked to the Avalanche Lake Trailhead. It was a short hike, and owing to Orson's age, I didn't want to strain him too much, especially on this first full day. The trail to Avalanche Lake is a fairly short one without a lot of elevation gain. I had brought my backpack, along with The Repository and some water and dog treats.

Since it was October, the trail wasn't crowded and Orson and I met few fellow hikers. We did come upon a couple of moose who were grazing at the other end of a large meadow that we were skirting. What large and majestic animals they are. I was a little concerned that they may pick up Orson's smell, but if they picked up our scent, they didn't show it and we ambled by unnoticed. We soon arrived at Avalanche Lake.

Orson waded in up to his waist and lapped up some of the lake water. He enjoys water, and he likes standing in it, but wasn't into swimming, making him very un-lab like. I took my hiking boots off and stood ankle deep, but did not stay in the water for long as it was freezing cold, the lake being mostly fed from the thawing of the surrounding glaciers. I couldn't blame Orson for not wanting to go for a swim. We both soon retired to a sunny rock and we shared some water and snacks, and afterwards began the walk back to the truck.

I was looking for just the right spot to spread some of the contents of The Repository and soon found what I felt was the appropriate place. It was at the base of a small tree, probably just three feet high, and I closed my eyes and spread some of the dust that was inside the old coffee can. I then took a small spade out of my backpack and mixed the ash of The Repository with some organic fertilizer that I had also brought along. I combined this mixture with the dirt and packed it around the young sapling. Orson served as my congregation as I said a few words of a Buddhist prayer, and he lay on his stomach with his paws stretched out in front of him. He seemed to understand the reverence of the occasion and when I finished I sat beside him and scratched his ears.

"With every breath I take today, I vow to be awake. And every step I take, I vow to take with a grateful heart.

So I may see with eyes of love into the hearts of all I meet.

To ease their burdens when I can and touch them with a smile of peace."

BUDDHIST PRAYER

A couple of squirrels ran up and down a nearby tree, and Orson barely raised his head in notice. Chasing squirrels seemed beneath Orson, and he gave them no never mind. I enjoyed watching the squirrels playing in the branches and coming closer as they sensed no danger from the four legged beast at my feet. I had some almonds with my snacks, and I tossed them towards the bushy tailed animals. They eyed them warily for a few moments, then made a break to gather them and take them to a safer spot for eating.

I was enjoying this communion with nature, its plants and animals, and I listened intently to the sounds of the forest, mixed in with the lapping of the lake as it gently kissed the shoreline. It was immensely peaceful.

This is what I had come to do, why I was taking such a circuitous route on this journey to Southern California and this was just the first full day. Orson and I shared the silence for a little longer and then we began the hike back to the pickup.

It was still mid morning when we got back to the pickup, and several fellow campers were just getting up and about, some making small fires to cook their breakfast. I love the smells of morning campfires, combined with coffee and breakfast makings, and I sat on the end of my tailgate and sipped some warm tea that I had made on my small backpacker stove. Orson snoozed at my feet, occasionally raising his head to take in a new scent or two.

Orson and I got back into the truck and continued on down the road, through Kalispell, onto highway 2, and headed towards Coeur d'Alene, Idaho. We stopped in Sandpoint and I enjoyed a chicken salad dinner, washed down by a locally made beer. We pulled into Coeur d'Alene as darkness was beginning to fall and we found a campsite at a local RV park. I have to admit that I felt somewhat out of place, my small pickup truck parked among several large RVs. While the park itself was quite nice, it wasn't nearly as peaceful as the night before outside of Glacier, with the sites being closer together and generators going on and off at different times.

Orson and I settled into our bedtime routine, me meditating, the both of us taking a brief walk, then some reading and afterwards, lights out. I journaled a bit, trying to capture my feelings of where I left some of the remnants of The Repository. I called Susan and hearing her voice gladdened me. Then I scratched Orson behind the ears and slept soundly.

. . .

In ancient China, there was a young woman from a wealthy family. When her only son was one year old, he fell ill and died. The young woman was struck with a paralyzing grief from the death of her only child. She gathered his lifeless body into her arms and she took him door to door though the village, pleading with all the people for news that could bring her child back to life.

Of course no one could help her, but she would not give up, so great was her grief. Finally a Buddhist teacher told her to go to the Buddha himself and ask him for help. She then carried her son's body to the Buddha and told him of her grief.

The Buddha listened with great patience and compassion, and he said to her, "There is only one way to solve this sadness. Go and find me four mustard seeds from a family in the village in which there has never been a death."

The woman set forth to visit every family in the village, but very soon she discovered that every family she visited had experienced a death. And she understood what the Buddha had wanted her to experience for herself - that suffering greatly is a part of life, and death comes to us all. Once she accepted the fact that death is inevitable to everyone, she was able to stop her grieving and celebrate life.

THEY CALLED IT NUTRITION BREAK, A PAUSE IN CLASSES for 20 minutes after the first two high school periods. This allowed students to go to the cafeteria and grab a quick snack. Even though it was called Nutrition Break, there was little nutrition offered in the way of snacks from the cafeteria. Often I would meet Otter there and we would chat or visit with friends, maybe flirt with a few girls. Sometimes I would get a snack, a donut or cinnamon roll, and that would necessitate waiting in line which could often be long. Otter never purchased anything, but he would hang out in line with me. The cafeteria at our high school, like a lot of school cafeterias in Southern California, was outside but covered.

I can't remember exactly what day it was, but it was a typical sunny May day in Southern California. Otter and I were stuck in the usual Nutrition Break line. In front of us were a couple of twelfth grade girls that were on the cheer leading squad, cute girls that definitely caught both our attention. They were chatting inanely about some class or teacher, who knows what, and giggling all the while.

While we were waiting, another twelfth grader, Roger Mooney, someone who I recognized was on the football team and currently on the baseball squad, came up and started a conversation with the cheerleaders. You could tell that they all obviously knew each other and the giggling was kept at a high decibel level. The line was moving slowly and Roger followed the girls along as we all barely moved.

Eventually the line got closer to the counter where we would order our food or drink and as it neared, Roger asked the girls if he could have "back cuts," to which the girls agreed while continuing their insipid giggling. Given this permission from the cheerleaders, Roger slid into line behind them and in front of Otter and me.

I did not have any reaction to Roger's cutting in front of us as this was not an uncommon occurrence in the high school social pecking order, and as tenth graders, Otter and I were on the bottom of the totem pole. I simply rolled my eyes. But then my eyes almost popped out of my head when Otter tapped Roger on the shoulder and told him that there were no back cuts and he needed to go to the end of the line.

I am sure that my mouth dropped open. I wanted to ask Otter what the hell he was doing, but he seemed intent on letting Roger know that he needed to go to the end of the line. I muttered under my breath, "Dude..." to Otter and if he heard me, he paid no attention. Roger just looked over at this punk who dared to question his obvious stature and gave a little smirk at the short haired Otter, whom he outweighed by at least forty pounds. Thinking that he had sufficiently dismissed the peon with this brush off, he resumed his conversation with the girls.

Otter tapped him on the shoulder again and said "Hey, no back cuts. Go to the end of the line."

Roger turned to Otter. I'm sure he sized him up as not much of a threat. "Back off, chrome dome," he uttered, a reference to Otter's short hair, and this time he gave Otter a little shove with the palm of this hand. But Otter did not budge, not even an inch. It was as if Roger had shoved a brick wall even though he had shoved Otter solidly. Otter didn't move or react. If he was afraid of this encounter with an obviously larger foe, he sure was not expressing any fear.

I stepped out of line, not believing what was happening. When I saw Roger shove Otter, I expected that to be enough to move Otter out of the way. But it wasn't. A thousand things were flashing through my mind, most of which were picturing two minutes into the future and Otter laying on the cafeteria cement, having been deposited there by this larger high school senior. I wanted to say something, but the intensity of the moment was growing and I was still wrapping my head around what was happening.

The cafeteria lines were crowded and this encounter seemed to be gaining notice, and several heads were turning towards what was beginning to look like a confrontation of some sort. No one was moving out of line, at least not yet, but there were a few taps on shoulders and fingers pointing toward Otter and Roger. As in most high schools, the anticipation of a fight brewing captured everyone's attention. The promise of blood was in the water and the sharks were beginning to circle.

Roger certainly noticed the crowd beginning to look his way and he extended the palm of his hand for a harder shove, and Otter grabbed his wrist folding Roger's palm inward. This was done so quickly, I barely registered it happening, but there was Otter pushing the back of Roger's wrist, folding it back towards his body, and Roger yelling out in pain. He tried to free his hand but Otter just pushed the wrist back a little harder, making Roger yelp even louder.

Someone in the line next to ours, another football player, was witnessing what was going on and he stepped out of his line, moving towards Roger and Otter. "Hey, need some help, Rog?" and he took a step closer.

Tom Smyly

Otter looked at him and simply said, "This doesn't concern you." As he said that he pushed harder on the back of Roger's wrist, dropping Roger to his knees. Roger was definitely in agony and he urged his friend to back up.

"No back cuts. End of the line, yes?" Otter said looking directly at Roger all the while keeping the pressure on the back of Roger's wrist. Roger yelped out a "Let go, asshole," to which Otter said, "Nope. Wrong answer," and he pushed back even more on Roger's wrist, eliciting more howls. "Back of the line?" Finally there was a "Yes….yes," Roger managing to get this out in between painful yelps.

Otter let go of Roger, who then got up from his knees, rubbing his wrist and hand. Roger looked around at the many faces of the crowd. It was clear he was embarrassed by this obviously inferior 10th grader humiliating him. And he was pissed. He looked at Otter. "You're a dead man." He repeated that statement again, this time with spit coming from his mouth. "You're a dead man." There was fury in his voice, the kind of fury that comes from the disgraced. I just knew that Otter was not going to come out of this well. I was petrified.

Roger stepped towards Otter and threw a wild punch. Otter pivoted out of the way with a casual ease and the punch hit nothing but air. Roger swung again and Otter glided aside with the same ease that he would stop the soccer balls that I had kicked at him. He didn't duck under the punches, he simply moved his head so the punches hit nothing, making Roger stumble forward, trying to regain his balance. Otter had no emotion on his face, but his eyes were focused entirely on Roger.

Roger stepped closer preparing to throw another jab, when he was hit by, I'm not sure, but I think three punches that came with such speed that I really could not count them by sight, only by the sound of them striking Roger in the face. It was smack!, smack!, smack!, in succession. This staggered Roger and he stumbled a couple of steps backward, blood beginning to come from his nose and the corner of his mouth. The rage intensified on his face and he stepped forward and threw a wild punch which Otter stepped away from. Otter then took a small step towards his opponent and stepped into a kick directed at the middle of Roger's chest, connecting with Roger with such force that he emitted a loud ooouf! and flew backwards into the arms of several students that were encircling the fracas. The crowd shoved Roger back towards Otter. Roger tried to throw another wild punch and Otter easily stepped aside and took Roger's outstretched arm, pivoted his back towards him and flipped Roger over his shoulder and onto the cement. All that could be heard was another loud ooouf! that emitted from Roger when the air was knocked out of him.

Just then a couple of teachers, led by my Government teacher Mr. Gearheart, pushed their way through the crowd and for a minute they simply stared at the scene. There was this baseball/football star athlete on the ground and this skinny short haired boy standing over the prostrate body. There was quiet, then Otter said, "I told you, no back cuts." It wasn't said with meanness or gloating, just matter of factly. The teachers on the scene simply stared for a few more moments, their own mouths agape. It was as if the teachers could not believe what they were seeing, just like the rest of us. A couple of students helped Roger to his feet and were instructed to take him to the school nurse. Mr. Gearheart asked who started the whole thing and the cheerleaders started talking about back cuts and so forth, making no sense, just jabbering. Mr. Gearheart looked to Otter and said that he needed to follow him to the principal's office, which Otter did.

Otter went by me as he followed Mr. Gearheart, his eyes down. I wanted to say something, but I was still in shock at what I had just witnessed. And everyone else simply starred at each other, confused by what had just happened. Then the warning bell rang, signaling it was time to go to our next class.

Everyone began heading towards the classrooms. I had forgotten all about my sweet roll.

HEAR THE DARK
By Mark Otter

Turn off all the lights.
All the lights.
Do you feel it?
Try again, lights off.
Do you feel it yet?

Even darkness has touch.
It has a feeling.
It has an embrace.
It is as real as a kiss,
    a grasp,
    a caress.
It has its own set of arms.

Most of all, it has a sound.
A sound all its own.

Do you hear the darkness?
Feel the darkness?

Can you can feel the darkness
    even though the lights are on?

That's when it's really dark.
Listen to the darkness,
it has its own sound.

Tom Smyly

OCTOBER 10

T HE NEXT MORNING DAWNED PARTLY CLOUDY AND after a brief stretching session in the camper, Orson and I made our way down to the shores of Lake Coeur d'Alene. There we walked in silence along the bank, every once in awhile stopping to admire the mountains in the distance and the majesty of this beautiful lake.

The sun was peaking out from the clouds here and there and it made a lovely checkerboard pattern on the calm waters. It was truly serene and peaceful, and I found a place to take my boots off and wade ankle deep into the lake. Orson ventured into the water to his chest and I thought he was going to go all in, but he seemed to think better of it and returned to the shore where he sat and watched me splash the water with my hands.

We continued wading down the lake for a bit, then I walked ashore where there were some azalea bushes and it was there I took The Repository out of my back pack. I repeated the mixing of both the contents of The Repository and the fertilizer and spread them under and around the bushes and said another prayer. Orson again respected the occasion and lay quietly a few feet away. After I finished patting the mixture down, I sat on the ground and looked out on the lake and felt peaceful, watching the sun dancing upon the water, grays and blues combining onto a beautiful calm canvas.

> *"May all be free from sorrow and the causes of sorrow; May we all never be separated from the sacred happiness which is sorrowless; And may all live in equanimity, without too much attachment and too much aversion; And live believing in the equality of all that lives."*

BUDDHIST PRAYER

Orson and I returned to the pickup and left Coeur d'Alene, driving west along Interstate 90, stopping in Spokane for breakfast and then heading for Leavenworth, Washington. After leaving Spokane and while on the road, I called my friend, Aaron, who was celebrating the double nickel birthday. He seemed to fret about this milestone, lamenting that he was turning the "double nickel", fifty five. I wished him a happy birthday anyway.

Aaron was one of the assistant basketball coaches at MSU and I think he was feeling his age hanging around these young athletes all the time. He was a good friend and Susan and I try to have dinner with him and his wife Debbie every couple of months. Susan would mostly come because she knew Aaron and I were friends, but she had little in common with Debbie, or either of Aaron's three other wives, two that we had known.

When I would see Aaron around campus, I would try and ask him about his kids, but it was hard to keep track of who was who. He had two children with his first wife, then one more with his second plus the one she brought to the marriage, one with his third plus her two kids, and then none with Debbie, but Debbie had three of her own. To his credit and my amazement, Aaron was still in the lives of not only his children but the step children that came with his other marriages. I don't know how he was able to keep everything straight.

With no children of my own, sometimes I am challenged to find understanding with others with children, especially as many as the hers, mine, and ours that Aaron had to deal with. Susan and I were in the dating stage, both of us in our late twenties, and I was often driving down from Bozeman to her home in Salt Lake City. I would commute to see her from my research position at Montana State to her job as a physical therapist. We had been going together for a while and were getting serious when one evening she told me that she was a cancer survivor, having been diagnosed with uterine cancer five years earlier. This entailed a hysterectomy and thus ended her chance to have children. I told her that she was important to me and that we would work through any regrets that both of us may feel in not being able to have children together. And thirty years later, I still have no regrets about having her as my partner.

During my phone call to Aaron, I teased him about his age, and even said that with all of his progeny and step-progeny around, he should get some good gifts. Aaron told me that he had purposely sent out an email to everyone, including Debbie, that this was a no present birthday. He seemed adamant that he was done with birthdays.

It bemuses me that people can become so stressed about turning a particular number, or the fact that we even celebrate these occasions, though I guess they are some cause for celebration. It's not easy or simple to live a long life and most of us seem to take it for granted. Though we are loath to believe it, we are not entitled to tomorrow. We are not entitled to live in a country free from war, or famine, or drought, or even from the biblical raining of frogs. We take so much for granted and I reflected upon that as I drove almost carelessly along the interstate.

Things change. It's our ability to adapt that gives us happiness, I suppose.

What's great about my age, and I'm in my sixties, is that I am over so many things. The age-vanity thing, being self conscious, worrying about how I look and what others think. It is truly freeing when you reach the age that you no longer give a damn.

And really, what age would you be if you didn't know how old you were?

My life doesn't feel like it's only been one life. I feel like I've lived many lives during this lifetime of chasing revolutions around the sun. Maybe they are actually chapters. The characters may stay the same, and even those can come and go, but everything else is different. Life is full of many lives.

Are we really only one age? Maybe by the calendar we are but I would like to think that I am sometimes many ages, often at once. I think that my wild and youthful 16 year old me, or my oh-so-cool 25 year old me, continue to linger around and want to make themselves felt. Sometimes I want to slip into them and feel their freedom, to feel that more simple life. And maybe they often want to slip into my current age and feel the wisdom that I have accumulated along the way.

I try not to complain about growing old. It is an opportunity not given to everyone.

Along the drive, Orson began panting, a sign that he needed to get out and do his business. I stopped at a gas station with a deli attached that was just off the interstate. I leashed up Orson and gave him a quick walk around the service station. He quickly relieved himself and I gave him a bowl of water, and since I was thirsty myself, I hooked his leash to a post outside the door of the deli and went inside to grab a bottle of tea.

The woman behind the counter was having a conversation with an older man, obviously someone she knew, who was dressed in farmer work clothes. His hands were calloused from a lifetime of working the land, at least that was what I surmised.

"What's the special today, Lois?," his voice boomed through the store as he addressed the counter lady.

"It's a French Dip sandwich with au jus" she replied, wiping a wet spot on the counter. "I'll pile it high with roast beef if you want me to, Henry." She gave him a smile and I wondered how many years they had conversed at this very spot.

Henry thought for a moment. "Nah," he said while moving in front of a rolling rotisserie. He pointed to an item behind the glass. "I'm not much for that foreign food. How about just giving me a couple of those burritos?" And he pointed at the deep fried objects rotating slowly in view.

"You got it," she answered without a hint of irony at what he just said. I smiled and enjoyed their exchange with one another.

I got back into my truck and scratched my co-pilot behind the ears. I felt grateful at being able to witness such a human exchange. I put the truck in reverse, backed out of my parking spot and pointed the truck towards the mountains and the town of Leavenworth, where I decided to spend the night in a motor lodge. I wasn't sure of the motel's pet policy, so I snuck Orson into the room, then I luxuriated in a warm shower. Afterwards, I ordered Chinese take out and watched some television. Another phone call to Susan, then some meditating and lights out. Talking to Susan gave me pangs of homesickness, but she encouraged me to stay on the mission that I had set out to do. What a blessing she is to me.

She did have one major question for me. "Honey," she said, "I had a glass of wine with some friends and I was telling them what you were doing, that you were on a quest to revisit some childhood memories."

"Okay," I responded, knowing something else was coming down.

"And the only thing they wanted to know," she hesitated. "How do you go to the bathroom while living out of your truck?"

"Well," I began. "Pretty much like everyone else. I use a toilet."

I understood the question. But one thing about traveling this country of ours is that there are bathrooms everywhere. There are rest stops located every so often off of every major highway. Every gas station, every store, every cafe, every coffee shop has bathrooms. Even most parks have at least a porta-potty, and though they may not be the most sanitary or pleasant experience to use, they are there in a pinch. All of the campsites I have slept in during my many campouts in life, they all had bathrooms. And I'm not against using a tree in the middle of the night if necessary.

"Really, Susan. Finding a bathroom is way down on my list of worries."

"What about showers? Bathing?"

"Well, that's why I will wander into a hotel every couple of nights or so. I just took a warm shower this evening." I teased her at the thought of this being a discussion around the glasses of wine. "I'm probably a little stinky. But Orson doesn't seem to mind."

"Well," Susan went on. "I just told them that it was part of your Buddhist philosophy to not shower and to go to the bathroom as few times as possible."

"Did they buy it?"

Susan laughed. "Probably."

"Well, we do have as a tenet of Buddhism to simply let that shit go."

Susan laughed again. "You always say that what you think you become, what you feel you attract, what you imagine you create."

I love talking with Susan. We have been together for over thirty years and we still talk, we still laugh. We are still friends. I signed off and closed the curtains of the small hotel room. I flipped on the television and surfed channels mindlessly for a few minutes. Then I turned it off along with the lights.

I closed my eyes and thought about all that I was grateful for. My journey was still young, but I was pleased with it so far. I was glad to be spreading the contents of The Repository in such beautiful spots. I thought about plans for tomorrow. I slept well, hearing from the floor Orson's gentle breathing as ambient noise.

...

A Zen master was given a beautiful cup as a gift. It was made of crystal and hand crafted. The master was very grateful for the gift and he would drink out of it every day and share the story of the generous present.

But every morning, as he held the glass in front of him, he would remind himself that the cup was already broken.

One day a visitor accidentally knocked the cup off the shelf. When the cup hit the floor it crashed into a hundred pieces.

The other visitors gasped in shocked but the Zen master remained calm. Looking at the mess of broken glass at his feet, he said, "Ah, yes. Now we begin."

He picked up a broom and started sweeping.

Previous ————————————————————————

THE NUTRITION BREAK INCIDENT WAS THE TALK OF THE school and by lunchtime everyone knew about it. I hung around the usual spot where Otter and I would hook up to go to the cafeteria for lunch, but he never came. It was the same at the end of the day as I waited by the flagpole, our usual meeting place, but again Otter didn't show. So I walked home alone.

I regaled my parents and Jenna with the Nutrition Break incident over dinner, but they seemed unimpressed. Except for Jenna, who would not believe the story and thought I was making it up. I ignored her doubtfulness and continued telling my parents about the fight. They seemed for the most part pretty nonchalant. Dad simply said, "Seems like there was too much chicken on that bone for old Roger." Dad loved homilies and he was always trying to make up his own. Then he said that there were more "beans in the chili than expected for that old boy," which would make my mom simply groan and left Dad smiling, as getting a reaction from my mom was his intent anyway.

I had the phone number for Otter's house, but I had never called it. Come to think of it, Otter had never called me on my house phone, even though we had exchanged numbers quite a while back. I debated about calling his house but I didn't, mostly because of fear. I was afraid that his dad would answer the phone. I'm not sure why I was afraid, I had only seen his dad that one time when we were walking home from school. I guess I felt nervousness when thinking about Otter's dad and what sentence awaited Otter for fighting in school. I remembered the bruises on his arm that he received for not ironing shirts correctly. And then there was the bruise under his eye and the cuts on his face. Otter never really implicated his dad in any of these last two, but I had my suspicions. But I swallowed my fear and dialed the number. I was relieved when his mom answered and she told me that Mark wasn't home, that he was out with his dad.

Otter's mom referred to Otter as Mark and that threw me off for a minute. I guess I just assumed that even his own mother called him by his last name. And hearing that he was with his father made me a little worried. I thanked his mom and hung up.

I suppose I was worried about the news that he was with his father. There were all of the physical elements. And then there was the haircut. I was worried about what would happen if fighting at school was the crime.

The next morning, I exited the front door of my house to start the walk to school and there was Otter, in his usual position at the end of my driveway. I just stared at him for a minute or two, and he grinned. "Bet I gave everyone something to talk about for the rest of the day," he said.

"Dude, that was bitchin'." I shook my head in disbelief. "I'm speechless. You kicked his ass!"

"I told you I take Tae Kwon Do classes."

I simply looked at Otter, this skinny short haired kid. "Yes. That's all everyone talked about for the rest of the day." I then asked about his parents reaction and he just passed it off, saying that his parents knew that he was defending himself. I have to admit that I felt quite a bit of relief and I let my concern drop.

The conversation continued on our way to school, me almost genuflecting at Otter's feet over the shocking results of the day before. Otter mostly pooh-poohed what I was saying, and I sensed that he was a little uncomfortable when I told him that the whole school was talking about the fight. He did want to know if any of the girls we knew had said anything, which I did not know.

Then, out of the blue, Otter said, "That was the first time I ever hit someone outside of Martial Arts." We kept walking. "It sounded different."

That took me back a bit. "What do you mean? Different?" I was interested in what he meant. "You mean, like, you guys are wearing face protection and stuff in class, right?"

"No." I could see Otter was thinking about what he was wanting to say and how he was going to say it. "Well, I mean, yes, we wear safety equipment." Then he stayed silent for awhile.

Finally I said, "Well? How was it different?"

"It was, it was... a different sound from when my dad hits me."

That statement sucked the air out of me for a few seconds. I thought about what to say next. We were getting closer to school and I could not think of anything to reply. We walked along in silence and I looked at my friend's face, feeling such sorrow that he was talking about this.

I'm sure Otter sensed how uncomfortable I was. "It's kind of like, well....when my dad hits me in the face, it sounds different than when I hit Mooney." He was quiet for a few more seconds.

"Is it louder?" I asked quietly.

Then, softly, almost so soft that I didn't hear him, like he was afraid anyone would hear what he was saying, "It sounds resentful."

We continued walking in silence. I thought about that description of being struck in the face. Resentful.

"I'm sorry, man." And I truly was. "That seems fucked up."

Otter put on a fake smile. "It's no big deal."

I didn't believe that for a second.

As we got close to the front gate of the school, Otter stopped. "Well, I can't come in so I'll be heading back. Let's meet over at the 7-11 and I'll walk home with you."

I was perplexed. "Why aren't you coming to class?"

"Dude, I'm suspended for a week." It was then I noticed that he had not brought any books or school materials with us on our walk to school. "I'm really not even supposed to be this close to the school grounds."

I looked towards the school and noticed several students stopping and looking at us as we stood outside the gates. There were a lot of hushed voices and fingers pointing in our direction.

"Alright, Otter. See you after school." And I went inside the school gates and I watched Otter begin retracing the steps that we had just taken.

HOUSE FIRE
by Mark Otter

It's hot in this house,
this house of shade, of shadows,
heat taking umbrage, indignation,
irritated at any attempt to cool it down.

Air is still, unmoving.
Hot air, hot blasts, seeping into corners,
and crags.
Just stillness, nothing moving,
making it hotter and hotter.

So hot that the house
bursts into flames.

How did you let the house
grow so hot,
hot enough to burst into flames?

Now it's too late.
No chance of putting the fire out,
or even contain it.

The house burns
    down

OCTOBER 11

THE MORNING DAWNED QUITE CHILLY IN THE QUAINT Bavarian themed town of Leavenworth and I put on an extra coat as I checked out of the small motel and leashed up Orson for our walk into town. The sun was slowly making its way up, peaking its head over the mountains that surround Leavenworth, and this slow rising was what was keeping it chilly. Orson and I plugged along until we found an offbeat little coffee shop. I hooked his leash to one of the outside tables, went inside and ordered a London Fog, a favorite tea drink of mine.

The barista could not have been friendlier as she asked about my day, and we exchanged pleasantries while my tea was steeping. I purchased an almond muffin and then did the balancing ordeal of trying to open the door without spilling the tea or dropping the muffin. But I was assisted by a kind gentleman who held the door open for me as I reunited with Orson.

I sat and enjoyed my warm drink and reflected upon these random acts of kindness that my day was beginning with and I made a mental counting of these kind actions of the last couple of days. There were the two from this morning, the lovely barista and the gentleman who held the door open for me. Then, while I was enjoying my tea, a young couple stopped to pat Orson on the head. We exchanged pleasantries.

It is true. As Aesop said, no act of kindness, no matter how small, is ever wasted.

I remembered the day before when I stopped for gas, the fellow traveler who gave me the squeegee so that I could clean the windows of my pickup. Then there was the clerk who offered me the "leave a penny, take a penny" change so that I could round my purchase to the nearest dollar amount. I appreciated that kind act as I dislike carrying change around in my pockets. There was the host at the motor inn who last night offered to bring by extra towels if I needed them. There was also the fellow traveler who helped me with the balky ice machine that didn't want to part with its ice.

And there was the truck driver at the rest-stop who offered a dog biscuit to Orson, saying that his pooch in the passenger side of his semi-truck was glad to share. I remembered exchanging several nods and hellos with strangers on the pedestrian path last night as I took Orson out for a stroll.

I made a mental note of all of these random acts of kindness as I had gone through my day. I was both surprised at the number of them and also at how many I had simply taken for granted. How much lovelier had my day been made in these many ways?

And what is the cost of these kindnesses? Virtually nothing. As I look backward thorough my life, I have never regretted taking the high road and simply being kind.

I reflected back to a lesson I had learned while studying Buddhism. In certain Buddhist temples, the monks are required to perform a daily "merit." This is an act of kindness which is important to the evolution of the monk's soul. These simple acts can take many forms, such as adding rice to someone else's bowl, or waking early and doing additional chores so that a fellow monk can get in extra study time. Maybe it's assisting a fellow student in their studies.

What a beautiful way to live, so soul enhancing. I thought of how doing these random acts of kindness could eventually become a habit, a way to live.

I have read studies that show that these acts of kindness not only help the recipient, but they also affect the giver in so many positive ways. Research on compassion and service show that giving improves the physical health of the giver, makes one less prone to depression, and can even extend one's longevity.

And perhaps the most beneficial consequence is that it makes one happier. These kindnesses give both the giver and receiver joy, and a more positive outlook. I remembered another of my Buddhist lessons. The fragrance of the flower stays in the hand of the giver. True.

I sat there with Orson and sipped my tea. The sun was just making it's way over the mountains and it was almost blinding in its light. I scratched Orson behind his ears and gave him the last bite of the muffin. I felt nothing but peace and gratitude thinking about these kindnesses that had been given so freely to me. What a beautiful day it was going to be.

I went back inside the coffee shop and put a couple extra dollars into the tip jar. I told the barista how much I appreciated her thoughtfulness, leaving her some money on the counter and asking that the coffees for the next couple of customers be paid with these funds. I wanted to pay my gratitude forward.

I gathered up Orson's leash and walked him to the pickup, opening the door, then lifting him into the back seat. He turned and licked my hand, thanking me for that kindness.

. . .

There is a story of two young boys who were walking down a road that bordered a farm when they noticed a poor farmer working the field, his good clothes neatly folded off to the side.

One boy looked at the other and said, "Let's hide this farmer's shoes so that when he comes in from the field he won't be able to find them. We can watch from the bushes. It will be so funny to see."

The other boy thought for a minute. "He looks poor. Instead, let's put a silver dollar in each shoe and then we can hide in these bushes. Let's see how he reacts to that."

The other boy agreed and they snuck over and put a silver dollar in each one of the poor farmer's shoes. They then hid behind some bushes. It wasn't long before the farmer trudged over to the spot where he had left his clothes. He first put one foot into a shoe and then stopped, feeling the silver dollar that was hidden therein. He pulled out the coin and puzzled over it and looked around to see who might have done such a thing.

He then put his foot into the other shoe and found the silver dollar that was hidden there. The farmer was overwhelmed at the surprise of these two coins and thinking he was alone, dropped to his knees and offered up a prayer of thanks, one that the boys could easily hear from their hiding place. They heard his tears of joy and relief as he spoke of his sick wife and hungry children. He expressed his gratitude for this gift from unknown providence.

The farmer soon began his walk back to his village and the boys came out from their hiding place and continued their walk home, themselves changed by knowing the good that they had done for this poor farmer. And their souls smiled, and made light for the rest of their journey.

AFTER OTTER LEFT ME AT THE FRONT GATE, I WENT TO MY first period class. At the first opportunity, my friends and I talked about the Nutrition Break Incident of the day before. We were still amazed at what we had witnessed. It was honestly something that we did not expect and could not compute into our teenage boy brains. But it was the talk of the school, how this skinny 10th grader took on the star of the football team. And lived not only to tell about it, but actually kicked his ass.

Everyone seemed to consider me the expert on all things Otter, since I was his best friend, maybe his only friend. I think most people liked Otter, at least what they knew about him. I don't think anyone disliked him. Otter was just a quiet guy and no one really knew him that well. Except me. And I wasn't sure how well I knew him.

Everyone wanted to know about Otter. Did I know that he could fight like that? What kind of martial arts did he use? Had Otter taught me any moves? Someone else asked if he liked girls, mostly to just be a smart ass. It just proved that no one knew him very well.

I was in English class when the lunch bell rang, so I left class and headed with everyone else towards the area where all of the covered tables were. I ducked inside the bathroom on my way to the cafeteria. I was standing at the urinal when Roger Mooney came in and started doing his business in the next urinal over.

I looked at him, probably stared a little too long, until he said, "What are you looking at?" I was simply wondering why he was at school since Otter had been suspended for a week. I didn't say anything and I turned back to the business at hand, but I was certainly perplexed.

I finished up and as I turned from the urinal Roger spoke. "I see your boyfriend got suspended." He had a stupid grin on his face. "Bet you're disappointed to have lost your cuddle buddy for a week."

I ignored his stupidity. "How come you didn't get suspended?" I said to him as he zipped up his pants.

Roger smirked. "Because I didn't start it. Chrome Dome did."

I shook my head. "Of course you started it."

Roger laughed. "Nope. Your girlfriend's lucky that I have a baseball game and I couldn't get into a fight. Otherwise…."

"Otherwise what?" I said, rolling my eyes, my tone full of sarcasm.

Roger puffed up his posture. "I'd have so kicked his ass. You wouldn't recognize him when you guys cuddled up together."

I ignored his crass comment. "You got your ass kicked. Everyone in the school knows it." I was smirking. "Dude, he wiped the floor with you."

Roger took a step towards me and started to get into a threatening stance, but then relaxed. "Tell Chrome Dome to stay the hell away from me or I will beat the shine right off his stupid head." Then he walked out of the bathroom.

I left right behind him and instead of going to the cafeteria I headed for Mr. Gearheart's Government classroom. Mr. Gearheart was the first teacher to arrive at the Nutrition Break Incident and he had walked Otter towards the principal's office. When I got to his classroom, he was busy going through some papers on his desk. I asked if he had a minute, that I needed to talk with him.

"What's on your mind, Jake?' he asked in a friendly manner. Mr. Gearheart was a favorite teacher of many students at the school and was my favorite so far in my first high school year. I told him that I had run into Roger Mooney and that I knew that Otter had been suspended for fighting and I wondered why the same punishment wasn't given to Roger.

"What did you see happen?" he asked and I told him of the whole incident regarding the back cuts and Roger pushing Otter twice and then how the fight progressed with Roger ending up on the ground. He asked for an explanation of what back cuts were, and I explained them the best that I could. I re-emphasized that Roger had started the fight and that Otter was defending himself.

Mr. Gearheart leaned back in his rickety wooden chair and it squeaked a familiar sound to those of us in his classroom. "That's not the way I heard it. I was told that Mark told Roger to go to the end of the line and when he didn't, Mark hit him three times, kicked him in the stomach, and then flipped him onto the ground. The story I was told was Roger did nothing to provoke Mark except not go back to the end of the line. And also that Roger did not even defend himself. I was told that Roger couldn't defend himself because he had a baseball game and it was against Coach Stenquist's rules, that he could get kicked off the team for fighting."

"That is not true," I stammered. "Roger totally started it and whoever told you different is lying."

Mr. Gearheart looked at me in his quiet and calm way, though he raised his eyebrows at my different version of the events. His voice was calm. "The person who told me this version of the story was Mark Otter."

I was speechless. The room was quiet except for the sounds of students coming and going outside the classroom. Mr. Gearheart continued with what he had been doing when I walked in. "Why would he tell that story?" I asked. My voice seemed to squeak, and I coughed quietly in hopes of getting the squeak to go away.

"I guess you'll have to ask Mark Otter," and Mr. Gearheart turned away to the blackboard to write the next period's assignment.

I planned to do just that and it was hard to keep my mind on my classes for the rest of the day. As soon as the bell rang, I headed to the 7-11, Otter's and my agreed upon rendezvous spot. He was standing next to the phone booths waiting for me and I came right out with it. "How come you told the teachers that you started the fight? How come you took all the blame? Why didn't you tell the truth? That Roger started the whole thing?" I was speaking fast and my voice was rising. I was getting worked up.

Otter stood next to the phone booths and listened to my ranting. After I finished, he checked for change in the two phones that were there, something I was sure he had already done. "I guess I thought no one would believe me."

"Not true, dude," I puffed. "There were tons of witnesses. Not everyone would have lied! I wouldn't have!"

Otter stopped going from phone booth to phone booth and faced me. "I know. Thanks." He began walking home and I fell into line next to him. "It's ok. I don't mind missing some school. And why should Roger miss school and baseball? There's no point in both of us getting punished."

We walked in silence for awhile. I didn't know what to say to counter this kind of logic.

"Anyway," Otter broke the silence. "Will you help me with the assignments I'm missing? I still have to turn everything in."

I nodded that I would. We continued home. Otter was sure a different kind of guy.

ROCK AND HILL
By Mark Otter

There is a hill.
There is a rock.
The rock must be pushed up the hill
each and every day.

Every morning the rock is at the bottom of the hill.
The day is spent pushing it towards the top.
And the next morning
the rock is at the bottom again.
Just as it was the morning before.
And the morning before.
And the morning before.
And the morning before.

Tired of this rock.
Tired of this hill.

OCTOBER 11

ORSON AND I LEFT LEAVENWORTH AND HEADED straight for Seattle, stopping only to park along the Wenatchee River to spread some more of The Repository. I found a small sapling just above the river line and spread my mixture and added my prayer. Orson and I stayed there for a few minutes and I tried to focus and meditate for a bit, but we were close to the highway and concentration was challenging. I still felt peaceful about the experience.

We drove straight over the mountain pass and I marveled at the beauty of the mountains and the woods, the leaves on the trees just beginning to change color. Driving down the other side of the mountain, I soon found myself caught in the usual Seattle traffic, so I pulled off the freeway and found an eccentric little sandwich shop, unusual because of its cow themed decor. There were paintings of cows, ceramic cows, cow tablecloths, cows everywhere. I ordered a cucumber, tomato and cheese sandwich and of course I saved the last bite for my traveling companion. Then we loaded back up and headed to Port Angeles where I picked up some supplies.

It was getting close to sunset, so I leashed up Orson and we walked along the pier to stunning hues as the sun sunk lower behind the horizon. It was as if the sun was going through a cheese grater, colors of reds and oranges streaking across the sky.

As I watched the sun fade from view, I thought of how much I appreciated these simple treasures of life, sunrises and sunsets, and that I am able to do so without some desperate need to own them or desire for them to last forever. I simply try to appreciate these moments when they occur and indulge in their beauty. I don't try and change them, change their colors or their timing. I let them fade away and watch in a certain awe as it occurs. I'm okay with that.

I then compared that feeling to so many of the wants and desires in my life, hoping certain feelings would last forever, and my forbearance to try and get them to do so. Life should be lived lightly, not fighting against the possibility of loss.

I decided to stop at a roadside deli and get some prepared food to have for dinner. I wandered around the deli, waiting for the checkout line to thin a bit. I picked up some chips and decided to splurge on a bottle of wine, then I got into the deli line to order a sandwich behind a few other patrons. I let my mind wander around the shop while I waited for my turn at the counter. I looked over other customers, and I tried to mentally place them with the cars that were in the parking lot, seeing if I could match person and automobile. It was something that I did to wile away the time while standing in line.

My mind came back to the present when the gentleman in front of me turned to me and said "Hey," under his breath, while nodding his head towards two men that were at the counter ordering.

I was unclear on what he was trying to point out, so I said, "What?" and he nodded his head more vigorously at the two men. It began to dawn on me what he was referencing as the two men at the counter were holding hands while ordering their food and one of them was rubbing the other's neck. It was obvious they were in a relationship together and sharing an affectionate moment.

Even though I thought this was what was disturbing the man in front of me, I thought there was still a chance that I might have misinterpreted his head nods. So I said, "What?" one more time.

That is when he mustered a sour look on his face and then said under his breath, "Damn faggots."

It is not like I have not seen this kind of bigotry before. I remember the word fag and faggot being fairly popular epithets during my teenage years. My friends and I oftentimes called each other fag or faggot, and it was certainly not the bigoted word that it has become over time. But I had not heard these words in several years before being reintroduced to them in such a crude way by the man standing in line in front of me.

I have seen this kind of quietly stated bigotry in my life, and I must admit that I have always been at a loss as to what to say, or even wonder if I should say anything and start a confrontation that may lead to further unpleasantness. I merely shook my head at this gentleman, and he turned away from me, still muttering under his breath.

I thought about how grateful I am that society has changed and bigots like this mostly lurk in the shadows, at least the shadows of polite society. The two gay gentleman finished their transaction and the bigot in front of me stepped to the front of the line. I don't think anyone else even knew what had happened.

I had a colleague at Montana State who has a gay son, and I remember when the son, who lived in Seattle, got married to his gay partner. My colleague was so happy and he would often tell me of the wedding plans whenever our paths crossed. I saw him a couple of days after the wedding and I asked him how it went. He talked on and on at what a lovely ceremony it was. It was fun to share in the excitement that this man had for his son and his son's new husband.

"I'm so glad it was such a good time," I said during our conversation. "And the weather seemed like it was perfect."

He smiled this large smile. "The weather WAS perfect." Then he got quiet and I could see tears beginning to well up in the corners of his eyes.

"Is everything okay?" I asked.

He dabbed a handkerchief at his face. "Jake," he began, "almost 28 years ago, my father didn't come to my wedding because I married this beautiful Jewish girl. He said it was an affront to his Christian beliefs. And now I just watched my father dance the night away, excited to be at his gay grandson's wedding."

I was so moved by this story. Then this colleague came over and we hugged each other. "The world only turns forward," he stated.

Yes. Yes it does.

Back at the deli, I stepped forward and ordered my sandwich and paid for my chips and wine and headed to the parking lot. There I watched the two gay men climb into the cab of their Ford F-150 and the man in front of me get into a Honda Accord. I smiled as I realized that I would never have matched that up. It reminded me that I had stereotypes too.

The sun was disappearing rapidly so I joined Orson in the pickup and headed towards Olympic National Park where we found a place to park and camp. I purchased some wood from a camp store and made a fire for Orson and I to sit around and we both enjoyed our dinner with gusto. I opened the bottle of wine and even indulged in a second glass, the mood simply perfect for it.

I journaled a bit by the fire as Orson crept as close to it as he dared so he could warm himself. I tried to call Susan, but reception was spotty and I decided after a couple of attempts to try again in the morning when I was further down the road. I took my flashlight and walked Orson around the campground and nodded greetings to fellow dog walkers. I wandered off the trail for a few yards and turned my flashlight off. The vista of stars in the sky was simply stunning and I found an old log to sit on as I listened to the sounds of the forest and studied the thousands of stars.

I decided that a night service for The Repository was what was called for and I took Orson back to our campsite and collected the old coffee can. I left Orson inside the camper, as he was moving slowly and was tiring of the several walks of the day. I went back to the log where I had been just a few minutes before and turned off the flashlight and knelt down and stirred my mixture into the soil. There were several mushrooms growing in and around the log and I thought it was a perfect place to leave the dust I have been carrying around, both figuratively and literally. And so it was.

I searched my mind for a few words to say, maybe a prayer, and I recited what was on my mind out loud. And I thought about how grateful I was that I and my many friends no longer called people that were different from us derogatory names. Stating my gratitude aloud seemed to give it more meaning, more importance, and that warmed me.

I recalled the words of the poet Maya Angelou. "Prejudice is a burden that confuses the past, threatens the future, and renders the present inaccessible." Wise words.

I stayed a few more minutes in the solitude, the quiet broken occasionally by some campsite noise as the campground was still fairly close by. My heart filled with gratitude. That feeling of gratitude is such a soft feeling and it's easily plowed under by a myriad of other feelings. It is easy to forget to give thanks.

After awhile I arose and walked the short distance back to where my pickup was and when I made my way back to the campground it was quiet, most of the campfires having been put out. I opened the back of the pickup and Orson did not raise his head in acknowledgment of my presence, but his tail thumped along the pickup bed. I climbed into my sleeping bag and Orson moved closer to me, luxuriating in my body heat. I gave more thanks.

I heard an owl in the distance, announcing his existence, probably preparing for his nightly hunt. It was tranquil and I slept peacefully.

Once there was a highly educated student who sought after a teacher to impress upon him all that this student had learned. So he set off and climbed many mountains and forded many streams in search of this renown sage.

When he came upon the sage's home, he was surprised to find it but a very humble hut. Inside was the teacher, with a long beard and bright eyes hunched over a tea kettle, humming to himself. Presently, the old sage looked up, and seeing this student, bade him to come inside.

They sat, and while the student boasted about his education, the teacher began filling up the student's tea cup with the hot tea that he had just prepared. As the student rambled on and on, so did the teacher continue pouring tea into the cup until it soon overflowed across the table and onto the student's lap.

"What are you doing old man?" The student admonished the teacher in a harsh voice. "You are spilling tea everywhere! Can't you see that my cup is already overflowing?"

The teacher calmly stopped pouring the tea and looked at him with his bright eyes. "Your mind is like this teacup. I'm afraid it is already too full for me to fit anything else into it. Else it too, will overflow and spill everywhere."

THE REST OF THE WEEK SETTLED INTO A PACE OF OTTER joining me in the morning and walking with me to school, then us rendezvousing at the 7-11 when school was over and he would walk home with me. There we would spend a few minutes going over his assignments. It never took too long and then we would play ping pong on the table in my garage or listen to music in my room and just chat. After that Otter would walk home and the next day we would do it again.

On the fourth day of the suspension, we were playing ping pong when my mom came in and told us that Otter's mom was here to take him home. This was unusual as Otter always walked home from my house, his house maybe a ten minute walk from mine, and this occurrence seemed to shake Otter a bit. He even said "Hmm…this can't be good."

I walked with him back into the house and Mrs. Otter was there, and nothing seemed out of the ordinary except that she had a black eye, bruising all around the left side of her face. She was standing in the doorway chatting with my mom.

"I know, clumsy, right?" Mrs. Otter was saying. "Slipped right on the bathroom rug and hit the corner of the sink." She saw Otter and gave him a little wave. "I mean, how many thousands of times have I gone in that bathroom and not slipped on that rug?"

Tom Smyly

My mom listened and nodded. This was the first time she had met either of Otter's parents, and the first time I had really seen Mrs. Otter. Mom was doing the usual chitchat thing. "Accidents do happen," she agreed. "Perhaps you should put some ice on it. Perhaps see a doctor."

"Oh, it looks worse than it is," Mrs. Otter replied. Otter slid by her and out our front door, telling me that he would see me in the morning. Mom waved to the both of them as they walked towards the driveway and she closed the front door behind them.

I started to go to my room when Mom called me into the kitchen where she was finishing up making enchiladas. "Did Mark mention his mother's accident?" she asked me.

I was totally oblivious to why my mom was wondering that. "Nope," I answered. "Why?"

"Have you noticed any other injuries on Mark, maybe like the one on his arm a while back?" Mom stopped shredding some cheese and wiped her hair back with her shirt sleeve. "Maybe you've seen other injuries on his mother?"

"I really don't see his parents very often, I've only seen his dad a couple of times. And this was the first time seeing his mom, except maybe from a distance. What are you getting at?" I was still oblivious.

"Because I don't think her bruised eye happened the way she said it did."

I didn't know how to respond to that. I simply thought she had blackened her eye the way she had described. I suggested that maybe I could ask Otter about it when I saw him tomorrow, to which mom said she was just wondering. And she left it at that.

Because of my mom's questions, I began to recall the times when I had seen cuts and bruises on Otter. I did begin to wonder if the story his mom told of slipping on the rug and hitting her face on the sink was true.

The next morning, the last day of Otter's suspension, he was at his usual place at the end of my driveway. I asked him if everything was okay and I mentioned that he seemed surprised that his mom came to pick him up.

"Yep. She just needed some help with something in the yard."

I continued walking along silently for a few steps. "That sure was quite the shiner that your mom had on her eye," I said, and I let that hang out there for a few moments. There was no response from Otter, so I ventured out a little more. "Slipped on the bathroom rug, huh?"

"That's what she said," and Otter continued walking along at the same pace.

"Is that what happened?" I tried to say this casually, like I was not implying anything.

Otter continued at the same pace, but he looked directly at me as I walked beside him. "That's what she said, wasn't it?" And there was a difference in the tone, a tone that communicated that this subject was over. This was a tone that Otter had not used with me during our friendship. So I let the discussion drop and changed the topic saying that he must be glad to get this suspension over. And he agreed, and I could tell he was glad to change the conversation.

I didn't think much more about our before-school walk and at the end of the day I headed towards our 7-11 meeting spot. Otter wasn't outside, so I went inside to see if he was there. A couple of times this week, I had gone inside and bought some gum or a drink when Otter and I met, so I was not unfamiliar with the clerk who worked there.

This time as soon as I stepped inside, the clerk came out from behind the counter and strode towards me. "You need to get out," he said gruffly. "You're not welcome here anymore." He met me just a couple of steps inside the store.

"What?" I was perplexed. "What did I do?"

The clerk was obviously agitated. "You and your buddy. I caught him stealing. Both of you…out! Don't come back."

"I didn't steal anything. I haven't done anything." I'm sure my voice rose an octave as it was apt to do when I was flustered.

"You guys are always together. How many times have you stolen something?" His voice was getting angrier. "You need to get out now or I'll call the police!"

"I haven't stolen anything," I retorted and I backed out of the store and out onto the parking lot. I walked out to the sidewalk. I looked both ways and I could see Otter in the distance waving to me, motioning for me to join him.

I quickened my walk until I met up with him. I was upset at what had just happened. "What the fuck, Otter? That clerk at the 7-11 was freaking out! He accused me of stealing!"

"I know, right?" Otter had this incredulous look on his face, but it seemed phony.

"He said you stole something. What happened?"

Otter turned away from me. "Oh…I had a couple of candy bars and I forgot that I had them and I accidentally walked out of the store. Then he comes running out of the store and grabs me and freaks out."

I wasn't buying the story. "Why didn't you pay him then?" I knew the answer to this question.

"I forgot my money at home. I told him I would bring it later, but he wigged out and told me to never come into the 7-11 again or he would call the cops."

We had stopped walking now and were facing each other. I softened my voice. "Dude, you never have money. You were stealing the candy."

Otter's voice softened also. "Dude, it's just a couple of candy bars. Don't you freak out too."

We looked at each other for several moments. "Do you have the algebra assignment?" Otter asked. He was clearly trying to change the subject.

I looked at him for a few more moments. "You can't do that shit," I said. "I'm not hanging out with this."

Otter looked down at the sidewalk, averting his eyes from mine. "You're right." He looked back up to my eye level. "I'm sorry. I won't do it again."

I still didn't say anything in response. "Honest," he was looking right at me. "I would never have done it if I knew he would have blamed you. It was just a spur of the moment thing."

I had always known Otter as a good guy. "Okay," I said. "Let's get our homework done quickly so I can school you in some ping pong." I was done with this subject.

"As if you could," Otter grinned. And we walked home.

EVIL IN MY POCKET
by Mark Otter

Jesus.
He walked upon the water.
He calmed the storm.
He fed the masses.

But what if-

He walked upon the water
Because it was easier than walking on the land?

He calmed the storm
Because he hated the rain?

He fed the masses
Because he was hungry?

Does it make it any more or less
A miracle?

Families are made of spider webs
And one gets caught in the morass.

I throw others upon the current
That I stand upon so still.

With evil in my pocket.

OCTOBER 12

THE NEXT MORNING DAWNED OVERCAST WITH PATCHY fog covering the highway, making the going damp. I decided to backtrack to Port Angeles and get coffee and breakfast there. Soon I was sitting outside the covered patio of a local coffee shop, Orson at my feet, and I was very much enjoying the warmth of my beverage.

I phoned Susan, now having cellular reception, and had a delightful conversation with her as she regaled me with tales of her physical therapy clients and her frustrations with insurance companies. I didn't say much, just listened with enjoyment at the sound of her voice and the passion of her living.

After an almost hour-long conversation, I purchased a refill of my coffee and sat next to Orson, enjoying watching the comings and goings of the citizens of this tiny coastal town. I thought of Susan, the ease of our conversation, and the love that we shared. I gave thanks as I warmed my hands on my coffee cup.

We first met when I was doing research in the canyon-lands of Southern Utah and she was doing an internship for her physical therapy degree from the University of Utah. She was working with a local orthopedist and I was doing research of migratory patterns of southwestern coyotes.

This was part of my research work with Montana State, a position that I had just started. It wasn't very thrilling, but I loved what I did, and I loved being in the outdoors. I was camping in Arches National Park with a research team and I was constantly waking up stiff and sore. Hoping to alleviate some of this soreness, I searched out a yoga class and found one in the nearby town of Moab. So I signed up and drove over one Saturday morning.

That's where Susan and I met, doing yoga poses next to each other. I struck up a conversation and I was taken by her easy manner, her strawberry blonde hair, the freckles on her nose, her clear blue eyes. And her lithe yoga body certainly stirred me. I was impressed at her ability to ask a question and then really listen to the answer. I asked her to lunch after the class and the relationship just sort of took off from there. Most of the time when people found out what I did for a living, they couldn't be more bored. But she seemed fascinated, and was an open book in talking about her life. I found myself smitten.

I knew from our first meeting that this was different. Maybe it wasn't exactly love at first sight, but still different. It was as if I knew her from another time, another place. And the universe conspired to bring us together at this exact moment in time.

All during our lunch I thought about how much I was enjoying her company and conversation. Then I began thinking of how I was going to ask her out. How would this work? She lived in town and I was camping out in the wilds of Utah. This was a time before cell phones. I knew that getting back in contact with her would take some effort. Risking rejection, I found a phone booth and called the number that she had given me on the back of a napkin. I asked her out for that very same evening.

We went out to dinner and I found myself wanting to get to know everything about her. Did she like the color turquoise? Did she wear slippers around the house? How many brothers and sisters did she have? Was she close to them? Did she like to play board games when she was young? Did she love the color of her coffee when just the right amount of cream was added? And I hoped that if in this tango of conversation we found ourselves drawn to each other's souls, then perhaps we would like to embrace.

I recall after the dinner was over, walking to another restaurant for dessert and her clasping my hand. And I remember thinking that there is no greater joy than in the first holding of hands, except perhaps luxuriating in the desire to do so.

It was obvious that we had a connection and we exchanged phone numbers and addresses. I completed my research project a few days later and when I got back to my home in Bozeman, I called her and we talked almost the whole night. It was simply....magic.

The relationship continued with me working in Bozeman and her finishing her internship in Moab. After her internship was over, she moved back to Salt Lake City, and we continued talking over the phone four or five times a week. After about a month of that, I made plans to make the 6 1/2 hour drive from Bozeman to see her.

I remembered pulling into her apartment complex and her running out to greet me. It was obvious that she had been looking out the window to see if I had arrived, something she would have had to be doing most of the afternoon of my scheduled arrival. Seeing her was simply joy.

The relationship progressed from there in the usual way. I kept working at Montana State and she started a full time position as a physical therapist in Salt Lake City. Soon I found myself driving the 6 1/2 hour drive from my house in Bozeman to see her as often as I could.

We decided to go camping for a week in the Yellowstone National Park area and we arranged our schedules to do so. I remember so vividly that week, and how wonderful it was. I recall stopping for lunch at a cafe in West Yellowstone, Montana. It was there that I fell into a deep enchantment to the sound of her voice as I listened intently to stories she had told me before. But each time she told stories that I had already heard, I learned something different, something new about her.

I was not one to talk much about myself unless prompted, so a lot of the conversation revolved around her. But I didn't mind. I wanted her to tell me everything, new stories, old stories, and with each telling I could feel my love growing. It was a magical week.

We spent a wonderful week backpacking in and around Yellowstone. When it was time to return to civilization, we hiked back to my car and started back to her house. She slept most of the return drive back to Salt Lake City. I remember looking over at her every few miles or so and I had such tender affection for her as she slept leaning against the window and I watched her breath come and go against the glass. Even when asleep, she was beautiful and I imagined our life together, all of the road trips we would take, sharing the same love and companionship that I was feeling at this moment. It was my job to get us safely home and I reveled in how she slept snuggled up in my jacket, soft tunes playing from the car radio.

As Rumi, the wonderful Persian poet said, "Close your eyes. Fall in love. Stay there."

When we got back to her place in Salt Lake City, I told her that I wanted to travel the world with her. I wanted to explore new places, eat spicy foods, drink wines and teas with her by my side. I wanted to hike strange roads and paths and get lost exploring mountains and rivers. And I wanted to rest at the end of the day upon each other, our bodies intertwined, whether it be in sleeping bags, fancy hotels, or simply on friends' and relatives' couches. Wherever it was, I wanted to be together. And always with her falling asleep in the passenger seat against the window or against my shoulder on every automobile or bus or plane that we found ourselves.

She agreed. Soon she joined me in Bozeman and joined a physical therapy practice there. We never had an official marriage, but we did invite close friends over as witnesses when we exchanged a vow of commitment to each other. It was a simple commitment - give each other room to blossom, always be there for each other, don't attribute each other's periodic unhappiness to something lacking in the other. Be optimistic and always assume each has value without them needing to prove it. And always love each other in such a way that the other feels free.

That was about thirty years ago and we remind each other of these commitments often.

That was what I was thinking about, sitting outside a coffee shop in Port Angeles on a foggy morning. I looked down at Orson and my heart was filled with gratitude for my beautiful companion back in Montana and the furry one at my feet.

I realized that I had been here for awhile. I walked with Orson over to a grassy area so that he could take care of his bathroom business, then loaded him back into the pickup. I filled up the gas tank at a local station, pulled out onto Highway 101 and headed towards the coast. I still had miles to go.

. . .

A Zen teacher saw five of his students return from the market riding their bicycles. "Why do you ride your bicycles?" he asks.

The first student replies, "The bicycle is carrying my sack of potatoes. I am glad to not have to carry them." The teacher tells the student that he is wise and will grow up not having to stoop over.

The second student says, "I love to watch the trees and fields pass by as I ride along. They are so lovely." The teacher tells this student that his eyes are open and he will see the world.

The third student says, "When I ride my bicycle I like to chant my Zen lessons. This way I can commit them to memory." The teacher praises this student and tells him that his mind will become sharp.

The fourth student says, "When I ride my bicycle I feel that I am in harmony with all beings." The teacher tells him that he is on the path to living with all beings in non-harming ways.

The fifth student says, "I ride my bicycle to ride my bicycle."

The teacher sits before the fifth student. "I am your disciple," he says.

Otter finished his suspension and we fell back into the routine of meeting at the end of my driveway and walking to school together. Most of the time we would see each other at lunch and then meet up at the end of the school day and walk home, though now we had to take a detour so as not to walk by the 7-11. We didn't talk about why we had to take the detour, but we knew it was because we did not want to rile up the store clerk again.

One morning I walked out the front door, and there was Otter at the end of the driveway, but looking different. Otter pretty much wore the same thing everyday, jeans and a t-shirt, but this morning he was disheveled. His hair was uncombed, and he looked he had just got out of bed and walked to my house.

"What the hell happened to you?"

"What do you mean?" Otter yawned and picked up a book that he had just dropped.

"You look like you just woke up."

Otter yawned again. "Yeah. My dad got me up in the middle of the night and made me wash all the dishes in the house."

I was perplexed. "Uh....why?"

"He found a dirty one, so I had to take all the dishes and pots and pans and silverware and wash them all again."

I just stared at Otter. "What?"

"He found a spoon that had a spot on it, so he got me out of bed and I had to wash all the dishes." He shrugged. "No big deal."

We started the journey towards school. "Seems a little harsh."

"What would your dad do? Don't you do the dishes at your house?"

"I do them with my sister," I continued walking. "But we have a dishwasher. We have to load them and unload them."

"Well, we don't have a dishwasher. What would your dad do if you had to wash the dishes and you left a spot?" Otter stopped and waited for an answer.

I turned to Otter. "I don't think he would notice."

"But if he did?"

I thought for a second. "Probably just tell me to do a better job next time."

We started walking again. I could see Otter was thinking about what I said. "Well. My dad makes me do all the dishes." Then, "He says it builds character." He said this with a smirk.

"You are a character," I lamely kidded him. And we finished the walk talking about girls.

Otter was a member of the Jehovah's Witnesses and I suppose I only knew this because at Christmas time, he told me that he and his family did not celebrate Christmas. I immediately thought he was Jewish, but he told me that he and his family were Jehovah's Witness. He didn't really expound much upon that and I simply forgot about it most of the time. It wasn't like he wore it on his sleeve. I did know that he wouldn't hang out much on Sundays, and that was no big deal.

One Saturday when we were playing ping pong in my garage, he mentioned that I should go to church with him sometime. I asked why and he seemed quite evasive. He hemmed and hawed over an answer and then he just let the matter drop, as did I. But I was a little mystified as the request seemed to come totally out of the blue.

A few days after that he brought it up again. I asked him why the interest in getting me to go to church and he said that missionary work was really important to the Jehovah's Witnesses faith and he was getting pressure from his dad to ask me to attend church with his family.

Then the truth really came out. "I've been telling my dad that I have been trying to get you interested in the church. That's why he lets me hang out with you as much as I do."

We were sitting in my room at the time, me laying on my bed and Otter reclining on the floor. I got up to change the record on the small stereo that I had. "Really?" was all I could say.

"That isn't why I hang out with you," Otter said by way of explanation to the puzzlement in my voice. "It's just that Jehovah's Witnesses don't encourage relationships outside of its members. I won't get into any hassles with my dad if he thinks that I am trying to recruit you." He paused for a second. "It just makes things easier around my house."

I thought about what Otter was saying as I took one record off of the player and put another record on. "So why do I have to go to church? Just keep saying that you're still working on me." I tried to lighten the mood. "Tell him that I'm a particularly hard case."

Otter seemed uncomfortable even talking about this subject. "I'm just getting some pressure about it. Maybe just think about it." Then he closed the subject. "It's no big deal."

This conversation stayed in the back of my mind when a week later I was walking with Otter towards his house, something I did on occasion though I had never been invited inside. When we got to the duplex that Otter lived in, his father came out and strode out to the driveway to get into his car. He saw the both of us and took a couple of steps our way. "What are you two doing here?" His question didn't seem friendly, but it didn't seem hostile either.

"Jake is just dropping me off. He was asking about an Algebra problem from our class." Otter seemed stilted and matter of fact. I could tell that he was nervous seeing his dad with me along.

Otter's dad turned to me. "So what did you think of The Watchtower?"

I was caught a little off guard. "What?"

Otter's dad's eyes stared directly into mine and he faced me directly. "The Watchtower. From our church. Mark said he gave you a copy."

"Yeah. I forgot what it was called," my mind raced as I thought of my next lie. "It's sitting on the table by my bed. I just haven't got into it yet."

"Well, read it and let's talk about it. You really should go to a meeting with us. We have an outstanding youth program in our church." Otter's dad turned back to his car and put some papers in the back seat. "You know that a relationship with God is so important now days." Mr. Otter paused for a second. "Mark invited you to attend church with us, didn't he?"

"Yes sir," I said. "But my parents wouldn't let me." I continued to lie.

He turned back towards me. "I could talk to them. I would like to tell them about how a belief in Jehovah is the only way to heaven."

"That's ok. But I'll ask them again."

Otter's dad began to get into the driver's seat of his car. "Good. Let's get you out to church with us. I'm sure you will love it. We have a great youth program." He had a smile on his face. But it wasn't a smile that was inviting in the least. It just seemed phony.

He pulled out of the driveway and I gave a little wave to him and he returned it with a nod of his head. I watched him drive away then I turned to Otter who was on his front steps. "Well, see you tomorrow morning at the usual spot. Don't let your meatloaf." He walked inside, then as I was walking away, he turned around and came back out on the porch. "Hey Jake." I stopped at the end of his driveway and looked back towards the front door. "Thanks for covering with the whole Watchtower thing." He then went inside and closed the door.

I watched him disappear into his house. I stayed at the end of the driveway for a minute or two more, thinking that he may come back out onto the porch. He didn't, so I turned back towards the street and walked home.

BRIDGES BURN
By Mark Otter

They tell you
not to burn your bridges
in case you want to go back across,
maybe start over.

But what if you want to burn the bridge
before you cross it?

Just destroy the future before it destroys you?

The hell with it.
No matter what you do
Bridges burn.

OCTOBER 12

LEAVING PORT ANGELES, I HEADED FOR THE WASHING-ton coastline. It was a beautiful drive, skirting the Olympic National Park, dense forests lining the highway. The fog persisted most of the way, but it broke up every few miles or so to spectacular sunshine. I was able to stream a podcast on traveling the Pacific Coast through the truck stereo and that added to the ambiance of the trip. Orson was mostly unimpressed with the landscape, and he snoozed in the back seat.

I decided to stop in the town of Aberdeen, drawn there for the Kurt Cobain Memorial Park. It is located in a small city park, land that was close to where he grew up. While I was never a big Nirvana fan, I did appreciate his talent and respected the many emotions that followed his suicide back in the mid-nineties. It was a quiet spot, set along the banks of a muddy river that I googled to learn was the Wishkah River.

The site is marked by a guitar and several Cobain quotes, and I don't know exactly why, but I was moved to spread some of the contents of The Repository there. That decision necessitated going back to the truck to obtain the container, and I left Orson in the back seat. I wanted to be as inconspicuous as possible in spreading a few of the fragments of The Repository. I stealthily dropped some of the contents around the monument, but I didn't need the subterfuge as there was no one around. Still, I felt good about this deed and I wandered over to the river and said a few words out loud.

I returned to the truck and drove to a local cafe and enjoyed a lunch of bread and cheese, of course sharing some with my traveling companion. Then it was back into the truck to continue driving west and south to the town of Long Beach, a small town on the Washington coast. I found an RV park in the late afternoon and Orson and I settled in for a couple of hours, me reading and journaling, him simply snoozing. As evening approached, we walked over to the boardwalk, through the grassy dunes, with beautiful ocean views all around. There were a few people flying kites over the beach and ocean and they added to the beautiful scenery. I took off my shoes and sat in the sand, Orson at my side, and contemplated my quest and what lay ahead.

The ocean seemed peaceful at this time of the evening, the waves gently kissing up to the shore in a sleep inducing rhythm. There is something that inspires contemplation when I'm close to any body of water, but especially the ocean. The waters of the ocean are the beginnings and endings of the earth.

I remember one of my first Buddhist teachings. It was in a class that I took in college about eastern religions, one that I took at a time that I was questioning much of what I believed. The discussion was one on enlightenment, a favorite topic of many Buddhist discussions. The instructor said something that I have always thought about, especially when I am sitting next to a body of water. He talked about how enlightenment comes when a wave realizes that it is part of the ocean. He went on to explain that human enlightenment can only occur when we truly realize that we as humans are simply a wave in the ocean, part of a grander whole. I have often reflected upon that remark, and the further teachings that we are all connected as spiritual beings having an earthly experience.

I scratched Orson behind his ears and his tail thumped the sand at my touch. I often reflect on Orson and his beginning and ending. Was he another being before this life? Will his soul live another existence after this life? Buddhism believes that there can be several "heavens", though they are not permanent. It has a belief that we can be reborn in other forms as Nirvana (the Buddhist perfection, not the Kurt Cobain band) is sought-after. Buddhism believes that all animals and humans are interconnected.

I have heard of a race of people in the mountains of Mongolia that believe that if a dog lives an exemplary life then it is possible for him to return to the earth as a human when his life as a dog is over. I thought about this as I scratched Orson's ears. I wonder if he knew this.

We have so many milestones in our lives - the first kiss from a lover's lips, the brand new driver's license, that walk down the aisle of marriage, bringing that newborn home from the hospital, the first breaking of the heart. All part of this life's first act.

At some point, new experiences are more and more infrequent, replaced by an endless parade of goodbyes, some chosen and some not, from life connections, whether they be jobs, clubs, friends, or lovers. Life can be compared to a sort of San Andreas fault, where the solid ground of loves and friendships can drift slowly apart. Pets come and go, your co-workers hold farewell parties for you, your friends say adios and then fade away, sometimes expiring without warning. You watch your parents age, perhaps even watch them struggle with their own memories of you….and their own lives. And then Father Time claims them. You will even kiss your lover that one last time.

And there is a cruelty to life. Sometimes there is an agonizing slow descent from a vibrant life to that of an incapacitated burden upon it. Often we are made painfully aware of our growing inability to care for ourselves as we once did, and unable to do anything about it.

The only way to live forever is to densely pack your life with creations and experiences and memories and people. Know so many people that it would be impossible for them to know the entirety of you. What matters is how you live, how much joy and meaning you shoehorn into every second. Too much for the world to hold. As the poet Atticus says, "I hope to arrive at my death, late, in love, and a little drunk."

Despite my Buddhist leanings, I am unsure about the whole reincarnation idea. But I cannot deny those times when I have met someone and I feel like I have known them already. Or maybe I'm in a strange place, but it looks so familiar. I sometimes have a deja vu experience, the experience that something has happened to me before. Maybe our souls do return to earth, to evolve, to learn, to grow. Maybe we even come in contact with many of the same people that we knew before. Maybe we even have a connection of the soul with these people.

I stayed on the beach for a while, continuing to be lost in my thoughts. After a bit longer, Orson and I retraced our steps along the boardwalk and got back into town where we found a small cafe. I had some delicious clam chowder, served in a bread bowl, and when I had finished the chowder, I broke the bread bowl into pieces and shared it with Orson. We then meandered back to our camp site where Orson received the rest of his dinner.

The campground wasn't very crowded, and it stayed quiet as night fell. I called Susan with an update and was again buoyed to hear her voice. She continued to support this quest of mine, this search for peace, and she had encouraging words, which I needed. Then Orson and I settled into the back of the camper. I read for a while longer, then was lulled to sleep by the sound of Orson's breathing. I slept comfortably, dreamless.

. . .

A wise sage was dining with a magistrate of the city. Between bites of food and sips of wine, he posed the leader this question. "If a man came running up to you and told you that there was a tiger loose in the city, would you believe him?"

"Just one man?"

"Yes. Just one man."

The magistrate thought for a moment. "No. If it were just one man, I would not believe him."

"What if it were two men?"

The magistrate thought longer about this question. After several moments he replied, "No. I would not believe only two men."

"What if it were three men," the sage asked?

The magistrate quickly said, "Yes, if it were the word of three men, then I would definitely believe them."

The sage sat back into his chair. "But there is still no tiger in the city."

Tom Smyly

THE SCHOOL YEAR SOON ENDED AND SUMMER VACATION began. I didn't see Otter very often, mostly because he had to go to summer school to try and improve his grades, something that he said was not a choice. He didn't have to explain for me to know that meant his dad was making him. Otter said he didn't mind, that it gave him something to do.

My summer was spent doing a few interesting things, going to a soccer camp, then a science camp. I also went on our usual family vacation to the San Juan Islands in Puget Sound. My parents rented a cabin there every summer and we would stay for a couple of weeks. Otherwise, my summer was nothing to get excited about.

I did see Otter a few times, and he joined my family for dinner and even spent the night at my house twice, sleeping on an air mattress on the floor of my room. My parents liked Otter and were always impressed with his manners and how polite he was.

My family enjoyed playing board games, Parcheesi, Sorry, Scrabble, things like that. If Otter was around he would join in, which he seemed to like. We had some rousing, friendly family battles.

Otter also taught me how to play Canasta, a card game using a couple of decks of cards plus the jokers. He said his dad taught him how to play the game, and Otter and I would sometimes play it for hours in my room, loser having to get the winner some lemonade or crackers, whatever was in the pantry at my house.

One weekday morning Otter came by my house to hang out and I noticed quite the bruise under his left eye. I asked him about it, and he said it was from Tae Kwon Do, and that seemed plausible to me. So I didn't say anything else about it.

When afternoon came, we went over to the park across the street and shot some hoops. It soon got hot so we headed back over to my house and after grabbing a couple of apples from the kitchen counter, we headed to my room. "Canasta?" I said, grabbing the cards off my desk.

"You bet," Otter replied.

"I'm going to beat you like a red headed stepchild," I said, obviously teasing.

Suddenly, Otter's mood changed. "Let's not play cards." It was clear that I had said something that upset him.

"Hey. Sorry. Did I say something wrong?"

Otter sat down on the edge of my bed. I thought for a minute he was going to cry. "We don't have to play cards," I told him.

Otter was quiet for a minute. "No, it's okay." But I could tell it wasn't.

I sat down in my desk chair facing him. "What's wrong?"

Otter looked up. "I was playing Canasta with my dad. He likes playing and he sort of makes me play with him."

"Okay." I waited for him to continue.

"Well, we were playing and I was winning and he accused me of cheating. So he slapped me with the back of his hand and his ring caught my eye." He touched the bruise. It was obviously still sore.

"Wow," I said quietly. "Were you cheating?"

Otter looked at me. I thought he might be upset by the question. "No. A couple of the cards had stuck together, so I had too many cards in my hand. That upset him."

"Sorry man." I shuffled the cards on my desk. I didn't know what else to say. We didn't play Canasta that day.

As I said, my family enjoyed Otter's company. He was funny and would often jump up to help my mom do something in the kitchen, to my and Jenna's dismay. Mom would tell us how much she appreciated Otter's manners, usually as a playful prompt at Jenna and me, encouraging us to be more helpful around the house.

My mom particularly enjoyed it when Otter brought flowers, which was often, and most of the time he brought hydrangeas. I don't know where he got them, as there did not seem to be any hydrangeas around the duplex where he lived, but he would bring one or two of the brightly colored flowers, sometimes in a glass mason jar, and other times just handing over a couple of stems. Mom asked him once why he liked this particular flower so much, and Otter would say that they made him feel peaceful. My mom liked that a teenage boy would feel peaceful about flowers.

One evening Otter joined us for dinner and while sitting around the table, my mom made some remark. I don't remember what it was about, and I responded with a snarky, sarcastic comeback. It was totally uncalled for and I'll just attribute it to my teenager-ness. Mom was annoyed by my unusual disrespect and she remarked that she thought Otter would never treat his parents with such rudeness.

Otter looked up from his dinner and said as casually as if he were talking about the macaroni and cheese he was eating, "If I did, I'd be gumming my food right now."

The conversation at the dinner table stopped and the quiet was a little eerie. Even Jenna stopped eating and took notice. Otter sensed the unease. "Kidding," he said to break the silence.

"Everything okay at your house, son?" my dad asked. He said it quietly and calmly.

Otter could sense the discomfort around the table. "It's fine." He looked at our faces. "Really." He paused. "Thanks for asking, but really, I was kidding."

I apologized to my mom and I turned the conversation to something else, but I could tell my parents were concerned. The next day each separately asked me what I knew about Otter's home life, and I honestly said that Otter didn't reveal too much about what was happening at his house. I had told my parents this before. But I knew they were concerned.

That incident passed by without much more comment and the summer kept flying by. One afternoon, a couple of weeks before school was to start up again, there was a knock at the front door. Jenna answered, then came and peeked into my bedroom. "Otter's here," she said. "And something happened to his arm."

I went out to the front room, and Otter was there with a cast on his left forearm. His hair had been cut again, so he was sporting a fresh buzz cut. "Dude, what happened?"

"Yeah, I broke my arm at Tae Kwon Do. Trying to break cinder blocks. Stupid." He held out his arm. "Want to sign my cast?"

I looked at his short hair. We looked at each other. I think Otter knew that I wasn't buying the Tae Kwon Do story. "Did your dad get pissed off about something?" I just came right out and said what was on my mind.

Otter ran his right hand through his short hair. I could tell he was evaluating what to say next. Then, "Yea. Cut my hair again. Hey, lets play ping pong. I can still whip you with one hand tied behind my back."

I knew he was trying to quickly change the subject, so I didn't press it. I was concerned about the broken arm but he assured me once more that he broke it while trying to split cinder blocks in Tai Kwon Do. We spent the rest of the afternoon playing ping pong, then went over to the soccer field where we took turns at goalie as the other kicked soccer balls. He seemed none the worse for having one arm in a cast.

When we came back to my house after playing soccer, my mom saw his cast and asked about it and Otter gave her the same story that he had told me. She later told the story to my dad, who seemed to shrug it off, even saying that it seemed kind of stupid to try and break cinder blocks.

A couple of days later, Dad came into my room as I was listening to music and reading a book that was on the summer reading list. He asked me if I had seen Otter lately and I told him I had not seen him since he came over with his arm in a cast.

"Well," my dad began, "I have one of the students in Mark's Tae Kwon Do class as a patient and he came in for a check-up today. I asked him if he knew a Mark in his class."

"And?" I asked.

"Well, at first he didn't know who I was talking about until I said Mark Otter. Does anyone call him by his first name?"

I closed the book I was reading. "I don't think so. Pretty much everyone at school calls him Otter." I reminded my dad that Otter introduced himself to me as Otter the first time I met him.

My dad chuckled at that. "He said he did know Otter, so I asked him about breaking cinder blocks and this patient of mine said they never did that." He sat on the edge of my bed. "So I asked him about Mark, and he said that Mark came to class with his arm in a cast."

"Maybe he broke it in another class, one that your patient was not aware of." I knew what my dad was getting at but I didn't really want to go there.

"Yes, maybe." Dad got up and walked over to the door. "Maybe ask Mark about it, if it comes up." And he walked out.

A couple of days later, Otter was over, and I decided to just come right out and tell him what my dad had discovered while treating one of his Tae Kwon Do classmates. Otter listened and then got quiet. We were out in my front yard tossing a frisbee back and forth. He caught the frisbee and held it for a few seconds, looking down at the orange disc. He was silent and I let the silence settle for a few moments.

Then he walked over to me, and he lowered his voice as if he was afraid someone might hear what he was going to reveal. "My dad did it. He was punching me in the arm because he was pissed off that I left one of his tools out of the toolbox. I couldn't stand the pain, so I threw up my arm to try and block one of the punches and his fist smacked my arm and it cracked my bone."

I was dead quiet. I didn't know what to say. Otter continued. "It hurt like fuck, so the next day my mom took me to the doctor for x-rays and they said it was broken. My mom said that we needed to come up with a story, that no one could know the reason that my arm was broken so I said that I broke it at Tae Kwon Do."

I was silent, I had no words. It seemed like silence was a blanket covering my front yard. Otter looked me in the eye. "Jake, you can't let anyone know the truth. It would piss my dad off so much. Promise me you won't tell anyone."

I looked my friend in the eye. "Dude, this is no good."

"I can handle it," Otter moved closer. "Please. Promise me you won't tell anyone."

I felt pulled in a bunch of different directions. I stood in front of Otter. He shifted is weight from side to side. I had never seen him look like this. He looked like he wanted to cry, but that there was no way he was going to cry. It's hard to explain how he looked or the silence in the yard. Finally, after what seemed like hours of quiet, I said, "Okay. I won't tell anyone."

Otter seemed relieved. "Thanks." He seemed like he wanted to say something else and I waited for him to do so, but nothing further was forthcoming. I wanted to tell him that I was here for him, not to worry about anything, but I didn't know how that would come out. I wanted to tell him that he should tell someone, a teacher, my dad, my mom. But I stayed silent as he walked back across the yard. He turned and reiterated, "I can handle it." He walked back to the other side of the yard, stopped, and spun the frisbee in my direction.

I caught it and sent it back to him.

I GO THROUGH
By Mark Otter

There is a wall,
tall and thick.
A brick wall.

And to get to the other side
you have choices.

Over.....too tall.
Under....too deep
Around....too far.

So
I go through.

It's painful, hard, almost impossible.
But it is the only way.

I go through.

OCTOBER 13

IT WAS ANOTHER FOGGY MORNING WHEN I AWOKE AND I started up my small backpacker stove and heated some hot water, using it to make tea and oatmeal. I walked and fed Orson, then loaded him into the pickup and headed south along Highway 101, crossing the Columbia River into Oregon and the town of Astoria. There I stopped and had some coffee and a danish. It was mid morning and I took my time sipping my coffee. I meandered in and out of several shops in the downtown. The sun was trying hard to peak out from the clouds, succeeding at times, but mostly just gently brightening the sky with reddish streaks.

After awhile, I found a bench with a view of the Columbia, and I watched as fishing boats floated around the dock, some going out, some coming back in. It was chilly out, but I was warm in my jacket, Orson at my feet.

I found myself watching the small trolley that rumbled along the riverfront and I debated getting on board to experience the short ride along the rails. But I did not know if Orson would be welcomed on board, so I demurred. I enjoyed the people-watching as they got on and off the trolley. And my mind began to wander as I thought about trains and how they could be a metaphor for our time here on earth.

Trains are similar to people in that we all have to arrive at a destination, a journey that necessitates stops along the way, both scheduled and unscheduled. Some trains can travel great distances without stops, settling on single destinations, while others make several stops along the journey. The purpose of the journey can change often, even the route can change as needed.

I love to travel, to see things that I have never seen before. Sometimes it can be a disappointment to arrive at the destination. Often it means that the trip is over. And the anticipation for the next journey begins.

Our lives stretch out before us like railroad tracks. Sometimes the tracks are straight, the two rails going on and on into the distant horizon without much deviation. Other times, curves and hills can obscure the tracks, much like our own vision of our own destinations. Sometimes we want to take the fastest routes to our journey's end, and sometimes we want to take in all the stops, maybe even disembarking to enjoy a particular place, taken in by sights and sounds. And life requires at times we get off one train and embark upon another, with a different destination, a different life path.

I found myself on the wrong path so many times in my life, wishing I had not boarded certain trains. But it was the realization that I could always change trains, go in a different direction, that was when growth occurred. So many times I have been given the opportunity to get on a different train. The many travels on my life's path have brought me to this point in time, sitting on a bench with a furry companion, watching the river flow out with the tide, being loved and loving others. I silently gave thanks.

I have always admired and appreciated those who know who they are and what their path is. My partner Susan is like that. She is the most comfortable in her own skin person that I know. She takes care of herself, physically, mentally, and emotionally. She seems to have the inner peace that I am always striving for.

A story that reminds me of Susan is found in a book that I read years earlier, *All I Really Needed to Know I Learned In Kindergarten*, by Robert Fulghum. He told of being left in charge of a group of 7-10 year olds. He had them play a game that he called Giants, Wizards, and Dwarfs, comparing it to a large-scale version of rock, paper, scissors. So he organized all the kids into groups and then had them all run to the appropriate spots for the Giants, Wizards, and Dwarfs.

The children were running around in quite a frenzy when he felt a tug at his pants leg from a small, young girl who asked in a concerned voice, "Where do the Mermaids stand?"

That took him aback for a second and he repeated the question back to this young girl, "Where do the Mermaids stand?"

"Yes. I am a Mermaid. Where do I stand?"

He looked down into this young girl's eyes. "There are no Mermaids in this game."

And he was answered, "Yes there are. I'm a Mermaid."

Then he realized that this young girl did not relate to being a Giant, or a Wizard, or a Dwarf. And she was not about to leave the game and stand over in the corner. She assumed that there had to be a place for Mermaids. And she intended to participate in the game as a Mermaid.

So Robert Fulghum told her that the Mermaids stood right next to him, the King, and inspected all of the Giants and Wizards and Dwarfs as they paraded by in wild disarray. And he came away with the belief that Mermaids truly did exist, for he had met one.

Susan is a mermaid, comfortable with who she is and what she is becoming.

Let's face it. If we don't change our direction once in awhile, we may actually end up where we are heading. And where is the fun in that?

After awhile, I gathered Orson and got back into the pickup and headed down 101. The Pacific came into view in several places, in spectacular vistas out to the west. I passed through several Oregon coastal cities, eventually pulling off the road for lunch in the small town of Manzanita. I gathered Orson and went for a long walk along the beach, Orson wandering leash free, and me carrying The Repository. I found a large log that had washed up along the beach and sat down next to it while Orson pawed at the clamshells that were littered along the sand.

The beach was mostly deserted, a rare jogger or couple wandering by and after awhile I took my trowel and dug a small hole and poured out some of The Repository into it. Since there was nothing that was going to grow here, there was no need for the fertilizer, and that container stayed in my backpack. I knew that the small offering from The Repository would get washed out to sea as the tide crept closer to the shore sometime this evening. But I liked the idea of that and I felt that was the perfect thing to do. I said a few words, a prayer from my heart, and Orson stayed out near the surf, keeping an eye on me and an eye on several seagulls that were darting here and there along the sand.

I stayed for awhile longer, maybe an hour, meditating to the sounds of the surf, then I whistled for Orson and he came trotting up. We walked back into Manzanita and had a small lunch outside one of the cafes there. I was in no hurry, though I was expected in Corvallis, Oregon, but not until later in the evening. Eventually I got back into the pickup and headed south.

I passed through a couple more coastal towns, some touristy, some more blue collar, all quaint in their own way. I loved the drive and stopped often at the many overlooks of the Pacific Ocean, reveling in the views. I took several pictures with my phone and texted them to Susan and always looked forward to her responses of "lovely" and "beautiful." It was a wonderful drive.

At the town of Newport, I turned and headed east towards Corvallis. This is where my sister Jenna lives with her husband Matt, and I was looking forward to seeing her and settling in at their house for a couple of days. I was sure she would pepper me with questions about this quest of mine. I looked forward to having someone to converse with.

• • •

Two monks were traveling home to their monastery during a heavy rain storm. The roads were quite flooded and filled with mud and travel was treacherous. Rounding a bend in the road, they came upon a lovely lady wearing a silk kimono with a colorful sash adorning her waist. She was unable to cross the road, so heavy was the rain and deep was the mud.

"Let me help," the first monk said and he picked her up and carried her across the road. Once on the other side, she thanked him and went on her way.

The second monk was aghast at the first monk, but he did not say anything until they had reached the temple that evening. Finally he could no longer contain himself. "Brother, you know that we are forbidden to be near females," he said to the first monk. "Especially one so young and beautiful as the one you carried across the road. What possessed you to do such a thing?"

The first monk merely put his hand gently upon his traveling companion's shoulder. "Brother, I left the girl back on the road. Why are you still carrying her?"

Previous

Summer soon ended and school started up, as did soccer and seeing Otter more often. We shared one class, Creative Writing, which was just after the morning nutrition break. He still showed up in my front yard most mornings and we would walk to school together when he did. But sometimes he wasn't there, which meant that I would wait for a couple of minutes and then just head to school myself. When I would see him in class, he would usually have some excuse for why he didn't show up in my driveway. It was no big deal.

Soccer started up and I had practice after school, so I did not see Otter then, but some weekends we would hang out, listening to music, maybe see a movie if he had a couple of dollars, or just toss some kind of ball/frisbee around.

I was somewhat surprised to see him in Creative Writing as it was an elective and he was never that comfortable with those kinds of classes. He just seemed better at Geometry, another subject we shared even though we were in different classes with different teachers. I would often ask him what answers he got on homework assignments as we walked to school. He answers were usually correct.

Soon it was October and then Halloween. Jenna was invited to a party and my parents were going to a get together that the hospital staff was having. Since I was too old to trick or treat, I thought I would hang around the house and hand out candy to the trick-or-treaters who came by, but the neighbors asked if I would babysit their seven and nine year old boys and take them trick-or-treating. Since I could always use a couple of extra dollars, I said yes, and with Jenna's help, made a vampire costume to wear.

I asked Otter what he would be doing on Halloween and he said that his family didn't really recognize holidays and stuff like that. He said that Jehovah's Witnesses did not believe in observing any celebrations like Halloween. He did say that he would hand out candy to any trick or treaters that might come by. I told him that I would be doing the same, thinking I might surprise him with a visit from a vampire that evening.

Halloween night I dressed in my costume and went next door and collected the boys. Otter and his family lived in a duplex on a street with several duplexes and when I took my babysitting crew over to the street where Otter's family lived, they were excited as they could get in a bunch of candy stops without having to travel too far a distance.

Watching the neighbor boys run from house to house and then compare their haul was fun. I remembered when I first went trick-or-treating. I was maybe five or six years old. My dad wasn't a big proponent of bringing unneeded sweets into the house, but he was a proponent of his kids having a good time, so he was the one who would walk up and down the street with my sister and I, while staying a reasonable distance away.

I remember my first costume was my hero at the time, Superman. I spent many hours watching the old black and white Superman, starring George Reeves, and my first young crush was on Lois Lane. This was a time before store bought costumes were all the rage. But my mom stenciled a

Superman S onto a blue t-shirt and I begged her to purchase the plastic, Superman-Clark Kent face mask and I was set. I just knew that I looked exactly like my superhero.

The face mask lasted just a couple of houses as no one could hear me yelling trick-or-treat behind the plastic Clark Kent, so I would yell it out and then spittle would drip down inside the mask and then down my chin. Then I was having to take it off so I could see, both to the next house and also to see what candy I was receiving. So I tried just holding the mask over my face, but then I couldn't hold onto the pillowcase that collected the candy when neighbors dropped those delicious morsels into it. It was quite the ordeal.

But I remember my trick-or-treating experiences with fondness and I tried to show the youngsters in my charge that same excitement. Though I did not think I would enjoy myself, I have to admit I was having a good time.

When we arrived at the Otter residence, unlike most of the other duplexes in the neighborhood, all the lights were off and I thought about passing it by. The boys were hesitant to go up to the door, having been told by parents not to approach any houses with the lights off, but since Otter said that he would be handing out candies I convinced the boys to go up to the door. While they rang the doorbell, I took a few steps back and stepped onto the lawn, just out of vision of whoever would answer the door.

Otter opened the door but turned on no lights, not even the porch light. I heard the boys holler out trick or treat and I saw Otter stuff something into their candy bags. He then closed the door before the boys could say thank you.

Afterwards, the boys ran down the walk and began the sprint to the next duplex. I yelled at them to slow down, that I wanted to know what they had received from the Otter house. The older one simply pulled a paper pamphlet out of his sack. "Just some paper," he said stuffing it back into his bag.

I told him to give it to me, and both boys handed over two pamphlets, both The Watchtower. "That's what he gave out, no candy?" I asked the boys.

Both boys said "Nope", in unison. And they were off to the next house.

The next morning, there was Otter standing at the end of the driveway, waiting to head out to school with me. As we began walking towards school I said, "You didn't see me last night?"

Otter looked at me. "No. Should I have?'

"I was dressed as Dracula. I took my next door neighbors trick-or-treating."

Otter kept walking. "That was a lame costume."

I matched his pace. "No more lame then handing out religious pamphlets to kids expecting candy."

Otter stopped, seeming surprised that I knew this. Then he laughed. "You think that I wanted to hand out that shit?"

"Of course not. But it was still lame." I have to admit I was kind of glad to hear that he didn't want to hand out religious pamphlets.

"Yeah, well my dad was pissed off. He thought it would be a great idea. But when he walked out of the house this morning there were a shitload of them scattered all over the lawn."

We walked a few more steps and I kicked a stick down the sidewalk. "Lucky you didn't get egged or something like that."

Otter kicked the same stick further down the sidewalk. "Well, I got yanked out of bed at 5:30 this morning to clean up all the Watchtowers that kids tossed onto the lawn."

We neared the school. Otter stopped and looked me in the eye. "Did you toss any on our yard?"

I studied his face to see if there was any anger in it. There wasn't. "No."

"Well, you should have." He began walking towards his first period class. "See you at Creative Writing." And he headed down the path towards the classrooms.

GARDEN IVY
by Mark Otter

The ivy creeps up the fence
Inching up slowly.
Slowly.
Day after day,
Slowly

So slow it is hardly noticed.
But it creeps

Soon the other plants
Begin to get smothered.
They never noticed
The creep.

And soon there are no other plants
Only ivy.
And no one noticed

Even though there are no other plants,
It continues to creep
Slowly.
Until there is nothing left in the garden
But the ivy

Tom Smyly

OCTOBER 13

I LEFT THE COASTAL HIGHWAY AND BEGAN THE CLIMB into the coastal range that travels north to south through the state of Oregon. It's a beautiful drive and I stopped in a couple of places, turnouts along the road, so I could marvel at the beauty and let Orson out to sniff around. There were a couple of local businesses along the way, essentially just curio shops, some with food and coffee, and I stopped in a couple of those. It was delightful not to be in any hurry on the drive from Newport to Corvallis.

At one of the pull outs along the highway, I stopped and looked out along the mountain vistas, spying some clear cuts in the distance. These barren, treeless hillsides are a testament to man's need for lumber. I debated at pulling out The Repository, but didn't, I'm not sure why. I just didn't feel the desire to do so.

Seeing the clear cuts made me think how decisions made today affect the future. How many inner scarred landscapes do I carry because of decisions made without regard for tomorrow?

It's not always easy to wrap my head around the fact that Today Me is given 24 hours until I have to hand over the living to Tomorrow Me. Only 24 hours. The same as everyone else, whether they be rich and famous, or poor and obscure. No one has a time advantage over anyone else. Everyone wakes up with the same allotment. 24 hours.

We all get the same opportunity as Today Me, the same 24 hours to make the choices that will affect Tomorrow Me.

So.........

Love is something that I can choose to give away without charge today.

Happiness is a choice that I can make in my daily comings and goings.

I can try and ease the suffering of others, in whatever small way that I may choose.

I can choose action towards a beneficial life, be less selfish, avoid a prickly heart.

My dad often said that the king and the pawn go into the same box once the game was played.

Because here is the universal truth: Once this minute passes, you cannot get it back. You can never relive this one minute. The minutes of our lives are not like cell phone minutes. They don't roll over. They don't accumulate in some minute bank account. They are simply gone.

As I stared out over the Coastal Range, Orson patiently lying by my side, I reaffirmed my commitment to hold precious the minutes that I have, not dwell too much on the minutes that have passed, and to leave Tomorrow Me with the time he needs to deal with the day that I give him.

I scratched Orson behind the ears and his tail thumped the gravel we were standing upon. He seemed to agree.

I reflected on the key to life as I have learned it. And that is we are all going to die. Every one of us. And it is only when we realize this that we can realize how precious and miraculous life is. And how fleeting it is. It is knowing that we are going to die and that we don't know when, it's this realization that allows us to start living. When we come to grips with this simple truth, when our hearts are opened, we give love freely, and we have the courage needed to face our fears.

This is what I first learned when I began studying the Buddhist path. This truth is what I try and stay focused on in my meditations. I am keenly aware that I will die. Not knowing when allows me to focus on the present moments that I have. It is when I am able to grasp this concept that I feel I am able to grow. The trouble is that I always think I have time.

Those are my thoughts this day.

Orson and I loaded back into the pickup and headed towards Corvallis. We stopped at a roadside convenience store for some tea and a snack. I perused the deli counter and marveled at the number of fried chicken tenders that were stacked neatly in rows against the glass. I wondered if this was a marketing ploy, something that perhaps made these greasy snacks a little more appealing. I felt sorry for whoever had to lean these chicken pieces against the glass case and wondered if he or she thought that this was a great idea - that this was all that was needed to get these birds to fly off the shelf. I chuckled at my ridiculous humor and exchanged greetings with the young woman behind the counter. I was feeling happy.

Just then, a well-dressed woman entered the small deli with what I assumed to be her child, a boy of about eight years old. She was impatient and she was either pushing or pulling him up and down the aisles, urging him to pick something and hurry.

The young boy stopped in front of the case where the rows of chicken tenders were stacked against the glass.

"I want some Chicken McNuggets," he said, with some vehemence.

"Those look gross," said the well-dressed woman. "How about something else? Look, they have burritos. How about a burrito?"

"I want Chicken McNuggets!" came the reply.

"Okay fine," said the exasperated lady. She looked at the girl working the counter. "Give us two Chicken McNuggets."

"They're not really Chicken McNuggets," the young lady said, in a polite voice. "They are more like chicken tenders."

"Does it look like I give a fuck what they are called?" The well dressed lady was starting to lose it. "Just put two in a bag, along with this root beer, and let me get the hell out of here!"

The young lady behind the counter was taken aback. She looked at this rude woman, then calmly went over to the display case where the chicken tenders were lined up against the glass. She slowly took one out, examined it carefully and placed it in a small sack. She then did the same with the second strip of chicken, first picking one up, then putting it back, before picking up another. She examined it and then slowly slid it into the sack along with the first. I glanced over at the well dressed woman and it seemed like I could feel the steam rising off the top of her head. The young woman behind the counter laid the bag of chicken strips on the counter, next to the root beer. "Will that be all?" she said with a sweet smile.

The lady stared at the young girl for a few moments before saying, "Yes, that will be all," through her clenched teeth. The young boy was taking all of this in while reaching up and grabbing the sack with the chicken. They then both stormed out of the store and got into a newer model

Mercedes Benz, reinforcing all of the stereotypes that I had about affluent people feeling entitled. I silently tried to correct myself from making that judgement.

I slid my bottle of tea onto the counter. "Just this please."

"Just the tea?" the young lady said politely.

"Does it look like I give a fuck what it's called?" I said, using the shrill tone of the well-dressed lady, though with a smile on my face.

The young lady laughed. "Thanks for that," she said.

"Thanks for the tea," I told her as I headed for the door and climbed into the pickup, Orson waiting patiently for me there.

I had promised Jenna that I would be at her house by dinner time. Jenna taught at the veterinary school at Oregon State University. She lived with her husband Matt, a skilled contractor with his own business, in a cute little home on the outskirts of Corvallis. She and Matt had two daughters who had graduated and moved away, one to California and the other to Colorado. The daughter in Colorado, Hannah, was married with a little girl of her own, Bethany. The other daughter, Sophia, was in Los Angeles doing the starving actress routine. But she seemed happy. I loved being their uncle and stay as close as I can. I call them once in a while and even send Sophia a few dollars here and there as needed. Jenna has a lovely family and I love the times when we are together.

I pulled into their driveway a little after 6 o'clock and Jenna came out of the house when she heard the truck. I let Orson out and he exchanged butt sniffs with Panama, Jenna and Matt's golden retriever. I grabbed my bag and followed Jenna inside where Matt had a cold beer at the ready.

It was good to be with family. The quest could wait for a couple of days.

• • •

A martial arts student desired to become the greatest martial artist in the land so he sought out his teacher. "Oh, teacher," he said. 'You are the greatest teacher and I long to be the greatest martial artist. How long will it take me to master it?"

The teacher looked at his student and casually said, "Ten years."

The student was visibly upset to hear how long it would take. "But teacher. I will work very hard. I will practice for ten or more hours a day. It will be all I will think about from the time I awake until I go to bed at night. If I do this, then how long will it take me to be the greatest?"

The teacher thought for a moment. "Twenty years," was his reply.

"But I do not understand," said the student with great disappointment. When I tell you that I will work even harder you say that it will take me even longer."

The Master replied, "When you have one eye on the goal, you only have one eye on the path."

Previous

ONE OF THE TOPICS THAT OTTER AND I ENTERTAINED quite often was girls. We seemed to be on the same page, in that we were extremely fascinated with the other sex, but pretty hopeless when it came to how to approach these creatures. We would talk big, often planning in painstaking detail how we would approach different girls, the lines and the schemes we would use so that we could get them to join us in our own particular orbits.

I would not say that either of us was terribly appealing to our female classmates, but we weren't bad looking guys. Otter did have short hair, which I believe contributed to his shyness around the fairer sex. And while we both were fairly thin, Otter had more muscle definition than I did. I think he was considered to be more of a loner than he actually was. But that may have been because I knew him better than others.

While I could strike up conversations with different young women, Otter simply wouldn't. This despite all of the planning and conniving on how to approach them. Whenever an opportunity presented itself, he became awkwardly stiff and would fade into whatever background there was. He was just too shy and unconfident to do anything.

That did not stop us from talking about possible conquests, which merely consisted of getting girls we liked to talk with us. Often while we were hanging out in the cafeteria or some other spot, a girl we knew would say something friendly. I could make some small talk, but it would be a stretch to say that I was comfortable creating a conversation. But that was miles ahead of poor Otter, who could barely mumble a simple greeting.

During our junior year in high school, I turned sixteen a couple of months after Otter. I began studying for that rite of passage, a driver's license. Otter was doing the same thing, but at a slower pace. We were both taking Driver's Ed in school, though at different times. When we talked about acquiring our licenses, Otter said that he didn't know if his dad would give approval so he was unsure when he would be able to take the test. That didn't stop us from talking about it, and talking about all the "dates with the ladies" we would be able to go on when we achieved that milestone. We each had our permits which allowed us to drive with a parent in the car. I was always bugging my parents to go somewhere and let me drive. Otter told me he did the same with his mom, but he wouldn't ask his dad, and by now I understood why that was.

The day came for me to go to the DMV to take the exam and my mom drove me to the testing center. Despite, or because of my nervousness, and the tester making ridiculous small talk, I passed. I mean, who asks a nervous teenager where his favorite donut shop was and how many boxes of shoes I thought a normal pick-up truck could hold? Anyway, I got an 89 out of a needed 80. I was an officially licensed driver.

There was a fellow junior in my US History class by the name of Debbie DiCamillo. I had been striking up conversations with her whenever the opportunity arose, and I thought she should be the one to win the "First Date with Jake" contest. The high school would put on a movie in the auditorium once a month, a free event for students on a Friday evening, and I summoned up the courage to ask her to go with me. And she said yes!

I had told Otter about my plans to ask Debbie out, and when we walked home the Tuesday before the Friday movie event, we dissected how I had asked her and what she said. We discussed possible moves to get some make-out time, how that might proceed, and how to be as cool and debonair as possible. We truly had no idea about any of this, but we laughed a lot as we contemplated all possible outcomes.

The next day when I saw Debbie in history class, she told me that her best friend Annette would also like to go to the movie. She asked if I knew anyone that could go with us and make it a double date. I mentioned Otter. "He's kind of weird, isn't he?," she asked, wrinkling her nose slightly. "I know he's your friend and everything, but....."

I assured her he was normal, just shy, and she said she would check with Annette. When I told Otter what I thought was great news, I could see panic in his eyes. Or maybe it was doubt.... no, it was panic.

"I can't, man," he gasped out.

"Come on, dude," I assured him. "Annette's cute."

"I know. That isn't it. But, I just don't know."

I convinced him to wait and see what Annette's response was. Otter agreed, and on our walk home he perseverated over the possibility of having an actual conversation with a female and I began regretting mentioning him to Debbie, mostly because he was freaking out so much.

But later that evening Otter called me and said he was in, that he could handle it. And then a little later, Debbie called me and said that Annette thought it would be okay to double with Otter. I procured the family station wagon for the evening and we were on for Friday night.

The next couple of our after school walks were spent plotting and planning for our big double date. Since Debbie and Annette were going to spend the night together, I invited Otter to do the same at my house. That way we could pick them up together and drop them off at the same time. We were both concerned about how the double drop off might impact any good night kissing/making out, but we felt that we could wing that part if necessary. I'm sure that less planning went into the invasion of Normandy.

On Friday night, Otter came over to my house and we drove together to pick up our dates. Things seemed to be going well, small talk was unleashed, and even Otter seemed to begin to loosen up and contribute to the conversations about school, bands, teachers, and other teen-agery stuff. We escorted our dates to our seats in the auditorium, where, as meticulously planned out by Otter and myself, we placed the girls in the middle with Otter and I on the outsides. Things were going as planned.

The movie started, a cornball comedy of some sort, and we all settled into our seats. A few minutes in, I pulled the old "stretch out my arms and settle the arm on her shoulder" routine. Debbie slid a little closer to me. Perfect.

A few minutes later, Debbie nudged me and shrugged her head towards Otter and Annette. I leaned forward and saw that they were intertwined together, making out. I leaned back, not sure if I believed what I had seen, and then leaned forward again to get confirmation. Yep. It was a definite make-out session. I didn't know what to think. Debbie had a slight smile on her face, but her eyes seemed as shocked as mine. It was fair to say that we were both rather amazed, and I was in awe of my friend's moves.

The movie ended, we walked the girls back to the car and drove to a local ice cream parlor where the date continued. We purchased two sundaes which were shared between the couples. We sat in booths, with Debbie and I on one side and Otter and Annette on the other. In between bites, Otter and Annette would kiss some more as Debbie and I uncomfortably shared some small chitchat. Afterwards, we took the girls back to Debbie's house and walked them to the door where I pecked Debbie on the lips while Otter swapped some more spit with Annette. I was ready to get home.

At home, I pressed Otter for details. How in the hell did he pull that off? I was amazed, astounded, and yes, a little bit jealous. To Otter's credit, he seemed as amazed as I was. We finally went to sleep and the next morning Otter went home.

That evening, Saturday, I got a call from Debbie asking what the hell was wrong with my friend Otter and why did I set her friend Annette up with such a fiend? She proceeded to tell me that Annette was in tears last night, that she had to fight Otter off the whole date, and that she was embarrassed. I listened for a while as Debbie disparaged Otter until I had enough. I pointed out that Annette did not seem like she minded the attention and that both she and Otter seemed to be going at each other equally. I told her there was no way all of that was one-sided, and Debbie then told me if that was what I believed, than I should not call her again. Which was a-okay by me.

When I next saw Otter while walking to school, I told him about the phone call from Debbie. He said that Annette had called him Saturday to tell him that she would not be his girlfriend, and when he told her that he did not ask her to be, she slammed the phone down, hanging up. We tried to analyze the situation but were both pretty flummoxed. We got to school and went our separate ways.

I was nervous about seeing Debbie in history class, but she smiled at me and thanked me for the nice evening last Friday. I told her she was quite welcome, and I was suspicious that something else was coming. But there wasn't. When I saw Otter at lunch, he told me that Annette came up to him and thanked him for the nice time and that she was sorry, but she just wanted to be friends, to which Otter agreed.

Otter and I stared at each other across the cafeteria table where we were sitting. And we just started laughing. We sure did not understand women. Little did we realize that we never would.

KALEIDOSCOPE
By Mark Otter

The broken colors
The fragments

Of the Kaleidoscope.

Glass broken joined together
By mirrors.
Turning, turning, turning.
Hopefully to find beauty.

Looks like my heart.

OCTOBER 13

O RSON AND I SETTLED IN NICELY AT JENNA AND MATT'S quaint little house on the outskirts of Corvallis. After dinner, we moseyed out to the fire pit in their back yard, sipping some Chardonnay, Orson and Panama stretched out beside us, worn out from their constant playing. The sun had just set and it was a beautiful fall evening.

Jenna and I caught up on all that was happening in our separate lives. She said that her girls were doing well, including her young granddaughter. Work was demanding in the usual way, and Matt chimed in that he was pretty busy, though he was trying to cut back. They both were edging towards retirement, could see it getting closer in the coming years. I could definitely relate, as I was contemplating the same in the next year or two. This was information that we often exchanged in emails and phone calls, but it's different when you're face to face and can ask questions and show interest. It was enjoyable catching up with people who I love so dearly.

We talked about some of the research that I had completed in the past couple of years. Jenna always kidded me about my "egghead" ways, always insisting that she was doing the "down and dirty" part of taking care of animals and teaching future veterinarians to do the same, all while

I was documenting how many fish were spawning in some lake or the other. I referred to her as a glorified cat doctor. It was good natured kidding, with Matt saying that we were both crazy and he had the only job that people actually needed.

Jenna was planning a trip to Arizona in the next month to see Mom. Dad had passed about ten years ago, yes - goddamn cancer. Mom and two of her close friends moved to a retirement village in Scottsdale, Arizona. I had visited her there a few times and she seemed happy and in fairly good health. She and her friends, all in their eighties, were still active and traveling, having just returned from a trip to Portugal. Mom was certainly trying to squeeze out all of life there was to live.

Dad was diagnosed with pancreatic cancer and lived about a year before it took his life. Disregarding his prognosis, he kept his medical practice, working right up to the very end, even while undergoing chemo. Jenna and I took turns going to Southern California as often as we could, sometimes to help Mom, but mostly to hang out with Dad. And then there were the myriad of FaceTime conversations we would share. He was one of those stiff upper lip types, never complaining, and honestly, most of the time you never knew he was sick. But the last few weeks were rough as his body wore out from cancer and chemo. I often talked to him about the Buddhist notion of the afterlife, that there were perhaps more opportunities after we died for the soul to continue to learn and progress. But Dad was agnostic, more of an "anything might and can happen" sort of belief. In some of our last conversations, he talked about the mystery of what came next. He looked at death as the next great adventure. At the end, he was simply worn out and ready to shed this mortal existence.

As he was nearing the end, I remember visiting with him sitting in the recliner in his home office, the same office in the same house where I grew up. We would talk about the news, or family stuff, or the Dodgers, or research that I may be working on. He would often doze off, and then I would just wait, read something or watch the TV in the room, then he would reawaken and pick up the conversation where it had been left off. I marveled at his ability to do that.

There soon came a point where he simply refused any more treatment, just some pain relief, which made him more tired. He was insistent on staying at home, and my mom was in total agreement, taking care of him with such gentleness and love. I always took for granted that my parents loved each other, but to see it played out in such a loving and caring way still took me by surprise. It seemed like everything they said to each other came from a bucket that had been dipped into and drawn from pure love. Words were infrequent as they communicated so much with their look, and even their touch. They smiled and laughed, often at their own shared jokes, not needing anyone else to get their humor.

The last time I saw Dad was on a weekend in September. I had flown down from Bozeman on a Friday night and I spent Saturday and Sunday beside him. He was now in bed 24 hours, visited by nurses and other hospice personnel coming in and out, as well as a steady stream of friends. He was still fairly cognizant despite the pain meds and he seemed to enjoy me telling him about my research project involving wildlife around the Yellowstone National Park area. But it was clear that the end was nearing, and he would often reference himself in the past tense.

I was sitting by his bed, trying to be helpful, offering him water or anything else he might want, with the TV turned to a football game that was playing in the background. Dad would fade in and out, and just when I thought he was sleeping, he would make a comment about something going on during the game. And I would comment back. Then it seemed like he would again fall asleep, his breathing slightly labored as his body systems began to switch off.

"Jake." I was startled to hear my name as I guess I was dozing off also. My flight back to Bozeman was in a couple of hours and it was getting close to the time when I needed to leave for the airport.

"Yeah, Dad?"

"I think this is about it." He turned his head and looked at me. He looked so frail. I had never noticed how much so until now.

"No. It's only the third quarter." I smiled into his eyes, making a lame reference to the football game on TV. I knew what he meant.

He tried to smile back at my attempt at a joke, and the effort made him cough a bit. "I'm so proud of you and Jenna. I hope you know that."

Tears began to well up in the corner of my eyes. "I do Dad. You always told me that." I touched his hand. "Thank you for always letting me know."

I pulled the covers up under his chin. "Anything I should know before you go?" We were always able to talk frankly even with the elephant of impending death in the room. He was a doctor. He knew about death.

He spoke slowly and softly. "I remember watching David Letterman when he had the musician Warren Zevon on." Dad tried to lift up a little taller and I helped him slide a pillow under his back so he could sit up in bed. "Warren was dying and this was to be his last show. David asked him a similar question." He settled back into the pillows a bit deeper. "Is there anything that those left behind should know?"

"What was the answer?" I put my elbows on the side of his bed and leaned in a little closer.

"Zevon told him that he didn't know that he was supposed to enjoy every sandwich." Dad turned his head in my direction. "I guess I've tried to do just that. Enjoy every sandwich."

Conversation was beginning to be labored for him and he coughed some more. "So that's what I would tell you, Jake. Enjoy every sandwich." And he leaned back into the pillows and closed his eyes.

> *"You put more value on every minute....You know I always kind of thought I did that. I really always enjoyed myself. But it's more valuable now. You're reminded to enjoy every sandwich and every minute."*
>
> WARREN ZEVON

I could not speak, my eyes were welling up, so I held his hand gently next to my cheek so he could feel the wetness as the tears ran down my face. I stayed there for a few minutes before straightening up and wiping my face with the sheets of his bed. "Dad, I'll see you next weekend. I already have my ticket."

The room settled in quiet, the only noise being Dad's labored breath. I waited for a response and I could see Dad trying to say something. Finally, "I don't know. I might not be here."

I could hear my breath slowly inhaling, then a slow exhale. I tried to say something to this wonderful man. I calmed my breath. "Where are you going, Dad?" My words were slow and measured as I tried to control my emotions.

Quiet once again settled in. Then Dad's eyes opened and his face shone in a smile as something on the ceiling seemed to hold his gaze. "I'm off to join the circus." Then he closed his eyes, but his smile remained and his labored breath returned as he dozed off.

Those were his last words to me. He died three days later.

Back at the fire pit in Corvallis, we toasted to our dad's memory, as we often did when we were together. Matt soon went inside, leaving Jenna and me to relax in the quiet of the night. Panama soon followed Matt inside, but Orson stayed close by, moving closer to the fire as the night grew chilly.

"Are you still chasing Otter's ghost?" Jenna was usually direct and to the point.

"There are just some things that I feel I need to finish up." I wasn't sure what to say. The question didn't bother me. I simply didn't have an answer. "Maybe I am chasing ghosts, I suppose." I finished the last sip of wine in my glass. Jenna slid the Chardonnay bottle towards me, but I demurred.

"Maybe a seance would be easier," Jenna smiled and even chuckled at what she apparently thought was funny. "Where's The Repository? Are you still dragging his ashes around?"

I leaned back in the patio chair I was sitting in. "Maybe that's the purpose of this trip. I think maybe it is. At least one of the purposes, to get rid of The Repository." I sighed. "I suppose it is." I told her about a few of the places where I had deposited some of the contents of the coffee can I was traveling with.

"You know that I'm teasing you. You do what you need to do." She smiled. Jenna and I were close as brother and sister. I always appreciated her sound advice. She was more practical than me. Always had been.

I smiled back at her. "I'm just trying to enjoy every sandwich." That made us both smile as we remembered Warren Zevon's advice given through our father. "Come on, Orson. Let's go for a walk."

Jenna came over and gave me a hug. "You know where everything is. Help yourself to what you need. Lock the door when you come back inside." And she walked back into the house.

My gaze followed her across the yard and inside the house. I attached the leash to Orson's collar. "Let's go, boy," I said quietly. We walked out the gate and into the front yard and down the street.

. . .

There was a Buddhist farmer who worked tirelessly at his crops year after year, barely making a living. But he had a first-rate horse, and this, along with a son, helped him get through the lean times. Then one day, his horse burst through the fence and ran off. Upon hearing the news, the farmer's neighbors came and expressed their sympathy. "Such bad luck," they said.

"Good or bad, who knows?" the farmer replied. "We will see."

The next day the horse returned, bringing with it three wild stallions. The neighbors returned to exult at the farmer's good fortune. "Such good luck," they said.

"Good or bad, who knows?" the farmer replied.

"We will see."

The next day, the son tried to ride one of the wild horses and was thrown off and broke his leg. The neighbors came back around. "Such bad luck," they said. "Now you have no one to help you work the fields."

"Good or bad, who knows?" the farmer replied. "We will see."

The following day, military officials came through the village to conscript all of the young men into the army to go and fight in the war. Upon seeing the farmer's son with a broken leg, they passed him by. And thus he did not have to go and fight in the war. The neighbors came back again to tell the farmer of his good fortune.

"Good or bad, who knows?" replied the farmer. "We will see."

Previous

SCHOOL CONTINUED AT ITS USUAL PACE AND I CAREENED into the spring of my junior year. I began taking more difficult classes and some college prep courses. I also started writing to colleges and began to explore the process of deciding where I might want to continue my education. School work became more intense and I was spending more time on homework.

I was seeing Otter less often, though not intentionally on either of our parts. Even at lunch, I only saw him once in awhile. There was a juggling club on campus that met three times a week during lunch and again once a week after school and Otter took a great interest in that. He got pretty good at it too, and he would often put on demonstrations for anyone who would sit still long enough to see him perform. My mom and dad especially loved his juggling acts and he would entertain both of them when he came around.

As I said, I didn't see Otter as much as before, but he would sometimes spend a Friday or Saturday night at my house. Saturday night was more of a pain though, since he had to get up early and get home so he could attend church. As I now had a driver's license and some limited availability to a car, we would go to a movie or drive around, maybe see some friends. We even one time saved some money and went to a local lounge and listened to some live music.

We would have interesting conversations, sometimes delving into deep topics. Once Otter asked me if I or my family had ever gone to church. I said that we had never attended any church, at least as far as I could remember. "How about God? Do you believe that there is a God?" he asked one Saturday.

"I suppose," I replied to his query. "I guess I really don't know. I mean, I've never really thought about it." I shifted the question back to him. "You? I know you attend church and stuff, but do you really believe?"

Otter furrowed his brow and seemed deep in thought. "I suppose so. I know I'm supposed to believe. But I guess I really don't know."

Otter was quiet for a minute. "I mean, I'm supposed to believe that there is a God who answers prayers and stuff like that, but it doesn't seem like there is."

"Do you pray?" I asked.

"Sometimes," was the reply.

"Does he answer your prayers?" I waited as Otter thought some more.

"Not that I know of," he said after some contemplation.

"What do you pray for?"

"Just stuff," Otter seemed to be getting a little uncomfortable. "Mostly just praying for me and my mom." The topic seemed to be getting a little too heavy for the both of us, so one of us changed the subject, I don't remember who.

We often talked about girls. I was dating here and there, and perhaps thinking about getting serious with one or two young ladies. Serious meaning that I would ask them for a second date. Otter, while interested in several girls in our school, just didn't date much. Though he had his license, he had less access to a car as his dad seemed to have all these pre-conditions for him to use it. That was what Otter told me. We did double date on a couple of occasions, but thankfully we did not have the same experience as the first time we did so. At least thankfully from my point of view. But we would still debrief each other and expound on our experiences. I'm sure like teenage boys have been doing since the dawn of time.

While I spent a good deal of time on school work, Otter seemingly did not. His grades were always so-so, and they were not close to being indicative of his smarts. He was especially good at math and I would regularly get him to explain some of the weightier concepts that I was enduring. We were taking the same math class, though in different periods. He would always ace the tests with little study. Math simply came easier to him.

He seemed to excel in classes which required some memorizing, math and science and such. But he struggled for good grades in English and Writing and those types of classes, though I think he liked them. He especially liked Creative Writing, a class that we shared together. When I did not see him before or after school, I would see him in Creative Writing.

The class was an interesting one, taught by an interesting teacher, Mr. Constantine, and by interesting I mean sort of peculiar. But I liked him and he was a popular teacher in the school, probably because of his unusual style. He challenged us to keep a pen and paper by our beds and to write down any dreams that woke us up. But try as I might, I could never remember a dream long enough to write it down, especially in the middle of the night. But Otter took to this assignment and he began to share some of his written dreams with me.

One dream he shared was one in which he was face down in a stream, and he would try and try to get up, for he could not breathe. Then right when he was going to pass out, he would be able to rise out of the water a little bit, just enough to get his face out of the water and grab a gasp of air. Then he would be plunged down into the water again. He said that in his dream, some one was holding him down, not letting him up, except for that brief gasp of air. He would try and try to see the person holding him down, but he never could. But he did see enough to know that it was someone that he knew and that he knew very well. Then he awoke.

We both agreed that was a pretty strange dream. Mr. Constantine would encourage anyone who wanted to share a dream with the class to do so. I tried to get Otter to share that dream, but he refused.

Mr. Constantine would give us a writing assignment for the week, usually consisting of writing about a particular subject matter, fiction or non-fiction, and it usually had a 2-3 page requirement. He then would read maybe five or six aloud in class, ones he thought were interesting for some reason, and then the class would critique them. This critique consisted of a few students stating what they liked about it and maybe asking the author a question or two about why they went in a certain direction. Generally it was pretty positive for I suppose that most students thought that if Mr. Constantine chose that particular assignment to read it must have some merit.

One assignment that we received was writing about what our dream automobile was and why. Mr. Constantine was not easy to bullshit in any assignment, you had to really tell him why your particular chosen car was important to you. I struggled with the assignment and finally turned in something about a station wagon being my dream car because then I could bring all my friends and family with me on my trip. The paper came back with a large "REALLY?" written in red ink. "Not sure I believe this" was written at the end. "But B for effort." So I was pretty much satisfied.

Otter wrote about his dream car being a 1968 Chevrolet Camaro. He wrote about it being cherry red and fast, so fast that it could outrun all troubles. And it would be so loud that it would shut out the rest of the world so he wouldn't hear the meanness, the cruelty of others. And it would be able to take him away from this life and vault him into another one, one that was different. A car that was fast enough to outrun all his memories.

Mr. Constantine read Otter's Camaro tale to the rest of the class and I remember thinking that it was a clever bit of writing. There were many comments from fellow students about how much they enjoyed it and how beautiful they thought the writing was. When Mr. Constantine handed back the assignments, "WELL DONE, MARK" was written in red marker.

There was one student, Dennis Mitchell, who had also written about his dream car being a Camaro, and while his essay was not read aloud, he stated the reasons for his writing about a Camaro was that it was the ultimate muscle car and great for impressing the opposite sex. He said that he did not understand Otter's essay at all and he thought that Otter had not been true to the assignment in writing about the Camaro since Otter gave it these other worldly features. But Mr. Constantine explained that the writer was free to interpret the assignment in the manner they wished. And that seemed that.

The bell rang and all of the students stood up to begin heading to their next class. I caught Otter's eye and gave him a thumbs up regarding his essay and he shot a smile back to me. I made some small talk with a couple of girls in the class and as I headed out the door, I saw Otter talking with Dennis, both of them up against a bank of lockers. Otter seemed irritated about something, and while he wasn't talking loudly, he was definitely making a point. Dennis was trying to back pedal along the lockers, but Otter kept his face right next to Dennis'. After a few feet of this, Dennis simply ducked away and went in the opposite direction and Otter continued towards his next class. I wasn't sure what had transpired, but I was uneasy about it.

I saw Dennis after school as we were heading off campus. I hollered at him to slow down and he waited for me to catch up, and I asked him what he and Otter were talking about after Creative Writing class.

"Your friend is fucking nuts," Dennis spurted out. "He told me that if I made any more comments regarding any of the details of his writing, he would rearrange the details of my face."

I was surprised. I didn't know what to say. This certainly didn't sound like Otter. "Maybe he was kidding," I said weakly.

"He's fucking nuts," Dennis repeated. "Jeez. It's about a fucking car."

Dennis strode off. I gave him a "sorry, man," as he walked away. I was trying to wrap my head around Otter's reaction. Dennis' comments had been pretty lame, but not at all confrontational. But Otter's reaction did seem out of character.

I mentioned it the next day to Otter, but I thought I'd kind of sneak up of the subject. "Hey, what were you and Mitchell talking about after class yesterday? It seemed pretty intense."

Otter was unfazed by the question. "I told him I didn't like his remarks on my essay."

"Who cares?" I looked him in the eye. "Why take it so personal that you threatened to kick his ass?"

Otter met my gaze. "Don't you think I could kick his ass?"

I shook my head. "That's not even close to the point. It was just his stupid opinion. Who cares?"

Otter began walking away. "Me. I cared." He was now a couple of steps ahead of me, heading to his next class. "Anyway, see you in Creative Writing." And he was gone.

During Nutrition Break, I saw him talking to Dennis Mitchell, but not nearly so animated as the day before. They were talking in hushed tones against one of the outdoor hallways. Then I saw Otter reach his hand out and Mitchell took it for a brief handshake. Then they departed.

Otter caught sight of me and walked over to where I was standing. Without explanation, "I apologized." He smiled. "But I could have kicked his ass." Then he was off again.

TRAIN TRESTLE
By Mark Otter

Legs dangling, on the bridge, hanging over the edge,
Looking down at the river below.
On the edge
Of the Trestle

Then a train approaches.

Three choices.

Run along the trestle, away from the train,
Get off the Trestle
And leap from the tracks.
Is it too far....can I make it?

Run towards the train
Get off the Trestle
And leap from the tracks.
Shorter distance, but I have to run
Towards the train.
Can I make it?

Or
Leap from the trestle
Into the river below.
Into the unknown.

Fucking Trestle

OCTOBER 14

I AWOKE EARLY THE NEXT MORNING, THE SUN STUMBLING in through the blinds of the guest bedroom where Jenna and Matt had put me and Orson up for the night. I put on some socks and padded to the kitchen and quietly started some hot water boiling in the kettle. I made a cup of tea and sat down at the table to read. Orson soon began sniffing at the back door, his way of saying that he needed to go out and take care of his business. I leashed him up, put on some shoes, and walked him around the block, sipping tea as I did. It was a beautiful morning.

Soon Jenna and Matt were up and off to their duties and I was left with the rest of the day in front of me. Leaving Orson with Panama in the back yard, I decided to check out a local Buddhist hang out, a Zen Center located near the Oregon State University campus. Arriving, I walked around the grounds for a little while, feeling the peace that inhabits such places. I then took in a Zazin service, a practice of meditation in the Zen Buddhist tradition. It is a meditation that I find particularly challenging; regulating my attention in a lotus or crossed legs position is difficult for me to sustain for an extended length of time. My aging bones and joints always have some complaints during and afterwards.

I remember a Zen meditation retreat, a weekend that I attended in my thirties. I was starting a new job, an instructor of Animal Science at Montana State and was feeling stressed out. I questioned if it was something that I could be successful at. Prior to that my academic career had been mostly research based. I was feeling inadequate at my abilities in front of a classroom.

I tried to convince myself that I, as much as anyone, deserved my own love and affection. So I thought that a meditation retreat was exactly what I needed and I went feeling confident in my ability to essentially be quiet for a whole weekend.

Looking back, keeping quiet was not the problem. It was the constant sitting without feeling cramped and restless. I remember one meditation in particular, called a sesshin, an intense meditation over a long period of time. After about an hour, my legs were cramping, my back was aching, my knees were hurting, and getting into a meditative state was becoming next to impossible. Everything hurt and my internal thoughts were becoming obsessed with eliminating the pain and discomfort. My eyes wandered around the room. Certainly there were others who were experiencing the same kind of agony. But everyone else seated around me seemed to be blissfully ignorant of any pain or hardship.

Then came the "I can't do this," and "I'm worthless," and "Why did I sign up for this?" thoughts racing around my brain. I recognized these thoughts and feelings as weights I often dragged along like a burden on my back. Then these thoughts dissolved into worry about my new position at Montana State; that I would be incompetent and soon exposed as a total fraud. The meditation session was becoming completely worthless.

At this point Rinpoche Soyuual, the leader of this particular practice, walked in and sat in a lotus position at the front of the room. And he started talking very, very slowly, quietly enunciating each word, each syllable. "The hardship and the difficulty that you are experiencing now," he let out a long and deep breath. I thought his next words would be "will go away" or "flow by like petals dropped in a stream," or something soothing of that sort.

But, "will be with you for the rest of your life," were the words that followed. That was certainly discouraging in my aching state. Then he explained that the practice of meditation is not to be soothing, or confirming, or to find some understanding. The practice of meditation is to be open to the whole range of experiences in our lives, including all of the hurt, and all of the discomfort. And all of the joy.

His words resonated with me and I took them to mean to make peace with whatever was at hand, whether it be pain or comfort, scary or brave, turbulent or peaceful. Each moment was one to be noticed and experienced. And when that moment was over, then the next moment was to be treated the same way. Even if the moments were fearful or painful, or negative, they were to be used to soften one's self and to become more kind and compassionate.

This wise Rinpoche taught that even in the most difficult of times, there was always some peace hidden among the superficial that so frequently weighs us down. There is always a rainbow waiting to come forward after the rain.

I finished my meditation at this Zen retreat, left a donation at the door, then wandered around downtown Corvallis for a little while. School was in session at OSU and the sidewalk cafes and coffee shops were filled with students and I meandered around them. It was a lovely day.

I wandered in a couple of bookstores in the downtown. I have always loved bookstores and have found that I can use up hours wandering around their shelves. This was a love from my early years, when I used to spend quite a bit of time at the local library. As I got older, I would spend more and more time in bookstores. Money was a lot tighter in those days and I would have to be deliberate in my choosing. I would take a book from the shelf, read the introduction and maybe a chapter or two, then carry it around while doing the same with other books. After an hour or so, I might be carrying six or seven books. Then I would have to eliminate five or six of them for budgetary purposes. Choosing was always such sweet sorrow.

I read a lot of fiction while in my teens, but that switched over to non-fiction in my twenties and thirties. I read to learn things about the world that I live in, different cultures, different times, different peoples. I loved the pursuit of knowledge of other lives, lives that weren't my own. I was fascinated about this.

But now I wander and read for different reasons. My early love of the great philosophers, Emerson, Thoreau, Nietzsche, have been replaced with the more Eastern wisdom of Lao Tzu, Siddhartha Gautama, Rumi. I read less about how to change the world and more about how to change myself. That's a positive. At least I think it is.

I left the bookstore without adding to my collection, secure in the knowledge that there were still several unread books, both in my pickup and on my nightstand back in Montana. I considered that a victory for my willpower.

That night, we had another delicious barbecue and another evening was spent sipping wine and watching the dogs play, then rest, then play some more, all around the fire pit. Matt regaled us with tales of construction projects gone wrong and I caught them up with some of my travels along the road. We even called Susan and FaceTimed her in, laughing the laughs of families that love and care for one another. It was a nice evening.

Before we all turned in for bed, I went into their garage to get a blanket that Jenna had offered for my road trip and I saw a familiar cabinet in the corner. I walked over and opened it up and saw that it was being used to store garden supplies and so forth. The cabinet looked aged, but was in excellent shape, and one could tell that it had been handcrafted, that it did not come from a big box store. I remembered the cabinet had been in the garage back home in California.

I asked Jenna about the cabinet when I went back into the house. "I took it from Mom and Dad's when Mom sold the house."

"Do you remember where she got it?"

Jenna thought for a minute. "I'm not sure. I just remember it being in the garage for years and years." She turned and faced me, "Why do you ask?"

"No reason. I thought it looked familiar." And I changed the subject. "Let's have lunch tomorrow."

"Great idea. Let me check my schedule and I'll give you a place and time." Then Jenna headed to bed.

I walked Orson one last time and settled him into the second-hand dog blanket that was laid out next to my bed in the guest bedroom. As I dropped off to sleep, hearing Orson's gentle breathing on the floor next to me, I thought about the cabinet that I had seen in the garage. Then I remembered where I first saw it. Sometimes you don't know the value of something until it becomes a memory. These were good thoughts and I slept soundly.

. . .

Five children were playing together when one of them asked the group what they would wish for if they had only one wish.

The first child said that he would wish for some ice cream as he loved ice cream. Everyone thought that was a good wish.

The second child wished that he would have an ice cream factory so that he would always have ice cream any time he wanted. All the children thought that was an even better wish.

The third child thought for a bit and then decided that she would wish for a billion dollars so she could build an ice cream factory and a cake factory and a pizza restaurant and whatever else she wanted. The first two children thought that was an even better wish and they regretted their wishes.

The fourth child said that he would wish for three wishes, that way he could wish for an ice cream factory with the first wish, a billion dollars with the second wish and then he could wish for three more wishes with the last wish. The first three children said that was the perfect thing to do with one's wish and that nothing would be able to top that.

The last child though for awhile and her wish surpassed all the other children. "I wish I had no wishes," she said.

School continued onward towards the summer break. I was getting more and more into my school work, trying to obtain scholarship attention from the universities that I was interested in attending. Otter was less and less interested in school work. Even in the Creative Writing class that he liked, he was drifting off to grade D territory. We were still hanging out, just not as often, but definitely still good friends.

One thing that Otter was interested in was wood shop and he was often talking about one project or the other that he was working on. He would bring some of his creations by the house and my mom would be especially taken by his obvious talent in this area, oohing and aahing over this or that design.

I remember a project that Otter spent hours and hours working on. He spent a great deal of time designing and making a wooden bird house. He would spend hours sanding and painting this birdhouse and it looked quite stunning. He was really excited about giving it to his mom, and he brought it over to my house after school to show it off.

My parents both thought it was quite impressive and I saw that Otter was pleased with their reactions.

About a week or so later, I asked him if his mom liked the gift of the birdhouse.

"Yeah," and that was all he said.

"Well, did she put it up in the backyard?" I asked.

Otter sighed a little. "She started to, but my dad said that he didn't want to attract any birds to the yard, that they would shit all over the patio."

I could see his disappointment. "Sorry about that. I thought it looked really nice."

"Thanks." And that was that about the birdhouse.

The next Saturday, there was a knock on the door and there stood Otter with the birdhouse. My mom had answered the door, and all I heard was, "Oh, Mark, I cannot accept such a lovely gift."

By that time, Otter had come into the living room. "It's okay," he said. "We really don't have room for it in my yard."

My mom took the birdhouse from his hand. "Well, if you're sure. I would love to have it in my backyard." Mom motioned for me to get up from the couch where I was sprawled. "Jake, get a hammer and some nails and let's put this beautiful birdhouse to good use."

The next hour or so was spent with Mom seeking advice from me and Otter about the best place to put the bird-house in our backyard. Otter was quite serious about its placement, talking about where the light would be the best, and where it would be easiest for the birds to find it. When the right position was found, we nailed it to the fence, and there it lived.

Another Saturday Otter was over and we were watching TV. It was about a week from Mother's Day, I remember, because my mom sat down and chatted with us for a bit and she asked Otter if he was making his mother something for Mother's Day. Otter said no, and when asked why not, he simply said that his religion did not recognize any of these holidays or celebrations. "Oh," was all Mom said.

A couple of days later, at the family dinner table, Mom began talking about getting a cabinet made for the garage to keep some of her canning supplies. Dad said that she should just go to a hardware store, or maybe even Sears or Penney's, and pick up one there.

"Do you think Mark could make me a cabinet, Jake?" My mom directed the question to me.

"I suppose so," I replied, sort of surprised that she would want a homemade cabinet.

"What's his number? I'll call him right now," Mom said with obvious delight at the thought of asking Otter to build a cabinet. She went over to the phone on the kitchen wall and called the Otter house.

I could only hear one side of the conversation, but I knew that Otter's mom answered the phone and my mom explained to her what she wanted Otter to build. Then I heard Otter get on the phone and my mom explained to him what she wanted built. The next thing I knew there was Otter and his mom at my house with a tape measure, taking measurements for the place my mom wanted the cabinet.

The next day after school, my mom picked Otter and I up and we went to the hardware store where there was an adjoining lumber yard. The three of us wandered around the stacks of lumber with Otter hand picking the wood that he would use to build the cabinet. He carefully ran his hand over the length of each board, checking to see if they were straight and knot free. After purchasing what was needed, we drove back to the school and had a janitor let us into the wood shop to store the lumber.

A couple of times while at the lumber yard my mom asked Otter how much he would charge her to build this cabinet. Otter would hem and haw and say that he had never done anything like this before and he didn't know how much to charge. My mom was insistent that she pay him what he thought would be a fair price for his labor. I smiled as I watched Otter stumble to find the right thing to say, and he looked to me for help. But I simply told him that this was his deal, not mine.

There was no time arrangement given as to when the cabinet project would be completed, but the next Saturday morning, there was Otter and his mom at the door, bringing in the freshly made and recently stained, wood cabinet. I have to admit, it was pretty impressive, attractive and well built, and it fit perfectly in the area of the garage where Mom wanted it placed. Mom did some more oohing and aahing, and even though Otter seemed somewhat embarrassed, I could tell he was quite proud of his work. And I could also tell that his mom was proud of what Otter had done.

My mom went and got her checkbook and asked Otter what was the charge for building the cabinet, but he refused to take her check. Even though my mother insisted, he stood his ground and refused any payment. I could tell that Mrs. Otter was proud that her son was doing this as a gift, and she insisted to my mom that it was something that Mark wanted to give her as a thank you for all the meals he had enjoyed at our house.

After a few minutes of this insistence, Mom pulled Otter close and gave him a hug and told him that it was a wonderful gift, one that she would always cherish. Otter told her that she was welcome and it was his pleasure, and he and his mom departed out the door and down the driveway.

A minute or two after closing the door, there was a knock, and my mom reopened it to see Otter standing there alone. "I wanted you to have the cabinet as a sort of Mother's Day gift."

Mom stood there in the open doorway for a couple of seconds. "Why, thank you, Mark. That means a lot to me."

Otter walked away and Mom closed the door. Then I helped her stack canning supplies in her new cabinet.

PROTECTED
by Mark Otter

Too much money?
Get a safe
Go to a bank.

Have valuable equipment?
Build a wall
Erect a fence.

Valuable car?
Buy an alarm system
Put it in a garage.

Beautiful house?
Build a barricade
Erect a blockade.

Delicate feelings?
Live with them
Don't be a sissy
Be a man

Protected
Not very much

OCTOBER 15

I STAYED AT MY SISTER'S ANOTHER NIGHT, ENJOYING THE relaxation of a comfortable bed. When morning dawned, I slept in. It was well after nine before I got out of bed and got Orson out for his business. Both Jenna and Matt had long since left the house and I got going slowly, rummaging through the kitchen cabinets, looking for coffee makings. I eventually found some, made a cup of delicious French roast, and settled in for some reading in the back yard, both dogs sprawled out in the sun on the lawn. It was heavenly. Having no plans often leads to the very best of days.

Around noon I met Jenna in downtown Corvallis for lunch. Corvallis is a charming college town, home to Oregon State University, and I enjoyed the changing colors of the trees while we sat and dined outside at a local restaurant. It was a nice way to spend time, and we continued our conversations from the night before, mostly talking about Mom and how she was doing. Talking about Mom's aging reminded me that soon my only relation left from my childhood would be my sister. I felt this sobering life conclusion.

"Hey, I have a question." Jenna's voice brought me back to the present moment. "Why do you nod your head to everyone?"

"What do you mean, I nod my head to everyone?" I was perplexed.

"Just that little nod of your head. You just did it when the waiter took our order."

I thought for a moment. I guess I did do that, pretty much to everyone, a sort of nodding of my head. "I guess it's from my Buddhist teachings. I was unaware that I even did it."

"You've been doing it for years. I assumed it was some Buddhist thing."

I suppose it was. I started bowing, a simple nodding of my head, in response to learning Buddhist traditions. Now I guess it was habitual.

When getting started in the ways of Buddhism, I found the custom of bowing to be one of the hardest to accept. Bowing is found in most Buddhist traditions. But I had the typical western cultural understanding that bowing is an act of submission. In Asia and other eastern countries, bowing has many functions and meanings, most often as an expression of respect. And in many parts of Asia, people bow instead of shaking hands. In Buddhism, bowing is a sign of humbleness and respect. Bowing towards the Buddha is a sign of respect for the teachings. Bowing to a teacher shows esteem for the teachings and those who embody them. And when students bow to each other, it is a recognition of the goodness in each of us.

An early Buddhist teacher of mine taught that bowing was a form of mindfulness, an in-the-moment awareness of humbleness and gratitude. That resonated with me and it has been a habit ever since.

Jenna brought me back to the present. "Hey, did you hear the one about the Buddhist who went into the pizza shop?" She was smiling at her obvious joke set up.

"No."

"He said 'make me one with everything.'" She chuckled with glee at her joke.

I responded back to her, "Yes, and he paid with a fifty dollar bill, and the pizza shop owner took the bill and placed it in the till and closed the drawer. 'What about my change?' the Buddhist asked. 'Change comes from within' was the answer."

Ah, the humor between brothers and sisters.

After lunch, Jenna left to go back to her teaching duties and I wandered along the trail that followed the Willamette River. It was a beautiful fall day, but I could see some wispy clouds in the distance, perhaps bringing in some drizzle soon. I discovered a path that allowed me to get close to the water and found a comfortable rock to recline against, letting the sun warm both my body and soul as I quieted my breath and listened to the beating of my heart. This was generally how I tried to meditate, flow with my breath and try to clue into the rhythm of my heartbeat. I have found that if I am able to quiet my mind, then I can tap into the longings of my soul.

I began my practice of meditation, and practice it is, during graduate school, desperately trying to control the creeping anxiety that threatened to overtake me. I had graduated a year before with a degree in Animal Science from Cal Poly. I was then in a Master's program, also in Animal Science, at the University of California, Davis. I was stressed; with school, with up-coming tuition payments, with life. I had wanted to take a year off after graduating from Cal Poly, but I didn't know what to do with myself. I was terribly unhappy.

I called home one weekend, a month into the Master's

program, and broke down telling my dad that I wanted to come home. He listened, like he always did, and then encouraged me to stay with it, perhaps drop a class or two and just take it more slowly. I thought that might be helpful. But when I went to my advisor he told me that rather than drop any classes I should discontinue the program and reapply for the next term. He also suggested seeing a therapist on campus, someone that could perhaps help give some clarity to the things that were bothering me.

So I set up an appointment, fairly reluctantly, but I was struggling. And I found out that it was exactly what I needed. During the course of my weekly visits, my therapist suggested I attend a meditation group that met on campus.

I remember that first meditation class. I was nervous, wondering what I was in for, as I saw pillows scattered around a classroom in place of chairs and desks that were pushed up against the wall. There were about 15 other students in the room, mostly female, all sitting quietly waiting for, I didn't know, the instructor? to come in.

I grabbed a pillow and looked around and tried to sit upon it the way everyone else was. Soon, an elderly gentleman, slight of build and with a kind face, came in and struck a small gong that resonated a soothing tone throughout the room. He then began talking in a calm and soothing voice, encouraging us to put our attention on our breathing, helping us to focus. He then was quiet as we all gently inhaled and exhaled for a few minutes. I struggled to concentrate on my breath, my mind wanting to wander, and my eyes wanting to check out what everyone else was doing, which I admit I did. But then the elderly gentleman would talk about simply bringing our focus back to our breath. He told us that our minds would wander, but to make no judgements, just continue to focus on our breath. He taught me that it was possible to feel the feeling, but not give into the emotion.

He talked about letting our worries go, freeing them to wander above us. I struggled with that image, but I kept focusing on my breath and with the image of letting my worries go, letting them wander, releasing them, making no judgements. And I began to feel a glimmer of peace, and I could physically feel my shoulders and my jaw and my eyes relax. Soon another gong was sounded and the fifty minute class was over. It had all gone by so quickly. I was astounded by how peaceful I felt, how relaxed I was. I was hooked and I couldn't wait until the next class three days away.

After the class, the same worries and insecurities returned. Then I would attend the meditation class and it would give me a respite from them. Afterwards I would revert back to my anxiousness. But I at least had the peacefulness of meditation class to look forward to.

After one of the classes I struck up a conversation with a young woman who I noticed had been in all the classes. She was an undergraduate student and I asked her how long she had been going to the meditation class. She told me that she had been meditating for years. "Oh, you have been taking classes for quite awhile?" I asked.

"No, I meditate at home, in my apartment, any quiet spot when I have the need to quiet my mind," was her response.

"You can do that?" I didn't think that I could meditate without someone guiding me through.

The young woman thought I was being silly. "Of course. It relaxes me. Why would I only want to get this feeling of peace and relaxation twice a week?"

After that I became a meditation devotee and it has been a part of my life since. I have even gone on several meditation retreats, helping me to get better and better at the practice of quieting my mind. I consider it as necessary for my life as exercise, a good diet, and adequate sleep. Meditation helps me to embrace my fears, my worries, and even my anger. It teaches me that I can have these emotions without giving in to them. That realization is very healing.

I stayed reclined next to the river for a while longer, occasionally hearing a bike or pedestrian go by along the path a few yards away. Mostly I just heard the water, gently flowing and touching the shore almost tenderly, brushing against the reeds and plants that grew along the water's edge. After some more time of listening to the world around me, I arose and walked back towards where I had parked my truck. I exchanged smiles with several fellow walkers along the path. The sun was still high in the afternoon sky, making the chilly fall day warmer.

I let my mind go back to the reason I was on this trip as I slid behind the driver's seat. And I began to miss Susan. I glanced at my phone, checking the time. I wanted to call her but I knew she was probably still at work. I would have to wait to hear her voice. I started up the engine. It was time to get going again.

There was a student who had been coming to a particular Buddhist priest for several years. He began to grow more and more frustrated with what he felt were the complexities of Buddhism. After one class, during the question and answer period, before all of the students had left the monastery, he remained to implore of the priest.

"Oh honorable one. I have been listening to your lectures for years," he said with a pleading tone. "But I am finding your lessons and teachings harder and harder to understand. Can you please simplify Buddhism? Can you put its essence into a more simpler form?"

Everyone, including the priest, laughed. Then the priest gently put his hand upon the student's shoulder.

"Everything changes." And then he asked for the next question.

Previous

I BEGAN TO NOTICE AN EDGE TO OTTER TOWARDS THE END of our junior year. It's hard to explain, and while no one would consider Otter easy going, he never seemed intense or in any kind of hurry. But this appeared to be changing, at least for me it did. He was spending more time alone, often making excuses or simply not coming along to our usual school hang outs, either at lunch or nutrition break. His work in Creative Writing was suffering. We would sometimes exchange stories or poems or essays that we had written for the class, but more often he would say that he had not completed the assignment.

That's not to say that we never hung out, it was that we seemed to be going in different directions. We did do some things together, an occasional overnight, always at my house, or maybe a movie. Sometimes we would meet at my family's next door neighbors, the Westersons, who had a pool and an open invitation for us to swim any time we wished.

I did go with him to one of his martial arts demonstrations. While having dinner at my house one evening, Otter asked if I wanted to attend one. I told him it sounded interesting, though that possibly wasn't truthful. But my parents jumped on the invitation, even though I don't think he was asking them to come. Anyway, we all showed up, and though the place was crowded with parents, Otter's weren't there. Otter said that they never came to any of these demonstrations so it was no big deal. I took him at his word as it surely seemed that he was used to them not being there. However, this distressed my parents, and though they tried not to show it to Otter, they certainly did to me. They came into my room that night asking me questions about Otter's parents, especially about his dad, questions that I did not have an answer for. How does Otter act around his father? Is he different around him? What have I noticed? The honest truth was that Otter did not talk much about his home life, even though we were good friends, and I didn't press him to.

Otter was very impressive in this Tae Kwan Do demonstration. It was obvious that he was very skilled and he was in his element. He won a couple of awards from the leader, the sensei, and I could see how much the other students respected him. I thought he appreciated that my family and I were there. Afterwards, the parents took Otter and me and Jenna to Farrell's, a local legendary ice cream parlor, and we pigged out on ice cream. It was a fun evening.

A couple of Saturdays after the demonstration, I was doing the teenager past-time of sleeping in. I was still in bed when I heard the doorbell ring. I sleepily heard my mom answer the door, and then her coming down the hall, peeking into my room and announcing that Otter and his father were here.

"What do they want?" I sat up rubbing some sleep out of my eyes, and candidly, getting an uneasy feeling in my stomach.

"They want to talk about church, I suppose." Mom came over to the bed and tapped me on the foot. "You need to get up and come out and be social."

I quickly threw on jeans and t-shirt and walked out of my bedroom, down the hallway, and into the living room and what should I see? My dad sitting in his recliner and William and Mark Otter sitting on the couch, the latter two dressed in jackets and ties. I almost felt like I gasped out loud, and I looked around at the faces to see if I had. I mean....I had seen Otter's dad on maybe three other occasions, but never in an ill-fitting jacket, an outdated tie, and shoes that had been polished so many times you could see the layers of wax on them. And sitting next to him was my friend, Mark Otter, dressed in almost the exact same way.

"Well, there he is!" Otter's dad announced my entrance in a booming voice as if I were a contestant on a game show. This unnerved me a bit, and Otter smiled weakly at my appearance. "Me and your dad were just talking about your interest in learning more about our God, the Great Jehovah." Otter's dad continued on for a couple more minutes, extolling the virtues of a "Jehovah" centered life. Dad listened quietly as Mom brought in glasses of lemonade.

After several more moments, Otter's dad finally stopped, probably to catch his breath, and my dad spoke. "I'm not much for religion, or God for that matter. But I can appreciate that you are, and I respect that. But I really don't think my family is interested in hearing any more."

If Dad thought that was going to end this religious discussion, he was mistaken. Mr. Otter continued talking about how important it was to have an individual relationship with God and how that was vital in this day and age. He referenced that we were in the throes of the last days. My mind simply was checking out of the discussion, and I watched Otter, who was silent and uncomfortable and fidgeting quite a bit.

"And I know that Jake has been asking quite a few questions about the Jehovah's Witnesses, at least that's what Mark has been telling me." This statement from Mr. Otter jolted me back to the present. Otter's dad looked at Otter, giving him a smile that gave me chills. I will always remember that smile, but I can't explain why it was so memorable. It was neither kind nor cruel. It was as if Otter's dad was reading a sales script and came to the part where it told the salesman to smile. That's the kind of smile it was. There was absolutely zero emotion in it.

"Well, Jake is curious about a lot of things, I'm sure." My father smiled over at me and I knew his smile was communicating kindness and understanding for the situation I found myself in. That was the difference in the two smiles.

There was a silence after my dad's remarks, before Otter's dad spoke again. "Perhaps we can leave you with our testimony of the God, Jehovah, before we go. Along with the latest copy of The Watchtower. Mark, go ahead and bear your testimony of Jehovah."

Otter fumbled nervously on the couch next to his father. "I don't think I can, Dad. I'm a little nervous."

Then came that smile from Otter's dad again. The same one. "Boy, if I tell you to jump, your only question to me is how high." A tense quiet fell across the living room and Mr. Otter looked over at my parents. "Teenagers, right?" The smile stayed on his face.

My dad spoke. "A testimony would be unnecessary. I am sure of the sincerity of both of your beliefs."

Silence continued. Then, "Mark," from Otter's dad.

Otter spoke. "I know that the Lord God, Jehovah, is the only true God. The way to heaven to be with Him is to accept Him as your God. The only way to be saved is to repent of your sins and call upon the name of Jehovah." He made the statement in a monotone. It was obvious that he had given this "testimony" many times before.

"There," Mr. Otter said tapping Otter on the knee. "That wasn't hard, was it?" Otter shook his head. Then Mr. Otter gave a similar testimony, and they got up and Mom and Dad saw them to the door and thanked them for coming. I stayed in my chair. I felt that it would embarrass Otter further if I followed the group to the door.

After they left, Dad came back into the living room. "Well, that was certainly interesting."

Later that evening, while the family was watching TV, my father got up and went over and turned down the sound. "Everything okay at Mark's house, son? I mean, as far as you know?"

I wasn't sure. "I suppose so. Otter doesn't talk much about home."

Dad was quiet for a few moments. "Maybe check in with him. I understand that diplomacy is called for."

"I will," I said. And I didn't think much more about that Saturday morning episode.

At school on Monday, I saw Otter at nutrition break. His already short hair was noticeably shorter, just a kind of fuzz on the top of his head. "What the hell happened?" I came right out and asked, but I was afraid of the answer. I was relieved when he passed it off, saying it was no big deal. But after school when we met at the flagpole, I asked if his haircut was related to the past Saturday.

"Maybe. I suppose. I smarted off to my dad about having to go over to your house." Otter looked tired and I could tell his haircut wasn't helping his self esteem. He shrugged. "It's really no big deal."

I looked him in the eye for a few seconds. "Dude. I think it is a big deal." I tried to make my voice soft. I was starting to get emotional and I could hear the catch in my voice. "Can't you say something? Do something?" It would be years before I realized the naïveté of that question.

"No. It would just be worse if I tried." And Otter paused. "Worse for my mom." His eyes began to water and he sat down on the curb.

I sat down next to him. "I'm sorry." The words fumbled out. Silence enveloped us for a minute or so. "Is there something I can do?"

Otter continued looking down at the curb. "No. I can handle it. It's just hair. It's no big deal. Honest."

"Okay. It seems like a big deal."

"I don't think he meant to cut it this short."

I let that hang in the air. I did not know what to say. We were just kids. It did not seem like there was anything I could do. "Just know I'm here," I said quietly.

We sat in silence for a few more seconds then Otter rose to his feet. "Thanks." I reached my hand up to him from where I was sitting and he grabbed it and pulled me to my feet. "I know you're there if I can't handle it. Just don't tell anyone about my hair. It's too embarrassing."

"I think others are going to notice." I stated the obvious.

"Yeah, well, I'm just telling everyone that I like it this way. If they object, I'll kick their ass." He said this with a smile, as if he were joking. I'm not sure he was.

He stood next to me and wiped his eyes with the sleeve of his shirt. "I can handle it," he said again. "It would just get worse for me and my mom." It seemed like he said that more to convince himself than for my benefit. He looked into my face. "I'll figure it out."

Then he walked off towards his juggling club. I watched him go and I tried to think of what I could do. I could not think of anything. I walked home feeling sad.

ENOUGH
by Mark Otter

Enough.
Said over and over
In many different ways.
That's Enough!
That's more than enough!
Enough said!
Enough of that!
Enough is Enough!
I've had Enough!

Enough!!!!

When is someone going to tell me that
I'm Enough?

OCTOBER 16

I SPENT ANOTHER LOVELY EVENING WITH JENNA AND Matt, one more cookout, one more time sitting around the fire pit sharing wine and stories. The dogs spent the time alternately playing and resting at our feet. I said my goodbyes and retired early, with the intention of getting up before the sun and finding a place to watch the sunrise. I have always enjoyed the quiet of the mornings, and this one was no different as I awoke and tried to exit the house as quietly as possible.

While I was loading the pickup with my gear, I saw a note from Jenna attached to the driver's door handle. "It was so great seeing you and Orson. I admire you for taking this trip and facing some of the unpleasantness of the past. Drive careful, stop often, and always live soft. My love to Susan. YMTM...Jenna."

Living soft was how Jenna frequently tried to describe her intention for life, and soft was how she wanted to treat all living beings, especially the creatures that she had spent her adult life taking care of. I always loved how she phrased that, to live softly as one goes along life's travels.

And the YMTM was a family reference, one that we all used with each other. It stood for You Matter To Me. It came from my father. He would always say, "Make it matter to you." It was his way of asking us to do our best. It was what he would tell his patients when he would prescribe a treatment or when encouraging them to adopt a healthier life style. Once, when he was being interviewed for a local segment in the newspaper, he was asked why he committed so much time to really listening to his patients and his response was, "They matter to me." I always remembered that, and I remember thinking of how true that was. My father conducted his life as though everything mattered to him, everything had a purpose, and you lived life with an intent. So we would often sign cards and letters and emails with YMTM. It made me happy to read those words from Jenna.

It was still dark as I loaded Orson into the back seat and slowly backed the truck down the driveway. I was headed for Alsea Falls, a lovely spot where water and meadows meet in a gentle waterfall. I had been there several years earlier on a previous visit and it was a place that felt peaceful. I was hoping to get there as the sun came up. I loved watching the sun cover the western slopes of the Cascades as it said good morning to the Willamette Valley.

I soon arrived at the trailhead and leashing Orson up, we took the short hike to the falls, arriving just as the sun was peeking through some scattered clouds. It was a beautiful, somewhat chilly morning and I pulled my jacket tighter around my chest as the spray from the falls lingered in the air. Because of the early hour, I was alone and the only noise was the waters of the South Fork of the Alsea River gently cascading over rocks and pooling into a small pond before continuing on towards its destination. I reveled in the quiet and the peace.

Watching the water move downstream is such a lesson for life. It teaches us to immerse ourselves in nature, going with the flow and natural rhythm of things. Slow down and meander through life. Be thoughtful of those creatures who live downstream. And always remember that the beauty is in the journey.

I had brought The Repository on the hike and I gently mixed some of the contents with the potting soil. I spread it around some willows that were growing wildly along the shore, then I sat back and said a prayer of peace, with Orson lying close by, his chin nuzzled into his front paws.

I began to seriously study Buddhism as my Master's program was coming to a close and I was soon to begin my doctoral program at Utah State. Buddhists believe that when the student is ready, the teacher appears. I may have not been totally ready, but teachers were beginning to appear.

I had contemplated taking a break from school once I graduated with my Master's degree. But I didn't. I always had a sort of dogged determination to keep moving forward in my education. Four years at Cal Poly, two years at UC Davis, and now I was heading to Logan, Utah. The way it was setting up, there would be no breaks and no pauses. I was also working part time jobs to assist in tuition payments, though my parents were helping as much as they could. By now Jenna was in college, and I was beginning to feel that maybe I wouldn't be able to finish what I had started. My determination was waning, as was my drive and self esteem. It was affecting my school work and my health.

I was constantly stressed and worried about my future. The term "over educated used car salesman" was always in my head. I feared that this would be my destiny. I had so much angst over an imagined future while weighed down with regret about things I couldn't change. I was feeling the need to attach to anything, especially physical things that I could touch, hold, and feel. I was always collecting stuff, both physically and metaphorically, as if these items could fill a hole within me. It seemed as if owning and collecting and doing were connected to my status. I was searching for an identity in things, in grades, in education, in the drive to get some letters after my name. I was looking for any distraction that would keep me from learning about myself. No matter what I did, I felt unfulfilled. I was confusing activity with accomplishment.

I was never satisfied, not with friends and relationships, not with professors and advisors, not with fellow students. But mostly I was never satisfied with myself. My dissatisfaction would then lead to running away. I felt that I was not meant for this relationship, or that friendship, or this class. I was constantly complaining and worrying, and always trying to force things to be done a certain way, my way. Even meditation wouldn't quiet these thoughts, often leaving me more frustrated. These things were taking a physical toll on my health, in the form of headaches and a sour stomach. Jenna mentioned to be more than once that she and my parents were worried about me, that it seemed like I was depressed and unhappy.

One day, about the time that I was graduating from UC Davis, a fellow student said to me, "You seem so stressed." I rolled my eyes, showing some contempt but knowing she was right. She invited me to a workshop on campus. It was a workshop about living in the moment and letting go of those things that were weighing you down. I balked at first, but then thought, "Why not?" So I went.

The workshop was taught by a visiting Buddhist monk, and the first words out of his mouth were about letting go of attachments, that nothing was permanent. Neither the good times, and certainly not the bad. He taught that there were three things to never be controlled by: Money, people, your past. To others this may not have been ground breaking information. But it resonated with me, deeply. And then he said, "Pain is inevitable. Suffering is optional."

There are certain moments in life where you remember where you were and how you felt at that exact moment. This was that for me. In a dingy, poorly lighted auditorium on the campus of UC Davis, this was my epiphany. But I still wasn't ready.

I waited around afterwards to talk with this learned monk and when he looked at me, I asked an incredibly stupid question. "How do you join the Buddhist religion?" This kindly, older gentleman looked quietly into my eyes and with nothing but love and kindness in his voice and manner, placed his hand upon my shoulder and simply told me that Buddhism is not a religion, it is a way of life, a way of study. He encouraged me to learn more and see if Buddhism was the path for me. I asked him how I would go about doing that and his eyes smiled as he told me he was sure that I would find the path if that was where I wanted to go. He encouraged me to learn as much as I could, but also to only believe what agreed with my own reason and my own common sense.

I visited a Buddhist temple that was located near Sacramento. I searched in the library for books and started learning more about the teachings of Buddhism. I searched these books for answers to the challenges I was having. I kept searching and studying, even going to some workshops and retreats. Eventually, it dawned on me - the question that I needed to find the answer to - what if there was no problem to search for?

And the evolution of that - I am not the problem since there is no problem. I began to accept that pain was always going to be part of life, but I did not need to give it transportation to go where it wanted to go. I am free to direct it to where I need it to go. And suffering was my choice.

The perfect version of me does not exist, no matter how much I chase it. The need to find that perfection was keeping me from growing as a son, brother, friend, and student. It was also keeping me from being happy. Though not easy, it was that simple.

No matter how much pain, or shame, or humiliation, or anger, or despair, or sadness that I may feel, these feelings were just part of life. And it is my narrative that makes them good or bad.

These are the things that I was reflecting upon as I lay with Orson among the willows growing along the river bed. It felt wonderful to reflect upon these beginnings in my life. I repeated my prayer of peace over the remnants of The Repository. Then I arose, as did Orson, and we loaded back into the pickup, started it up, and aimed it down the road, heading south. Traveling softly.

One day a horse came galloping at a high rate of speed down the middle of a well traveled road that connected two villages. Several travelers were forced to leap to the side of the road in order to save their lives and belongings. One traveler shook his fist at the rider of the horse and demanded to know where he was going in such a hurry.

The man on the horse merely shook his head. "I don't know. Ask the horse."

Previous ———————————————————————————

AS MY JUNIOR YEAR OF HIGH SCHOOL CAME TO A CLOSE, I started writing to different colleges and universities, trying to decide where I would like to continue my education. I was drawn to the sciences, especially biology and related subjects, and I was beginning the process of applying to universities with good programs in these majors.

Often Otter and I would discuss our future plans for getting out of our respective houses and how our lives would look once we were on our own, anticipating our senior year of high school. The difference in our plans was I was going to college, since there was never a question in my house; college was what you did after you finished high school. Otter's plans were more up in the air and he was not very interested in college, nor did his parents seem to push such a plan. Otter was thinking more along the lines of an apprenticeship route, perhaps electrician or plumber, doing something with his hands. He was looking into some of the local junior colleges.

We both wanted to get out of our respective houses and experience life on our own. I was looking and planning for a college dormitory experience and Otter was just looking to get away from his home life. That was pretty evident.

The summer between our junior and senior year found us with our first official jobs, ones with pay checks and taxes taken out. I worked a morning shift at the local Jack in the

Box. I wasn't a fan of either the food or the early morning clientele, but it was an easy job, except for having to wake up at 5:30 a.m. I was either assigned to the counter or the drive through, and afterwards I had the rest of the day to lounge or read or apply to colleges.

Otter hired on as a helper for a landscape service company. He was working mostly full time, 5-6 days a week, in the hot Southern California sun. He liked the physical part of the work and it got him out of the house and making some money.

Because of our jobs, we didn't see each other often, but sometimes we would chat on the phone or maybe hang out at a local donut shop when we had some time off. Things seemed to be going okay for Otter, though he did complain about his parent's rules sometimes. That was not out of the ordinary. I think for different reasons we were looking forward to our senior year in high school.

One morning after my shift at Jack in the Box, I called Otter, knowing it was one of his rare days off. I suspected he would still be in bed, but I also thought that both of his parents would be at their respective jobs. He answered the phone groggily, but perked up when I told him I was on my way over with some egg sandwiches, leftovers from the breakfast service at Jack in the Box.

Otter was sitting out on his front steps when I arrived. I sat beside him and we snacked on the breakfast sandwiches and downed some cartons of milk. He mentioned that he had recently purchased what he called a Shaolin Wooden Dummy, something to assist him with his martial arts training. I didn't know what he was talking about and asked him to show me this weird-sounding device. We finished off the sandwiches and walked through a small courtyard and went in the back door to the garage located in the front of the house.

The double car garage was without cars and it looked like it would only accommodate one vehicle because boxes were lined up along both side walls as well as the back wall. The boxes were all the same size and shape and they were each marked with a date in black marker. I could see that the dates were several years in the future. These boxes were stacked from the floor to midway up the wall, and even to the ceiling in some spots. There was a section of the garage where there were some typical storage items, a rake, a shovel, implements like that. But it was mostly boxes. Boxes and boxes.

In the middle of the garage was a wooden contraption, an upright log with several dowels sticking out in different directions. Otter went over to it and started throwing martial art punches in between the dowels. At first he was slow and deliberate, but then he progressed faster and faster until his hands were just a blur as he snapped punches in between the dowel arms. It was impressive.

Suddenly the side door to the garage flew open, banging against the wall, and there stood Otter's dad. The sound of the door slamming against the wall scared the absolute shit out of me, making me feel like I jumped six feet into the air, or out of my skin as the saying goes. I'm sure I let out an audible gasp, so startled I was at the surprising and loud entry.

Nobody said anything for several seconds. Otter and I were staring at Mr. Otter. He was staring at us. Then, "What are you doing in here?" came from Mr. Otter. It wasn't said loudly or softly, but there was an edge to it, the question coming out not as a question, but more of an accusation.

"I was just showing Jake my Shaolin dummy," Otter's voice was high, and I could feel a panic in both his voice and my stomach.

Otter's dad took three, maybe four steps across the room until he was standing in front of Otter and myself. We had turned from the dummy and were standing next to it. "You're not supposed to be in here." I didn't know if he was addressing me or Otter. Then, without warning, Mr. Otter hit Otter in the face with the back of his hand, the sound reverberating around the garage. I will never forget the sound of his hand hitting the side of Otter's face. Otter dropped down to one knee with the force of the blow. Mr. Otter turned to me, and for a split second I braced for the slap I was positive was coming. I closed my eyes and waited. Nothing came, just silence, then I opened my eyes.

"You need to go home," Mr. Otter said, in the same voice, neither loud nor soft, but more like it just dropped out of his mouth.

I glanced down at Otter, still on one knee, and I headed for the side door. "I told you no one was to be in here." I heard Mr. Otter's voice echo around the garage. He was now directly in front of Otter, towering over my friend. "Now look what you made me do." That I heard as I exited and I closed the door behind me. I froze. I didn't know what to do. I listened for any sounds coming from the other side of the door. I was scared. Then it came to me that Otter was right so many months ago when he said his father striking him sounded resentful. That was how it sounded. Resentful. Full of resentment.

I crossed the courtyard and then followed the sidewalk down to the street. I hesitated and looked back at the front garage door that was closed and I listened for any other sounds. I couldn't hear any. I thought about waiting for Otter, but I was not sure what to expect, my head was spinning in a million different directions. What had I just witnessed? I began to feel my lip quiver and I felt tears start to run down my face. I walked briskly, trying unsuccessfully to control the tears. I got home and was glad no one was there. I went to my room and collapsed on my bed, sobbing into the pillows.

I did not know what to do. Should I say something? I knew that I could talk to my parents, maybe should talk to them, but I had promised Otter that I would not let anyone know what I knew about his home life. But this was different. It felt different. I decided to give it a day, see what might happen tomorrow. I was so mixed up, astonished, and feeling ashamed for my friend.

The next day turned into another day, and then another. I did not hear from Otter. No calls, no Otter dropping by my house, no Otter swinging by the Jack in the Box. I was too scared to call his house. What if Mr. Otter answered? What if I just dropped by unannounced? Pretend that nothing was different? I felt so alone, with a secret that I could not tell anyone.

The days after the garage incident turned into a week, then two. My family went on our annual vacation to the San Juan Islands in Washington. I sent Otter a postcard from the islands, but I heard nothing in return. We visited a couple of the universities that were on the list of schools I might want to attend after graduating. Soon the summer was over and it was time for school to start. I still heard nothing from Otter. My parents asked a couple of times and even Jenna was curious about why I wasn't hanging out with him. They wondered why Otter never came around anymore. I said that he was working and just really busy. I felt that I could not share his shame without at least talking to him. But I didn't know how to do that.

The summer ended and school was ready to begin. It had been four weeks since the garage incident. Would Otter be at school? What happened after the incident?

I had always been excited about the beginning of a new school year. And this was to be my last year of high school. But I was worried about my friend.

THE QUESTION
By Mark Otter

The question is asked,
If a tree falls in a forest
And no one is around to hear it,
Does it make a sound?

If love is given
And no one is around to feel it,
Is it love?

If hurt is given
And no pain is felt,
Is it really hurt?
Is it really pain?

Someone has to be there
Or it doesn't count.

Does it?

That's the real question.

Tom Smyly

OCTOBER 16

I DECIDED THAT IF I WANTED TO GET TO CRATER LAKE National Park and have time to set up camp, I needed to get going. So I left Alsea Falls, headed east towards Interstate 5, then turned south. Just past the city of Eugene, I veered east towards the Cascades. Driving into the mountains I marveled at what a lovely state Oregon is. A few days earlier I was immersed in Pacific Ocean views and now I enjoyed the vistas of mountains and lakes as I headed over Willamette Pass.

I stopped for gas and refreshments outside of Oakridge and found a pleasant rest stop with picnic tables and a dog area, so Orson and I were both able to snack on a few provisions and take a short walk to stretch our legs.

We finished our stroll through the trees and returned to my pickup. While we were away, an older pickup truck had parked next to me. This truck was in disrepair and I wondered how it had made it down the highway to this point. It had a dilapidated camper shell attached, one with a door that exits to the rear. A window on one side of the truck was barely being held in place with duct tape and another window was missing, having been replaced with a cardboard cutout. The camper shell, along with the pickup, had several spots where the metal had rusted clean through. It truly was a traveling tenement house.

But this is not what made the vehicle remarkable. It was covered with stickers and homemade signs, all with essentially the same couple of themes. One was that we should repent, that America was sinful and it would be destroyed if said repentance did not occur, well, I guess within the next couple of hours. And the other theme was that the owner of the vehicle was not a fan of abortion. There were several pictures of fetuses in different stages of development, and the gist was mankind was murdering all of them. And just for additional flair, there were several anti-government stickers and additional homemade signs with this similar message placed in several spots.

I popped my truck canopy open and threw Orson's water bowl in the back and as I did, a thin, bearded man appeared from the other side of the vehicle. Our eyes met, and we both looked each other over. I nodded a greeting, and he asked me if I had repented of my sins. This caught me somewhat by surprise and at first I thought he was talking to someone else so I looked over my shoulder. Finding no one there, I turned back and asked, "Who, me?"

His question didn't seem like it was asked in anger as he certainly did not seem agitated. It was more of an information gathering kind of question, like being asked how I want my steak cooked or when the next bus would be coming by. He was what best could be described as grizzled. His beard was unkempt and his face was hardened, but his eyes were soft and not at all confrontational. His voice was raspy, and I could see the cause of that was probably the package of cigarettes popping up from his shirt pocket.

"Do I need to?" I followed up. I was trying to keep my gaze at his eyes, though it was hard not to let my eyes wander over to the many placards posted on his vehicle.

"Brother, we all need to." He said this as he walked back around the other side of the truck, the same direction from which he had come.

"Amen to that," I told him, and I watched his boots from underneath the pickup continue walking on the other side, stop, then reverse themselves and come back around to the rear where I was standing.

"You better repent now brother," he said with some admonishment in his voice.

And I responded back, "Now? Where's the fire?"

That got his eyes ablaze. "IT'S IN HELL BROTHER!! WHICH IS WHERE YOU'LL BE GOING IF YOU DON'T REPENT NOW!!"

Our eyes met again. I didn't say anything. And though his words were said with passion, I didn't sense that they were said in anger. I waited to see what was next.

After a few seconds, he said, "Have a good day, brother." and with that, he climbed into the cab, and tried to start his pickup. The engine sputtered and he turned the key twice more before the engine came to life. He backed out and gave me a wave as he rumbled down the frontage road of the rest stop. I watched the pickup with all of its stickers and signs merge onto the highway.

And I thought - it's good to have a hobby.

As I pulled back onto the highway to continue my journey towards Crater Lake, I remembered a gentle admonishment from one of my Buddhist teachers. I had told him that I was trying to perfect the action of "going with the flow." I thought this would be a worthwhile goal to achieve, something that indicated that I wasn't getting bogged down with what others thought or what might hinder me along my way. I told him that I was forcing nothing, simply trusting that wherever I went would be for the best.

This teacher told me about how he liked to canoe down the local rivers, the peacefulness that it gave him. Then he asked me, "What would happen if I put my canoe into the stream, laid my paddle down, and went with the flow?"

I was confused for I thought that he would praise me for my "go with the flow" attitude. And knowing that a lesson was forthcoming, I sat silently and let him continue.

"If you go with the flow, the current has the power to take you where you might not want to go, perhaps into rocks, damaging your canoe and possibly putting your life at risk. But if you understand the current, and appreciate its power, you can move in harmony with it. You can work with the current, dance with it, sliding smoothly around rocks and paddling around eddies. You can do this with minimal effort unless you try and fight against the current. You must have an active engagement with the current, knowing of its power and majesty and working in accord with it." Then he said, "Don't go with the flow, be the flow."

I reflected on this as I sped down the highway and tried to think of the times that I had worked against the currents of life and how much unhappiness this had brought me. It was a good lesson.

While on the road, I called Susan and visited with her for a good part of the drive, having to call back on a couple of occasions as I traveled along the hills of Southern Oregon which resulted in a brief loss of reception. It was good to hear her voice and to hear of her plans to go to Boise, Idaho for a couple of days to see her sister. She was feeling a little lonely by herself, and I admitted to her the loneliness that I felt without her. But she encouraged me to stay on the path of what I was doing. What a blessing to have her as my life companion.

Orson and I pulled into Crater Lake National Park in the late afternoon and quickly found a quiet place with which to set up our simple campsite. I eschewed making a fire, even though the evening was getting quite chilly, but I stayed outside the camper and waited to see the first stars come out. I love that time when the stars are first appearing, counting them as they show their light, then losing count when literally thousands of stars become visible. This was a clear night, though cold, and I bundled up to stay out and count the stars. I was treated to a brilliant light show, even seeing a few shooting starts here and there. It was a spectacular sight.

After a while, Orson and I went for a brief walk and I bundled up to ward off the chill. Back inside the camper I meditated for a bit, making it easy for me to doze off as soon as I turned off the battery powered lantern. Orson was sleeping right beside me, his chest moving gently up and down with his breath. It was a perfect night.

. . .

There was a wise teacher who every year would have a retreat for the study of Buddhism. Even though this retreat was several weeks and quite intense, it was highly sought after to attend. During one of these retreats, a student was caught stealing and the matter reported to the teacher with the request that the offender be immediately expelled. The wise teacher ignored the matter.

Later, the same student was caught stealing once again and the matter was reported to the teacher, who again ignored it. This ignoring of such a blatant offense incensed the other students, who drafted a petition demanding that the offending student be expelled. Furthermore, they stated that they would leave the retreat if the situation wasn't resolved.

When the wise teacher read the petition he gathered all of the students around him. "You are wise brothers," he told them, "and you know what is right and what is not right. You may go and study elsewhere if you wish, but this poor brother does not even know right from wrong. Who will teach him if I do not? The rest of you may leave if you wish, but I am going to keep this brother here."

The student who had stolen broke down in tears upon hearing of the caring and love that the teacher was offering him. He apologized and repented of his offense and soon became the most dedicated student at the retreat.

Previous

THE NIGHT BEFORE THE FIRST DAY OF MY SENIOR YEAR IN high school, the phone rang at my house. Jenna answered and by the way I heard her talking, I knew that she was talking to Otter. It was an amiable conversation from what I could hear. Jenna always liked Otter, though she did think he was a little strange. She was asking about his summer, telling him about our family trip, and just chatting with him about various things. Then, "Jake, phone.... it's Otter!"

I went over and took the phone from Jenna. "What's up, man? Long time no hear from."

Otter's voice came over the phone. "Yeah, let's catch up. Want to walk to school together tomorrow? First day of senior year!"

"Can't walk tomorrow," I responded. "I'm driving to school."

Otter chuckled. "Well, la-di-dah Mr. Bigshot."

I laughed in return. "Yeah, it's my mom's station wagon. I'm sure everyone will be quite impressed," I said sarcastically. "Hey." I paused. "I have an idea. Come over early. We'll go grab a couple of donuts before school."

"Great. I'll see you in the morning."

When I hung up the phone, I thought about the last time I had seen my friend. It was definitely good to hear from him and he sounded good. But I wondered if the garage incident was going to be talked about. I was nervous about bringing it up, but I was still shaken by the events.

The next morning, there was Otter standing at the end of my driveway, the same spot where we had often met for our first two years of high school. We sort of hugged/patted each other, awkward as we had never done that before, but I think we genuinely missed seeing each other. It had been four weeks since the garage incident. On the drive to the donut shop, we talked about our summers, me working at Jack in the Box and his landscaping job. We ordered donuts and sat in a booth and continued our discussion. I filled him in on the family vacation to the San Juan Islands and on the universities that we visited. He told me that his family didn't go anywhere and that he was able to work a lot of hours and save some money. But it was obvious that we were both waltzing around the elephant in the room. I wanted to bring up the garage incident. And as I was telling him all the details of my life for the past four weeks, I was trying to think of a way to broach the subject. I couldn't think of any way to start this difficult conversation, so I kept hoping that he might bring up the subject first.

My avoiding the issue paid off. After a few more minutes of chit chat, Otter broke the ice. "Hey, sorry about that day in the garage."

I looked at my friend in the eye. "There's nothing for you to be sorry about."

His gaze met mine. "I'm just sorry you had to witness that whole thing."

I was glad to have the ice broken. "I didn't hear from you after that. I have to admit I was a little worried."

Otter rubbed his short crew cut. "I understand. I guess I got kind of busy. And I knew you would be going on your family vacation." He paused and quiet settled over us for a second. "I suppose I didn't know what to say."

"What set your dad off so much? I mean, was it the boxes?" I was curious about what was in all of the boxes that lined the walls of the garage.

"Yeah. They're full of food storage."

That perplexed me. "Food storage?"

"My dad thinks that the apocalypse will be coming one day soon, so he wants to have enough food to last through the end of times." Otter took a bite of donut and the filling squirted out along his chin. He wiped it with a napkin. "He doesn't want anyone to know that we have all this food. You know, in case of the apocalypse." He paused. "It's a religion thing."

I chuckled in that nervous way that one laughs at something that isn't really funny. "Sorry to laugh but that seems a little weird."

"I would agree. But it's a big deal to my dad. So that is what upset him. He doesn't want anyone to know of this secret food supply." Silence settled over us, the only sound being the bell that rang each time someone else came into the little donut shop. I didn't know what to say and it was starting to get uncomfortable. Finally Otter spoke again. "Did you tell anyone about it?"

"About seeing all the boxes of food? No."

"No. You know....about my dad hitting me."

I looked at Otter for what felt like a long time. Otter had blue eyes that would brighten up when he was excited and soften to an almost gray color when he was more somber. I had seen both of these colors over the couple of years of our friendship. His eyes were that soft gray now. "No. I didn't," I told him. I waited a few more seconds. "I thought about it, I wanted to, but I was worried about you. What might happen to you if I did."

Otter looked down at the table then back up again. "Thanks for not telling anyone. It would have made it worse."

I wanted to ask him how it would be worse, but I guess I just didn't want to contemplate what worse looked like. "Have you ever thought about leaving? Going somewhere?"

Otter's eyes looked down to the table. "Like where?"

"Maybe a relative, I don't know."

Otter breathed out a long exhale. "That would make it harder on my mom." He crumpled the napkin that was in front of him. "Really, I can handle it." I kept my eyes focused on his eyes and maybe I rolled my eyes, I don't remember. I know that I looked like I didn't believe him. "I can," he reiterated.

I thought I saw his lips quiver just a bit, but he quickly finished the milk he was drinking. "Let's go," he said. And then he smiled. "First day of Seniors' Rule!"

I got up and tossed my napkin and empty milk carton into the garbage. "Yep, Seniors' Rule!"

We walked out the door of the donut shop and got into my mom's station wagon. We didn't say much on the drive to the student parking lot. Once there we compared our class schedules and saw that we did not have any classes together. That wasn't unusual as I was taking two college prep classes and his schedule had a couple of shop classes. We went our separate ways as the warning bell rang in the school yard, giving us notice that classes were about to begin. We agreed to get together at lunch.

I didn't tell him that I did not believe that he could handle it. I didn't remind him that he had said these same words many times during our friendship. But I had a bad feeling that he couldn't.

DAMAGED GOODS
By Mark Otter

There's a bin that's away from all the other bins.
Half Priced,
Damaged Goods.

Sign says there is minor damage
everything still works.
Just cosmetic.

Half Priced.
Damaged Goods.

And if nobody still wants the
Damaged Goods?
Return to sender.

Damaged Goods.
Still good,
Just a blemish or two

Unwanted.

Return to sender.

OCTOBER 17

I AWOKE EARLY IN THE MORNING, FEELING THE COLDNESS of the air that surrounds Crater Lake, the frost glistening on the ground and on the windshield of the pick up. I was feeling the age in my bones and as I attached the leash to Orson, his stiff stretching indicated that he was feeling his age also. I walked him a few hundred yards down the pathway and he was especially entranced by the smell of bacon frying from a nearby campsite. It was early and the campground was mostly still asleep, but another dog began to bark from inside an RV when it picked up Orson's scent. That was followed by "Hey! Quiet down!" from inside the RV. After a loop around the campground, Orson and I walked back to the pickup and I poured some kibble in his bowl and lit the butane on my camp stove to heat water for my tea. The odor of bacon was still in the air, and Orson and I longed for a couple of slices, perhaps with pancakes on the side.

I was feeling the urge to go for a morning hike, the sun just starting to appear above the mountain tops that ring this lovely lake. I left Orson in the camper and he didn't seem to mind being left behind as he snuggled down into the covers. I thought the cold morning air might make a hike difficult for him so I left the windows cracked and grabbed The Repository, placed it into my day pack and headed down the trail.

Summer had ended weeks earlier, so this national park wasn't as crowded as it could be, and there were several empty camp sites as I hiked out of the campground and onto one of the many trails that meander through the park. It seemed like I had the trail to myself, perhaps owing to the earliness of the morning. I quickened my pace to warm myself and I quickly heated up with the exertion of hiking at altitude.

Crater Lake was in constant view as I hiked along the trail that wandered in and out of the trees. The sun rose higher in the sky and it soon became noticeably warmer, and I slid the jacket I was wearing off my shoulders and tucked it into my backpack. Soon, I ventured off the trail, not far, just enough to have some privacy in case any other early morning hikers ventured close.

I thought about how I wanted to distribute some of the contents of The Repository and I began collecting rocks and stacking them on top of each other, trying to construct a cairn. Cairns, or stacked rocks, have carried several meanings throughout history and I had seen many over the years. Most were used to mark the trail, a symbol that one was on the correct path. I had a Buddhist teacher tell me that constructing a cairn was a practice of patience, and like our lives, each rock needed to be placed gently and carefully in order to create balance. He taught that each rock should signify thankfulness, an intention of grace, and a sign that we ourselves are on the right path. In Buddhist tradition the stacking of stones asks for good fortune to be bestowed upon the stacker and their families. With each stone placed, a specific wish or designation of gratitude can be made. So I tried to place each stone with intention.

I remember learning that cairns are often used as guideposts throughout history. My Buddhist teacher would say that we should take what we have learned and use it to guide others on their journey, using our own knowledge and experience as a cairn for others. He taught that cairns are not only a map through various pathways, but they can guide us through uncertain areas of life as well. The act of attentively, patiently, gathering, and balancing our intentions can reassure us that we are on the path of right effort and right action.

Afterwards, I stepped back and sat a few feet away from my just created cairn. I closed my eyes and breathed in the clean mountain air. After a few minutes, I took out The Repository and gently spread some of the contents around the intentionally stacked stones. I took note that often cairns were used to indicate burial grounds, a memorial of sorts. I liked that thought as I patted down the earth, all within the breathtaking views of Crater Lake.

I spent a few more moments at my makeshift memorial, then I gathered everything up and headed back to the campground to my pickup with a snoozing Orson in the back. I gave him one more quick stroll as I munched on a granola bar before breaking camp, then helped him back into the truck and headed out. It was still morning, but the day was definitely starting to warm. I drove down the mountain, back to the interstate, and after a few miles I turned west, heading again towards the coast.

The road towards the Pacific Ocean was full of twists and turns. It wound through the forests, meandering back and forth through switchbacks, crossing the beautiful Smith River several times until I finally arrived at Highway 101, the north to south coastal highway. I turned south and crossed into California, stopping in the little coast town of Crescent City. I pulled over at a small cafe and ordered some fried chicken and coleslaw. Orson and I found a picnic table outside the cafe doors and we settled down and enjoyed our lunch.

As I was finishing my meal, a shaggy-haired, middle aged man, dressed in worn jeans and a dirty sweatshirt approached me and Orson. He was followed by a dog attached to a leash that the man held in one hand. The man had a dark complexion, possibly Hispanic or maybe Native American. The dog was an older mixed breed. They both stopped a few feet away and he hesitantly asked "If you're finished with the chicken, could I have the bones for my dog? He loves them."

I tried to project a kind face for this man who seemed down on his luck. "I'm not sure that chicken bones are too good for dogs." I tried to say that with no judgement and I hoped that I did.

"It's okay. He just crunches them up with his teeth. Really, it's fine."

I gave him the paper tray containing the left-over chicken bones. "Of course," I said. He thanked me and took the tray and walked back around the corner of the cafe.

I stayed with Orson for a few more minutes and finished off the rest of my iced tea. I picked up Orson's leash and started walking around the side of the cafe to the parking lot. As I rounded the corner, I encountered the man again, except this time he was sitting with his back up against the wall of the cafe, and he was gnawing on the chicken bones that I had just given him, trying to get the last bits of meat off.

Our eyes met, and he looked down, seemingly embarrassed. "I was just cleaning them off a bit before giving the bones to Jake here." He nodded at his dog that was laying by his side.

"Jake? That's my name." I gave him another smile. "What's yours?"

"Artemis." His eyes came back up and met mine.

"Nice to meet you, Artemis," and I extended my hand which he accepted and shook. I squatted down so as not to continue to tower over him. "Let me buy you and Jake lunch."

"That's not necessary. These really are just some bones for old Jake here."

"I know it's not necessary. I would just like to buy you lunch."

He hesitated. "Please," I continued. "Allow me."

"That's very nice. Thank you." And Artemis rose to his feet as did old Jake.

We left the dogs tethered outside the cafe while Artemis and I went inside and ordered a large fried chicken platter, with some boneless chicken tenders thrown in for Jake. Artemis thanked me again, we shook hands once more, and I loaded Orson back into the truck and continued south on Highway 101.

I was in such a good mood. I needed that.

. . .

A student went to his meditation teacher and lamented at how poorly his meditation studies were going. "My meditation is horrible! I am often distracted or my legs hurt or I am constantly falling asleep. It is horrible!"

"It will pass," the teacher said kindly.

A week later the student returned to the teacher. "My meditation is going wonderfully. I am so aware and at peace!"

"It will pass," the teacher said kindly.

Previous

Senior year clipped along for me and Otter. We saw each other occasionally and talked on the phone once in awhile. We did try to get together sometimes. We weren't hanging out as often as we did in previous school years, but that wasn't by design. It was more that we were just doing different things.

I was taking college prep classes in advanced English and Math. Otter was concentrating more on Wood Shop and Metal Shop, classes like that. He liked those classes and he was good with his hands. I was always impressed with some of the things that he created. He certainly had talent.

A lot seemed to be changing with my friend. He seemed edgy and moody, often snapping at classmates for seemingly no reason. I will say that he never did with me. But it seemed he was always on the verge of an argument with somebody over the smallest slights. He even got into a couple of shoving matches with other students, which got him sent to the principal's office a couple of times. They were always such seemingly minor issues, someone bumping into him in the hallway or something like that. He would even admit to me afterwards that it was stupid for him to be getting upset over such trivial things, but they continued to bother him.

One Saturday we planned a beach trip, something we did once in awhile when I could get use of the family car. We liked going over to the beach, flexing our skinny teenage muscles, and generally checking out the girls in bikinis who frequented the beaches of Southern California. So we drove over the hills of Topanga Canyon Drive and headed for Malibu one fall day.

We parked and found a spot to lay out our towels, went in and out of the water a few times, and flirted with a few of the girls that were around. After about an hour or so, Otter said that he wanted to show me what he had made in Metal Shop. He pulled out a metal flask that he had fashioned. It looked pretty cool and as I held it, I could tell that it was full of something. "What's in it," I asked, perhaps a little naively, as I was pretty sure what the flask contained.

"Just some Jack Daniels," Otter replied a little mischievously, and he unscrewed the top and took a swig and handed it back to me.

This was not my first time having a taste of alcohol. I had been to a couple of friends' houses and we had snuck a sip or two from a parent's liquor cabinet. At my house I had snuck a few sips of wine from my parent's supply. They only kept wine in the house, maybe an occasional beer, but no hard liquor. One time Otter and I split a beer at my house when no parents were around, and though we tried to pretend that the taste wasn't that bad, it was obvious that we had not acquired a taste for beer as of yet.

But this was the first time that I was not at someone's house, and I have to admit to being a little nervous that someone I knew might see me and word would get back to my parents. Otter shook the flask in front of my face again, and I took it from him and swallowed a taste. The whiskey burned the back of my throat, but not too badly, and I gave the flask another pull before I passed it back. We shared it back and forth for the next few minutes before it eventually was empty. It was a small flask and it didn't start full, but Otter and I felt pretty grown up as we passed the flask back and forth. I have to admit to feeling a little, I suppose tipsy, but we got back into the water and flirted with girls for another couple of hours before the drive home. I was cognizant of making sure that I felt totally in control before getting behind the wheel of the family station wagon. We left the beach as night began to fall and drove uneventfully home.

To be honest, we were just not into alcohol or drugs or even pot, which was fairly prevalent around the high school. It was the seventies after all. Once, at a party, a joint was passed around. Otter passed it over to me without taking a hit, but I tried it and immediately began coughing up a lung, it burned so much. Later when we were headed home, I asked Otter why he didn't even try it and he said that his martial arts leader was really opposed to any kind of drug. This sensei said he would not teach anyone who used illicit drugs, so Otter was pretty adamant about not using them. And I never really had much desire.

So it came as quite a surprise to me when two weeks after our beach trip, Otter was suspended from school for bringing alcohol to campus which was found in the same flask that he had brought to the beach. The alcohol was found when the school administration did a search of his locker. I had seen Otter at nutrition break earlier that day, but then he was called into the office and sent home. It was the talk of the school.

I was genuinely shocked. It just did not seem like Otter. I wanted to call him, but I was too afraid that his dad would answer. I was concerned and worried and just all around uneasy. The rumor around the school was that someone alerted the office that there was contraband in a locker. They

Tom Smyly

then searched Otter's locker, and alerted law enforcement officers when the alcohol was found. I began to wonder who would have known that Otter had alcohol in his locker. I would think that if I, as his best friend didn't know, then who would? Then I began to worry that maybe Otter thought it was me who told the school office. Of course I didn't. But I began to worry that he thought it might be me.

Otter was suspended for one week. I didn't hear from him, nor did I try and contact him during that time. Two days before the suspension was to be lifted, around dinner time, there was a knock on the door. My mom answered and there was Otter, looking somewhat sheepish. Mom invited him in and he stood in the entryway, seeming not to know what to do or say. But Mom did. She went over and gave him a gentle hug. "How are you doing, Mark?" There was a kindness in her voice, one that I recognized easily. "We've missed you around here."

Otter started to say that he had been suspended from school but my mom cut him off. "Come and sit down. We are just getting ready for dinner. Why don't you stay."

"Thank you, really." Otter shifted his weight back and forth. "I can only stay a minute. I have to get back home. Is Jake here?"

I stepped out of the hallway, not letting Otter know that I had witnessed the exchange with my mom. "Here he is," Mom pointed over to me. "Mark?"

"Yes, ma'am?"

"We've been worried about you."

I saw Otter's lip quiver just a bit. "Thank you."

I touched his shoulder. "Hey. Let's go outside." We both walked out and stood on the porch.

"Everything okay?" I wanted to know where we stood.

"Well, it's kind of a mess, but I'm trying to figure it out."

"So, what happened?"

"I'm not sure. I think it was because I got into a fight after Tae Kwan Do one evening with one of the students at the school. We got into an argument. So after class we went out back and I kicked this kid's ass."

"What did that have to do with the suspension?"

Otter sat down on my front steps and I sat next to him. "His mom is Mrs. Kelso."

"Old lady Kelso?" I registered some surprise. "Front office secretary Mrs. Kelso?"

"Yep." Otter sighed. "So I think she got them to open my locker and that was that."

I had to admit to Otter that I was a little relieved as I thought he might be blaming me for the discovery in his locker and I mentioned that fear to him. "No, man. Never," Otter assured me. "But I did have the stuff in my locker."

"Why there?" I asked.

"Can't keep it at home." Otter grinned, or at least tried to. "So you can imagine how happy my dad was to get the call. It's been hell. In fact, I've got to go. My dad thinks that I'm at martial arts." Otter got to his feet and moved quickly down the steps. "I'll see you in a couple of days." And he was off.

I went back inside the house. Mom was waiting and I sort of debriefed her with what Otter had told me. She listened intently, like she always did. "Otter's a mess, Mom."

"I know." She rested her hand gently on my shoulder. Then she went into the kitchen to finish preparing dinner.

The next morning, I went out the front door headed for school and there on the porch was an ordinary kitchen glass with three starkly purple hydrangeas sticking out of the top. There was a note leaning against the glass. "Thank you" was all that was scrawled on it.

HYDRANGEAS
By Mark Otter

White Hydrangeas
Gently misted, as if cotton collected on its petals.

Pink Hydrangeas
Bearing a dainty hue, kissed by God.

Purple Hydrangeas
A regal statement, stately and queenly.

Yellow Hydrangeas.
Reflecting sunshine and mornings, dew glistening.

Red Hydrangeas.
Bringing power and dynamism, drawing all eyes.

All bringing a peace, a calming influence
On all who receive this beauty.

But no water makes them brown
With leaves flaking, falling away
And littering the ground.

Now made worthless.

OCTOBER 17

I CONTINUED SOUTH ALONG HIGHWAY 101, PASSING though stands of enormous, stately redwoods. I stopped often to admire these beautiful trees. I took one of the many roads that branched off from the highway and drove deeper into the forest, weaving among the giant redwoods and sequoias. Other trees, the deciduous ones, were beginning to turn color with the passing fall month. I stopped at a state park visitor center and took in the exhibits and film showings. Many of the short films about the park I remembered from the times when my family would visit on the way to our annual trip to Friday Harbor in the San Juan Islands.

Eventually Orson and I made it to a camping spot at Redwood National Park. We set up camp and I dined on a vegetable stew that I had bought in town and Orson had his usual. I reclined in my camp chair, Orson at my side, and I read as the setting sun was beginning to fade behind these giant trees. Though it was fall and not the busy summer months, the campground was full of fellow campers. Most of these were in larger RVs and trailers, but a few had tents laid out on flat portions of ground. The din of the other campers melded in with the odors of fires and dinners being prepared. The sunlight filtering through the trees waned and it became darker. I turned on my battery powered lantern as I settled into my chair.

I was reading some of the teachings of Lao Tzu. His instructions about living in the present were particularly impressing me this evening. "If you are depressed, you are living in the past. If you are anxious, you are living in the future. If you are at peace, you are living in the present." I was becoming immersed in his gentle counsel.

In the campsite next to mine was an older couple in a large RV, the kind that take up tons of space and hardly seem like camping vehicles but more like traveling houses. The quiet of the evening was shattered every now and then as the generator they used to power various electrical devices would kick on and then power off. I tried to ignore the noise, as it was pretty standard fare in many of the campgrounds that Orson and I had bedded down in. But the whirring of the generator seemed particularly loud and obtrusive this evening, made even more so with the beauty of the giant redwoods that were towering over us. I contemplated going over and asking them to maybe shut it down as it was growing dark, but I worried about the confrontation that might provoke.

So I sat in my camp chair, grinding my teeth and muttering to myself. I looked down at Orson who seemed oblivious to the noise pollution that was engulfing our campsite. I had a combination of admiration for his being able to do so and disgust for his ignoring what was obviously a blight on what had started out as a beautiful evening. The Buddha taught that holding onto anger was like grasping a hot coal with the intent of throwing it at someone else. You were the one who was going to get burned. It seems like Orson was more learned than I was in this regard.

Night fell and I continued to sip my tea and read a book by the light of my lantern. I began rereading The Tibetan Book of Living and Dying, skimming through some of the passages I had underlined in times past. I was almost lost in this reading and had mostly blocked out the offending generator noise. Then I heard a gentle "Excuse me," and I turned and looked over my shoulder at my next door neighbors standing a few feet from me. They were the owners of the large RV with the loud generator. "Sorry to bother you," the wife said softly.

I stood up and turned around as Orson lifted his head and peered at the couple over his nose. "Good evening," I politely said. "What can I help you with?"

The husband spoke. "We saw that you had a yellow lab and we just wanted to come over and say hi. Is he friendly?"

I motioned for them to come closer. "I think yellow lab and friendly are pretty redundant phrases. Yes, please come over. He loves people."

The older couple, I would guess they were in their seventies, moved closer to Orson and he responded with a thumping of the tail and he unhurriedly climbed to his feet. "He's an old fellow, so he's moving a little slowly," I explained his slow rising. "His name is Orson."

"Aren't we all moving a little slowly?" the husband said smiling, responding to my statement as he patted Orson on the head. We were all quiet for awhile, me standing and the couple leaning down beside Orson, scratching him behind his ears. They knew just the spot where labs loved to be massaged and Orson emitted a low, grumbling sound from his throat, something that he often did when he was happy and content.

Then the wife stood up and rubbed her eyes. It was obvious that she was crying and she gave a giant sniff to try and stem her runny nose, as her husband continued to stroke Orson. She looked at me and I could see the tears glistening down her cheeks. "Are you okay?" I gently asked.

She put her hand over her face. "Excuse me," she sniffed and walked back over to their RV, opened the door and went inside.

I looked over at the husband who was scratching Orson under his chin. We were silent for a few seconds, his eyes staying fixed on Orson. I didn't know what to say, so I stayed quiet. The husband gave Orson another pat on the head and stood up. "We had to put our yellow lab down two days ago. Suzy. She was old and this road trip was a little hard on her."

I looked at this older gentleman in silence for a few more moments. I saw the pain in his face. It was the pain of losing a beautiful companion. All dog owners know of it. "I'm sorry," I said softly. "Truly their only fault is that they don't live long enough."

"It was especially hard since we were on the road. We're from Nebraska. So we had to find an emergency vet. The old girl had a stroke." He bent down to pat Orson again and Orson wagged his tail in thanks and even slid closer to this gentleman, putting his head on his knee. Orson knew that there was sadness being talked about.

I told the gentleman again that I was sorry and he expressed his thanks. He patted Orson one more time and he took a couple of steps towards his RV when the door opened up and the lady stepped down the steps and walked back over to my campsite. She was carrying a cloth bag full of various items. "Did you tell him about Suzy, Jim?" she asked as she came closer.

The gentleman nodded his head. The lady came closer to me and held the bag out in front of her. "These are some of Suzy's snacks and play toys. I though Orson might like them." And she put the bag on the picnic table.

I smiled at her. "That's very kind. I am sure he will." I stepped closer to her. "I'm Jake by the way."

Introductions were made. They were Jim and Jane Sanderson, from Omaha. I invited them to sit for awhile and offered to make them some tea. They passed, but they sat at the picnic table and I turned my chair around to face them. Orson slid closer to them, lying at their feet in easy distance for them to continue to scratch him around the ears. He knew that they needed some comfort, of that I'm sure.

Jim and Jane had been on the road for about three weeks and had always wanted to see the Pacific Ocean and the redwoods. They planned on staying on the road for a couple more weeks before heading back to Nebraska. I told them that I was merely on a trip to clear my head, thus explaining the simpleness of my camping accoutrements. They stayed at my campsite for about 30 minutes and we had a most pleasant conversation. The evening ended with hugs and exchanged email addresses. They patted Orson one more time on the head and went back inside their RV. After a few minutes I heard the generator start up again. This time it didn't bother me.

Before heading to bed myself, I leashed Orson up and hiked down the campground road, trying to get a good cell phone reception. I eventually did and I called Susan. A call to her always made me feel better, for I missed her so. I told her about Jim and Jane, my new Nebraska friends. I left out the part where I was so annoyed about the humming of their generator. I suppose I was a little embarrassed about almost letting such pettiness spoil my evening.

I found a tree stump to recline on and talked with Susan for quite awhile. When I headed back to my campsite most of my fellow campers had put their fires out and turned their lights off, including Jim and Jane. I heated water to make chamomile tea and opened the bag that Jane had given me. There were a couple of chew toys and some dental chew treats, as well as two cans of dog food. I gave Orson one of the dental treats, which he took into his mouth, then dropped it on the ground, sniffing at it for a good minute.

"It's okay. It's from Suzy. She wouldn't mind." I picked the treat up off the ground and gave it back to him. He devoured it with gusto.

I sipped my tea for a few more minutes until it was no longer hot, then I tossed the remainder on the ground. I lifted Orson into the back of the camper and we both snuggled in for the night, and I pulled the covers up to my chin. It was getting chilly here in the redwoods. I silently gave thanks and made a mental checklist of the many things I was grateful for. They included my new friends, Jim and Jane.

. . .

There once was a monastery that was very strict. Following a vow of silence, no one was allowed to speak at all. But there was one exception to this rule. Every ten years, the monks were permitted to speak just two words. After spending his first ten years at the monastery, one monk went to the head monk. "It has been ten years," said the head monk. "What are the two words you would like to speak?"

"Bed... hard..." said the monk.

"I see," replied the head monk.

Ten years later, the monk returned to the head monk's office. "It has been ten more years," said the head monk. "What are the two words you would like to speak?"

"Food... stinks..."

"I see," replied the head monk.

Yet another ten years passed and the monk once again met with the head monk who asked, "What are your two words now, after these ten years?"

«I... quit!" said the monk.

"Well, I can see why," replied the head monk. "All you ever do is complain."

Previous

I HAD MY FIRST GIRLFRIEND IN THE FALL OF MY SENIOR year. Well, sort of girlfriend. Jessica Hanks. We started hanging out often, sometimes at each other's houses or somewhere in between. I took her to the Homecoming Dance, doing the whole taking pictures with both sets of parents. It was fun. She was smart and cute and had a great sense of humor.

Jessica was also involved in the drama department at school and had the lead in the musical Man of La Mancha, playing Dulcinea. I talked Otter into going with me to one of the Saturday night performances. It was well done and was a thoroughly enjoyable performance. And Otter loved it! We went backstage afterwards and congratulated many of our classmates on such a fine show. Then a bunch of us, including Otter, went out for ice cream afterwards. Otter was fairly gushing over how good the play was and how much he enjoyed it.

On the following Monday, I was meeting up with Otter to walk to school together. I walked out my front door to be greeted with Otter bowing before me. Then, in a passionate and dramatic voice, "I shall impersonate a man. His name is Alonso Quijana, a country squire no longer young. Being retired, he has much time for books. He studies them from morn till night and often through the night and morn again, and all he reads oppresses him; fills him with indignation at man's murderous ways toward man."

Otter smiled at me before continuing, his voice reso-nating with deep feeling, "He ponders the problem of how to make better a world where evil brings profit and virtue none at all; where fraud and deceit are mingled with truth and sincerity. He broods and broods and broods and broods and finally his brains dry up. He lays down the melancholy burden of sanity and conceives the strangest project ever imagined - to become a knight-errant, and sally forth into the world in search of adventures; to mount a crusade; to raise up the weak and those in need. No longer will he be plain Alonso Quijana, but a dauntless knight known as Don Quixote de La Mancha."

I was impressed. "Dude, what's that all about?"

Otter shrugged his shoulders. "I dunno. I just liked the play so I went over to the library yesterday and checked out the book. I guess I got to memorizing a few passages."

"Wow, quite impressive," I said. "I guess you really did like it."

We finished our walk to school and then went our separate ways to class. I was hanging out with Jessica and a couple of friends at lunch when Otter approached. He greeted everyone with a nod, then to Jessica, he said, "Hello, fair Dulcinea." And he bowed.

Jessica smiled and curtsied. "Why thank you, Sir Knight."

I weighed in. "I think Otter really enjoyed the play."

Jessica turned to Otter. "You should try out for drama. They're doing the musical Carousel next spring."

Otter smiled. "I can't sing, though."

"Well, you should try out anyway. Most of us can't sing either." Jessica was kind in her encouragement. I could tell Otter appreciated that.

Otter spent the rest of the day and the rest of the week, quoting Miguel Cervantes. He even responded in class to a question posed of him by a teacher, "Facts are the enemy of truth." Then there was the pronouncement during wood shop, "It is the mission of each true knight...his duty....nay, his privilege, to dream the impossible dream." I heard Otter said that when asked about building a planter box. He certainly seemed taken in by the school musical.

As the school year continued rolling along, I saw Otter less and less, probably because I was spending a lot more time with Jessica and not as much time at my house. I would see him at lunch and he would hang out and shoot the breeze, often with Jessica as she and I would spend lunches together. Everything seemed fine with Otter, though I knew that he was drifting away from schoolwork. He often did not show up to school at all. But I was not sensing that there was anything out of the ordinary.

The following story happened about two weeks after seeing Man of La Mancha. I have to tell it second and even third hand as I was not there and did not witness the actual events.

There was another student at our school, an 11th grader named James Chamberlin. I did not know him, but knew of him, having seen him around campus and here and there around the neighborhood. He was, to put it mildly, a different kid. He was skinny, had acne, and also wore black, nerdy eye glasses. He was constantly being teased by a certain crowd of boys, the type that look for those who are different and think it's okay to bully them. I never saw him being teased or bullied, but often heard about it, and knew that most everyone regarded Chamberlin as an odd duck.

One day at lunch, Chamberlin happened to be walking along the fence that bordered the school, off by himself. My high school, like a lot of Southern California high schools, was a closed campus that was surrounded by a chain link fence. Apparently, three of the usual suspects, high school senior boys with nothing better to do than pick on other students who they considered different, surrounded him and began telling him to "hump the fence." And that is what Chamberlin proceeded to do. He began pantomiming having sex with the chain link fence. Why he would do that, I'm not sure. I suspect he may have been told by parents or well-meaning adults to simply comply with what the bullies tell you to do and then they would leave you alone. In any case, this merely egged on the three bullies. They proceeded to push Chamberlin up against the fence and 'helped' him in the act of humping the fence. As I said, I wasn't there, but I can imagine it was not a pleasant scene.

Apparently Otter happened by, intervened, and told the senior boys to leave Chamberlin alone. At this point, the boys said something to the effect of 'make us.' Which, it seems, Otter then proceeded to do. Otter had a reputation around the school as someone who could take care of himself, so most of the bullies generally left him alone. But I'm sure, buoyed by numbers, the bullies felt no real fear from this Otter guy, who they thought should be minding his own business.

So there was a fight and blows were delivered and received from both parties. And here is where the story takes a turn, maybe for the worse and certainly not for the better. A knife was pulled. The stories differ on who brought the knife, who pulled it out, and who threatened to use it. But what is not in debate was that by the time a small crowd of witnesses had gathered, and then school administrators showed up, the knife was in Otter's possession.

When the adults arrived, there were five male students out by the back fence. One student was still leaning against the fence, Chamberlin. Another was on the ground with a broken arm. And the other three, including Otter, had assorted injuries from blows to faces and bodies. Several other students gathered when they saw the commotion, and saw the scene as described, with Otter holding a knife.

Once teachers and administrators arrived, the three bullies immediately said they were just having a little fun, kidding around with their friend Chamberlin, when Otter came up threatening them. They then got into a physical confrontation in which blows were thrown and they were only defending themselves. When it became obvious that Otter was getting his ass kicked, as they told the story, he pulled out the knife and began swinging it at these poor innocents.

Chamberlin's story was that all four boys were hassling him, then the four boys got into a fight, and he just wished everyone would leave him alone.

Otter's story was pretty much as I described. He was minding his own business, saw a commotion out by the fence and decided to check it out. He did not like seeing the treatment of Chamberlin so told the three bullies to leave Chamberlin alone. When the bullies heard this, they attacked Otter, giving him a cut over one eye, along with other assorted bruises. Otter delivered a couple of black eyes as well as other injuries to his attackers. One of the bullies then pulled a knife, at which time Otter took it from him. When doing this, he broke the attacker's arm.

As you might imagine, it was the talk of the school. I heard about it and went to the school office and saw Otter sitting there waiting to see the principal. The other three boys had already been to the office, telling their side of the story. Otter filled me in on what happened. I believed him. I had never known Otter to carry a knife, I knew that he could handle himself in a fight with three punks, and defending Chamberlin was something he would do.

"I guess I should have probably just minded my own business." He touched the bump over his right eye and winced a bit.

"You did what you thought was right," I told him.

Otter looked at me and with no drama in his voice, quietly said, "One man, scorned and covered with scars, still strove with his last ounce of courage to reach the unreachable stars. And the world was better for this." And he smiled.

I told him I believed him and for him to tell the truth and it would turn out okay.

Otter was suspended from school for fighting and bringing a weapon onto campus. Things were starting to spiral out of control.

CHEAP SUIT
By Mark Otter

There is a man who wears a cheap suit.
Frayed at the sleeves
Worn at the elbows
The hem unraveling.
He sits in the front pew every Sunday.
Almost invisible,
Quietly,
Reflecting.

There is another man who wears a cheap suit,
Shiny suit.
Trying to appear that it cost more than it does.
He sits in the front pew every Sunday.
Oblivious,
Saying amens,
Praying so that everyone can see.

That is church.

OCTOBER 18

THAT NIGHT IN THE REDWOODS I HAD THE SAME DREAM that started this journey that I am now on. In the dream, I was at the now familiar starting place with trails leading away from me in various directions. I remember thinking in my dream - here I go again. Just like before, I picked a trail and started walking, trying to go at a good pace. For some reason there seemed to be a sense of urgency to get to wherever it was that I was going.

After hiking for a short period of time, I came to a mountain, and remembering Otter's urging from before, I started to climb. It was slow going, and hot, and I was getting frustrated at my slow pace and the difficulty of the climb. I sat down several times just to rest and catch my breath, and my frustration level continued to rise. I would climb and climb and then I would look up, but I could see no end to the trail. It seemed like it went on and on. After a while I sat down, rested for a few minutes, then turned around and headed back to the start.

In the dream, I trudged back to the place where I had started, feeling totally defeated. As I approached the area where all of the trails converged together, I saw Otter. He was sitting on a rock, looking just as he had in the last dream, the one I had before leaving on this trip. His hair was straight and long. He was constantly flipping it out of his eyes and he was wearing his usual jeans and a t-shirt. He was reclining, obviously waiting for me.

"I knew you would chicken out and end up back here." Otter said this with no malice in his voice, but no understanding either.

"It's hard," I said sitting down next to him. "I don't know if I can do this."

Otter looked at me. "Endurance is one of the most difficult disciplines, but it is to the one who endures that the final victory comes."

I stared back at him. "So now you're quoting the Buddha?"

"I'm just trying to speak in a language you can understand," he said, a wide grin spreading across his face. His voice softened. "What are you trying to do?" Otter asked. I was silent. "You don't know, do you?"

I thought for a while. He was right. I shrugged. I didn't know what I was doing. "I thought I was doing something for you," I told Otter in this dream.

"You don't have to do anything for me," Otter said, sliding off the rock where he was sitting. "Really. There is nothing you need to do for me. Whatever you're doing, just do it for you."

I looked at my friend who I had not seen face to face in almost forty years. "I'm not sure it gets easier no matter who I'm doing it for." And then I started sobbing, wailing with the tears held in for years and years; tears for Otter, tears for my father, tears for myself. Just raining tears, loud, drawn out, circles of moans, misery pouring out onto the ground that surrounded us.

I felt embarrassed, ashamed at this flow of emotion.

But I couldn't stop and the grieving continued. I saw the ground get wet beneath me as my tears lingered on. The dream seemed so real.

Otter kept quiet through my display of sorrow. Eventually I stopped and wiped my nose and eyes. "What do I do now?" I gasped out the words.

"Finish what you started," Otter replied, still sitting next to me. "Hey, I appreciate what you are doing. Just finish it." He arose and extended his hand down to mine. "Come on. I'll go with you."

I grasped Otter's extended hand and he pulled me to my feet. "Which way?" I asked.

"You lead," Otter replied. "I'll follow you."

We started down one of the trails, me in front and Otter behind. Then I awoke from the dream. I was covered in sweat, the sleeping bag soaked. My nose was runny and my eyes were wet. I had obviously been weeping in my dream. Orson was down at the foot of the sleeping bag, having moved there from his usual position next to me. His ears were back and he was eyeing me nervously, upset, probably because I may have been kicking at him in my sleep. I unzipped the sleeping bag and kicked it towards the foot of the bed and patted the mattress beside me, inviting him closer. He crawled up and slid his head on top of my hand, awaiting a scratching underneath his chin, a reassurance that things were okay. I spoke to him soothingly and calmed him.

I felt good, despite the obvious thrashing that had taken place through the night. The sun was just beginning to peak through the trees and the campground was quiet. I opened the back tailgate and slid out, helping Orson down. I decided not to leash him, knowing that he would follow me as I walked through the campground. We found a trail and hiked a few hundred yards. I then laid down on a soft patch of moss and looked straight up at these enormous trees that had been there for hundreds of years, watching the sunlight begin to peer through them. It was quiet. It was spiritual.

I was practicing the Japanese art of Shinrin-yoku. This art has been Americanized with the term Forest Bathing, a term that I dislike. It is not simply walking and meandering around a forest, as some take it to mean. It is the active practice of going to the forest to receive mental and physical healing. When we come in contact with the quiet and solitude of the forest, with practice, one can almost smell the oxygen the trees emit in exchange for the carbon dioxide they absorb.

When we walk through or sit amongst the trees, nature flows into us and helps us to reconnect with the nature inside of ourselves. Beneath soaring pines and giant redwoods and majestic oaks, our thoughts naturally become expansive. As we walk and reside under these trees, we can connect with the harmony that they live in and we become aware of how interconnected we are with the heartbeat of nature, and the reciprocal relationship we have with all things growing. It helps calm and center our minds.

I decided to walk back to my campsite and grab The Repository, which probably confused Orson quite a bit as he followed along faithfully. I went back to the grove of redwoods where we had just been and carefully spread some of The Repository around, gently patting it down with the trowel. I said a prayer and Orson sat quietly a few feet away. I felt such peace. I think this feeling of extreme peace is within all of us. We just don't realize it.

Orson and I stayed there for some time, enjoying the solitude. Soon, though, we heard signs of the campground awakening and campers beginning to rise and start their days. We made our way back and I fed him some kibble and I mixed in some of the canned food that Jim and Jane had given me. Orson can sometimes be picky about different food, and he sniffed at this concoction for a bit before deciding that it met his approval, and then finished it with gusto.

I heated up some water on my little backpacker stove and made some tea and oatmeal. I noticed that my next-door neighbors, Jim and Jane, had not yet emerged from their RV. I gathered up the bedding that was still wet from the night before and thrust it into a laundry bag. I loaded Orson into the truck, started it up, and pulled out of the campground.

I drove along the narrow road winding through the campground and finally made it out to Highway 101, gathering speed as we headed south. When we got to the coastal town of Eureka, I found a laundry mat and scrounging the floor of the truck for quarters, threw the bedding, as well as some dirty clothes, in a washer. Then Orson and I walked a couple of blocks to a small cafe delightfully decorated in pig decor. I ordered French toast, which was quite delicious, and even ordered some scrambled eggs for Orson, which he devoured as if it were his last meal. We both relaxed, me with a cup of coffee, and him spread out beneath me as we sat at the outdoor dining tables.

Afterwards we wandered back to the laundry mat, put the now clean clothes and bedding into the dryer, waited for that to finish, then it was back into the truck and onto Highway 101.

Despite the dream, or maybe because of it, I was invigorated. I rolled both windows down, and Orson and I headed south towards Highway 1.

. . .

Once upon a time in ancient China, a disciple was talking with his teacher. "Master," said the disciple, "It is said that all you really need to know in dealing with people is to always treat others as you would want to be treated yourself. What do you think?"

"Let me tell you about how the Marquis of Lu entertained the seabird," the Master responded.

"One day a rare and beautiful seabird was blown far off course by a storm. It came to earth in the capital of Lu. The Marquis of Lu was delighted and made the seabird his special guest. He had performers sing and dance for it day and night, and he presented it with fine roast meats and excellent wine. But the bird was terrified and confused, and it ate and drank nothing. After three days it died.

"The Marquis of Lu entertained the seabird the way he liked to be entertained, not the way a seabird likes to be entertained."

I SAW OTTER A COUPLE OF TIMES WHILE HE WAS SERVING his latest suspension. He was accepting the fact that because he had missed almost a month of school during his senior year, he might not graduate with the rest of the class. In any case he would have to go to summer school for credit recovery. He told me that his dad was thinking he should drop out of school entirely. However, at the end of the suspension, he did return to school and I would see him during most lunch periods. Jenna was now on the tennis team and I would attend some of her matches. Sometimes Otter would join me and help root her on. But outside of that, we didn't hang around much after school. Otter was still working with the landscaping crew he had worked with during the summer. In fact, he had been able to increase his work hours during his latest suspension and he often went to work after school. He seemed to be doing well and in good spirits.

I knew that his schoolwork was suffering and the suspensions didn't help any. He used to be exceptionally smart at math, but now had to drop out of those classes because he had missed so much time and was unable to keep up with the assignments. Apparently, his mom would come to school at the end of each day and pick up the assignments from his classes. I offered to pick them up, but Otter said that his dad had decreed that his mother was to pick them up, that was her punishment for Otter's getting suspended. That perplexed me and I asked Otter about it, but he just shook his head and mumbled something negative about his father. His father's need to punish his mom was never quite clear, and I let it go.

I did ask him about how things were going with his father, especially since the recent suspension, but he was pretty evasive about it. He would say that things were always shitty and that it was remaining that way. He often said things similar to this.

I have to admit that ever since the incident with his father in the garage the previous summer, I stayed away from his house, and even avoided calling on the phone.

One Friday at school during lunch time, Otter was hanging out with me and Jessica and a couple of other students, just shooting the breeze. Jessica mentioned that she was going to the mountains with her family for the weekend and Otter, hearing that, asked me if I would like to go to a movie that night and just hang out, which I thought sounded fun.

I procured the family car, picked Otter up, and we went and saw the movie The Trial of Billy Jack, Billy Jack being a favorite martial artist of Otter's. We were infatuated by Billy Jack's prowess and we left the theater kicking and punching our way back to the car. We ended up grabbing burgers afterwards at Jack in the Box. It was around midnight and we were heading home when Otter said that he knew where Roger Mooney, his old nemesis from tenth grade, lived. I replied with "so?" and wondered what Roger was up to. Otter said Roger was going to a local junior college, playing baseball there, and was still living at home.

"So why did you bring up Roger?" I had not thought of Roger for a couple of years, certainly not since he graduated two years ago.

"I know what car he drives. Let's just go let the air out of his tires," Otter was grinning. "That way when he goes out in the morning....." Otter chuckled at the thought.

That did not sound like much fun to me, and I certainly did not want to slash anyone's tires, but Otter assured me he merely wanted to let the air out of the tires through the valve stem. No slashing would be involved. So I said, "What the hell?"

We drove to where Roger lived, which was in the country a little ways off the main road, if you can call anywhere in the Los Angeles area country. He lived in an area where the houses were spread out, on a winding road, a road that curved through the hills and led to the beaches on the other side of the mountain.

We parked a couple hundred yards away from the actual driveway and snuck up towards the house. There was Roger's car, an older Camaro, parked in the circular driveway. While I stood lookout, Otter snuck over and crouched on the side of the car that faced away from the house, which was dark and seemed empty. Otter had taken a screwdriver from the glove compartment in my car and he used it to press down the valve stems on two of the tires. I nervously watched from the street as the tires went flat. He then snuck back towards me and we giggled as we ran back to my car. It was a fairly innocent prank and we both laughed at the thought of Roger coming out the next morning and finding his car temporarily inoperable. And of course, he would never suspect who had done such a dastardly deed. Just a couple of rapscallions we were.

The next day, Saturday, I found out that I had been accepted at my first choice in colleges, Cal Poly, in San Luis Obispo, for the upcoming fall term. I was even offered a partial academic scholarship. Destinies were being set.

HUSH UP CHILD
by Mark Otter

When he was a baby
He was impossible to hold
Fussing during the day
Giggling at night.

He always had a lot of questions
But hush up child.

He believed the stories they told him
That he could be anything
Anything he chose
The world was his paradise.

But when he asked what he could be
Hush up child
He believed that the adults would protect him
Make him safe from boogie men
And monsters under the bed
And lava on the floor.

But when he asked for help
Hush up child.

Soon the questions stopped
No more questions
There were no answers
Hush up child.

Tom Smyly

OCTOBER 18

CUTTING OVER FROM HIGHWAY 101 TO HIGHWAY 1 IS a slow, arduous process, winding through the costal range in Northern California. The trip from Eureka down Highway 101 is beautiful, snaking through great redwoods and quaint little forest towns. Eventually you come to the Highway 1 turnoff that goes up one side of the coastal range and back down the other side, navigating switchbacks and around trees until you finally begin to hug the Pacific. It's easy to get behind slow traffic, keeping you from going your intended speed, with RVs and log trucks constant company along the way. Finally I arrived in Fort Bragg, a small coastal town on the Pacific Ocean. It is a town that attracts visitors for its Glass Beach, an area that was created by years of dumping garbage in this area of the coast. It is also a popular spot because of the Skunk Train, an old train that winds it way through the redwoods. My family took the trip when I was in middle school and I remember how much fun it was.

I decided to stay in one of the many motels that line Highway 1. It was time for a decent shower and a shave. Orson approved, as this time I paid the extra $15 pet fee. Upon checking in, he immediately gave the room some extra sniffing, perhaps smelling some odor left from the previous occupants, and then quickly settled down and sprawled out on the carpet.

I fed Orson his usual kibble and gave him a rawhide treat to gnaw on and left him in the motel room. I had decided to wander down the main drag of Fort Bragg and check out a bar or two that I had noticed while driving into town. There were several eating out possibilities that were all within walking distance from the motel, and I grabbed a jacket as the fog was moving in quickly. The temperature was dropping, but the fresh air felt good after being in the pickup driving the winding roads that led me here.

I walked a couple of blocks and found a tavern that seemed inviting. I sat down at the bar, and ordered a beer and some nachos. There was an older gentleman, bearded with a cowboy hat, setting up some speakers on a small platform that served as a stage. He hooked a microphone to a stand and took a guitar out of an old beat-up case. He settled onto a stool, adjusted the mic, and then starting some soft strumming, checking the sound as it was reverberating around the small tavern. The guitar was old, with scratches and worn spots along its body. I imagined that the guitar and the cowboy were old friends as he strummed and fingered it with gentleness, and it responded with a deep and soulful sound. It sounded lovely, and he began playing a little louder.

The cowboy stopped playing for a minute, got up and adjusted the mic stand, sat down again, and then began singing cowboy music. His voice was gravelly, probably from years of smoking, but the pitch was perfect, and he played songs that invoked a bygone era, an era of cowboys out on the range watching over their cattle. It was just him playing with a raspy voice and the soft soulful guitar, and

I was mesmerized. It was beautiful. There were about 25 customers in the bar, and I may have been the only one listening. Often I had to strain to hear the lyrics over the clanging of beer glasses and banging of forks on plates. But I throughly enjoyed this old cowboy and his old songs.

I added a hamburger to my nachos and beer and ate slowly, enjoying the music and ambiance of this small bar. After about 45 minutes, the singing cowboy stopped, announced to nobody in particular that he was going to take a break, and placed his guitar back in the case. He left it on the small stage and wandered off towards the back door. I decided that it was time to settle up my bar tab and I motioned for the bartender to give me my bill. I laid cash on the counter and walked outside, where darkness had now fallen over Fort Bragg, and the fog had definitely settled in.

Out in the parking lot, leaning against an old Ford pickup truck, was the cowboy, attired in his cowboy hat and Levi's. He was smoking, kind of slouched against the passenger door of the pickup truck. I walked towards him and I nodded as I caught his eye. "I sure enjoyed your music," I told him. "It has such authenticity"

He took a long draw from the cigarette that was hanging from his lips. "Thanks, I appreciate that." He took another puff. "Sometimes it's hard to know if anyone is listening or not."

I stuck my hand out. "Jake Campton," I said, and he shook my outstretched hand.

"Cory Willis, and thanks again."

"How long have you been doing this?" I asked.

"Wow," Cory thought for a minute. "Since my teens, I reckon. Had always hoped to make a living at it, but that never turned out. Now it's just for beer money here and there."

"I guess we all had dreams when we were younger," I said.

"Yeah. I gave it my best shot, lived out of my car for a few years. But got tired of being broke all the time." He tossed the cigarette butt aside. "First your money, then your clothes." He smiled.

"Well, you're really good. I think you're honest to your craft." He seemed to be perplexed with that description, raising his eyebrow. "I mean, you're you. You look the part. And you sing the part."

Cory chuckled. "No one has ever given me that handle. Honest to my craft, huh?" He opened the door to the passenger side of the pick up and rummaged around a small duffle bag and produced a CD case. "Here. Take a CD. Good for calling cats and dogs and the occasional varmint," he said, keeping the smile on his face.

"Thanks," and I put the CD in my jacket pocket. "Can I buy you a beer?"

Cory looked at this watch. "It'll have to be a quick one, I reckon. I'm due for my second set. Can't keep my fans waiting." I appreciated his deadpan humor.

We went back inside the tavern. There were a couple of different customers at a couple of different seats. We went up to the bar and the bartender noticed Cory and came right over. "A beer before you go back on, Cory?"

"Yep. And one for my friend, Jake." The bartender slid us a couple of beers. I took out my wallet to pay, but the bartender waved my cash off and told me it was on the house. It was obvious that Cory had played here before and was liked by the staff, and the only waitress came over and said hi to him, and he introduced her to me.

Cory and I talked for a few more minutes, then he

excused himself and went back to the stage, pulled the old, beat up guitar out of its old, beat up case, and resumed singing more cowboy standards. I stayed for about 20 more minutes, continuing to be enthralled by his simple tunes sung with such soul. After finishing my beer, I walked over and put a generous tip into the small jar that was next to the stage. Cory nodded his head in thanks. Then I left a tip on the bar and walked out onto the foggy main street. I was feeling good after a couple of beers and the wonderful live music. I walked quickly back the few blocks to my motel room where Orson was waiting to be taken on his nightly stroll.

I grabbed his leash and back out into the cool evening I went, though this time I spent the walk talking on the phone with Susan. I told her all about Cory and she could hear the enjoyment in my voice. She told me that she looked forward to listening to the CD that Cory had given me, caught me up with the comings and goings around our house, and then bid me goodnight.

I was really beginning to miss Susan and our house. It was time to finish up this quest or crusade or journey, whatever it was called. I made some tea and went to bed, renewed for the rest of the trip.

．．．

A young student approached his Master. "Master, I have just entered the monastery. I beg you to teach me."

The Master replied, "Have you eaten your rice porridge?"

"Yes," the young student said.

"Then go and wash your bowl."

At that moment the young student was enlightened.

"Master," he approached again. "I have obtained enlightenment. What shall I do now?"

The Master looked at his young student. "What is it you did before you obtained enlightenment?"

The student responded, "I chopped wood and I carried water."

"Then chop wood and carry water," the Master responded.

MY SENIOR YEAR PROGRESSED INTO THE SPRING AND headed towards graduation and the summer break. I broke up with Jessica, went with Kate Villers for a few weeks, and then broke up with her. I say broke up, but the actual truth is that the relationships were not that serious and they pretty much died a natural death and relatively good friendships remained. Good for high school dramas, I suppose.

Otter began hanging out with a junior girl, Emily, whose last name I can't remember. They went out on a couple of dates and hung around at school some. She was cute and quiet and a good student. That seemed to motivate Otter to care more about his classes and that was a good thing.

When it came time for prom, I was still hanging out with Kate, so I asked her and she accepted. My parents agreed to host a group of prom goers for appetizers and pictures, so I asked Otter if he wanted to come over and join in, assuming that he would ask Emily. But Otter declined without explanation.

I saw him after school a couple days later and checked in with him and I tried to gently encourage him to come over to my house before prom. "I'm not going to prom," he told me, expressing it without emotion and I couldn't tell if he really didn't care or if there was something else.

"Everything ok?" I asked as I had not talked with Otter for several days, not since we went to the movie together.

"Even if you aren't going to prom, you can come over and hang for a bit."

"Nah, thanks anyway." Otter shifted his weight from one foot to the other and I knew that meant that he had more to say. "My dad says no prom. It's kind of a churchy thing."

"Ok, I get it." But I really didn't. "Well, the invitation stands if you can make it." Otter nodded his head in appreciation and went on his way.

Prom was fun. My parents hosted five couples and we all had a good time. I didn't get home until well after midnight, but no real hankie-pankie went down, except for some making out in the driveway of Kate's house. Someone brought a flask of vodka and several of us had a couple of sips while at the dance. Nothing real serious. It was fun.

The next evening, Sunday, I was watching TV with the family. I think it was Walt Disney's Wonderful World of Color. Suddenly there was a knock at the door which startled my parents as it was around 9 pm, late for visitors. My dad left the couch and answered the door. "Hello Mark. Kind of late to be visiting, isn't it?" he said in his calm, friendly manner.

"Yes, sir. I'm sorry, but I needed to talk to Jake." I started walking towards the door when I heard Otter speak.

"Hey, what's up," I said and my father opened the door wider and motioned for Otter to come inside the house.

Otter looked downward and stepped inside. "What's going on son?" my father asked kindly.

"My dad is on the rampage and I just had to get out. I don't know if I should go back home." Otter seemed on the verge of tears and it was noticeable how difficult it was for him to say what he had just said. "I'm sorry to bother anybody but I just needed somewhere to hang for awhile."

Just then the phone rang. "I'll get it," Dad said, mostly so no one else would answer the ring. It rang a couple more times. Then three, then four. After the fifth ring the phone was silent. After a minute, the phone began to ring again.

"I believe that's probably your father," my dad said and he moved into the front room to the phone. "Hello." Pause. "No, he's not here. He stopped by for a second, but then he left." Another pause. "Of course. If I see him, I'll tell him to head home."

My father stepped back into the entry way where Otter and I had remained, listening to one half of the phone call. "It was your mother, Mark." He placed his hand on Otter's shoulder. "She said that if I saw you to tell you that things were okay now and for you to come on home."

Otter and I were still standing in the same places that we were when he first came into the house, Otter still looking down at the ground. "What would you like to do, Mark?" Dad was standing next to Otter, and Otter gave an almost imperceptible shrug. "Why don't you stay here for a bit longer?" my father said as he closed the still open door behind everyone. Then, "Anna Lee is dishing up some ice cream as we speak," my father added. "Isn't that right Anna Lee?" and I heard my mom and Jenna both get up from the couch.

"Just dishing up now," she said from the kitchen. Otter followed Dad and I into the dining room. "Get out Parcheesi. You guys play while I get the ice cream ready."

We sat down at the dining room table. "I think a rousing game of Parcheesi is just what Mark needs right now," Dad said as he spread out the game board. Otter, though seated, was still looking down and I could tell that he was embarrassed about....well, about everything, I suppose.

"It'll be fun, Otter," I said, trying to relieve some of the tension that I thought he was feeling.

"Sure. That sounds fun," he said looking up for the first time.

"I'm blue," Jenna chimed in, and my dad said that the guest got to choose their color first, and Jenna pretend pouted. My dad spread the game pieces into their appropriate places.

"I think I know the rules," Otter said, and he sounded somewhat more like himself.

"Okay, where are the dice?" my father asked, looking through the Parcheesi box. He found them and slid them across the table to Otter. "You roll first, Mark." My mom brought out the dishes of ice cream and handed my father the bottle of chocolate sauce. "Okay, who wants some chocolate?" and he squirted chocolate sauce out of the bottle onto his bowl of ice cream.

"Yes, please," Otter said, and he smiled just a bit. We played two games of Parcheesi, and then Otter said he should be getting back home. Dad insisted that he not walk, so the three of us got into the car and drove Otter the short distance to his house.

We pulled up to Otter's duplex and he got out of the passenger seat and held the door open for just a second. "Thank you," was all he could say before choking up and he stopped before saying anything else.

"Are you going to be okay?" my father asked.

"Yeah. I'm okay." And I have to admit that my stomach dropped just a bit as I had heard that "I'm okay" so many other times. Dad and I watched from the car as Otter walked up to the front door of his duplex, stooped down to pick up a key under the mat, let himself in and closed the door behind him. Then we drove silently home.

I saw Otter at nutrition break the next day at school. "Everything go okay when you got home?" I asked.

He sat down at one of the several tables in the lunch area. "Yeah. Both my mom and dad were asleep when I got home and my dad was gone when I got up for school. And mom acted as though nothing happened."

I didn't know what to say so I simply offered up, "That's weird."

"Yeah." Otter was quiet for a moment, and I listened to the nutrition break noise going on around us. "Thanks for last night. Please thank your parents for me."

"Sure." I left that in the air for a minute, looking at Otter as he was looking around the lunch area. I wished there was something I could say, something to tell him that I understood, that I was here if he needed someone. Or simply ask if there was something I could do. I thought back to the garage incident. If that was what was happening when someone outside his family was there, what must be happening when no one was looking?

Otter must have sensed my uneasiness. "I'm okay, really. I can handle things."

And there it was again. The "I'm okay." "Sure," I said again. And we parted and headed to our separate classes.

TOO
By Mark Otter

Too tall
Too short
Too smart
Too dumb
Too pretty
Too ugly
Too rich
Too poor
Too unseemly
Too pleasing
Too argumentative
Too agreeable
Too hard
Too gentle
Too repulsive
Too beautiful

Life is about the Toos

Try to live in between.

Tom Smyly

OCTOBER 19

I HAD A GREAT NIGHT'S SLEEP AFTER THE LIVE MUSIC AND the wonderful chat with Susan. I awoke with renewed vigor, made some tea in the motel room, gathered up my belongings, rounded up Orson with his leash, and marched out the door. I was invigorated.

The left rear tire of the truck was flat.

I stood staring at it for a good three minutes, I guess hoping that it would magically inflate. I got down on my hands and knees and felt around the tire tread. I found the culprit. A nail was stuck dead center in the tread, and the tire had been slowly losing air throughout the night. I debated trying to drive the truck with the bum tire to a repair center but decided that driving might ruin the tire completely. So a change was necessary.

I know how to change a tire, have changed many over the years, but this seemed like a particularly unpleasant time to have to do so. It was a cold and foggy morning, and the thought of having to crawl around the parking lot of this dingy motel was quite unappealing. I was beyond frustrated with my bad luck.

While taking the jack from the storage compartment I remembered a lesson taught by a Tibetan monk who I met while visiting Colorado. I was attending a series of lectures by different monks who were doing service around the spiritual town of Crestone. It was a peaceful place to me, this mountain town devoted to finding a spiritual path, no matter what it may be.

The lesson being given was one about the unpredictability of life. No matter how much one may plan and prepare, life remains unpredictable. Life is uncontrollable. Life is ambiguous. It is when we accept these simple truths that we become more in tune with our own path and our own nature.

I thought about this as I was changing the tire. I long ago accepted the fact that life is unpredictable. And I have long stopped fighting the belief that there is nothing certain about life, at least this life that we are living now. But this Tibetan monk cherished unpredictability, gave himself over to it. The phrase that he used over and over was, "Embrace the ambiguity." He knew that because everything in life is uncertain, there must also be the realization that anything in life is possible.

This, he taught, is the basis of Wabi-sabi , the Japanese principal of accepting life's imperfections. He taught me that when this acceptance happens, you are then on the precipice of making the most of your life.

Wabi is an understated elegance, a basic simplicity, a focus on the principal that less is more. This learned monk posed the question, do we really need the choice of fifty different cereals in the cereal aisle? Many are simply the same choice repackaged. He was not implying that choice is a bad thing, but rather that we expend energies making choices between differences that are actually similarities.

And Sabi is taking pleasure in the imperfect, the damaged. It's the finding of beauty in the flaws. Thus Wabi-sabi is the finding of beauty in simplicity, in economy, in austerity. Wabi-sabi accepts three simple realities: nothing lasts, nothing is finished, and nothing is perfect.

An example of Wabi-sabi in Japanese culture is the art of kintsugi. This is where cracked or damaged pottery is restored with a gold glaze as a way to highlight its repaired cracks, showcasing the beauty of the damaged piece instead of trying to hide its imperfections. The cracks and breaks in the vases are seen as lovely and necessary, not as something to hide. The resulting uniqueness makes the pottery stronger and more valuable. As Leonard Cohen famously said, "There is a crack in everything. That is how the light gets in."

As I tightened the lug nuts on the spare tire, with Orson sitting a few feet away, eyeing me critically, I reflected on the pursuit of perfection that often drove me in my life. It is this desire that also resulted in my unhappiness, my misery, my suffering, when this perfection became unattainable. I was miserable because I never felt that I measured up to the perfection standard that I had made for myself. The practice of Wabi-sabi invites me to focus on the blessings that are often hidden in everyday occurrences. Even the discovery of a flat tire. It invites me to give thanks and have gratitude for the way things are rather than the way that I think things should be.

Wabi-sabi celebrates authenticity.

And Wabi-sabi is not only the discovery of beauty in imperfection, it is the acceptance of the cycle of life and death.

I try and use my morning tea preparation as the time to practice Wabi-sabi. Making tea is a simple exercise and as such, it would be easy to do so absentmindedly, without thinking about each of the individual tasks that go into the preparation. I try and focus my mind on each of the simple tasks, creating a sort of minimalistic tea ceremony. I focus on the tea kettle, listen to the water as it fills, feel the heat as it warms the water. I trace the handle of the teacup, smelling the tea that is steeping inside, warming my hands on the cup. I remind myself to not expect perfection and order in life, that these things aren't necessary for my happiness. It takes a mind quiet enough to appreciate the simple, the absence of ornamentation, to strip life to its bare necessities. Nothing we see or hear or do will ever be perfect. But it is in this imperfection that perfection resides.

I finished the tire changing and hoisted Orson into the back seat and drove to a tire repair shop that was located on the main drag of Fort Bragg, just a few blocks from my motel. They promised to get the damaged tire fixed within the hour, so I took my backpack with The Repository, leashed Orson and wandered down to the beach. The fog was still fairly heavy, and the beach had few fellow wanderers.

I stared out to the horizon for a few minutes, enjoying the brisk breeze in my face, appreciating the smells of the saltwater and various sea life. I took my shoes off and wandered into the surf a few steps. Orson hung back, nosing a clam or two, keeping me within view. I had The Repository with me and I opened and poured a small batch of its contents into the surf. Then I watched as the particles rolled out with one wave and then wandered closer to the beach with the next. Then out again and back in until I could no longer make out any fragments left from the original pour. I felt moved to pour out a little more and the particles repeated the going out and coming back of the first batch. It was calming after the energy expended by changing the tire and I felt mesmerized with the process.

As I watched the particles from The Repository move towards the surf, then back towards the shore, then out again, I harkened back to the times I spent with my friend Otter at the beach. We would play tag with the waves, running towards the surf, then back towards the shore as the waves came closer. And we would laugh and giggle at the silliness of it all. I smiled at this memory.

Soon it was time to call Orson, walk back into town, pay the tire repair bill and hit the road again.

I continued down Highway 1, stopping for coffee and danish in the artsy town of Mendocino. I once had plans to stay the night in this lovely town, maybe find a close-by camp site, but my motel desires had found me in Fort Bragg instead. But now I found myself wandering through a couple of the art galleries that dot this small town.

When Susan and I got together over thirty years back, she gifted me her love of art and artistic endeavors. Many is the time we have spent wandering around art colonies from California to New Mexico to Vermont, collecting original art work from local artists. Art is a skill I have never mastered, but Susan likes to work the potter's wheel on occasion, and our house is scattered with her creations. They give the house a warm vibration and add a peaceful ambiance to the home we have created.

I thought that maybe I would find something to add to our collection, but while I found many beautiful pieces, nothing moved me enough to spend any monies. Orson and I enjoyed walking around this lovely costal town, Orson sniffing at all of the water dishes left out for dogs. Many shops had dog treats and Orson would sniff them quite snootily before deciding if the treats met his sophisticated palate. Most did.

Soon it was time to get back on the road. I wanted to make the Bay Area and find a camping place before dark, but I would probably have to find something in Wine Country, north of San Francisco and Marin County. Then it would be on to Southern California, towards a conclusion to this journey.

. . .

Two men visit a Zen Master, looking for advice. The first man says, "I'm thinking of moving to this town. What is it like?"

The Zen Master asks, "How was your old town?"

"It was terrible. Everyone was mean and jealous. I hated it."

To which the Zen Master replied, "This town is much the same. Don't move here."

After the first man leaves, the second man enters and says, "I'm thinking of moving to this town. How is it?"

Again, the Zen Master asks, "What was your old town like?"

"It was wonderful. Everyone was very friendly and welcoming."

The Master replies, "This town is very much the same. I think you will like it here."

Previous ────────────────────────

As my senior year of high school was drawing to a close, I saw a recommitted Otter trying to improve his grades, at least improve them enough so that he could graduate with our class. I would sometimes see him for a few seconds after school, and he always seemed to be headed to a classroom to connect with a teacher about something or else he was going to the library to study. I commented on it a couple of times, kind of a "way to go" pep talk, and while he always seemed to shake it off, I could tell that he appreciated me noticing his extra effort.

That was why it was baffling when he missed a day of school with only a month to go until graduation and summer break. Then it was two days in a row, then three. I wondered what might be going on and I got a sinking feeling in my stomach that something was definitely wrong. Then when he missed the fourth day, I really began to worry.

I thought about calling his house, but decided against that, again afraid that his dad might answer. I contemplated just dropping by, maybe hoping to time it when his dad would not be home, but dismissed that idea as too risky. I needed a reason to stop by his house.

Jenna provided me one. She was selling raffle tickets for the tennis team to travel to an away tournament. It was mostly asking friends of parents to make a cash donation, but I talked her into going over to Otter's house to try and sell a ticket to his parents. She wasn't particularly up for doing that, but I told her that my motive was really to see if there was anything going on with Otter, so she agreed to go over as long as I went with her. That evening after dinner, we walked the few blocks to Otter's house.

Jenna knocked and Otter's mom answered the door with a polite greeting that was immediately followed by the voice of Otter's dad, "Who is it and what do they want?" that came sight unseen from the living room area.

Jenna quickly explained our purpose. "It's Mark's friends, Jake and Jenna," Otter's mom said while looking over her shoulder, as if concerned her husband would appear. "They are selling raffle tickets for Jenna's tennis team."

"We're not interested," the voice from the living room replied.

Otter's mom turned back to Jenna and myself, and with a kind of sad smile she said, "I'm afraid not today."

"Is Mark around?" I quickly asked before the door shut.

"Yes," Otter's mom said softly. "I think he is in the garage working out."

"Could you please tell him I would like to say hi?" Otter's mom hesitated. "I'll wait," I said this just as softly.

"Sure. You two wait here." And she quietly closed the door.

Jenna and I waited for a minute until she decided she was going to head back home. I told her to go ahead, that I was going to wait a few more minutes. I nervously sat down on the steps of the front porch. I could hear music coming from the duplex next door, classical music of some kind.

After a few minutes with no Otter appearing, I began fidgeting, fearful that his dad would come outside and find me still there. Finally, Otter opened the door and came out, closing the door behind him. "Hey." And he sat down next to me.

I got straight to the point. "Where have you been?"

Otter let out a sigh. "I dropped out. I thought you knew."

"How would I know?" I let that startling news settle for a minute in my brain as I tried to wrap my head around what Otter had just told me. "I thought you were wanting to graduate." Those words seemed to sputter out of my mouth.

It was quiet for a few moments, the only sound the classical music coming out of the screen door in the neighboring duplex.

"My dad is setting me up with an electrician apprenticeship with one of our fellow church members. So he said that I didn't need a high school diploma and there was no need to finish school. I can just get a GED if I need to."

Otter stared at the ground as I let his words settle. I searched for something to say. I wanted to tell him how messed up that sounded, but I wanted to be understanding. "Wow." That was all I could think to utter.

"It's okay. It's not a big deal." There was Otter saying once again that everything was okay.

I looked at the ground and we both kept our heads down for a minute. "Is this what you want?" I broke the silence.

"Not really. But I don't have a choice."

"I don't understand that. Of course you have a choice."

We were quiet for a few more seconds. Then Otter spoke, still looking down at the ground. "I don't know how to say it. My dad says I'm done with school. I'm done with school."

His words sounded foreign to me. I could not understand. I repeated, "What do you mean? Your dad says you're done, so you're just done?"

There was no answer. I knew he was getting upset, I could see it in his face. He was clenching his jaw and his breathing became shallow. He was still looking down and away from me. He bit down on his upper lip, as if he wanted to say something but was telling his lips not to move.

"Tell your dad that this is not what you want. You are going to finish school. Simple as that."

Otter slowly turned his head. "It's not that simple, Jake." His teeth were clenched. I could feel his animosity settling over the both of us, like a fog.

"Otter," I turned my head to face his. "What could possibly happen? So he gets mad. So what. Do what you want to do!"

Otter raised his head and stared straight ahead. "I DON'T have a choice."

And that made me mad. I don't know why. Maybe it was all of the times that I heard Otter tell me that he could handle things. Maybe it was the helplessness of the situation. Whatever it was, I could feel the anger growing inside of me. "The fuck you don't." I felt my voice rising and getting louder, and I made a conscious effort to speak more quietly so my words would not carry beyond the steps. But I was angry, angry for my friend, angry that no one seemed to care about this. "Damn it! Say fuck no! Say this is your life and you'll decide what you want!" I was trying to be quiet, but my voice came through clenched teeth.

Otter went back to looking at the ground, his shoulders slumping even more than his usual hang dog posture. I continued. "Well? Say that! Say something!"

Otter was quiet for what seemed like a very long time. I was immediately regretting, maybe not what I said, but the clenched teeth tone that I used to say it. Otter raised his head, turning it towards me. I could feel the anger and frustration welling up inside of him. I didn't know what to do or say as he stared at me, so I stayed silent as I met his eyes.

"Pretty fucking easy for you to say." His words were measured, but in his voice I could feel a rage at what I had said. "Do you wake up each morning worrying what kind of mood your dad is in? Not that you give a damn what mood he's in, but just wondering if you're going to get slapped, or punched, or kicked? Or even just called fucking names? Worthless? Piece of shit?" He was just winding up and I knew to be quiet. "Do you dread footsteps coming towards your bedroom, not knowing what they might bring?"

I turned away from his stare and looked to the ground. Otter wasn't finished. "Do you sometimes have to start an argument with your father, maybe take a blow or two, so that he doesn't slap the shit out of your mother? Or even step in and say 'bring it here' so your mom doesn't get hurt? Or hurt more?"

He was silent for just a moment, and I started to say something, but I didn't know what to say. I felt my mouth open, then close, no words coming out. Then he started up again. "Ever go to church, watch your father strut around like he's some special person of God, like everyone should look at how righteous and good he is, knowing that as soon as you get home you're going to get slapped for some infraction? Do you see all of these people at church proclaim what a great 'family' man and 'man of God' your dad is when you know that isn't the truth? And you want so badly to tell everyone the real truth?"

He was quiet for another minute and then he turned his gaze back to the ground. "But you can't tell anyone the real truth. No matter how much you want to, you can't.... say....nothing."

We both were quiet for a little while. Still looking down, I finally asked, "Why can't you?" I said it softly, almost too quiet and I wondered for a minute if Otter even heard me.

Finally he looked over at me. "Because as bad as things may seem, they can always be worse."

I met his gaze. "I'm sorry." I wished with all my heart that there was something else to say. But there wasn't. "I'm sorry," I said again.

Otter sighed. "It's okay. I can handle it." And I winced at hearing these words for what seemed like the millionth time.

"Okay," I said, standing to my feet and I reached down and pulled Otter up from the steps. "But let's go to a movie or something sometime. Just hang out."

"Yeah." Otter started heading back to the door of his house. "I'd like that." He opened the door. "Thanks for dropping by." Then he went inside and closed the door.

I waited for a second or two, maybe hoping he would come back out. He didn't so I turned and headed towards the street. I thought about how different our lives were turning out. The images of what I just heard played over and over in my thoughts. I felt tears dripping down my cheeks and the breeze made them turn cold against my skin. I trudged home.

ELEPHANT
By Mark Otter

There is an elephant
Who lives in my room
And follows me around.

"How are you, Mark?"
"I'm fine, thank you."

And the elephant says
"What about me?"
"Introduce me to your friends."

I ignore his pleadings.

No one talks about the elephant.
Everyone sees him.
No one talks.

Eventually I no longer see him.

I miss that elephant.

OCTOBER 19

L EAVING MENDOCINO, ORSON AND I HEADED SOUTH along the winding coastal highway. Soon I was faced with the decision of leaving Highway 1 and heading over the coastal range and joining up with Highway 101 and traveling towards San Francisco through the many vineyards along the way. The other way was to continue on Highway 1, skirting along the Pacific. This route would be more time consuming. I consulted with Orson. We decided to stay on Highway 1.

It is a spectacular drive. Following the road south led me through many tiny coastal towns that dot the beaches of Northern California. Orson and I traveled slowly through the town of Sea Ranch, enjoying the views and seeing the many cabins that line the cliffs. I was on the lookout for the Sea Ranch Chapel, a small non-denominational church that I had read had a unique architectural style. I found it off to the east of the highway and it was stunning. It is a small building with a winged roof, looking like it wants to take flight out over the ocean. On top of the roof is a bronze spire that seems to point to the heavens.

I parked in the small parking lot, leaving Orson inside the cab with the windows rolled down. I went up to the teak doors, opened them and went inside. I was greeted with a lovely, sculptured ceiling embedded with sea shells and sea urchins in a beautiful pattern. The sun filtered through gorgeous stained glass windows. I sat down in one of the hand carved pews, hewn out of local redwood trees, and closed my eyes to take in the tranquil environs. It was a peaceful spot.

I took some time to rest here. I pondered the last several days on the road. What had I accomplished? Was accomplishment important? I tried to tune into my feelings. I knew I was chasing something, I just wasn't sure what that something was.

Have you ever played the card game Hearts? We used to play it in my family while I was growing up. The object of the game is to be the player with the fewest points. The player with the most points loses. However, if you collect every point possible during the playing of one hand, you get zero points and everyone else loses. It's risky trying to collect all the points, because if someone else gets just one point, you are saddled with the rest and sure to lose. Trying to collect all the points is called "shooting the moon." I loved trying to do that while playing Hearts. That was always the fun part in playing the game for me, trying to shoot the moon.

As I sat in this beautiful chapel, I wondered if this was what I was doing. Trying to shoot the moon. Was I collecting the experiences of this journey, leaving these pieces of myself along the way, only to find that I missed collecting one point? The point I needed the most, making all the other points irrelevant.

I was jolted out of my reverie by a voice coming from the doorway. "That your truck outside with the dog?"

I turned to see a small woman, perhaps in her seventies, but probably older looking than she was. She was wearing worn jeans and a tattered sweatshirt, her hair tied back by a bright red scarf. She also wore a long raincoat, the hem fraying below her knees.

I stood up. "Yes. That's Orson. Is he bothering anyone?"

"Nope," the lady responded. "I just thought he needed a reading. But I wanted to check with the owner first. Is he friendly?"

I began walking towards the exit in her direction. "Thanks for checking. Yes, he is quite friendly," I said, trying not to express wonder at her meaning.

Without saying anything else, the woman turned and walked out the door and by the time I got to the entrance and opened the door of the chapel again, she was already standing beside the pickup scratching Orson on his head.

I walked over to the pickup and stood behind the tailgate, watching this lady pet my dog. Her eyes were closed, and she seemed to be in some sort of trance as she stroked Orson's head. I continue to observe the woman as she moved her hands up and down Orson's back, eyes still closed. She was doing it with a gentle hand, and it was obvious that Orson was enjoying the attention.

This went on for a couple of minutes, Orson's head and back being messaged and this older woman lost in a rapture, her eyes closed. She moved her hands gently over Orson. Finally she stopped and with one last pat on his head, she turned and started to leave.

"You seem to really like dogs," I said. "It seems like you have a real connection with them."

The lady stopped and turned back towards me. "Oh, I talk to dogs," came the reply. "And I listen to what they have to say."

"So you really are communicating with them?" I asked, trying to sound friendly.

"Oh yes," the woman said. "It's a gift. I've been able to communicate with animals my whole life. If you talk to them kindly, they will hear and communicate back to you."

I moved to the truck window and scratched Orson behind the ears, his tail thumping the seat as I did. "That is a pretty unique gift to have," I said, trying to be polite rather than to initiate any further conversation.

The lady stepped closer. "Animals exist in all of us, and they communicate with us in many different ways. I allow myself to be still so that I can not only notice that they have something to say but realize that they need to be heard. I find communication with them quite natural."

She paused. "Is there something you would like to say to, who is it again? Orson?" She seemed very earnest.

I thought for a second. Was there was something that I would like to say to Orson? "No, not really. Orson and I have been together for quite a while. I think he understands most of the things I say." And that was the truth.

"Well, okay. If you're sure there is nothing you would like to tell him." She seemed disappointed. She turned to walk across the parking lot.

"Maybe there is something that Orson would like to say to me?" I asked, still trying to be polite to this kind person.

She turned back and smiled. "I'll ask him." She moved to the window of the truck as I stepped aside, and Orson stuck his head out the window. She began again to touch Orson behind the ears and stroke his back, all done while her eyes were closed. It seemed like she went back into a trance, a calm expression on her face. After a couple of minutes, she gave him one last pat on the head and turned back to me.

"He says he appreciates all you have done for him in his life. You have been a good friend." She said this matter-of-factly.

"He has been a good friend to me. And a good companion."

"He says that he is entering the last portion of his life and that he wants to spend it with you as he prepares for his next existence." I nodded at her words.

"He also says that he would appreciate a few more snacks, especially in the afternoon, because he gets a little hungry waiting for his dinner."

I gave a quick laugh at this. "Well, he is a lab. I think they all want more treats than they are given."

"I'm not kidding," she said abruptly. "He said he needs a little more food than you are giving him." I looked at her and could hear that there was a seriousness to her tone. "That's what he said," she emphasized.

I saw the kindness and concern in her face for this dog that she had just met. "Well, that makes sense," I said. I walked to the back of the truck and opened the canopy, and pulled out a dog biscuit, one that had been given to me by my Nebraska friends Jim and Jane the night they were lamenting the loss of their lab, Suzy. I extended it to this kind woman. "Why don't you give this to him. I'm sure he would appreciate it coming from you."

She smiled and took the biscuit from my hand, turned and gave it to Orson. She patted his back as he crunched up the biscuit. When he was finished, she gave him a scratch on his ears. Turning back to me she said, "This isn't one of his usual biscuits, it was another dog's."

I stared at her. "How did you know that?" I sputtered.

"He told me. But he said he was okay with that." She

moved away from the pickup, picked up her backpack and started walking towards the road. She stopped and looked at me over her shoulder. "Safe travels," she said and continued on her way.

I was speechless. I started to say something, then stopped. All that came out was, "Thanks for visiting with Orson." She gave me a little wave. "Can I give you a ride somewhere?" I asked.

"No thanks," she said, not turning around, letting the wind take her words towards me. She continued out of the small parking area and then she was gone.

I watched her disappear down the road. I opened the door for Orson to jump out, and he looked up to me as his feet hit the pavement. "Really worked that lady didn't you?" I said as he wagged his tail. "I need more snacks. Really?" I scratched my friend behind his ears and we walked around the outside of the Sea Ranch Chapel, me admiring the beautiful and distinct architecture and Orson finding a few interesting scents. Then we loaded back into the truck and continued traveling south on Highway 1.

We traveled along the Pacific, through Jenner and Bodega Bay, lovely places to stop for the night. But I wanted to try and get closer to San Francisco. Finally, we arrived in the Stinson Beach area where I stopped at a deli and purchased my dinner. I saved it to eat for when I got to a campsite, a few miles south of Stinson. I found a campground that also had cabin rentals and I thought about renting one and staying inside but decided to bed down in the truck for the night. We found a nice spot and made a small fire and enjoyed our dinner as the sun was setting over the Pacific. It was a beautiful picture show of reds and yellows and oranges. I read and journaled for a while, then made a call to Susan.

I had now been on this journey for almost two weeks and I was missing my dear companion back home. And the truth is.....I still wasn't clear on what the mission was. I tried to explain all of this to Susan, but it tumbled out in dribs and drabs, like paint streaked on a canvas with no clue to what the picture is supposed to be.

As usual, Susan listened with kindness. "It seems like you're carrying some awfully big mountains," she said. "You're only supposed to climb them, you know." I appreciated her gentle wisdom. "You'll know why it's important when you're through." And I believed her.

I sent all of the love that I could muster through my cell phone to hers, climbed into the back of the pickup, and curled up next to Orson. I looked him in the eye. "I'll give you more treats starting tomorrow, my dear friend." He licked my hand in appreciation and we let the sound of the waves rolling up to the shore send us to sleep.

A man and his wife were traveling with their donkey.

On the first day, both rode on the donkey's back. When they got to town, they heard the townspeople whispering, "What a selfish couple, putting the weight of two people onto this poor animal."

On the second day, the man rode and his wife walked along beside them. Then the townspeople whispered, "What a heartless man, forcing his wife to walk while he rides upon the donkey."

On the third day, the man walked and his wife rode on the donkey. Then the people whispered, "What a careless man, letting his wife ride alone on the donkey."

On the fourth day, both the man and his wife walked beside the donkey. Now the townspeople said, "What a stupid couple. Why walk when they could both ride on the donkey."

One should never try to please the rest of the world.

Previous ———————————————————

GRADUATION FROM HIGH SCHOOL CAME A COUPLE OF weeks after my talk with Otter out on his front steps. I saw him once before the graduation ceremony, when we met for an early morning donut run, and he seemed his usual self. He was working six days a week for the landscaping service, and his thin body was definitely becoming more muscular and he was getting quite tan working under the Southern California sun.

Otter asked about the graduation ceremony, if my parents were both going to be there, who was going to speak, who was the class valedictorian, stuff like that. I tried to discern if he was feeling remorse about not being there, but as usual, it was hard to detect how Otter really felt about certain topics. I didn't push further the conversation we had on his front porch.

The night before graduation, my mom asked about Otter, wondering if I had seen him lately. I told her that we had met a couple of days ago at the donut shop. I had told my parents that Otter dropped out of school, but I did not tell them the reason, just that he would probably have to go to summer school to make up the credits he lacked.

"Do you think Mark misses graduating with his class?" Mom asked.

I thought for a second. I really wasn't sure. And I told my mom that. "I think a little bit. There is probably some regret. How could there not?"

"Well, I worry about him. Tell him to come by and say hi sometime." I knew both of my parents were concerned about Otter and the situation he was in. But I supposed that, like me, they were unsure of any action to take. I understood that.

One of the popular students, Steve Fine, was having a swim party at his house the night of the graduation. Steve was a good guy, a football player, and he was also in the school's production of the musical Carousel. It promised to be a pretty innocent party by high school standards. His parents were going to be there, but they had agreed to stay upstairs. And the swimming pool was in the backyard where the party was going to be.

There were about 30 graduates there and nobody really paired up with dates. But the male to female ratio seemed to favor the guys. That was fine with me since I wasn't dating anyone. There was some booze going around, a couple of guys had brought a flask, but at Steve's constant urging, it stayed hidden in jackets. The flask was brought out a couple of times to liven up the punch and sodas. One of the girls brought a joint, but it was of poor quality and fell apart as it was being passed around, which made all of us laugh.

Steve's mom made an appearance around 11, just reminding us that the music couldn't be played too loud, and then to ask if anymore food was wanted. Steve's parents had provided a bar-b-cue and tons of snacks. She also reminded us that we would all need to leave the party by 1am. It was fun and laid back.

Some of us were swimming, some sitting around the pool, and all of us were laughing and having a good time. Around 11:30, Steve came over and tapped me on the shoulder and asked me to follow him a few steps away. I was a little irked at this as I was flirting with a cute blond named Jessica, but he was insistent, so I got up and followed him to a corner of the yard.

"What's up, Steve. Couldn't you see I was a little busy?"

"Dude. Otter is at the side gate." Steve seemed a little shook and I wasn't sure why. "Says he needs to talk to you."

I tried to calm Steve. "No big deal. Tell him to come on back. He's cool."

"I told him that. But he said no, he just wants to talk to you."

"Okay." I shrugged. I didn't have any idea what this was about. "Is he still by the gate?"

"Yeah." He stopped me as I turned to walk to the gate and I looked back. "I think he's drunk," Steve said.

I knew that a lot of classmates were always inferring that Otter was stoned or something, mostly because they needed something to say, and also because Otter had a perpetually sleepy look about him. I knew that Otter had done the alcohol thing a time or two. We all had. But I also knew that he didn't do anything harder than a swig or two of booze because he was committed to his martial arts. So as I walked over to the gate, I just assumed that this was another "man he's stoned" type of comment.

But as soon as I saw Otter standing unsteadily at the side gate, I knew that he had been drinking. I smelled it as I got near and I could tell that he needed to lean against something, and he almost collapsed against the wooden fence.

Otter saw me and tried to stand more erect. "I'm free!" He exclaimed this quite loudly and the first words out of my mouth were to exhort him to be quiet. All Steve needed was for his parents to think one of the teenage guests was plastered.

"Sorry," Otter said as he tried to stand more steadily. "Hey. I'm free."

"Fill me in. I don't know what you mean."

Otter straightened up. His words were a little slurred, but he was easily understandable. "I had enough, so this time I hit back. So then we had a family meeting and the family decided it was time for me to go."

"A family meeting?" was all I could say.

"Well, I suppose it was a meeting. I mean I wasn't invited. But it was decided that I should leave and not come back."

"Hey, let's sit down for a minute," I said to Otter while helping him slide down and rest against the fence. "How did it start?"

"Father dear said I needed to go with him on another one of his missionary trips to knock on doors and I said no. I'm through with that shit. Then he smacked me. And this time I hit him back, right in his fat face." Otter rested his head against the fence. "Then he went into his bedroom like a fucking pussy. Mom follows after him, like a little wiener dog, and then comes back out and says that I needed to leave and not come back. Like I was planning on staying anyway."

I was silent taking all this in. Otter continued, "She said that she would put all my clothes out on the steps, and I could pick them up tomorrow. But I was not to come back. I would not be welcome back home. How about that shit?" Otter then coughed and I could tell he was trying to keep from crying as he tried to catch his breath.

"Hey, take it easy," I told him. I watched him lean against the fence, and his breath slowly returned to normal. "So your mom said you needed to leave?" I did not know what else to say.

"Yep." Otter let out a huge sigh. "My dear fucking mother said that."

I leaned back against the fence. I wanted to say something, but I couldn't think of anything.

"So I left. I went to the liquor store and gave some dude some money and had him buy me a bottle of Boone's Farm. And I slammed it down. The whole fucking bottle." Another sigh. "Then I wanted you to be the first to know my fucking good news!" Then Otter began to cry.

I swallowed hard, sorting through what Otter had just told me. And I also gagged a bit at the thought of anyone downing a bottle of Boone's Farm. We sat in silence for a few more minutes, the only sound being the party noises in the distance and Otter's somewhat labored breathing. Eventually his breathing settled down.

"What happens now?" I broke the silence. "Where do you go now?"

"I got it covered. My boss said that I could shack up in his garage. He's got a cot." Otter rose to his feet, balancing against the fence. "I've been wanting to do this. Now it's happened."

Otter walked out to the street and I followed him. He picked up the bike that he had laid down on the sidewalk and threw his leg over the bar, straddling it and using his leg on the ground to balance. "I'm okay, really," he said, answering a question that wasn't asked. And then he pushed off the curb and rode off, weaving a bit across the road until he got up enough speed to coast, then he pedaled some more.

I watched until he was out of sight, then went back through the side gate and rejoined the party.

LOVE
By Mark Otter

Love,
How you mock me.
How you laugh at me.

Is this Love's sense of humor?
The jokes are all at my expense.

Love
Laughs at me.

But it isn't funny

OCTOBER 20

O RSON AND I AWOKE TO A FOGGY AND CHILLY MORN-
ing, the cold air settling in all around us. We both did
our bathroom business and then climbed into the pickup. I
fired up the heater and we sat in the cab and warmed ourselves. I decided a trip into town was needed to procure hot
beverages, so I drove towards Highway 101 and Mill Valley.
There we found an overpriced coffee and Danish spot, and
Orson and I sat outside and watched the sun make its way
through the fog.

Getting back into the pickup, we headed south. I have
been over the Golden Gate Bridge several times in my lifetime and I am always in awe at the view of San Francisco
when traveling across this iconic span. I get goosebumps
every time. I tried going slowly in order to enjoy the trip
across, but the traffic patterns dictate how fast or how slow
you go over this bridge. It was stunning as the fog was
hanging about in wisps of clouds across the bay. I enjoyed
the whole trip across.

I wound my way through traffic, heading towards Highway 1 and joining it in Half Moon Bay. There Orson and I
found a place to take a quick beach break before continuing
the journey southward. Soon we came to Santa Cruz and
drove on through towards Monterey and Carmel, where I

stopped for lunch and some tea at an outdoor cafe on Ocean Street. Orson and I took a break from the car and walked around the quaint shops and popped into a couple of the galleries. We ended up at the beach, where we sat for a bit, enjoying the last morsels of our lunch. Then it was back into the pickup where we headed towards Big Sur.

Big Sur was one of the must stops on this trip. It was at Big Sur where my Buddhist beliefs really took root. I wanted to visit a couple of the places that I was familiar with and feel the spirit that I had felt there in the past.

Nearing graduation from college with a Master's degree in Wildlife Biology, I was unsure of my next step. I knew that doctoral work was in my future and I had been accepted at Utah State University in their Animal Science program. But I had no confidence in any work that I was doing, and though my grades were good, that was only because I had no other life outside my coursework.

Personally I was a mess. I felt anxious all the time. I was short tempered and impatient with others. I really had no friends. I dated a time or two, but mostly for sex. I would have several one-night stands and then would leave without as much as a phone call. Yes, I was that guy.

I knew my family was worried because Jenna told me so. My unhappiness and lack of social life had become obvious. On one visit home, Jenna confronted me, telling me my brooding mood and short temper were becoming tiring. I felt embarrassed I was treating people so poorly but didn't know what to do to change.

Then I remembered a class I had taken a couple of semesters earlier about eastern religions. The professor was a kind old soul, a Buddhist by belief, and I remembered how learning about the keys of Buddhism had resonated with me. I was beginning to explore some of the tenets of Buddhism, but I needed some assistance. So I sought him out.

I was still living in Davis, getting ready to move to Logan, Utah to start the doctoral program there. I found him in his office at the university and he was gracious enough to invite me to sit down. I told him about how I was searching for some meaning in my life and he encouraged me to take some time off and find that meaning. He suggested I go to Big Sur, about a three hour drive from campus, and take in some of the surroundings there. He told me there were many sects of different eastern philosophies to be found in and around Big Sur. He especially encouraged me to visit the Esalen Institute, a retreat center perched high on the cliffs overlooking the Pacific. He said that he would make a call and perhaps there would be a space in one of their upcoming retreats. I told this professor that I didn't have the funds to attend such a retreat. He told me not to worry about the cost, simply to contribute what I could. He had connections there because he often taught workshops at the institute in the summer. I thanked him for such a wonderful gift and I made plans to leave and attend a workshop on meditation and spirituality.

It was a time that changed my life and started me on a more self-aware path. It helped me learn to quiet my mind, to live more in the present, and to accept life on my terms.

It was the discovery of the need for mindfulness that moved me the most. Mindfulness is the principal pathway through which to become aware of the causes and sources of suffering. All of this was pretty heady stuff, but I felt that I finally connected with my soul.

A month later, before leaving for Utah to begin my studies, I attended another workshop at the Tassajara

Zen Center in Big Sur. There I started down the pathway of Zazen Meditation, the primary meditation in the Zen Buddhist tradition. I was intrigued by Zazen Meditation's focus on the breath and remaining in the present moment. The goal with this meditation is to stop the mind from careening about in aimless and pointless streams of thought. And that is exactly what I needed at this stage in my life.

I remember to this day the instruction about meditating that I got from one of the monks at Tassajara. He told the group of students that we needed to learn to meditate like an old cow pissing. We, of course, were quite perplexed with that description.

"Go and look upon a young cow. When they pee, they pee all in a rush, all at one time. Now look upon an older cow. When they pee, it comes in dribs and drabs, a little here, a little there. Be like an old cow when you meditate, a little here, a little there."

I have never forgot that advice. And every time I see a herd of cows, I remember this teaching.

Orson and I came into Big Sur in the late afternoon, and I drove to the Esalen Institute, its campus on the cliffs overlooking the Pacific. I left my furry companion in the truck and I walked the grounds. I have attended a few workshops here over the years, so I was familiar with my steps.

It felt good to reflect on my first visits in this wonderful spot. It is where my Buddhist awareness started. And it is a practice that saved my life. I know that statement can be a cliche, and I don't mean that it saved my actual life, but it saved me from a life of pettiness, of unkindness, and lack of purpose beyond the fulfilling of my own desires and wants.

That's not to say that I was magically converted when I took my first retreat here. I still had fights with my thoughts, questions that imperiled my peace. But this started me on the journey that I am still on today, the search for a more enlightened mind.

I walked out to the cliffs overlooking the Pacific. Out in the distance, a fog bank was beginning to form and roll towards the shore. I reflected on where my life was so many years earlier, when I first came to the institute. And I thought about the journey that I was currently on. It was becoming clearer to me about why this was so necessary. I think it was to give meaning to lives lived so many years earlier, not just other lives, but also my own. And to bear witness to these lives. People can become eternal when they are not forgotten. And they are not forgotten as long as there is someone to say their names.

I spent so many years trying to figure life out. What should I do? Who should I become? How could this or that person benefit me? Those were such wasted energies. I can now look backwards, see those years, and reflect upon those thoughts. I see now that I spent too much time developing a lifestyle that was too consumed by what others thought, owning a chilly heart. How much of my life was consumed by this?

Only now do I see that there is no sense to be made of life. Maybe there is no great purpose to fulfill, no to-do lists to check off, no expectations to measure up to, no bucket list to complete. There is only this unique moment in time. Every moment is simply this - a moment we are given to breathe, to be kind, to love all beings. Life is lived in the simple moments, the ones that often pass us by.

My father was fond of saying, "There are no deserves in life." That is true.

So I try to not complicate my heart. I want to be present, to be here now, wherever that may be. My journey is simply my journey. When I embrace it, there is beauty to be found in this exact moment.

I spent a couple of hours at Esalen, finding a quiet spot to meditate. I was nervous for what was to come, the conclusion to this journey, and meditating calmed me.

After a while, I went and got Orson out of the truck and walked him around the grounds, letting him partake in the spirit of this beautiful place. Then we got back into the truck and headed towards Highway 1. I thought about detouring to Tassajara, but it is quite a drive back into the coastal mountains, and I decided not to make that journey. It would be a trip for another time.

The sun was beginning to set out over the Pacific, turning the sky into a stunning array of oranges and reds. I pulled off the highway into one of the numerous turnouts and parked facing west, watching the sun call it a day. Orson arose from laying down and sat up in the back seat. We both sat quietly, reverently, watching the sun sink lower and lower.

I grabbed The Repository, got out of the pickup and stood against the railing. As the sun disappeared, as that last spark of light departed, I took some of the dust out and gently tossed it into the calm breeze and then I watched the particles waft away from me. Some settled onto the various plants that were lining the turnout, while others caught more of the breeze and floated out in the wind until they were no longer visible. I took another pinch of dust and repeated the tossing, and I watched the specks reflect the last bit of light. Orson and I stood watching the Pacific several feet below us, the waves gently kissing the shore and then rolling back out to sea.

It was with some reluctance that I loaded Orson back into the truck, for I was enjoying the peacefulness of the moment. But we continued on a few miles south to a campground, where I paid the fee for the night's stay at the drop box just inside the park. Orson and I set up camp in the dark, made dinner of chili and tortilla chips, and Orson's kibble. I journaled a bit, wrote a love letter via email to Susan, and then crawled into the back of the pickup and slid into the sleeping bag. It had been a satisfying day and my heart was full of gratitude.

. . .

There was a student who was quite full of himself. He prided himself on his wisdom and he enjoyed showing off his intelligence by debating his teacher. One day he challenged his teacher. "People think of you as an enlightened monk, but I find you stupid and boring."

His teacher placed his hands in a prayerful position. "Oh, dear student, to me you look like a Buddha."

The student went back to his home wearing a triumphant smile, knowing that he had bested his teacher. His sister asked him what happened.

"Today I out smarted my teacher." And he recalled to his sister the event with his teacher.

"Oh brother. I am sorry to tell you this. But you lost badly," his sister told him.

"What do you mean?"

"Don't you realize that the world mirrors the heart? Your teacher sees you as a Buddha because he is a Buddha. What does that make you?"

The student turned beet red at this realization. Then he became enlightened.

Previous —————————————————————————————

I LEFT THE GRADUATION PARTY AT ONE IN THE MORNING, hung out for a bit longer with some friends, flirted with a few more girls, then headed home and went to bed. It was a fun night, and I didn't give too much more thought to Otter and his situation. Actually, I thought that since he was a little drunk there was a possibility some of his story had been exaggerated and there was a good chance he was already back home.

The next morning, Saturday, I stumbled out of bed around 11 and mumbled good mornings to my parents who were outside on the deck sipping their morning coffees. My dad motioned for me to come outside, and I grabbed a glass of orange juice and walked out through the sliding glass doors.

"Did you see Mark last night?" Dad asked, catching me a bit by surprise.

"Yeah," I said, sliding into one of the patio chairs. "He came by Steve's house, but didn't come inside. He just wanted to tell me that he had been kicked out of his house."

My dad leaned back. "Well, that explains a lot."

"What do you mean?"

"Mrs. Otter called a couple of times..."

"Three," corrected my mom, who had previously been sitting quietly reading the newspaper.

"Three times," Dad corrected himself. "The first two calls were to ask if we had seen Mark."

"Which we had not," my mom chimed in.

"And the last time was to tell us that Mark had attacked his father," my dad continued. "As a result they had been forced to tell Mark 'to leave and to not come back.'"

I mulled over what my dad was saying for a few moments. "That's essentially what he told me, except he said that his father had hit him first when he refused to do some missionary work for his church."

"Do you know where he is staying?" Dad asked, peering over his glasses.

"He said something about staying with his boss. I assume he meant his boss at the landscaping company." I paused. "Why all the questions?"

My dad was slow to answer, and I knew that this meant he was choosing his words carefully, something he often did. But this longer pause meant he was taking even greater thought before speaking.

"It seemed to me that while Mrs. Otter was talking she was being told what to say, at least on the last phone call when she made clear that Mark was not welcome back at their house. I thought I heard someone making threats if Mark was to come to our house."

I said what we all knew. "Otter's dad was threatening? Who?"

"I think that I heard some veiled threats if Mark was found over here. I can't be sure."

"You seemed sure last night," Mom corrected Dad. Then to me, "We care about Mark but we have to be very careful."

Dad nodded but added, "I think Jake knows the situation, Anna Lee,"

"Does he?" Mom questioned. "Does he know how unsettling this is?"

"Otter didn't ask about coming here, or staying here, or anything like that." I offered this up without being prodded but I felt that this was where the questioning would eventually be going.

My dad was silent once again, mulling over his next statement. "Even if he does ask, I'm not sure that staying here is an option at this time," he finally said.

"Well, he didn't ask," I snapped. For some reason I felt that I needed to defend Otter, but I'm unsure why. My parents weren't responding to anything Otter did, just to his mom and dad. All because of the phone calls.

"Slow down, Jake," my dad calmed me with his soft voice. "You know that we like Mark. We are concerned about him, but we're also worried about his father's volatility."

"I know," and I did know. "I'm just a little unwound by the situation. I'll let you know if I find out anything more."

And that was that. The weekend passed, and I started my summer job at Jack in the Box, the same place I had worked the previous summer. My goal was to save as much money as possible to supplement the partial scholarship I had received.

On the next Tuesday, after I got home from doing the dinner shift at JITB, I collapsed onto the couch and was kicking my shoes off when the doorbell rang. Dad went to the door and I heard him say, "Why, hello Mark."

I heard Otter respond with, "Good Evening Dr. Campton."

My mom replied from the other room. "Hello, Mark. Come on in."

"Thank you, Mrs. Campton. I will."

Otter walked into the living room where I stood up, still in my work shirt with my name tag on it. "Hello, Jake is it?" Otter intoned, squinting at my name tag. "I'll have a quarter pounder with cheese and please say hi to the Hamburgler for me."

"I'm sorry, sir," I spoke like my voice was coming through drive-thru speakers. "You are confusing us with the far inferior hamburger from McDonalds. Perhaps you meant the Double Jack with Cheese? With extra secret sauce, sir?"

We sort of bro hugged. Otter sat down on the couch for a few minutes as my parents peppered him with questions about his life. He didn't seem to mind, assured them he was fine and said that as far as he knew, his parents were fine also. He told my parents he was living temporarily in his boss's garage. But one of the crew members that he worked with had a room open up in his apartment and he planned on moving in there soon.

After a few minutes, I motioned for Otter to follow me to my bedroom. "So what's the real story?" I asked as soon as the door was closed.

"Jake, it's good," Otter had a large smile on his face. It was so good to see him smiling. His whole manner seemed relaxed. "It really is. I get up, I work 10 hour days, but the money is decent. Then I go and pick up something to eat, read some, and then go to bed."

I studied his face. He really seemed happy, which was what I told him.

"Jake. No worrying about my dad's moods. I feel free. I can actually sleep at night." He paused for a moment. "I do worry about my mom, though." He got up off the bed.

"And I can't stay here long. Julio, my boss, doesn't want the garage unlatched too long after dark. I told him I wouldn't be late. Besides, I get up at 6 o'clock."

I bro hugged him once more. "I'm glad things are good. I don't leave for school for a couple of months. Let's hang some."

The smile returned to his face. "Yeah. Cool." And then he was out the door and with final shouts of "See ya around" to Jenna and "Good bye" to my parents, he was off.

I came out to the living room where my parents had the TV on. "It was good to see Mark," my mom said. "So, Jake, is the real story different than the bullshit he was slinging earlier?" That made Dad smile since Mom rarely cursed. "I mean, everything is just coming up roses? That seemed to be what he was saying."

"Mom. He just seems happy. The story I got was even better than the one out here." Then I added, "And no, he didn't ask if he could stay here."

"Sounds like the boy is in a good place. I'm sure we are all glad about that." And my dad changed the subject, asking about the location of the latest TV Guide, and who in the house was continually hiding it. A typical night.

It was good to see Otter so happy. And so content.

THE BREATH OF GOD
by Mark Otter.

Where do we come from?
Why are we here?
Where do we go after this?

What are we here to do?

God breathed his breath into Adam
Giving him life.
And then what?

Are we all waiting for God's breath
To bring us home?

OCTOBER 21

THE NEXT MORNING DAWNED COLD AND CLOUDY. SINCE it was dark when I checked into the campground, everything was new to me when I slid out the back of the camper shell. I slipped on my tennis shoes and hit the ground with a thud and turned back to Orson, who arose, shook himself and waited for me to help him down. I hitched him to the leash and started a walk around the camp site. There weren't many other campers at the campground, and most of those were in larger RVs.

I walked Orson around the camping loop and as I came back to my truck, I noticed something on the windshield. As I got closer I saw that it was a purple hydrangea. I walked around to the front of the pickup and scanned the area to see who might have left this flower. I could see no one. I looked around for a hydrangea bush, and then remembered one that was by the entrance to the park. I kept Orson on his leash and retraced my steps to the entrance, where I saw the hydrangea bush next to a large RV that housed the camp hosts. The hydrangea bush had mostly purple and pink blossoms. I tried to ascertain if a blossom had been picked or cut off, but I didn't want to get too close to the RV, not wanting to arouse suspicion. I could not see anything amiss.

I'm a scientist by profession and by nature, so I usually require proof before believing anything. But this finding of the hydrangea unsettled me. I knew in my head that there was a perfectly logical explanation for the flower appearing seemingly out of nowhere on the windshield of my pickup. Perhaps the camp hosts placed one on the windshield of those who have just come into the campground. There could be several explanations. But I couldn't come up with one to soothe my racing brain. I have to admit it took me back to my dream of a couple of nights earlier, where Otter encouraged me to finish what I had started.

As children we have no trouble believing things that don't seem explainable. Did our brains become too big? Or maybe our hearts too small?

My brain raced. I wondered if this was a sign.

I fed Orson and heated some water. I sat on the back tailgate, sipping my tea and scratching Orson behind the ears. I contemplated on what I was doing, and what I was hoping to accomplish. I knew that this was all coming to an end, that I would soon be arriving back to where I grew up, the place where I was trying to find some.....closure? I still didn't know. But I did know that it was time to get going. I was frustrated that I had been on the road for a couple of weeks and it seemed I was no closer to knowing the purpose of this trip, at least a purpose that I could understand.

I quickly packed up and helped Orson into his usual position in the backseat. I took the purple hydrangea blossom off the windshield and placed it gently into a paper sack for safe keeping. I reasoned that I could find a more appropriate vase somewhere. Then I was off, starting the truck and winding my way through the foggy, damp campground.

I had to backtrack some, going north on Highway 1, back to the Monterey area, and then take a road over the mountains that eventually connected back with Highway 101. I headed south towards San Luis Obispo. I planned to spend a little time at Cal Poly, wandering around the campus, perhaps doing some reminiscing.

I arrived in SLO a little before noon, and I stopped at a cafe just off campus. Even though I had been back to Cal Poly on several occasions over the forty years or so since I graduated, I am still surprised at how different everything looks. Everything changes, I suppose. That is the true constant in life.

School was in session for its fall term, and as I walked the campus grounds, I was surrounded by students coming and going. Most of the campus was very different from when I went to school, but I did recognize some similarities, such as the quad area and where the student union was located.

Memories flooded back to me as I walked around the campus. I had a difficult emotional time during my four years of school here. I reflected back on how much had changed over the years. I thought about trying to seek out any professors that I knew from way back when. But of course, none were here from that long ago. It was simply too many years back, and the truth of the matter is that I made few friends during that time since I mostly kept to myself and focused on my schoolwork. It was a long time ago.

I found a bench to sit and contemplate how life changes, sometimes quickly, sometimes slowly, but it always changes. And I thought about how often it can change in the blink of an eye. I wasn't feeling sad or happy. I was enjoying the sitting and contemplating. Then all of a sudden I began sobbing, not just tearing up, but full blown wailing. I tried to cover my face, burying it in my hands and leaning over my knees as I sat on the bench only bringing up my head to sniff loudly. I was hoping no one would notice this old man sitting on a bench in the middle of a college campus, crying.

I don't know why I felt suddenly emotional. It was if all the sadness and grief and heartache that was deep inside my soul decided that it needed some air. My heart deemed that now was the time and they came gushing forth. Tears streamed from the storm inside of me. I wished I had a tissue or a handkerchief of some sort. But I didn't, so I kept wiping my nose on the sleeve of my sweatshirt. I must have been quite a site, an old man, three-day old stubble, needing a shower, sobbing on a bench on the quad of a major science and engineering university. But if anyone noticed, they didn't appear to slow down their pace at the sight of me. Perhaps they even quickened it.

And then as quickly as the sobbing started, it stopped, and I gave my nose one last wipe from my sleeve, now covered in wet. I got up and walked back to the pickup, gathered Orson and walked around the main street of downtown San Luis Obispo. I ducked into a couple of shops and spent some time in a local bookstore. I also stopped in a convenience store and purchased some wet wipes and went into a bathroom and cleaned myself up. I was planning on spending this evening in a hotel, taking a much needed shower, and the reflection I saw in the mirror cemented that thinking.

Orson and I shared a chicken salad sandwich outside a popular deli that used to be a plumbing supply store when I was living in the area. Orson was quite the star as many a student stopped to ooh and aah at this handsome boy. It definitely brightened my spirits seeing the excitement of these young people. It was hard for me to believe that I was once as young.

I marveled at Orson and a dog's ability to live in the moment. I knew that this trip had been hard on him physically, his old age definitely showing now and again. But he always was a good sport, ready to go on any adventure or wait in the truck if that was what was required. The present moment was all that mattered to Orson.

Soon it was time to "get to going", as my dad liked to say, and I loaded Orson back into the pickup. I was headed to my home of so many years ago. I rolled down the windows, Orson stuck his head out and barked a couple of times, a final goodbye to this college town, and off we went.

· · ·

There was a Master teaching at his temple when he was challenged by a priest of a different sect, one who believed in salvation through the repetition of the Buddha of Love. This other teacher was quite jealous of the large following that the Master had. So one day, in the midst of a lecture given by the Master, this other priest loudly spoke out and challenged him.

"The founder of our sect," boasted the priest, "has such miraculous powers that he once held a brush in his hand on one bank of the river, and while his attendant held up a piece of paper on the other side, wrote the name of his God through the air and it appeared on the paper. Can you do such a wonderful thing?"

The Master listened respectfully, then replied, "Perhaps your teacher can perform such a trick, but that is not the matter of zen. My miracle is that when I feel hungry, I eat and when I feel thirsty, I drink."

Previous

THE SUMMER-BEFORE-LEAVING-FOR-COLLEGE WAS MARCH-ing toward its conclusion, with me leaving for San Luis Obispo and the freshman dorm experience in just a few weeks. I filled my hours with work at Jack in the Box, reading books off the freshman reading list, going on a few dates, and working on my tan in the backyard.

Otter and I got together a number of times; saw a couple of movies, went bowling once, and spent several hours listening to music in my room. He was working a lot of hours with the landscaping crew and seemed to be adjusting to his new life without parents. He once brought over a catalog of classes from the local junior college, and we went over some of the subjects that he might be interested in taking. These were mostly classes in auto repair, plumbing, and electrical work, and he seemed interested in taking courses to improve his employment outlook.

One Wednesday found me working the morning shift at Jack in the Box, relegated to the back room sorting and stacking a recent delivery of buns, condiments, and so forth. I had been doing that for an hour or so, when the shift manager poked his head back where I was working.

"Jake, some dude wants to see you out front."

"Who?" I wiped sweat away from my face with my shirt sleeve.

"How the hell would I know?" came the reply. "I'm not your secretary. He's out front."

I put another box on the shelf and headed for the front counter area. I thought the person waiting for me was probably a friend from high school, maybe even Otter, though it wouldn't be like him to drop by my work. I went through the door that divided the back kitchen from the front counter and there, standing by the counter, was William Otter.

I was surprised. I had not seen Otter's dad since the garage incident of almost a year earlier, but he looked just the same. There was something in his look, in his countenance, that felt unnerving whenever I saw him. But even though I was surprised I didn't want him to know it.

"Hello, Mr. Otter. What can I do for you?" I tried to sound unsurprised, trying to make like it was no big deal for him to drop by.

He smiled his usual phony smile. "Hello, Jake. I was wondering if you had seen Mark lately."

I measured what I wanted to say, choosing each word carefully. "I saw him a couple of days ago. Why?"

"Oh, no reason." He walked a little closer to the counter that separated us. "The police were asking about him, so I thought maybe you might know where he was."

I'm sure my face registered some surprise at the news of the police asking about Otter. That made his smile grow even larger, though just as phony. "Oh, you hadn't heard that he was arrested, had you?"

I tried to desperately exchange my surprised look for a 'whatever' look. I wasn't sure if I was successful. But I tried my best not to register much surprise. "Oh?" I said, raising my voice at the end to sound like it was no big deal.

"Don't you want to know what for?" Mr. Otter said with that disgusting smile still plastered on his face. "I'm sure you do." His expression never changed.

I wanted so badly to ram my fist down his smiling, repulsive face. But, of course, I didn't. I simply said, "Well, if that's all, I have to get back to work."

"Shoplifting. Stealing stupid stuff from the Ralph's Grocery." Mr. Otter put his hands on the counter, leaning closer like he was going to tell me a secret. "I really thought that him hanging around you would be good for Mark. I really did." The smile never left his face. "That's why I allowed it. But even a nice kid like you couldn't help him. He's worthless. Has always been worthless."

I could feel my face flush and anger welled up inside of me. "No," I said, my teeth tightly clinched. "He was always treated like he was worthless."

The smile remained. "No. He fooled you like he fools everyone. Just a dishonest, lying little shit."

We stood staring at each other for a couple of seconds. I could feel the hatred that I had for this man taking a hold on me. Finally I said, "You need to leave."

"No. I don't think I do. I think I'll order some breakfast." And he took a step backward to look up at the menu.

"You need to leave." My teeth were still clinched.

"Let's see.......I think I'll have..."

He was then cut off by Matt, a fellow employee and member of the local junior college football team. He had overheard the last few words of the conversation that I was having with Otter's dad.

"No, sir," Matt said. "Jake said you need to leave. I think you need to leave." And Matt flipped up the counter divider and began walking toward Mr. Otter.

Otter's dad turned toward Matt. I don't know what he was thinking, if he was considered squaring off with Matt, and I found myself wishing he would, knowing Matt would pound him.

"It's okay, Matt," I said. "Mr. Otter was just leaving."

Otter's dad looked at both of us. "Yep. I was just leaving." He turned and walked to the door, then looked back at me. "Good to see you, Jake. If you see Mark you might want to let the police know where he is." Then the smile left his face, almost like he turned the smile light off. "I'd hate to see a nice kid like you get into trouble." And then he walked out the door.

I thanked Matt for his help and went back to what I had been doing before Otter's dad showed up. But I was shook up, my stomach was upset, and I had a piercing headache. I finished my shift and headed home.

I didn't tell my parents about the meeting with Mr. Otter. It's not that I didn't want to, I just thought I would get more information before I did. I went about my usual business, reading, listening to some music in my room, and by dinner time, my stomach had settled a bit and my head felt better.

That changed when the phone rang. My dad answered and I listened to the one-sided conversation. "I'm fine, Mr. Otter. Thank you for asking. What can I do for you?" Then, "No I haven't seen Mark in several days." Then, "Well, I don't expect to see him." Then, "I don't know if Jake has seen Mark recently." Then, "No, I will not ask him." Then, "No, the police have not come by." Then, "I think this conversation is over." And my dad hung up the phone.

The rest of us were still seated at the table when Dad returned from the living room. He sat down at his usual place and started finishing his meal that had been inter-rupted by the phone call. He continued eating like nothing had happened. We all sat and watched him chew his food, and if he noticed our stares, he ignored them. Finally, my mom broke the silence. "Well. What did he have to say?"

As was my dad's way, he thought for a few seconds before saying anything. "Not much. He was wanting to know if we had seen Mark." He then turned to me. "Tread carefully, son. Make sure of your footing here. There are a lot of banana peels just waiting to be slipped on."

I appreciated my father in that moment. He often spoke in similes, and I knew what he meant. "I don't know much more than you do," I said. "I haven't seen Otter for a couple of days. But I'll be careful."

"I know you will. Now what's for dessert?"

Mom got up and served dishes of strawberry ice cream. Then we played a game of Parcheesi. I wondered about Otter the whole time.

TEARS
by Mark Otter

Don't want to shed tears for what
Might have been.

Don't want to shed tears
For what is to come.

Don't want to shed tears
For hope of what might be.

Don't want to cry at all.

OCTOBER 21

I LEFT SAN LUIS OBISPO AND HEADED SOUTH ON HIGHWAY 101, catching glimpses of the Pacific while passing through Pismo Beach. When I reached Santa Barbara, I exited the freeway for a quick pass through the town. I have always loved Santa Barbara and wished I could spend a day or two there, but I was feeling homesick and wanting to finish this journey. I felt that Montana and Susan were calling to me. After a quick cruise through the downtown area and a quick drive by the beach, it was back on the highway.

I hit the San Fernando Valley during rush hour, but when is it not rush hour in the Los Angeles area? I have been back to the home where I grew up many times over the years, but not since Mom moved to Arizona. Even though I had experienced the many changes in the area since the days of my youth, the traffic and differences always surprise me. But I think the same thing about my adopted home of Montana. The only certainty in life is change.

I remember a quote from the poet Rumi. "Although the road is never ending, take a step and keep walking. Do not look fearfully into the distance....On this path let the heart be your guide for the body is hesitant and full of fear." I was definitely feeling nerves for what was to come. I tried to stay focused on the present and not worry about the next day.

I decided to check into a nicer hotel, upgrading myself from the campgrounds and motor lodges of the last two weeks. I even paid the pet fees, not trying to sneak Orson by the front desk.

Once in the room, it was time for the both of us to get a good hosing down. I lifted Orson into the tub and gave him his first bath of the last couple of weeks. I brought a towel in from the pickup and used it to dry him off, massaging his head and back. He emitted a low contented rumble, showing his approval.

Then it was my turn and I stayed in the shower for quite a while, finally getting out when the hot water ran dry. I shaved the two weeks of stubble that I had accumulated and splashed on some aftershave, perhaps putting on too much, making Orson sneeze when I walked back into the bedroom. I kicked back on the bed, enjoying the smell of cleanliness as I surfed the TV channels. I was feeling the exhaustion of the last two weeks of travel.

After a bit of channel surfing, I ordered pizza, and while waiting for its delivery, left Orson in the room and went across the street to a small convenience store for a bottle of wine. When I got back to the room I poured the wine into a hotel glass taken from the bathroom. The pizza tasted delicious, as did the wine, and I even shared the last slice with Orson, who wolfed it down with relish. I think we were both getting tired of being on the road and we were looking forward to getting back to our own beds.

I called Susan and we talked for a quite a while, and the closeness that I felt for her spanned the many miles that separated us. I told her about my breakdown at the campus earlier today, and how I sobbed for no apparent reason.

"What do you think your body is telling you?" I could hear the concern in her voice.

"I'm not sure," I replied. "I didn't feel particularly emotional. Maybe I'm just tired." I paused for a second. "I'm feeling a little nervous about tomorrow. I hope this whole quest thing was a good idea."

"There is no right or wrong decision," Susan reminded me. "We've talked before that If you obsess over a decision being right or wrong, you are essentially saying that the universe rewards you for one decision and punishes you for another. The universe has no fixed agenda, it works around the choices that we make. There are no shoulds when it comes to things like this. There are just possibilities that come with each choice."

I knew she was right. But that didn't explain my sudden emotional breakdown.

She continued. "Jake, I see how much anguish you heap on yourself by beating yourself up over the things that you couldn't change."

Then my dear companion started dictating what she thought I needed to do next. "Do you have any chamomile, maybe some lavender oil?" I didn't, but I knew Susan was big on essential oils for healing, and I had often experienced great relief from physical ailments by following her advice. "So you need to go and get some."

"I will," I promised.

"That's not all." I knew she would have more.

"What else, my love?"

"Ashwagandha. Make yourself a tea and use Ashwagandha powder. Add it to a chamomile tea. That should help you relax and prepare for tomorrow."

I knew how effective her advice was. She grew many

healing herbs around our garden and knew of their beneficial properties. I also knew that she would check up on her admonition to me, making sure that I had followed her recommendations.

Off I went into the Southern California evening. It was quite pleasant outside, a perfect temperature, not too warm and not too cool. It was weather I took for granted while I was growing up here, but weather I had come to appreciate on the occasional visit. The hotel where I was staying was close to the house I grew up in, and even though the neighborhood had changed much over the years, I still felt that I knew my way around.

I found my way to a natural food store and picked up the herbs and supplements that Susan had suggested. I also procured a few snacks for the drive back to Montana. I spent some time wandering around the aisles, looking at the variety of chips and crackers. I was browsing the rows of snacks in the cracker aisle, when a woman reached across me. She picked up a box of crackers with a polite "excuse me" and began reading the ingredients.

There was something familiar about her and it seemed like I had seen her before. But I couldn't place her face.

Our eyes met and she spoke, "You look familiar."

"So do you," I said. "Did you grow up around here?"

"Jake? Jake Campton?"

I looked her in the eyes again. "Yes," I replied. "You look familiar, but I just can't place your name."

"Jessica. Jessica Hanks. Well that's what it was back then, anyway."

"Yes." Now I remembered. We had dated a bit in high school. "What a good memory you have." We exchanged the "How have you beens" and the "What have you been doings." She looked as I remembered. Though she probably colored her hair, keeping it the blond that I knew from long ago, there were wrinkles around the eyes (and didn't we all have those at our age). But she was still lithe and petite, just like in high school. I secretly sucked in my stomach.

We kept visiting in the aisle of the grocery store, just chatting, when she said, "Hey, do you want to get some coffee? There's a Starbucks next door."

"It has to be decaf," I said. "Getting close to my bedtime."

"Yours too?" And we both laughed at this reference to our age.

We sat down at the Starbucks with our coffee drinks. Jessica sipped her beverage. "What brings you to SoCal? You moved away, right?"

"Oh, just taking care of some business. Yeah, I've been in Montana for quite a while."

We discussed what we had been doing for the last forty years. She was a retired schoolteacher, teaching high school social studies and history, and she had been retired for the last three years. I told her of my education and job at Montana State. "Ooooh. So it's Doctor Jake," she said with a smile. "You have never come to any of the reunions. Did you ever get the invites?"

"Yeah, I did get some. Montana is a long way from here. And I'm not much of the reunion type."

"Are you married?" she asked.

"No. But partnered. I've been with her for thirty years. You?"

"Not at the moment. Been through three marriages though. You knew my first husband, I think. Steve Fine?"

I did remember. "Yeah, he was in our graduating class. I liked Steve."

Jessica smiled. "We were married for about eight years. We're still friends. He retired from being an accountant a couple of years back. Lives down in Orange County." She leaned forward. "Have any kids?"

"No. My partner had uterine cancer at an early age. So that wasn't an option."

"Oh, I'm sorry to hear that. I've got two boys and a girl. Two with Steven and one from my second marriage. My third marriage ended last year." She shook her head. "Winner, huh?" She smiled and seemed somewhat embarrassed about her number of marriages.

"I think it's probable most of our classmates have had a divorce or two," I said.

"But I've got four grandkids. Three girls and a boy. And that's a blast."

We continued talking about our parents. She had lost both of hers and I told her that my mom was living in Arizona. "Do you keep up with anyone from the high school days?" She asked.

"No. I went away to school and never really saw anyone." Jessica mentioned a few names of classmates from long ago, names that I had not heard in years and what they were doing. One owned a car dealership, another a construction company. Some names I didn't remember.

Jessica had graduated from Cal State, Northridge when she married Steve, divorced, and then stayed in the valley for her second husband. After retiring she moved to San Diego for the third husband, but that marriage ended after only a year. She had a good sense of humor when talking about her husbands and said only good things about them. She seemed content with her life. I like that. It seems to me most people aren't.

"I remember that guy you were friends with who knew martial arts," she said, furrowing her brow as she tried to come up with the name.

"You mean Mark?"

"No, I don't think so." She wrinkled her brow searching her memory. "I thought it started with an O. Oscar?"

"His name was Mark Otter." I was not surprised that she did not know Otter's first name.

"That's it! Otter!" She seemed relieved to have remembered the name. "He was kind of a weird guy. But he was nice. I remember when he kicked that guy's ass right in the middle of the cafeteria!"

"Yeah, I remember that too. It was Roger Mooney."

"Right. And Mooney was this big senior football player. Wow. That was something." Jessica got quiet for a minute. "I was sorry to hear about what happened to Otter. That was a long time ago." More quiet between us. "Did you stay in touch with him after you left for college?"

"A little." I didn't know what else to say. I was feeling uncomfortable. I'm not sure why. I thought about telling her that Otter was why I was here, thought if I told her it might make my purpose clearer. But I suppose I didn't want to talk about Otter any longer. "Tell me about your grandkids." I changed the subject.

We visited for a half hour longer, then I said I needed to get back to my dog. We exchanged phone numbers and email addresses with a promise that we would reach out if I came back to the area, or if she got up to Montana. But I think we both knew that probably wouldn't happen. And I think we were both okay with that.

The trip back to the hotel found me thinking about Otter, but more of Otter in the present. I wondered what

Otter would be doing if he were still around. Married? Kids? Career? Then it made me think about why I was here and he wasn't. I didn't deserve the life that I had any more than Otter deserved the life that he had been given. Then my mind went to shoulds and should nots, one of the worse places you can take yourself. But Susan was right. There are no shoulds and no should nots.

And Dad was right also. There are no deserves in the lives we live.

We all make mistakes. We all have regrets. No matter the intention that we may have. But we are not our mistakes. And we have the power at any moment to shape our own futures.

I arrived back to my hotel room with the supplements that Susan encouraged me to get. I applied them and then made some tea using the hotel room microwave. I leashed Orson up and took him for his nightly constitutional. Afterwards, we sat outside the doors of the hotel, relaxing on a bench. I nodded and Orson added a thump of his tail to people coming and going.

After some time sitting, we both went back to the room. I hoisted Orson up on the bed, giving him the rare treat of sleeping on a soft mattress. I crawled in next to him. Soon his breathing became heavy and I listened to its rhythm. I thought about Orson. I thought about Jessica. I thought about Jenna. I thought about my dad. I thought about my mom. I thought about Susan. I thought about Otter. Then I went to sleep.

. . .

One evening, as a teacher was meditating in the temple, a thief with a sharp sword entered and demanded that the teacher give him his money or he would take his life.

The teacher said, "Please do not disturb me. The money is in the drawer." He then resumed his meditation.

As the thief began taking the money and stuffing it in a sack, the teacher said, "Do not take it all. I need to pay taxes in the morning."

The thief took most of the money, but left some of it on the table and as he left the teacher said, "Thank a person when you receive a gift." The thief then thanked the teacher and left.

A few days later, the thief was caught by the authorities and he confessed to many robberies, including the one of the teacher. When the teacher was called as a witness, he said, "This man is no thief, at least as far as I am concerned. I gave him the money and he thanked me for it."

After he finished his prison term, the man went to the teacher and became his disciple.

OTTER CALLED MY HOUSE ONE EVENING, A COUPLE OF DAYS after I saw his father at Jack in the Box, and we made plans to meet at a bowling alley. While lacing up our shoes, I told him about his dad coming by my work.

"Really? Jeez, sorry about that." Otter let out a big sigh. "I hope he wasn't too big an asshole."

"He said that you had been arrested." I said this casually while knotting the rented bowling shoes.

Otter was silent for a few moments, then let out a slow breath. "Yeah. I did something really stupid. After putting down a deposit and some rent money, I didn't have any left for food and I was still a few days away from payday." He stood up to go over to the rack of bowling balls. He walked up and down the row of balls, rolling several of them back and forth in the rack before continuing. "So I went to Ralph's Market and stuffed some food down my pants and in my jacket. A loaf of bread and some peanut butter. Some Top Ramen too."

I joined him over at the bowling ball rack. "You should have dropped by my work. I probably could have snuck something to you."

Otter looked over at me. "Don't think I didn't think about doing that."

"Or at least loaned you a couple of bucks."

"Thanks." Otter chose a bowling ball. "But I can't do that. Anyway, guess who works at Ralph's."

"Who?" I grabbed a ball and we both headed back to our lanes.

"Roger Mooney." Otter stood erect, preparing to roll the ball down the lane towards the pins. "Anyway, he saw me. He didn't say anything, tried to pretend that he didn't see me. But I'm pretty sure he reported me to the manager who called the cops."

I let this digest as Otter rolled the ball down the lane, knocking over seven pins. "I thought I had got away with it," Otter continued. "But the next day, right at my work site, two police officers came over and arrested me for shoplifting."

Otter placed his hand over the air blower that is at every bowling alley, drying his hands. "Boy, was my boss pissed at the cops showing up. He was all worried about the client seeing the cops. I had to beg him not to fire me."

Otter finished his turn and I got up to take the next attempt. "What proof did they have?" I asked, getting ready to roll. "Just Mooney's word?"

"Nah. They had security cameras. It showed me cramming the stuff in my jacket. So I was cooked."

"So what happens now?" I rolled my ball down the lane.

"I'm pleading guilty, so I'll have to spend the next few weekends picking up garbage along the freeways."

I picked up my ball to roll again. "That sucks."

"Yeah. So that's my next few weekends. Hope the weather is decent."

We bowled for a couple of hours and then parted and went our separate ways. I noticed that Otter was drinking whiskey, which he sipped from a flask that he would pull out of his pocket. I asked him about his increasing alcohol use. He said that everyone on his crew was drinking throughout the day, and even some did drugs, mostly pot. I asked him if he ever did drugs.

"Nope. I mean I tried a couple of times. I just don't like the way it makes me feel. But the booze relaxes me."

I didn't think too much about his drinking. He wasn't driving, he always rode a bike when we got together. And I knew that was how he got to work.

But I became more concerned as each time we got together, for a movie, or just shooting hoops at the park, he was always taking a pull off his flask. He always offered me a drink, and I said yes a couple of times, but straight booze was too strong for my tastes.

We double-dated once, both of us going with girls we knew from high school, and he and his date drank quite a bit during the movie. I was nervous that an usher or someone else would come and kick us out of the theater. I became even more uneasy when Otter and his date started giggling during a serious moment in the picture. They were obviously tipsy.

The movie ended and we all went out for ice cream afterwards. But the next day I told him that I wished he would cut back on the alcohol, at least when we were double dating. Otter apologized and promised he wouldn't drink when we were on dates together. But the summer went by without us double-dating again.

As the summer came to a close, I prepared to leave for college. Otter seemed genuinely excited about this next adventure in life for me. He was always asking about the classes I was going to take and what did I think I would major in. I sometimes detected some envy, but not jealousy, and we made a pact to continue to write each other while I was away. And I told him that he should come up and see me. That is if he could stop stealing groceries long enough to get a weekend free.

"Hey. Low blow!" He said with a laugh.

The last weekend before I left for San Luis Obispo, Otter and I decided that we would go to Sir George's Smorgasbord, a favorite place to eat when one cared more for quantity than quality of food. It would be the last time we would hang out together, at least until Thanksgiving, or maybe even Christmas. I wasn't sure of my schedule since I planned to try and get a part time job.

We both looked forward to our last hang out together.

SIN
by Mark Otter.

We are told
To hate the sin
But love the sinner

The world is the sinner
I am the sin.

Tom Smyly

Previous

OTTER AND I PLANNED A LAST GET TOGETHER THE SATUR-
day night before I left for college. I spent the weekend
packing for the trip, preparing for life in a dorm room. The
plan was for my parents and Jenna to make the trip with
me on Sunday morning. They would drop me off in time
for freshman orientation.

That Saturday morning, Otter called me from a pay-
phone near the apartments where he was living. "Dude. You
don't have to pick me up," he said with some excitement in
his voice.

"What do you mean?"

"I'm going to pick you up! Just meet me by the soccer field."

I spent the rest of Saturday packing and getting ready for
the next day's drive. When evening came, I wandered over
to the soccer field across from my house. Waiting by the
soccer nets was Otter, holding a soccer ball. "Hey. Want to
try and get one by me, for old times' sake." He was grinning.

We had not kicked a soccer ball around in quite a
while. But we had fun kicking the ball and trying to get it
past one another into the net. After a few minutes, I asked
Otter what he wanted to do on this, my last night before
leaving for school?

"There's a band playing at The Alley," he said, referencing a place that we had gone to before. It was one of the few
places that minors could go and listen to music.

"So....how are we getting there?" I knew there was a surprise coming.

"Follow me," and Otter led me out the gate and onto the street. We walked a few yards, until he stopped in front of an older maroon Volkswagen Beetle. "Well, what do you think?" He searched my eyes for clues to what I thought about his car.

"It's cool, man. Did you just get it?"

"Yep. Last night. Jump in."

We both got into the car, me in the passenger side and Otter in the driver's seat, and we were off.

We first went to The Alley and listened to a band made up of guys barely out of high school. And they were awful. But we had fun watching them play. We especially enjoyed the people watching, with many in the crowd dancing shirtless and barefoot. We flirted with some of the girls, most of whom were in groups of four or more. We had a good time.

Otter did have his usual flask, and he pulled it out frequently. He would discreetly take a swig out of it, ever on the look-out for bouncers who would love to throw out a couple of punk teenagers. He went outside once, and I found out that was mainly to refill the flask from a bottle of Jack Daniels that he had stashed under the seat of the Beetle.

After spending some time at The Alley, we decided against Sir George's Smorgasbord, and instead we went to Tommy's Hamburgers, a popular place in the Valley. There we pigged out on burgers and fries and also cokes, to which Otter added some Jack Daniels. I could tell he was getting a little tipsy, but we were still having a good time. Otter was doing his impressions of other diners, and we couldn't stop snickering. I worried that our loud laughter would get us kicked out. But eventually we finished the burgers and decided to go to a pool hall that was popular with our age group. But this time I told Otter that I needed to drive, that he was having more to drink than I thought someone driving should.

Otter looked at me, and then shrugged. "Know how to drive a stick?"

"Yep." Otter tossed me the keys and I drove the short distance to the pool hall. We spent a couple of hours there, playing pool, flirting with more girls, challenging other guys we knew to some doubles matches, and continuing the good time. Both of us were pretty lousy at pool, so often we would just haul off and whack the cue ball as hard as we could and hope some balls would magically end up in one of the pockets. They rarely did. It was fun anyway. We met up with some fellow high school graduates, and we all shared stories about what we were doing after high school. A couple, like myself, were going to college. Another was joining his dad in the mattress business. Otter simply said that he was still deciding.

It was late, well after midnight, when we both decided to call it quits. We shot one more game of eight ball, then headed out to where we had parked the Volkswagen. I still had the keys so I got in the driver's seat and Otter slid into the passenger side. Otter was definitely intoxicated, and though I had taken a couple of swallows from the flask, I felt fine.

"One more thing I want to do before I go home," Otter looked over at me.

"What's that?"

"I need to pay Roger Mooney back for squealing on me."

I looked over at Otter who was grinning like the proverbial Cheshire Cat. "What do you mean by that?" I asked.

Otter reached behind the seat and pulled out a baseball bat. "This."

I shook my head. "Dude, you're not going to whack Mooney with a baseball bat. No way."

"Don't be ridiculous. It's not for his head, it's for his mailbox."

I still didn't know what he meant when he said "for his mailbox", so I continued to stare at him.

"I'm going to take out his mailbox." Otter slapped the bat into the palm of his hand. "You drive by his house, I'll lean out the window, and bam! Take his mailbox out."

"Man, that sounds stupid." I was thinking that I didn't want to be part of this payback of Mooney.

"Come on, man. I have to do something. And this is harmless."

I was still against it. "Let's just let the air out of his tires again."

"Nope. Mailbox." And Otter slapped the bat into the palm of his hand again.

I rolled my eyes. "Okay." And we headed off in the direction of the hills that separated the Valley from the coast.

I know it was after 1 am, probably closer to 2, when we came upon the house where Roger Mooney lived. I drove by the house at the speed limit, not wanting to slow down just yet, while Otter cased the mailbox position. It was a standard mailbox, one with the little red flag on the side, and it was positioned just alongside the winding road. There were no streetlights in this area of town and it was a moonless night, and the only way to see the mailbox was with the headlights shining directly on it. The house was on the right side at first pass, and after passing the house, I continued on a block or so, then I pulled into a driveway on the other side of the street in order to turn around.

We made another pass of the house, now on the driver's side, and Otter leaned forward and peered out the driver's window. "Okay. Got it," he said. "Let's do this," and he readied his baseball bat and rolled down the passenger side window.

I drove another block past Mooney's house, this time in the opposite direction, and again I pulled into a driveway and executed another u-turn. I then started towards the Mooney house, this time with Otter hanging out of the passenger side window. As we neared the mailbox, I drifted the Volkswagen closer, but the car began to skid on the dirt that was just off the pavement, forcing me to correct back onto the road. Otter swung his bat at the mailbox, but because I had to make that quick correction, he missed.

"Damn it," he exclaimed. "I missed." He settled back into his seat. "Okay. Just turn around again."

"Man, just let it go," I said.

"No! Turn around. I'll get it this time. You have to drive a little closer."

I sighed and prepared to turn around in the same driveway that I had turned into before.

It was a cloudy night, no stars, no moonlight, and no streetlights lighting the way. The street was canopied with trees. The only lights in the area were the two small headlights of the Volkswagen Beetle, and they peered out in front of me as I turned into the driveway so that I could turn around.

I never saw what I hit. All I knew was that I hit something solid and I saw an object go across the windshield. I immediately braked and took the car out of gear. "What was that?" I was shaken.

"What the fuck was that?" Otter was jolted. He had not seen what I had collided with either.

I pulled up the emergency brake and opened the door. In front of the car was a bicycle, now crumpled, laying on the ground off the right front bumper. My stomach immediately dropped. I let my gaze follow further down the road, maybe ten yards or so, and there was a pile of clothing lying beside the pavement. In the darkness I had a hard time seeing what it was. I froze in place, standing outside the open door.

Otter had already exited the passenger side and walked around the front of the vehicle. He saw the bike and then saw the crumpled pile of clothes and starting walking towards it. I couldn't move. I watched Otter approach the pile of clothing and kneel down beside it for just a second.

"What is it?" I asked. But I already knew. "Is it someone? Did I just hit someone?" I took a couple of steps towards the body lying beside the road. "Is it a dog?" But I knew it wasn't a dog. I could see that whatever it was had been wearing clothes, for goodness sakes. I guess my mind couldn't process what had happened.

Otter got up, walked back towards me and grabbed me by the shoulder. "You got to go!" And he began to push me back towards the road and behind the Beetle.

"No. We have to help this guy." I was trying to wrap my head around this scene.

"No! You got to go!" This time he said it more emphatically.

I stood my ground. "Is he dead?"

"I don't know. I'll stay here. I'll get him some help. But you got to go! Now!"

I wasn't having this. "No. I didn't see him. It was an accident. We need to get some help."

"You need to go now!" This time he shoved me more forcefully down the road.

"Stop it." I was getting angry. "I can't go and leave this."

Otter grabbed me by the shoulders. "Dude. The car is stolen!"

My head started spinning. My stomach went queasy and for a second I thought I was going to throw up. "What?" I was trying to process what Otter just told me. "What do you mean?"

"I stole the car! It isn't mine."

I stood in place, placing my hands on my knees. I tried to catch my breath.

"The car is stolen. I've been drinking. The smell of booze is everywhere. You're going to college tomorrow." Another shove. "Go now!"

A million things were going through my head. I desperately tried to quiet my mind. "But he needs help," I said this pleadingly.

"Look. I'll stay here. I'll get him help. You got to go." And he gave me one last push down the road. "Jake. You have to go! Now! Don't say anything, I'll take care of this."

I stood still. "Jake." Another push. "Just get home, shut your mouth, I'll take care of this."

I stood and watched Otter go back and kneel down next to the body that was inside the pile of clothes, maybe ten, maybe fifteen yards from where I was standing. I then turned away and started jogging in the other direction. When I was about fifty yards away, I stopped, turned and looked back towards Otter. He was still kneeling, but it was hard for me to see through the darkness. Then I saw head-lights coming from the other direction and Otter stood up, waving the car to a stop. I thought about going back. Then

I thought about having to leave for college in a few hours. How my life was changing in such a split second. I made my decision. I turned away and starting sprinting back towards the valley, towards home.

. . .

Four monks decided to meditate without speaking for two weeks. They lit a candle as a symbol of their commitment to their practice and began. By nightfall of the first day, the candle flickered and then went out.

The first monk said, "Oh, no. The candle has gone out."

The second monk said, "We are not supposed to talk."

The third monk said, "Why did you two have to break the silence?"

The fourth monk said, "Ha! I'm the only one who remembered not to speak!"

Previous ———————————————————

IT TOOK ME A COUPLE OF HOURS TO WALK/RUN HOME, stumbling in around 4am. I let myself in and quietly slunk to my room, trying not to make any sound that might wake my parents or Jenna. I laid on my bed, wanting to take a shower, but afraid it would wake someone up and questions would come. But I couldn't sleep. I lay awake, still in my clothes from the night, millions of questions rambling around my brain. But one question kept rolling through my head, over and over.

What the hell just happened?

Around 7:30, I thought it safe to venture into the shower. I stood under the water, letting it wash over me for several minutes, hoping it would erode away the events of the previous night. I heard my dad downstairs, he was an early riser, and I knew that he was sitting at the table, sipping coffee and reading the newspaper. I panicked for a second, thinking that there may be a news story of the night's happenings, but then I realized that it would be too early for any newspaper coverage. That relieved me some, but not much.

I stayed in the shower for a while. I knew that the family was planning on a ten o'clock departure to drive to San Luis Obispo to drop me off at my dorm room. Freshman orientation was going to commence tomorrow. My parents were going to make the trip, up and back, in one day, because Dad didn't want to take off any time from work. My mind raced in a million different directions. Should I tell my parents what happened? Should I tell them I was sick and delay the trip for a few days, maybe giving me enough time to figure things out? I just didn't know. My mind did not work well under this kind of stress. I had never been in trouble before. I was panicked. I decided to just pretend last night didn't happen. At least for today.

I wanted to call Otter, ask him what happened to the person that I hit with the car. But I wasn't sure that Otter even had a phone where he lived. He always called me from a pay phone. And then it dawned on me. He probably was not home. Certainly the police had been called.

I finally got out of the shower, dressed, and went into the kitchen. There my mom was making a breakfast of pancakes, eggs, and bacon which were being served in my honor. I plastered a smile on my face and slid into my chair. "Man, am I starved." It was an Academy Award winning acting job.

"Someone was up early this morning," my dad said peering over the paper. "Must be excited about the day."

"Just a little," I said while downing some eggs and bacon, hoping that my queazy stomach would allow the food coming its way.

"Did you and Mark have fun last night?" my mom weighed in.

"Yeah," I said in my most casual tone. "We just ate and shot some pool. Nothing much." I gave more information, talked about the lousy band that we had seen, hoping to stave off the questions about what we did.

I ate as much as my squeamish stomach would allow. I then excused myself to finish packing, though I was mostly packed. I needed some time to myself to try and calm my nerves. I thought I had made it through breakfast without revealing my panicked insides. Now just to make it through the rest of the day.

Ten o'clock saw the family load into the car and we departed for San Luis Obispo. I tried to bury myself in a book on the trip, and I was relieved that Jenna did also, and my parents mostly just chatted with each other. All I could do was read the same line over and over. Halfway there, I just decided to close my eyes and pretend I was asleep.

We arrived on the campus of Cal Poly and found my dorm room with the help of some of the older students who were tasked with orienting the freshmen. Fortunately, the family was already familiar with the campus because we had taken a trip to the area the previous summer. I plastered a look of normalcy on my face, trying to reflect an excitement for the upcoming school year, but also reflect some degree of cool. Normal was as far away from how I felt as one could get.

The family helped me lug my suitcases into my dorm room, then we left campus for a nearby hamburger restaurant. We had burgers and fries, and I think I was beginning to feel a small bit of excitement at being a freshman. I was actually able to place some of my anxiety to the side. Soon we were back on campus, with the parents and Jenna giving me hugs and Mom doing the requisite mother duty of crying as her first born went off to college. They soon left, and when I was alone, all of the weight that had been piling up engulfed me. I collapsed onto the bed in my dorm room.

My roommate, Jason Phillips, who was someone that I knew from a neighboring high school back home, popped his head in and invited me to join one of the freshman activities. I declined, saying that I was not feeling good, which was the truth. So I was left alone. I slid off the bed to a sitting position on the floor, leaning against the small single bed in this small dormitory room, wondering what to do.

After a while, exhausted, I finally pulled myself onto my bed and fell asleep, still in my clothes. I didn't even hear Jason come back to the room. When I finally awoke, the Monday daylight was just starting to filter between the gaps in the curtains. I got out of bed, grabbed my shower tray and walked down the hallway to the showers. No one else was there this early in the morning, and I stood letting the warm water rush over me. Afterwards, I felt better and I formulated a plan.

I decided that I needed to find a way to see Otter and understand what was happening. And then come clean. I didn't do anything wrong. I didn't know the car was stolen. I had not been drinking. It was nothing but a horrible accident. At least that was what I was telling myself. Anyway, maybe Otter had a plan. And I simply had to know if I had killed someone. That was what was weighing most heavily on my mind.

There were two days of freshman orientation before classes began on Wednesday. Most of these two days were filled with ice breaker kinds of activities to introduce us to fellow freshman and get us used to being on campus. I thought that I could miss at least one day. Knowing that Jason had a car, I asked him if I could borrow it. I told him that I needed to break up with a girl in person, that I had intended to do so before I left, but had not, and I couldn't be a cad and do it in a letter. It was a wild story and I'm not sure Jason bought much of it. But he was a good guy and he tossed me the keys. I assured him that I would pay for my own gas and leave his car with a full tank. Then I was off, retracing the same route that I had traveled the day before.

The whole 3 1/2 hour drive was spent with me wondering how I was going to get in touch with Otter. I was clueless, but I thought I would figure it out when I got closer to home.

When I arrived back in the Valley, I pulled over at a newsstand and bought today's newspaper, wondering if the events of the night before last had made the news. Skimming the pages, I quickly found what I was looking for. In the back of the Local section was a brief article:

"Approximately 2am on Sunday morning, a bicyclist was struck by a vehicle on Topanga Canyon Drive. Edward Jamison was admitted to West Hills Medical Center in serious condition. Mark Otter, 18, was arrested at the scene on DUI charges and also charged with vehicular assault as well as vehicle theft. Otter was lodged in the County Correctional Facility."

I consulted a map in the glove compartment of the car, and I headed towards the jail.

WOLVES
By Mark Otter

The wolf
Quietly he endures
He suffers in silence
Patience is deep within.

The wolf
Is in love with the moon
And each night he sends
His love call.

He waits
He watches
He moves in the shadows.

Throw me to the wolves
I will return as leader
Of the pack.

Previous

I ARRIVED AT THE JAIL AROUND 1 PM AND WENT TO THE front counter. It was very intimidating as I had never seen the inside of a police station. I never had the occasion. It was nothing like it was portrayed in the movies, TV shows, and books. It just seemed so...normal. It was like any other office that I might walk into. Though there was nothing overtly intimidating, my stomach had still not calmed down from the recent events. It was turning and turning, giving me bouts of nausea.

I made the inquiry about visiting a Mark Otter and was told to put my name on a signup sheet and to check back at 2pm when visiting hours were in effect. After signing my name on a yellow legal pad, I went outside, sat on a nearby bench, and waited.

The day was bright and sunny and as I sat there, several people walked by on their way into the jail. I began to worry and have the irrational fear that maybe someone I knew would recognize me, so I got up and walked down the street and around the block. Walking helped me feel calmer, and I began to feel a little more normal, if that were even possible. Soon, it approached 2 o'clock and I went back to the jail.

There was some more waiting and some forms to fill out, then I was ushered into a large room that was used as a dining area when it wasn't being used for visits. There were several other visitors sitting alone at different tables, some in pairs but most just singles, and every once in a while, a door opened and a prisoner from the jail was escorted to a table, where they sat down and began their visit. I waited and waited for Otter to be escorted out, and I worried that maybe he didn't want to see me. Worries were taking my mind in wild directions and I began to feel nauseous again. Finally, after about twenty minutes of waiting, a skinny teenager was escorted to the table where I was sitting. Otter was wearing what the rest of the prisoners were wearing; matching pants and shirt, a flat orange color, dulled from hundreds of washes. He slid into the seat across from me, and except for his clothes, the place we were in, and the general circumstances, he looked like Otter. I don't know why that surprised me, but it did.

"Hey," he said, with a sort of half smile. "I'm glad you dropped by."

I looked him in the face for several moments. "Man, I am a mess," I said as the understatement of the century. "What is going on?"

"Have you told anyone about what happened?" He returned my gaze, leaning in across the table and speaking quietly.

"No."

"Not even your parents?"

"No one." I found myself also leaning in closer.

"Okay. Good."

We sat in silence for a few more minutes. I waited for him to reveal more information, to let me know what was next. If I wasn't supposed to tell anyone....well, he was the one in jail. What the hell?

"So, how is school? Did you get to the dorms? Have classes started?" He actually asked this with a straight face, as if he really wanted to know how classes were going.

"Are you shitting me?" I kept my voice down, but I was angry. And still freaking out. "What is going on? This isn't some high school suspension. You're in fucking jail."

"Oh, really," the sarcasm dripped from his lips. "I hadn't noticed."

There were a few more moments that passed in silence, the only sound being the soft murmur of other conversations going around us. "Look," Otter began. "Don't tell anyone you were with me. This is on me. I stole the car. I wanted to take out Mooney's mailbox. I was the one drinking. This is on me."

"But I was the one driving."

Otter sighed. "Look. I am in no less trouble than if I were driving the car. All you do by telling everyone that you were driving, well, that just gets you in trouble. You need to go back to school. And tell nobody. We went our separate ways after shooting pool." He said this last sentence with more emphasis. "Tell NOBODY," he reiterated.

I asked him the question that was on my mind. "How bad was the guy hurt? Did he die?"

Otter looked at me, and I felt the concern in his voice. "I think it looked worse than it was. I was told he was pretty banged up but that he should come out okay. But I'm not positive."

I looked him in the face again. "I appreciate what you're doing," I started. "I do. But I was driving. I'm losing my mind. It isn't fair. I need to come clean." I felt I was beginning to babble. I leaned in closer. "You don't know that you would be in the same trouble."

"But I do." Otter leaned back in his chair before leaning forward again. "And you would be in big trouble. Trust me. No one will believe that two teens were out driving at two in the morning, just cruising around in a stolen car. The police questioned me about why I was driving in that neighborhood at that time of night. I told them I was just joy riding in the car. They think I was out casing the houses. Said there were some recent break ins. So they're trying to tie me to those."

I dried my hands on my pants legs. They were wet from sweating. "No one will believe that we were driving there just to drive there," Otter went on. "It is not worth both of us getting in trouble. And this is on me. I won't let you take even part of the blame."

"You can't decide that for me," I said, pronouncing each syllable slowly and with emphasis. "I get to decide that. I've got to come clean."

Otter leaned closer. "I won't let you do it. I'll deny that you were driving. I'll say that you were so drunk that you forgot that I had dropped you off earlier. I'll just keep muddying up whatever you say."

I shook my head. Otter shifted his weight. "Let me take the fall. It's okay. I'm on the hook anyway."

Now it was my time to sigh. "I appreciate what you're doing. I do. I just don't know if it's the right thing to do."

"Five minutes," announced the guard who was standing next to the door that Otter had entered.

"Just don't tell anyone. You went home after we finished shooting pool. That's the story. I go to court tomorrow. I'll know more after that."

"Court?" I asked. That part of the equation had not occurred to me.

"Yeah. I've been told that it is mostly to get assigned an attorney."

There was a notepad at every table, along with a pen, and I slid the pad in front of me and scribbled down my dorm address and passed the pad to Otter. "Write me. I need to know. And here is my dorm room phone. Call me. Let me know what is going on."

"I will. I promise." We stood up and Otter stuck out his hand and I shook it, like we were closing some kind of deal. "Do well in school. You've worked hard for this."

I squeezed his hand. "Is there anything I can do for you?"

"There is something," and Otter stepped closer. "My dad should be at work right now. Drop by my house and tell my mom I'm okay. I'm sure my dad won't let her reach out to me." He turned and started to walk away, but then stopped and came back. "Just tell her we were together until we finished shooting pool."

I looked at Otter. "Anything else you want me to tell her?'

Otter shrugged. "Nope. Just that I'm okay."

"I'll tell her." And Otter left and went out the same door that he came in.

I immediately left the jail and drove to my old neighborhood and parked out in front of the duplexes where the Otter family lived. If I was going to get the car back to my roommate as promised, I needed to give Mrs. Otter the message from her son and then get on my way. I sat in the car for several minutes, trying to work up the courage. I wasn't used to lying, and I didn't look forward to telling her this lie about how Otter and I spent the evening. But I was more worried that his father would be there. Finally, after several minutes, I summoned up enough courage and I walked up the familiar walk.

Not wanting to announce my presence too loudly, I knocked gently at the door. I could hear some stirring in the house and I waited patiently, but no one came. I knocked gently again, and once more I heard stirring from inside the house, and finally footsteps approaching the front door. It opened slowly, then more widely when Mrs. Otter recognized me. "Oh, hello Jake. I thought I heard someone at the door."

"Hello Mrs. Otter. Can I come in? I have some news from Mark."

Otter's mom looked spooked, as if she were afraid someone would come out from behind the bushes. But then again, she always looked like that.

"No. Let's just talk out here on the porch." I got the sense that she was afraid of letting anyone inside and Mr. Otter finding out. That was the feeling that I had.

I wasn't sure what Mrs. Otter knew or didn't know, so I just came out and asked, "Did you know Mark was in jail?"

"Yes. I was told he stole a car and hit someone that was on a bike." The words came out softly and slowly, she seemed so tired. "Have you seen him?"

"Yes ma'am. I just visited him at the jail. That's why I'm here. He just wanted me to tell you that he's going to be okay. I think he's worried about you."

I thought that might make her pause, or maybe ask why I thought that, but if it did, she didn't show it.

"Well, he's on his own. That's what he wanted." I thought she was going to cry, but again, she always seemed to have that going to cry look. We looked at each other in silence for a few moments. I was thinking of what I might say next. Finally she said, "Anything else, Jake?"

There was my chance to come clean, maybe figure out a way to turn back time, to change these events, or at least alter them going forward. But I didn't. "Mark told me it was an accident. And that it would all get straightened out."

Mrs. Otter nodded. "Well, perhaps you should go, before...". She didn't finish her sentence, but she didn't have to. I could tell she was worried about being seen, or about her husband coming home.

I didn't know what to say so I said something stupid. "I don't think the car was stolen, I think he borrowed it and it's just a mix up. I'm sure they'll figure it out." Why I said this, I don't know. Perhaps it was to cover my cowardice in not being truthful.

Mrs. Otter looked like she was going to close the door, so I stepped a few inches closer. "I think he is really worried about you, ma'am."

She looked at me in silence for a few seconds. She always seemed on the verge of tears, but this time was different. She didn't look well. Not only did she look like she was going to cry right there on the front porch, but she looked like she might faint. She looked so tired.

I waited for her to say something. Finally, after what seemed like an eternity, she said, "He isn't my son."

I processed those words for a few seconds. Thoughts flew around my head. I knew that she could not mean this in the literal sense. "I know that he has made some bad decisions, but he is your son. You don't get to just walk away from that."

She continued to look at me, but it seemed as if she were simply looking straight through me. "No. Mark is not my son."

A wave of dizziness came over me. "I don't understand," I said and I placed my hand on the railing that ringed the porch so that I could steady myself. "What do you mean?"

"Mark was my sister's son," she said in an almost whisper. I leaned in to hear her more clearly. "She wasn't married but she got pregnant. It was a sin. So God punished her. She died in a car accident when Mark was three weeks old. There was no one to take him, so William and I decided to get married and adopt him."

My mouth hung open. I leaned against the railing for support. I thought I might fall over. I don't know how long the silence hung in the air, like smoke. Finally I said, "I'm not understanding. What do you mean? Does Mark know this?"

Mrs. Otter took in a deep breath and let it out slowly. "We are his parents as far as he knows. The family members that know have all kept it from him. We think it's for the best that he doesn't know the sinfulness of his mother." Then her voice raised just a bit. "You should not tell him. It will only make things worse."

My mind summersaulted. I desperately tried to slow my brain down and process what I was hearing. I felt my breathing shallow out and I tried to gulp some air. "Why are you telling me this?" I felt anger coming out of the question.

"I want you to know why I cannot help him."

Then I did get angry. "It doesn't matter! You are his mother! He is your son!"

"No he isn't. We only took him in because it was what God wanted us to do." She said that with as much feeling as if she were giving me instructions on how to make pancakes.

I looked at her, looked at the place where she lived, looked at who she was living with, and I felt such pity for her. "I'm not sure you're an expert on what God wants."

She looked deep in my face and raised her voice slightly. "Do not tell him," she repeated. "It will make things worse." She paused. "For everyone."

I looked at her and she looked at me. It was almost as if we were in a starring contest. It's often a cliche when people say they are speechless, but I truly did not have anything to say, or the ability to say anything if I did. My mouth agape, I simply continued to stare at her.

"Thank you for coming, Jake. You're a good friend to Mark." And she closed the door, leaving me alone on the front porch.

I stood there for a few moments before I turned and stepped off the porch. I thought for a minute that I was going to throw up. I felt as if I couldn't catch my breath. I stopped on the sidewalk and tried to breathe, tried to take in as much air as I could. I stood in the same spot for several more minutes, trying to slow my breathing.

Eventually I walked down the sidewalk and leaned against my borrowed car. I wanted so much to get in and drive around the block and just go home. I wanted to climb into my own bed and pretend these last couple of days had never happened. I opened the car door and slid into the driver's seat. The events of two nights ago, a lack of sleep, seeing Otter in jail, and now finding out this ugly secret, pressed down upon my chest. I leaned my head against the steering wheel and cried.

. . .

There was a man who was very successful in business. But in obtaining this success his marriage ended in divorce, he was estranged from his children, and he was physically unhealthy. Then someone told him that there was a wise old man who knew three secrets to a happy life. So the man quit his job, sold everything he had, and began a search for this man and the three secrets to a happy life.

He traveled the whole world enduring many hardships, but he finally found the wise man, sequestered high on a mountain, who knew these secrets. He went before this wise man. "Oh wise sir. I have traveled long and hard to find you and learn the three secrets of happiness. Please tell them to me."

"Most certainly," replied the wise man. "The first secret of life is to pay attention."

The traveler was ecstatic. He most certainly could do that. "What else, old wise one?" the man begged.

"The second secret of life," said the wise man, "is to pay attention."

"This is unbelievable," thought the weary traveler. He knew that he certainly could do that. "And the third secret?"

"The third secret of life is to pay attention," said the wise man.

And the man who had sold all of his possessions now had knowledge of the way to happiness.

Previous

I sat in the car in front of the Otter duplex and cried for awhile, I'm not sure how long. Eventually I realized that I needed to get going and return the car to my roommate. For one fleeting moment I thought about driving to my dad's medical office and telling him what happened the Saturday night before. I sat in the car for a few minutes and tried to weigh what would happen with that decision versus just doing what Otter asked me to do and not tell anyone. I felt this would be the last time I would have to come clean and clear my conscience.

I thought about what I had just learned from Mrs. Otter. Was it true? Was he truly not their birth son? Was this just something she was saying now so that she could cut all ties with Otter? I remember asking Otter once why his parents didn't have any other children, why he had no brothers or sisters. He said he had asked his mom about it once and she told him that his dad wasn't able to do so. Otter wasn't sure if that meant that his dad was sterile or just couldn't be sexual. If Otter knew anything different, he never told me.

And I thought about the meaning of "It would make things worse." Worse for who? Otter? His mom? I couldn't think straight.

I drove by my house. I didn't think anyone would be there and it didn't look like there was, but I hunched down behind the steering wheel, just in case. Then I got nervous about somebody recognizing me, so I straightened up in the seat and drove off towards the freeway.

The drive back to school was a blur. I drove in silence, no radio and the windows rolled down, the noise of the wind drowning out my wails. I remember nothing about the drive, no scenery, no traffic, not anything; just a complete blank.

When I got back to San Luis Obispo, I went straight to my dorm room and gave the car keys back to Jason, thanking him for letting me take care of some loose ends back home. Apparently, I had made my decision.

A few days after my classes started, I got a letter from Otter. He said that he had been assigned an attorney and that he had a court date to enter a plea and perhaps get bail established. He said that jail wasn't awful, but that it was pretty boring. He also said he made a couple of friends and they seemed like pretty good guys. If he was distressed at all about being in jail, it wasn't coming through in his letter.

I sent him a letter, trying to be chit chatty, talking about the classes I was taking and so forth. I told him that I went by and saw his mom and gave her the message that he had for her. I didn't tell him about what I learned from his mother. I told him to let me know when he could call and I would make sure I was by a telephone.

I tried to follow any news in the newspapers available in the campus library. But I never saw anything mentioning a Mark Otter. I just put my head down, focused on my classes, and waited for some information directly from Otter.

After a few days, I got a brief letter from him saying he would try to call me at my dorm room the next Saturday. I was nervous about what news he may have. I knew this call would be after his court date. At least I would find out something.

Waiting for the coming Saturday was nerve racking, but the appointed time finally came. After answering in the affirmative to "Will you accept a collect call from Mark Otter?" and after exchanging the "How's it going?" and so forth, Otter got down to letting me know what was happening. "I've got a court date next Wednesday, at which time I make a plea. My attorney is trying to set up a plea deal. He thinks that I should get just a couple of years here in county jail, which could get knocked down to a year with time served and good behavior and stuff."

I was quiet for a few moments. "Did you hear me?" Otter asked." And I'll have to make some restitution to the bicyclist and do some community service."

"What about the bicyclist?" I had to know this; it was constantly on my mind.

"As for the guy I hit with the car...," Otter started.

"You mean the guy I hit with the car," I interrupted, emphasizing the I.

"No, the bicyclist I hit with the car," Otter emphasized the I. "He is banged up but not too bad. A concussion, a broken arm and a cracked rib. He is out of the hospital."

Though that wasn't terrific news, especially for the poor guy riding his bike, I had been preparing myself for worse. So I was a little relieved.

"My attorney says that the police think the bicyclist may have been out casing some of the cars in the area to break into since he didn't live close by. I mean, who is out riding their bike at 1:30 in the morning?"

Somehow, this information didn't make me feel any better.

"So what happens now?" I asked. "You make it seem like all of this is no big deal."

I could hear Otter breathing on the line. He lowered his voice, perhaps making sure he was not being heard on his end. "I'm okay." He paused, then continued. "My situation would be exactly the same if you came forward. All it would do would be to put you in the shitter along with me."

I sighed. "I know all of this. But isn't fair for you to have to take all the blame."

"Listen. I appreciate what you're saying. But I did this. I was so stupid. I saw the car idling outside the 7-11, I thought I'd take it for a couple of days. Just for fun. Then I'd park it somewhere and book it. And no harm done." I heard Otter sigh though the phone line. "But like everything else, I manage to fuck it up."

I didn't know what to say. Finally I asked, "Have you heard from your parents?"

There was a pause. "No. I wrote my mom, but I haven't heard anything. I don't really expect to."

I didn't know what to say to that. So I said, "I'm here. You can call me anytime."

"Thanks. Calling is kind of a hassle. But let's keep writing letters. The worse thing about this place is the boredom."

I committed to writing letters. "Okay."

"Sounds good," Otter replied. "Don't let your meatloaf." And then he hung up.

I went about keeping my head down, concentrating on school. I often thought about Otter sitting in a cell. Guilt racked me. Should I be in the jail cell with him? Here I was, acting the part of a college freshman, believing that maybe I should be getting, if not the same punishment as my friend, at least some punishment.

I was hoping that maybe he could make bail, but then I didn't know how he would be able to raise any money to do so. It was hard to shake the image of my friend being in jail.

I knew that Otter was going to court on a Wednesday, so after that day, I went to the dorm mail center hoping for a letter from him. A letter eventually came. In it he told me that he had pled guilty and accepted a plea deal. He was sentenced to 18 months in jail, $1500 in restitution to the cyclist, and 200 community service hours. He also said that he could probably get out in a year with good behavior and time served. Otter made it sound like he got a great deal. I did not see it that way. But his letter was upbeat. I returned an equally upbeat letter, telling him that was good news and to stay busy and the time would fly by. I didn't feel that way, but who was I to be the downer in the conversation.

I received another letter saying that he would try to call the next Thursday, and that it would have to be collect, as that was the only way he could make calls. He did say in his letter that he had tried to call his mom, but that his dad was obviously answering the phone and would hang up as soon as he heard Otter's voice. That made me incredibly sad, and I asked him about it when he called me collect, but he shook it off and said that was what he expected.

The rest of the semester, even the entirety of my freshman year, I threw myself into my schoolwork. I added to my class loads. I did extra credit work. I got a job tutoring other freshmen in science. I also got a job at a local print shop, getting paid minimum wage to take printing orders.

I had no spare time, or at least I took no spare time. I didn't date. I didn't hang out with friends. I didn't go to movies. Most of the time, I went to the dormitory dining hall by myself. I lived a hermit-like existence.

I would call my parents about once a week, and if the topic of Otter was brought up, it was always in the context of sadness at the direction of his life, how off course it had gone.

I didn't go home my first semester. I didn't know how much my parents knew of Otter's situation, and if they did, if they connected any of it to the night that we were together. If they knew anything, they never mentioned it to me when I called home. Jenna would call me and ask if I had heard anything from Otter and would ask me if he ever talked about jail or about the car he stole. She was the one who would ask if I ever heard anything about the bicyclist that was injured. I told her that I knew nothing about the cyclist and that Otter had written me a letter a couple of times. But outside of that, I didn't know much more.

The rest of the school year went by, with Otter and I exchanging letters about once a week and then every month he would call collect. I always felt bad that I had to watch the clock so the phone calls would not last too long. I just didn't have a lot of extra dollars to spend and collect phone calls could be quite expensive. But Otter didn't seem to mind the short duration and it was always good to hear from him.

He seemed to be in good spirits if his letters were any indication. He would tell me stories about other inmates, and that as often as he could, he would volunteer to go out on the work crew and pick up garbage. He liked getting outside. I would tell him stories about how my classes were going and maybe some stories about dorm life. He would always ask about my coursework and about the girls I was dating. He found it hard to believe that I wasn't dating and he teased me about that. I didn't tell him that it was because I felt so lousy about what I had chosen to do regarding that ill-fated Saturday night.

The guilt was continuing to gnaw at me.

HOLY GHOST
by Mark Otter.

The Holy Ghost
Is the ghost that inspires the spirit.
It is the music in our lives.

It inspires you for good.
We receive God's instructions through this spirit.
We invite his goodness into our lives
Through meaningful prayer

He is our constant influence.
Constantly directing,
Constantly comforting

The Holy Ghost is the way
To know the truth of all things

My Holy Ghost
Is haunting me.

He tells me not to be scared of death.
But to be scared of where I will end up.

THE MONTHS FLED BY, ALMOST LIKE THEY WERE TRYING to run from something. As was I. Otter and I continued to communicate, mostly via mail, and sometimes the occasional phone call. I went and visited him during my Christmas break. It was a brief visit, he looked good, but he seemed more hardened. That sounds cliche, but I don't know how else to describe it. Maybe I was simply imagining the hardness because of the jail surroundings. I asked him if anyone ever came by to see him and he said that all of his friends, except me, were in jail with him. This was said matter of factly.

I asked him about his parents, and he said that the last time he saw either one of them was the night he left, that night he came by Steve's house at the graduation party. No visits, no phone calls, no letters.

My mom did bake Otter some cookies and dropped them off at the jail, but she didn't stay for a visit. My parents would occasionally ask if I had heard from him, and I would tell them what he would say in his letters. A sadness seemed to come over my parents when Otter was mentioned. Though their regrets were different from mine, I sensed they had some also.

My freshman year ended and I stayed in San Luis Obispo and worked during the summer. Then my sophomore year started, and I threw myself back into my schoolwork. I still wasn't doing much socially, and I mostly stayed to myself. I did move off campus with a couple of acquaintances (I had not made many friends) and with my parents help, purchased a used Toyota Corolla. It was good enough to get around town and campus, but not reliable enough to travel much further than that.

I tried to move forward and ignore my misery and guilty conscience . Mostly I did, but I still had a pit in my stomach and would wake up nights with horrible stomach acid, necessitating me eating antacids like they were candy.

Otter got released in October, having served about 13 months of his sentence. I invited him to come see me and sent him bus fare. He came and spent the night, bunking down on the couch in my apartment. It was good to see him and he got along with my roommates, but he didn't stay long and I could tell he was antsy to leave. Maybe he felt uncomfortable around college students. We mostly hung out in my apartment. I did treat him to burgers at a popular hangout spot and we went bowling. And while we did enjoy seeing each other, things were different. He seemed quieter, more reserved. And more cynical. It was obvious we were both changed since that Saturday night of long ago.

Otter said he had a job interview back in the valley and he left the day after arriving. He also had to set up his community service or he would have to go back and serve the remainder of his time. He was staying with a friend that he had met in jail and this friend was getting him an interview with a construction crew. We agreed to continue to exchange letters.

Slowly the letter exchanges became more and more infrequent. I would get a letter from him, and it would sit on my desk until a couple of weeks later when I would return a letter back. And then a month or so would go by and the routine would continue.

Otter ended up for a time in San Bernardino, doing construction work in that area. He moved in with a girl-friend, I think her name was Louisa, and he said he was doing well and things were good. Then I got a letter with a return address from the San Bernardino jail. Otter said that he had been busted for marijuana possession, and he was jailed for about a month. When he got out he moved back to the valley. I don't know what happened to the girlfriend. He never mentioned her in any letters after his stint in jail.

Every letter I would get would have a different return address, he was moving around a lot. We talked on the phone a couple of times during my sophomore year, but none after that.

His letters were always upbeat, telling me what work he was doing. I tried to encourage him to register at the junior college and do the apprenticeships that he often talked about when we were younger. He always was going to do that, but he never seemed to follow through. I also suggested that he continue with his Tae Kwon Do, maybe even getting a job at one of the many martial arts studios that were around. He always said that he might check that out. I don't think he ever did.

School continued and I dedicated myself to my major in Animal Science. I was also tutoring and getting paid for that and I still worked at the Print Shop. I made little time for anything else.

One weekend during the spring of my sophomore year, I came home for Jenna's birthday. Dad and I were setting up some decorations in the back yard when out of the blue he said, "I ran into Mark Otter's father the other day."

I had not thought about Otter's dad in months. "Where?" I asked.

"At the grocery store." Dad straightened up the table-cloth and I waited for him to continue. "It was uncomfortable to say the least."

I continued spreading out a paper tablecloth on a folding table. "What did he have to say?"

"Well, I asked him if he had heard from Mark, how he was doing and so forth. He simply said, 'Mark who?' He thought that was pretty funny." Dad settled into one of the patio chairs. "He did say that he had hoped that Mark hanging around you would have made a difference in Mark's life. He said that you were a good influence on him."

I sat down in a chair across from Dad. "Yeah. He told me that once. Maybe Mark's father should have been a better father."

Dad leaned back in his chair. "Possibly." He seemed quite reflective. "He said that Mark was always a troubled person and that he and his wife had done all they could. Said something about Mark turning away from God."

I was quiet for a minute. "Mr. Otter is an awful human being."

"Don't know if I can disagree with that. He said that he no longer considers that he has a son."

I flashed to the conversation with Mrs. Otter on their front porch months ago. "Not surprising," I said. "Otter told me that his parents have never reached out to him since he left."

Dad got up and re-arranged a bouquet of flowers that was in the center of the table. "I surmised as much."

I looked across the table at my father. He was silent, looking up at the trees in the backyard gently swaying with the wind. He seemed lost in thought, and he took his glasses off and rubbed the bridge of his nose. "I wish I had done something for Mark. It seemed like he was reaching out. I wish......". He didn't finish that thought and he put his glasses back on, letting out a sigh as he did.

After a few more moments, I broke the quiet. "Was he friendly?" I asked.

Dad brought his attention back to me. "I'm not sure I would describe anything that Mr. Otter did as friendly. He always seems to have an odd expression on his face. Like an emotion that is painted on."

I got up and moved a chair underneath the table. "I know. It's like he says something, then pulls from a Rolodex what emotion his face should have. Then he puts that on his face."

I thought about Mr. Otter's comment of not having a son. "Dad?" I began. "I had a conversation with Otter's mom awhile back. She told me that Mark wasn't really their son, that he was her sister's son."

My father raised his eyebrows. "Really?" He slid back onto a chair. "How so?"

I let some silence settle between us as I gathered my thoughts. Dad didn't break the quiet, he just waited patiently for me to continue. "Apparently her sister had a son out of wedlock and died in an auto accident three weeks later. So Mr. and Mrs. Otter got married and adopted Mark."

There was more quiet in the backyard as my dad processed this information. I let my eyes wander to all of the decor set out for Jenna's eighteenth birthday. I knew that my dad would say something, and he would take his time and measure his words.

"When did you find out this information?"

I wanted to choose my wording carefully, not wanting to completely come clean, but not wanting to add too much fabrication to the tale. "It's been a while. I went over looking for Otter and she told me. She told me not to tell Mark, that it would be better for everyone involved if he didn't know." I was silent for a moment. "I'm not sure I know what she meant by that."

"And you believed her? That they adopted Mark?"

"I guess so. I mean, I don't think she would tell me this if it weren't true. What would be the point in that?"

Dad leaned back in his chair. "You're probably right." He reached across the table and poured himself some lemonade from a pitcher. "So you didn't tell Mark about this conversation? That must have been difficult."

It was a question without guile or judgement. I so appreciated my father in this moment. He understood the dilemma I was in.

"I didn't know what I should do. I didn't know if she was afraid for herself, afraid of Mr. Otter, afraid of what might happen to Mark." I sighed. "I didn't know how to tell him. Or even if I should."

Dad let another moment of quiet pass between us. "Mark is a grown man now. Maybe he deserves to know."

I looked up into my father's eyes. They were filled with compassion for the spot where I found myself. "I suppose you're right. I don't see Otter anymore, at least not much." I got up from the chair. "If I get a chance, if I can figure out the words, if...." and I let that trail off.

Dad stood up to finish moving some balloons around. "I'm sure you'll find the words when the time comes." He stopped and looked at me, giving me a smile. "Mr. Otter gave me a copy of The Watchtower." And he chuckled.

I didn't see the humor in that at all. It reminded me of what Otter told me on the steps in front of his house. When he said "Ever go to church, watch your father strut around like he's some special person of God, like everyone should look at how righteous and good he is, knowing that as soon as you get home you're going to get slapped for some infraction? Do you see all of these people at church proclaim what a great 'family' man and 'man of God' your dad is when you know that isn't the truth?" That's where I went in my head.

Once again I thought about telling Dad about that Saturday night of seemingly long ago. And I wondered again how much he already knew. But emotions swam around in my head, and I was beginning to feel that familiar sour in my stomach. I quickly decided against that thought and I returned Dad's chuckle about The Watchtower. I had already made my decision in that regard.

School continued to progress for me and my contact with Otter became less and less. I heard from him about every other month. It was hard for me to stay in contact with him as a few of the letters I would write would come back "Return to Sender." I'm sure that was because he was moving quite a bit. He was employed in different jobs in different towns, so he said, always in the construction field.

After a while, I would only write him after I got a letter from him. His letters were usually the same; he was staying with some girl, he was thinking about going back to school, he was getting screwed by the foreman of whatever job he was working. But he would always ask about how I was doing, how classes were going, what I wanted to do when I graduated. When I told him that I had been accepted into the Wildlife Biology Master's program at UC Davis, he sent me an actual congratulations card, where he was effusive in his excitement for me.

In my letters to Otter I always tried to stay positive and tried to encourage him to go back to school, and he always wrote back and said that he looked into a program or two. But there was always an excuse of why he couldn't attend - he filed too late, he didn't have the requirements, or he didn't have enough money (even though I offered to help him out). I just think that he didn't want to go.

So the months continued to go by and my life moved along its path, as did everyone else's, I suppose. I thought about Otter often.

. . .

There were two monks washing their bowls in a river when they noticed a scorpion that was drowning. One monk immediately scooped it up and dropped it upon the dry riverbank. In the process, he was stung. The monk went back to washing his bowl when the same scorpion fell into the water again. The monk saved the scorpion again and was stung once more.

The other monk looked at his fellow brother who had now been stung twice and said, "Friend, why do you continue to rescue the scorpion when you know that it is in his nature to sting you?"

"Because," the monk replied, "It is in my nature to save him."

Previous

THE LAST TIME I SAW OTTER WAS IN THE SPRING OF MY senior year at Cal Poly. I was preparing to graduate and I had been accepted into the Wildlife Biology graduate program at UC Davis. My mom called and left a message that Otter was trying to get in touch with me, and that he did not have a phone, but I could leave a message at a friend's house. I called the number that he left and a woman answered and she didn't seem too interested in taking my message for Otter. But he must have eventually received it as he called back late one evening and left a message with one of my roommates. And on and on it went for a couple of more days.

We played phone tag for these two days, but finally connected, and he told me that he had been busted for possession of prescription drugs that were in the glove compartment of a car he was driving. He then told me a long, convoluted story about a car he had borrowed from a friend, which was reported stolen. There were some legal issues with that. The gist of it was that he was asking if I could write a character reference letter to the judge, "you know, that I'm a decent guy, has somewhat decent integrity, just a little down on my luck" sort of letter, which I agreed to do. He said that his court appointed attorney told him that a letter would help.

We planned to meet at a coffee shop that was located

close to where he was living, actually close to where my parents lived, and I awoke the next Saturday and made the three plus hour drive from my apartment in San Luis Obispo to the San Fernando Valley, pulling into the parking lot of the coffee shop a couple of minutes early.

Otter was already sitting at a table in the corner of the shop, a cup of coffee in front of him that he seemed to be absentmindedly stirring. I stood inside the door and watched him for a few seconds, unobserved by him. I was surprised at how different he looked in his jeans and t-shirt. It was hard to say how he looked different, he was still lean and muscular. And he was wearing what he usually wore. I know we were the same age, but he seemed to look so much older. I wish I could explain that further, but I can't.

He caught sight of me and half stood up when I approached and we gave each other a sort of brotherly hug. He seemed tired and there were bags under his eyes, as if he had not been sleeping well. His hair was slightly longer than I remembered, and also uncombed. His face had the starting of a beard, but it was patchy and only made his face look unwashed. It was good to see him. I had thought about making an excuse and simply mailing the letter he had asked for, but upon seeing him, I was immediately glad that I had not chosen that option. That feeling surprised me.

I got a cup of coffee and sat across from him and we caught up with each other's lives, though in a cursory manner. During the years of our friendship, Otter had a way of asking a question and then really listening to the answer, thoughtfully turning things over in his mind before responding, and he did that this morning. He asked questions about my mom and dad, about Jenna, about how school was going, if I was getting excited about graduate school and moving to Northern California. He always had a sincere interest in the lives of others, at least in those lives he cared about.

He was not as open and engaging about his own life, but I did find out that he was living with a quasi-girlfriend, meaning it seems that she thought they were boyfriend/girl-friend, and he, not so much. He was working construction, whenever he could find some work, but that seemed a hap-hazard existence at best. He was also picking up handyman jobs when he could, mostly stuff like setting up TV rooms and stereo systems. I asked lots of questions, what were his plans, if he saw anyone that we both knew, and while he didn't seem evasive in these answers, the responses were short and to the point. I wanted to ask about his parents, but I was uncomfortable bringing that subject up. I thought I would let him make the first move in that regard, which he never did.

After a few minutes of this kind of banter, I slid the letter of character reference across the table. "It's pretty weak," I sort of half smiled. "I wasn't sure how to say what you needed."

"I'm sure it's okay." He folded the paper, putting it in his pant's pocket without reading or even glancing at the words. "It's mostly a formality. I got a foreman buddy of mine to write one also." Otter looked down at his coffee and again began stirring it around and around the cup with his spoon.

"So how'd you get in this jam?"

"I borrowed a friend's car, and I thought it might be stolen but my friend insisted that it wasn't. What I didn't know was that it had a busted taillight, so I got pulled over." He stopped stirring for a minute. "And then the cops claimed that they smelled pot in the car, so they searched the glove compartment. In the glove compartment, there were, like, six prescription bottles of codeine with different names of people on the bottles. So that got the cops pretty excited. And I was driving with a suspended license."

"Didn't your friend vouch for you taking the car?"

Otter gave me a look of astonishment, one that I had seen hundreds of times. "A stolen car? Yeah, I don't think so." He began stirring again. "He said that he had never seen the car and that I had told him it was my car, even though he had never seen the car. And then there was a totally different name on the registration. I don't think the cops believed either one of us, but I was driving the car..."

I sipped my coffee for a few seconds, letting some silence settle over us. "Do you think you'll get jail time?"

"Nah. At least my lawyer doesn't think so. A public defender who's not too excited about his job. Probably probation, maybe some community service." He then smiled in my direction. "I'm becoming a saint with all the fucking community service I've had to do."

Silence again settled over our table, even though there was quite a bit of background coffee shop noise.

"Anyway, thanks for the letter." Otter continued stirring his coffee. "And for driving all the way down here."

I simply nodded. Otter was quiet. I was stuck in that spot in life where one wonders if the time was right to leave or was it too early. I wasn't in a big hurry and I thought I would stop and see my parents for a couple of hours before heading back to school. So I sat sipping my coffee and listened to the din of the coffee house.

"Have you ever seen the movie "It's a Wonderful Life?"" Otter never looked up from his coffee while asking such an out-of-the-blue question.

"The Christmas one? The one with Jimmy Stewart?"

Otter nodded. I sat quietly, not quite understanding where this was going. But Otter was not forthcoming with the reason for such a strange question. Finally I said, "What? Are you taking a poll? What makes you bring that up?"

Otter was quiet for a few more moments before replying. "You know how George Bailey gets into financial trouble, and thinks he has lost all of his friends and has no reason to live? He wishes that he had never lived, and wonders if everyone would be better off if he had never been born? And he gets to see the lives of others in the town, how their lives would have turned out if he never existed?"

"Yes," I said, "And he gets to see how he made a great difference in everyone's life, how he truly had a Wonderful Life."

"Yeah. That angel Clarence." His stirring continued, slower than before.

I leaned in a bit, the noise of the coffee shop seemed to be getting louder. Or maybe we were just getting quieter, our voices getting softer. "Why the interest in this old movie? It's not even close to Christmas." I smiled while saying that, as if trying to find some humor in the conversation.

Otter stopped stirring for a second and looked into my face. He had these eyes that narrowed a bit when he was emotional, and that's what they were doing now. "What if you got to see how life would have been if you had never been born......and everyone's life was better? That people were happier? That everyone was better off?" He restarted the stirring, looking down at the brown beverage going around and around in his cup.

Though the noise continued around me, it felt so much more silent at the table. I searched my mind for the reasons that made Otter bring this subject up. "That seems silly. One, you can't know that. And two, it's just wrong. And three, well, you can't know that."

Otter didn't look up. "I'm sure you're right." Stirring. Stirring. "It would be easier if I just saw life as it is. Am I right?"

"I suppose so," I responded, not quite knowing where he was going in this conversation.

Someone called across the cafe to someone they knew on the other side, breaking the constant drone of the conversations going on around us. Then the din settled in once again and I felt the silence between our chairs, across the table. "Hey, Otter," I said quietly, almost whispering. "Are you doing okay? Everything all right?"

Otter looked up and stopped stirring his coffee. He had been sitting with his legs crossed and now he uncrossed them and slid his chair and legs underneath the table. He looked me in the eye, silent for a few seconds. Then, "I have lived over fifty years and I have seen life as it is. Pain, misery, hunger...cruelty beyond belief. I have heard the singing from taverns and moans from bundles of filth in the street. I have been a soldier and seen my comrades fall in battle...or die more slowly under the lash in Africa. I have held them in my arms at the final moment. These were men who saw life as it is. But they died despairing. No glory, no gallant last words...only their eyes, filled with the question, whimpering the question 'Why?' I do not think they were asking why they were dying but why they had ever lived."

Otter paused. This performance, taken from Man of La Mancha, was very impressive. He gave it with such meaning, such significance. It was as if he had transported himself to the stage.

But I was his only audience. Our eyes met across the table. He continued in the voice of Miguel Cervantes. "When life itself seems lunatic, who knows where madness lies? Perhaps to be too practical is madness. To surrender dreams, this may be madness. To seek treasure where there is only trash. Too much sanity may be madness! And maddest of all....to see life as it is...and not as it should be."

It was a beautifully delivered soliloquy. I wanted to applaud his memory of Miguel Cervantes over these many years. I stared at him. It was a brilliant performance.

Otter started stirring the coffee again. "Yeah, everything's okay." He smiled, really smiled a genuine smile for the first time since I had sat down. "Maybe I just need an angel. One like old Clarence."

We sat in silence for a while, and I began to feel a little uncomfortable. My mind was wandering, looking for something to say, playing out conversations in my head. Otter sat silent, still twirling his spoon around the cup, which sometimes gently clanged against the sides, breaking the silence, stirring his coffee even though he had not added anything to the black drink.

My mind was spinning in so many different directions as I sat in a wooden backed chair, across from this person who was my best friend in high school, as snippets of coffee shop conversations whirled around me. We both sat for awhile, not speaking.

I broke the silence. "Do you remember the time after that Saturday night, in the jail, when you asked me to go by your house and tell your mom that you were all right?"

Otter stopped stirring and raised his eyes to meet mine. "I remember," he said.

"She told me that your mom and dad, that William and Linda weren't your real parents." I let that sink in for a second. Otter continued to look at me with no change in his expression. "She said that her sister was your real mother, that she died in an auto accident a few weeks after you were born. And that she and William then got married and took you in."

I looked down at my hands and they were shaking. Otter's expression stayed the same. Quiet enveloped us like a heavy blanket that weighed upon our table.

Finally, in monotone, Otter spoke. "And they took this baby in because this sister had this child without being married? That she died in sin? And God commanded his faithful servants, William and Linda Otter, to take this bastard child and raise it as their own? So they obeyed the Lord, their God and got married?"

Otter was quiet again, but his expression remained unchanged, his eyes still locked on mine. I started counting my breaths, my breathing all that I could hear, despite all the noise around us.

He continued. "Then they found out that they were unable to have children of their own. So they were stuck with this one... bastard... child."

I leaned back in my chair, keeping my eye on Otter and the unchanged look on his face that had remained through his statements and questions, even the rhetorical ones.

"You already knew, didn't you?" I returned forward. It was quiet for a few seconds more. "How long have you known?"

"A cousin told me when I was twelve. I didn't believe him at first. Then I asked my grandmother just before she died and she told me." He resumed stirring his coffee. "I promised her that I wouldn't tell anyone that I knew this 'embarrassing' family secret." He was silent for a minute. "Hush, hush, you know."

I felt tears welling up in the corners of my eyes. I felt such sadness for my friend. "I'm sorry." I wiped my nose on a coffee shop napkin. "That should not have been a secret that you needed to keep."

Otter nodded, almost as if to thank me for my words. We were quiet a bit longer. I did not know what to say.

After a few minutes of this silence, I stood up and pushed my chair back, scraping it along the tile floor of the coffee shop. "I gotta get going. I've got a long drive ahead of me," I said this even though I planned on running by my old house and seeing my parents.

"Thanks again for bringing the letter." He was still looking down.

I stood leaning over the table. "It's been good to see you Otter," I said, and I immediately regretted how insincere that came out. I hoped it came out more sincere than it sounded to my ears.

"Good to see you," he returned, not looking up from his coffee and he did sound sincere. He had not taken a sip of his coffee the whole time of our visit and I resisted the urge to point that out to him.

"What are you up to now?" I shifted my weight back and forth.

"Right now? I'm going to hang here and finish my coffee. No plans." There was no emotion in his voice, the words coming out flatly, quietly across the table.

That really wasn't the answer to the question that I was asking. But I let it drop. I walked around the table and put my hand on his shoulder, resting it there for a few seconds before taking it off. "OK. Be well. Take care." I didn't know what else to say. My goodbye was returned with silence, just another slight nod of his head.

I started walking towards the door, stopped midway and returned a couple of steps. "Mark," using his first name for maybe the third time in all of the years that I had known him.

He looked up and stopped stirring his coffee. "Yeah?"

"I just want you to know that you matter to me."

Otter nodded his head, I guess meaning that he heard me. And I said it again. "You matter to me."

I took a couple of steps towards Otter, mostly so I wouldn't have to speak too loudly. "You're a good guy. Really." I said these words softly, Otter didn't raise his head, merely letting his eyes look up to me. "I can't be the only one who knows that." I said that softly, hoping he could hear those words over the noise in the coffee house.

I took one, maybe two steps closer. "Does it ever bother you that it seems like no one wants to see the good in you? That it seems like everyone only wants to judge you for who they think you are?"

I let that sit in the air for what seemed like several minutes, but I'm sure it was just a couple of seconds. Otter began stirring his coffee again. I resisted the urge to break what seemed like an eternity of silence. His eyes fixed on mine. "No. It doesn't bother me. Everyone needs to tell themselves something." His eyes looked downwards toward his cup and he watched his coffee go around and around, creating a small whirlpool. "We're all terrible in someone's story."

I stood in place for a few more seconds, then I turned and walked to the door and held it open for a lady and her young daughter to come in as I went out. The sunshine blinded me for just a second until my eyes adjusted and the door closed behind me. I took one last look through the window at where Otter and I had been sitting, and through the glare I could see he was still there, stirring his coffee, not drinking.

I walked down the street towards my parked car. We just were not the same people, Otter and I, that we were once. I suppose no one really is. He was right. We are all terrible in someone's story.

VALUE
by Mark Otter

Water has only value to the thirsty
Food has only value to the hungry
Friendship has only value to the friendless
Shelter has only value to the homeless
Clothing has only value to the naked

But death
Death has only value
To those who have already died.

I GRADUATED WITH MY BS IN ANIMAL SCIENCE AND MOVED my meager belongings to Davis, California, where I started work on a master's degree in Wildlife Biology. I continued to place a great focus on my schoolwork, continued to do fairly well, and soon I was applying to doctoral programs around the country.

I received maybe seven or eight letters from Otter in the two years that I was in graduate school. The last five were forwarded by my parents, as Otter simply addressed them to that home address with the direction to please forward them to me. The letters were pretty similar; he was working construction, building houses, laying pipes, putting on siding, hanging sheet rock, and other jobs along these lines. The letters came from various locations, San Bernardino, Bakersfield, even one from Indio, out in the desert. They were upbeat, always asking questions about how I was doing and how my family was. They never mentioned anything about his family and in my return letters, I didn't ask.

There were also a couple of phone calls, both collect. They were mostly "How's the weather" type of stuff. Because of the cost of collect calls, we both were cognizant about keeping the conversations brief. But it was good to hear his voice.

He did have to go to jail for the incident that he told me about while at the coffee shop, when he was driving a stolen car with prescription drug bottles in the glove compartment. He joked that my letter didn't help. At least he said he was joking. He ended up doing three months for possession of a controlled substance. They waived the stolen car charge in the plea bargain.

As part of the plea deal, he was told that he needed to go to "some stupid bullshit recovery program," as he called it. Stupid because, according to Otter, he didn't have a drug problem. He told me he wasn't involved in any drug use, just alcohol, and he did not see that as a problem.

He did talk about the community service that he had been court ordered to do. He was teaching Tae Kwon Do to inner city kids, and he talked excitedly about that. This was something he really enjoyed doing.

He also talked about a couple of relationships with a couple of different women. He would state that he thought they were getting too serious and that it might be time to end the relationship soon. That was another topic that I generally steered clear of.

I worried about my friend. Our lives had taken such divergent paths. Perhaps our backgrounds, our family experiences, had made this growing apart inevitable. He was my best friend in high school, we shared so much together. But now it seemed we only shared that long-ago Saturday night. At least, it seemed that way.

After graduating with my Masters degree, I started the doctoral program in Animal Science at Utah State University in Logan, Utah. Before starting the doctoral program, I wrote to Otter at the last address that I had for him, hoping he would receive it. I told him about getting accepted into the doctoral program. As it turned out, he did receive it, called my parents for my phone number, and then called me late one night to congratulate me. It was good to hear from him and he was effusive in his excitement for me and my news. For over an hour we talked and caught up on each other's lives. He kidded me that when I graduated from Utah State, we would have to go out to dinner so he could have me paged. "Paging Dr. Campton," he said several times, giggling each time he said Dr. Campton.

I told him how that would not be a big deal for me as I heard that page many times for my father. Otter laughed some more. "You're going to take me to the best steakhouse around and I'll have them page Dr. Jake Campton. Oh, this is going to happen." I appreciated his excitement at my news.

I asked how his life was going and he mostly shrugged it off, saying that it had its ups and downs. He said he was living in a studio apartment in San Bernardino, wasn't dating anyone, and was trying to find some work. Each time I asked about his life, he would give me a short answer and then ask about my parents or Jenna. I told him that Jenna had been accepted to Veterinary school, and that set him off again, chortling with excitement and genuine glee. He talked about sending her a congratulations card and I gave him her address.

We talked for quite a while. I encouraged him to keep trying to go back to school and get more skills, telling him that it would make him more employable. He said that he would look into it as soon as he got more steady employment. We said our goodbyes. It was really good to hear from him.

That was the last time I heard from Otter. I soon moved to Utah and started my doctoral program. I did send him a letter giving him my new address and telling him a little about the work I was doing. But it came back with no forwarding address. He had moved again and did not leave any information about where he was.

I threw myself into my work in the Animal Science program and I was really enjoying what I was doing. I was a teaching assistant for a professor, which paid a little, and I was liking the coursework. I was beginning to explore subjects for my doctoral dissertation. I dated some, and I was becoming sweet on this nice Mormon girl, an undergraduate at the university. I was continuing my studies in Buddhism, which I had become interested in the last year. Life was going well.

Late one evening, I got a call from my dad. I knew something had to be up as Dad never called. It wasn't that I never talked with him, but it was always when I called home and he answered the phone, or when my mom called and would hand it over to him to say goodbye. But it seemed like my suspicions weren't true as Dad engaged in several minutes of small talk, asking about how my program was going and then telling me about a couple of his patients.

Then, "I need to tell you something, Jake" and my stomach rose in my chest. I was right that something was up. I braced myself. "Son, Mark Otter was killed two nights ago."

Have you ever heard something, but your brain simply cannot compute what it had heard? That was me at this instant. "Otter?" I whispered into the phone. I had heard the words that my dad said, but did I really? I remember standing in the small kitchen of my studio apartment, holding the phone that was connected to the wall, leaning against the wall and sliding down to the floor.

"Jake?" I heard my dad's voice through the phone still pressed up against my ear. "Are you there, son?"

"I'm here." I leaned my head back, bumping it against the wall with an audible thud. "What happened?"

"Well, the details are still a little sketchy and I only know what I read in the paper this morning."

"When did it happen? What happened?" My voice was barely above a whisper.

"According to the paper, Mark was involved in a single car accident. He was driving on Topanga Canyon about three in the morning when the car left the road and plunged down an embankment. Apparently he was not wearing a seatbelt and was thrown from the car. His body was found the next day."

I had studied science throughout my academic career. I was a scientist. In science, some things make sense, they can be proven, and some things don't make sense, they can't be proven. Science meant dealing with a body of facts or truths that hold to the operation of general laws. The systematic knowledge of these truths and facts are gained through observation and experimentation. This is science. This was what made sense to me. What I was hearing did not make sense. My head could not wrap around what I was hearing.

I was silent, listening to the words from my father. I was in total shock, and questions swirled around my brain. Whose car was he driving? Why was he driving on Topanga Canyon at 3 am? How could he be dead? Why? Were drugs or alcohol involved?

I don't remember the rest of the conversation. Dad offered to pay for my flight if I needed to come home for a few days. I told him that I needed to figure out what I wanted to do. Then I hung up.

Immediately after hanging up, I got a call from Jenna. All she said was "I'm sorry, Jake."

I don't remember my reply.

After a sleepless night, I called home and talked to Mom, trying to get more information. She didn't have any, but she gave me the name of the Los Angeles Times reporter who had written the story. I called him, explaining I was a friend of Mark Otter, and he was nice enough to give me the information that he had. Apparently Otter left a girlfriend's apartment around 2:30 am, taking her Datsun. While driving the winding Topanga Canyon Boulevard west towards the beaches at a high rate of speed, he failed to negotiate one of the curves. He crashed through a guard rail, flipping several times. He was not wearing a seatbelt and was thrown from the auto. The car and his body were discovered the next day. Law enforcement did not find any evidence of drug or alcohol use and there were no skid marks and no evidence of braking. They attributed the death to lack of visibility (there were reports of patchy fog in the area) and a high rate of speed.

I thanked him for the information. "Can I ask you a question?" the reporter asked.

"Of course."

"Do you know if Mr. Otter was depressed? Did he seem down, or did he talk about suicide?"

I thought this was an unusual line of questioning and I took a second to mull over my response. "No. I haven't talked with him in a while, but in my last conversation he seemed very upbeat." I thought a second more. "Why these questions?"

"I've seen these kinds of accidents before," the reporter replied. "No drugs or alcohol involved. High rate of speed. No evidence of slowing down. I was just wondering. His lady friend said that they had an argument before he left, though she did say it was no big deal. She said that Mr. Otter stated that he was going out for a drive, getting some fresh air."

I thought about what he was telling me. "As I said, the last conversation I had with Mark, he was quite upbeat."

"Well," the reporter continued, "his girlfriend said that he had been discouraged. He had recently been laid off from his job and was having a hard time finding any other work. She said that he seemed moody and depressed recently."

I didn't respond and the phone line was silent for a few seconds. Finally I broke the quiet. "Why would you tell me this?"

"I was just wondering," the reporter concluded. "I didn't mean to be rude or anything. I apologize if I was."

I thanked him again for giving me this information and hung up the phone. I knew what he was alluding to. I thought about what he said, hoped it wasn't true, but was unsure. I wondered about my friend's last few hours on this earth.

The next couple of days I was in a fog, and went through my daily actions robotically. Three days after the phone call from my father, I received in the mail a large packing envelope. It had no return address. When I opened it, there was a stack of neatly handwritten poems, all with the byline "by Mark Otter." On top was a scribbled note, and while all of the poems were neatly hand written, the note on top seemed to have been hastily scrawled.

"Jake. Hope you like these poems. I've been writing them for the last couple of years. I know they're not very good, but I thought you might like to have them. You're a good friend. I remember the first time we met, on the soccer field, thinking

what a cool guy you were. And what a lousy soccer player!
You're definitely going places Dr. Jake. Do your thing. Don't
let your meatloaf.......Otter"

I called my parents and asked about a service. They told
me they had been looking for any information with regards
to one, but had not been able to find any mention that one
was planned. Dad said that he went over to Otter's parent's
house, but no one answered his knock and that the duplex
looked closed up. Dad talked to the neighbor next door and
they told him they had not seen anyone around the Otter
house in quite a while.

I asked if there had been an obituary in any of the local
papers and dad said that he had not seen one but would
keep a lookout and let me know.

I called Otter's parents as I still had the number from
where they lived. The response was a recording on an
answering machine. The voice was one that I did not
recognize. "You have reached the home of the Otters.
William and Linda have left the area for a few weeks to
do missionary work for the Lord God, Jehovah. If you
are calling asking about Mark Otter, the Otters have not
heard from him in several years. It would be appreciated if you did not call again." Then the phone hung up,
taking no messages.

I called the LA County Morgue and asked about the
procedure for the disposal of deceased bodies, and I asked
specifically about Mark Otter. I was told the morgue would
keep unclaimed bodies for a period of one month, then they
would be cremated and the remains kept for three years.
If no one claimed them after that period, they were given
an interfaith funeral and buried along with others in the
same situation.

I was in shock. Though I had not heard from Otter for a few months, I could not believe that I would not hear from him again. Ever.

I didn't know what to do next. So I kept going to my classes, kept teaching undergraduate courses in animal science, kept going out with friends once in a while. Just kept moving, the cliche of putting one foot in front of the other. I thought about Otter often, then once in a while, then occasionally. But never not at all.

Six weeks after his death, I received a certified check from Western Alliance Life Insurance for $10,000. There was no explanation, just a check. I called the insurance company. They apologized for the delay in issuing the check, but needed to verify the death. Still perplexed, I asked for some additional information. They told me that Mark Otter had taken out a life insurance policy in the amount of $10,000 and Jake Campton was named as the sole beneficiary. I thanked them and hung up the phone.

After two months I called the coroner's office and asked if anyone had claimed Mark Otter's remains. No one had. That next Christmas break, I traveled home and went to the LA County Morgue and made a request for Otter's remains, paid the $85 handling fee, and received his ashes in a plastic bag that were placed inside a cardboard box. On the outside of the box was the label - OTTER, MARK FLOYD. I remember staring at the name when the box was given to me. Floyd. I never knew Otter's middle name until then.

After picking up the remains, I sat on a marble bench in front of the county morgue, holding the cardboard box. I looked at the label again. OTTER, MARK FLOYD. I smiled. I wished that I had known his middle name when we were in high school. I would have loved teasing him that he was named after Floyd the barber from the Andy Griffith show. Then I remembered that one of Otter's favorite imitations was of Floyd the barber. Now I knew where that came from.

That was a good memory. Other good memories followed, and I smiled as I thought about them, holding a box, outside the county morgue.

I took the box with me when I went back to my apartment in Utah. I found an empty coffee can, poured the remains into it, and placed a rubber band around the top to help insure that none fell out. I put the can on the top shelf of my closet.

Life went on. I chopped wood. I carried water.

. . .

A man went to a Buddhist monastery for a silent retreat. After he finished, he felt better, calmer, and much stronger. But something was still missing. His teacher told him to talk to one of the monks before he left.

So the man sought out one of the monks and talked with him at great length. Finally he asked him, "How do you find such peace?"

The monk said, "I say yes. To everything that happens, I say yes."

When the man returned home, he was enlightened.

OCTOBER 22

I AWOKE IN MY HOTEL ROOM AFTER A NIGHT OF SLEEPING hard. Hard in that I never remember waking up, rolling over, or dreaming the whole night. I took another long shower, washing the sleep from my body, and dressed for the day. I packed my clothes in preparation for checking out.

I walked Orson down the stairs and through the lobby that was full of business travelers getting started on their days. It was a typical busy mid-week Southern California day, the weather was again perfect, and I gave gratitude. I walked Orson down the street, letting him do his morning sniffing, walked into a local coffee shop and purchased a London Fog and a scone. I sat at one of the outdoor tables, feeling the sun warming my body. I closed my eyes and tried to picture my day.

After finishing my breakfast, I walked back to the hotel and checked out. I then hopped into the pickup and it was on to the first stop of the day, a doggy daycare center close by. I had made a reservation for Orson, letting him enjoy being a dog for the day, rather than my travel companion. Upon arrival, as I got him out of the pickup, he caught the smell of the dozen other dogs there, and his tail began to wag excitedly. I left him with the doggy daycare staff, leaving a few dog treats behind to be given to him during the day.

I scratched him behind the ears as a goodbye, and then he was off to make some new friends.

My next stop was at a local branch of Wells Fargo Bank. I walked up to the teller and asked how to go about closing an account and I was directed to a professional looking woman, dressed in the business suit of bankers. I sat down across from her desk and stated my objective of closing my account.

She introduced herself as Rachael. "Well, we hate to lose you as a customer, but I can assist you with that," she said smiling. "Is there a reason for wanting to close the account?"

"Not really," I said politely. "Just need the funds elsewhere." I produced my account information as well as some ID.

"Let me call up that account," she said, clickety clacking on the keyboard to her computer.

After a couple of seconds of typing, she paused. "Is your account at this branch?"

"No. I think I opened it in Utah many years ago."

She clicked a couple of more keys on the computer. "Yes. I see where the only activity on this account is a deposit once a year on May 3rd". She typed some more keystrokes. "It looks like a ten dollar deposit every year on May 3rd for…" she paused as she did some mental math. "Well, it looks like it has been about forty years."

I agreed with her. "I guess I sort of forgot that I had money here. Is that a problem?"

"No. I don't think so. Just let me check with my manager." And she was off to consult with a gentleman on the other side of the bank.

Both of them returned after a couple of minutes and the bank manager introduced himself. "This is quite unusual, to have such little activity on an account over this length of time. We would be happy to move this to a higher yielding savings account. You could make a great deal more interest. Or perhaps you would like to set up an investment account? Our returns have been quite impressive."

I eyed the both of them. "No thank you. I just want to cash out and close the account."

"Okay," the manager spoke again. "I'm going to have Brad help you out with that." He picked up some papers that were on the desk. "Rachael," he said turning to the young woman who had been helping me. "Will you explain the situation to Brad, please?"

"Is there a problem?" I asked again. "I simply want to cash out this account and close it."

"No problem at all," the bank manager assured me. "Brad is the person who handles these types of accounts."

"And what type of accounts would that be?" My frustration level was rising.

The manager gave me a smile. "Oh, just the accounts that have seen little activity on them for a long length of time."

Rachael started walking towards another part of the bank. "Hold just a second," I said, turning to her. I turned back to the manager. "The funds are in the bank, correct?"

"Certainly." The bank manager shifted his feet uncomfortably.

"And I have provided appropriate identification as the owner of the account, yes?"

The manager looked towards another part of the branch, perhaps hoping Brad would appear suddenly and take care of this matter. "I just thought you would like our investment counselor to explain the many different investments and opportunities for your funds that are available at Wells Fargo."

"Well, you thought incorrectly," I told him. "I would like to close out this account and receive the funds that I have in here."

The manager turned back towards Rachael, who had returned behind her desk. "Well, that certainly is not a problem," he said in a voice that wasn't far from sarcasm. "Rachael will be able to help you with that."

"Of course," she said as the bank manager walked away. "How would you like to receive these funds?" she asked politely.

"Please make it a cashier's check. Here is the name it is to be made out to." And I slid a piece of paper across the desk.

The rest of the transaction was done quickly and soon I was headed out the door with the cashier's check in my pocket. I then drove over to my old neighborhood and the house I grew up in.

Arriving there, I parked across the street from my family home. I had not seen the old house for a few years, not since mom had sold it and moved to Arizona. I sat in the pickup for a few minutes and I checked off the differences from when my mom was last there until now. It was like those pictures side by side where one is asked to find the subtle differences between the two. The house numbers were displayed differently, a hedge had been taken out, some rose bushes planted, and pavers had replaced the walkway from the garage to the house. But outside of those minor changes, the house looked the same. I looked at the neighbor's houses on each side, and they looked much different from when I grew up, different paints, one having an addition added. Those houses had changed ownership a few times over these many years.

I did not feel much nostalgia, and that surprised me. I thought seeing the place where I grew up, especially in connection with this trip, would move me more. They just seemed like houses now, though they looked smaller than I remembered. I guess that's how memories go.

I reached into the back seat and got The Repository out and walked over to the park. I must have been in this park hundreds of times during my life. It had certainly changed, the old metal play structures of my youth having been replaced with much safer plastic ones. Some trees had been taken out and replaced with others. Some of the older trees were now much larger, giving more shade and making the area more visually appealing. I walked through the park towards the fenced in ball fields, another walk that I had taken more times than I could count.

The fields seemed in better repair than when I was spending hours on them. The soccer field was better marked and the goalie net cemented into the grass. There was no one out on the field because school was in session and all of the school age kids weren't around at this time of the morning. I leaned against one of the goal posts, quieted my mind, and thought about that time when I first met Mark Otter so many years ago on this very spot.

I let my mind wander to the many times that Otter and I had met at this soccer field, a sort of halfway point between our houses. Though my mind wanted to go in several different directions, I kept trying to bring it back to reflect on the times that Otter and I shared on this field. I remembered when we first met. I remembered when he taught me how to visualize my kicks, to see the result in my mind before I tried the kick. I have used that lesson that he taught me, to see the target before I acted, many times in my life. I let that memory lead to other memories of Otter.

I try to treat these recollections with tenderness as they have led me to this place in my life. I try to give them no values, no good or bad, no shoulds or should nots. They have been the stones that I have stepped upon to become who I am.

After a while, I got up and took the lid off The Repository and sprinkled some dust around the goal posts. I said a Buddhist prayer, trying to do so surreptitiously as I didn't think people would appreciate me spreading this dust around. I didn't spread too much, The Repository was starting to get low in volume, a testament to the length of this journey that was now past two weeks.

I replaced the lid and headed across the field towards the gate that led to where the duplexes that Otter and his parents had lived. The duplexes had long since been replaced, their old and tired structures razed and townhouses built in their stead. It was an improvement in the neighborhood appeal, if aesthetics were the goal. My mom and dad thought the townhouses looked quite "cookie cutter," as they liked to say. And I suppose they did. But change is inevitable. I didn't think the new looked too bad and I was glad to see the old go. Perhaps my memories of them were different than my parents.

It was hard to imagine where the old duplexes were in relation to the townhouses, but I guessed where the Otter garage must have been and I recalled the many hours of practice that my friend put in on his Shaolin dummy. And I remembered the garage incident. And I wondered how many other garage incidents occurred in Otter's life. I sprinkled some dust from The Repository into the wind and let it settle over where I thought the garage must have been so many years ago.

I walked back towards my old house and put The Repository into the back of the cab of the pickup. I then walked to my old high school, in the same place it was so many years ago, still standing. When I got there, I noticed that some of the old buildings were no longer there, having been replaced with shiny brick and steel buildings. I entered the administration wing and noticed that it looked different from when I was a student. Just outside the administrative office was a trophy case, crammed full of trophies, both athletic and academic. I looked for trophies from those years when I was there, but there weren't any. In fact, I didn't see any trophies older than ten years. No room I suppose. I wondered where those trophies went.

I walked into the office and was greeted by the front secretary with a warm "Hello, may I help you?"

"Yes you may," I said, and I moved closer to the counter. "I would like to make a donation to pay off all the lunch bills that students may have that might be in arrears."

"What is that again?" the secretary asked politely.

"All of the students with lunch debt, I would like to pay it all off and wipe their slates clean."

"That's such a nice thing to do," she smiled. "We have a form right here for donations of that sort." She slid the form across the counter. "How much would you like to donate?"

"I have a cashier's check made out to the school for $34,059.83."

"I'm sorry. Again?" She was still smiling.

"I have a cashier's check made out to the school for $34,059.83."

She took the form back across the counter. "Wow. That's a significant donation. Let me get Mr. Kincaid, the principal."

I watched her go to a back office and knock on the door. I felt somewhat out of place, and even though I had recently showered and shaved, I was still feeling grungy from two weeks of camping and traveling. I watched students come and go through the door. Schools are always such hubs of activity and youth, and I could feel the energy emanating from these young people.

A gentleman with a tie and jacket came out to the counter where I was standing. "Hello. I'm Jonas Kincaid, the principal here." He had a youthful look about him, though he was probably in his early forties. "Come have a seat in my office, if you would."

I followed the gentleman into his small office just off the bigger office of the school. He motioned for me to sit down. "You would like to make a donation, what is it, 34 thousand and...?"

"$34,059.83. I used to be a student here a long time ago," I stated by way of explanation. "I received some monies from a fellow student. I sort of forgot about it, but I'm wanting to make the donation now."

"That's a very generous gift. And much appreciated." He was sincere in his remark. "And you want to pay off all of the student debt as it relates to lunch monies owed?" He handed me the same form that the secretary up front had given and then taken away from me.

"That's correct. I would like all lunch debts wiped clean. Is that enough to do that?" I started filling out the form.

"Oh, it's more than enough. Where would you like the rest to go?"

I stopped filling out the form. "I would like it all to go to cover lunch monies owed."

"I think that amount is about $8200. There would be a significant amount left over."

I thought for a minute. "Can it be used to create a fund to go through the year?"

"Yes. We could do something like that. Let me ask you a question.... I'm sorry, I didn't catch your name."

"It's Jake Campton. I graduated from here back in the seventies. But the donation is not from me. Like I said, it was given to me years ago and I am now giving it to the school. And I know that this donor would want the money to cover lunch debts."

"Well, Mr. Campton, we have many students that not only struggle in paying for lunches, but also activity fees, library fines, school supplies, stuff like that. Would it be okay with the person who gave you the money if the school could use some of these funds to help out more needy students with these different kinds of fees? We have an account set up for these kinds of expenditures. Perhaps the donation could go there?"

I thought for a second. I had not counted on this event. I really wanted all of the money to go to paying off lunch debts. I didn't know if that would be a good use of this life insurance payout of so long ago. My eyes wandered around the room. Just then a knock came on the door. "Come in," Mr. Kincaid said.

The same secretary that I had talked with earlier came into the room. "Someone just delivered flowers and these are for you, Mr. Kincaid." And she placed on his desk an arrangement of hydrangeas, purples, pinks, blues, whites, a total assortment. "Aren't they lovely?"

she gushed. "I think they are to thank you for your help with the assembly last week."

"They certainly are beautiful," Mr. Kincaid said. Then he turned back to me. "Mr. Campton? Would it be okay to use those funds for needy students for more than just lunch debts?"

I was staring at the arrangement of hydrangeas. They were beautiful, full of vibrant colors. My eyes were fixed on these beautiful flowers. And then I remembered that the universe is always speaking to us, sending us messages in many different forms. It is always reminding us to stop and look around, often giving us guidance in what to do.

"Mr. Campton?" the principal broke the silence.

"Of course," I said. "That would be fine."

I pushed back the donation form. "I'm not feeling the need to fill this out if you don't mind."

"Well, it's for your taxes and we like to recognize a gift of this size with a plaque in our library. We would love to put a name to the gift."

"No. The giver would not want his name mentioned."

"Anonymous it is then." I handed him the check that was made out to the school. "Please thank this generous person for me personally, if you would."

I shook his hand, "I will." I walked from his office into the outer office and thanked the secretaries for their help. I walked out the door of the school and retraced my steps back to my childhood home. I thought of Otter and the many times we had hiked this same route. I hoped he was pleased with his donation. I'm pretty sure he was.

I walked the route slowly, trying to take in everything. Though the houses were much different, some of them gone and replaced, I felt like I was seeing them as they were when

I walked home from school many years before. I knew this would be the last time seeing this neighborhood, the school, my childhood home. I wanted to take it all in.

I got back to the pickup, started it up and headed to the freeway and turned north. I was traveling out of the valley. The traffic was its usual high intensity, and it was making me homesick for my simpler life in Montana. Driving further and further from the Valley brought me past what used to be uninhabited rock and dirt, acres of hills. Uninhabited no more. I looked out to what used to be Vasquez rocks, a place where Otter and I used to go hiking. It was houses and more houses now. I was headed to Santa Clarita, a city that barely existed when I was growing up. Now it was just elongated suburbs of the San Fernando Valley and Los Angeles.

I passed the exit to Magic Mountain, now an enormous, sprawling amusement park, one that was just getting started as I grew up. I had been a couple of times with friends and I remembered that Otter and I had always talked about going there, but we never quite made it.

I took one of the Valencia exits and headed towards the foothills. I noticed my heartbeat was quickening. I took some deep breaths and turned into a parking lot. Second guessing began.

DIG A LITTLE DEEPER
by Mark Otter

I think I just killed a man

I woke up and the whole damn world was on fire.
I tried running
But my legs were broken
And there was no where to go.

When you are born
In the middle of the ocean
You better learn to swim.

You start digging.
And you dig a little deeper.
And you dig and dig
And you dig even deeper
Until you realize you are buried alive.

In the darkness, everything is different.
The air is thicker.
And when you close your eyes
It just gets darker.

Time to pay the piper.
Don't have enough money?
Just dig a little deeper.

OCTOBER 22

THE SIGN OUTSIDE THE BEIGE STUCCO BUILDING SAYS Haven of Rest Convalescent Center. Underneath, in smaller lettering, We Put the Care in Assisted Care Living. It is an unremarkable building, all one story, in a u-shape with a courtyard in the middle. It is landscaped in a unimaginative sort of way, some grass and some shrubs, not well cared for but not ignored either. The grass is mowed, but a lot of it hangs over the sidewalk, looking like it had not been edged in quite awhile, and dandelions poke out in several patches. Next to the building there are flower beds, dirt areas where some flowers are growing, but most choosing not to. It certainly is not an appealing spot.

I park in the lot among other vehicles scattered here and there. There doesn't appear to be a lot of visitors at Haven of Rest, as most of the cars are in designated employee spaces and mine is the only vehicle in the visitor parking area. I sit in my pickup for a few minutes, gathering my thoughts and reflecting on the events of the day thus far. I can see the breeze picking up outside, and the trees beginning to lose their leaves as the wind picks them off their branches, swirling them around the parking lot. I step outside the pickup and lean against the door and I feel the breeze in my face. The smell of landscape bark hits me and makes me sneeze, and I see where bark has been spread unevenly around the flower beds.

I walk up to the front veranda, a covered area where people can be dropped off. There is a bench outside the front door and four Adirondack chairs of a sad color of brown line the sidewalk. On one of the chairs is an older woman, rocking back and forth, humming to herself. She looks up at me as I approach and I try and give her my warmest smile, but her expression doesn't change and she goes back to rocking and humming.

I push open the double doors and there is a small waiting area of over-stuffed chairs where a couple of male residents are sitting, one reading a pamphlet of some kind and the other talking in a soft voice, but it seems like no one is listening to whatever it is he is talking about. They both raise their heads at the sound of the door opening and I say, "Hello. Good afternoon," and they both blink a greeting before going back to what they were doing.

Just inside another set of double front doors is a counter separating me from three desks and a host of file cabinets. No one is at the front counter or at any of the desks, and I wait by the sign that says Please Check In Here, though there is no one to check in with. I contemplate writing my name on the yellow sign-in sheet that is on the counter, but I decide not to, as I don't know where I'm going. Off to my right is a dining area with several tables and 5-6 chairs at each. A couple of tables have someone sitting at them, I can't really see what they are doing, if anything. Behind that is a hallway, appearing to contain resident's rooms. I look to my left and see a sign over a door that says "Nurse" and past it look to be more rooms.

I turn my attention back to the office area and I see that the counter wraps around in a square and there is an entrance to the kitchen off one side and on the other is an entrance to a small courtyard. I look out onto the courtyard and see that it has similar landscaping as the front of the building. There are several outdoor chairs scattered around and several older women and men are occupying a few of them.

I wait for several minutes and no one presents themselves, so I walk around the counter and down a hallway that opens up into a lounge of some sort where it looks like two aides are doing something with a remote control to the television that hangs from the wall. I watch for a few seconds as they talk politely with one of the residents, telling him that Jeopardy does not come on until after dinner. One of them turns the channel to Wheel of Fortune and that seems to satisfy the older gentleman and he settles into a chair.

The aides notice me. One says, "Hello. Can I help you?"

"Yes," I say. "I was hoping to check in."

The aide gave me a friendly smile and walked back towards the entryway and to the front counter. "I can help you with that."

I retrace my steps and follow her. "Just write your name and who you are visiting on the sign in sheet," she says.

I write my name on the yellow sheet of paper and then under "Visiting" I write William Otter.

The aide takes the paper from me and reads what I have written. She looks up at me. "Willie Otter?" It is in the form of a question.

"I believe so. I didn't know him as Willie."

"Well, I don't think he has had a visitor in quite a while." She turns and looks over her shoulder and talks to another aide who has come into the area. "Amber. This gentleman is here to see Willie Otter."

I could tell that surprises Amber. "Wow," she says. "I don't think he has had a visitor in a long time. In fact, I don't ever remember him having a visitor."

"I know," said the aide with the name tag of Kathy pinned to her blouse. "That's what I told this gentleman." She then turned back to me. "Is Willie family?"

"I'm a friend of the family." I look around at several of the residents that are within view. "Is he around?"

Kathy swings part of the counter open and steps to the front. "He's around someplace. He may be in his room, it's not quite dinner time." She motions for me to follow her. "He's such a sweet old man. I'm glad he finally has someone to come and see him."

We start walking through the dining area when she stops. "There he is," and she points to an old man sitting at a table in the corner of the room. He is eating something, I can't make out what it is from where we are standing. Kathy walks over to the man and I follow her. She puts her hand on the man's shoulder and he looks up. "Hi, Willie. You have a friend here to visit."

I don't recognize this old man. He looks nothing like the William Otter that I used to know. I feel like maybe this is a different William Otter; that all of my searching and googling to find the person that I once knew, and finding that there was a William Otter at Haven of Rest Convalescent Center, well... is this the one I was looking for?

He looks up from his dish and I see that he is eating a bowl of applesauce. He looks me in my eyes and smiles. And then I know without a doubt that I have found the William Otter that I was searching for. The eyes are without passion, a smile without meaning, looking like it was painted onto a face for appearance's sake. I could never forget that look. Like my dad said so many years ago, it was something in his countenance.

"Who are you?" He asks, his smile never leaving his face.

"Hello, Mr. Otter." I give him a mirrored smile. "I'm Jake Campton, a friend of your son Mark."

Mr. Otter continues to eye me, the smile still on his face. "Are you Mark?"

Kathy starts to walk away. "I'll leave you two to catch up." Then as an aside to me, "I'm afraid that he doesn't remember too much. Don't be surprised."

I turn back to the old man eating applesauce. "No, sir. I'm not Mark. I'm his friend, Jake."

Mr. Otter's gaze leaves me and he turns his attention back to his applesauce and resumes spooning it into his mouth. "They have good applesauce here."

I watch him spoon some more into his mouth. "Mr. Otter, I've come here to talk to you about your son, Mark." I settle into a chair next to his, scooting it underneath the table.

He looks back up from his bowl. "Are you Mark?" He asks again.

"No, I'm not Mark." I watch him eat for a few seconds. "Do you remember Mark?" Nothing. "Would you like me to tell Mark something?" He continues eating. "Is there something you would like to say to Mark?"

Mr. Otter stops his spoon midway from the bowl to his mouth. "No." Then he finishes his spoonful. "Mark's dead."

I shift in my chair. "Do you remember when Mark died, Mr. Otter?" I watched the old man slowly chew his applesauce. "How did Mark die, Mr. Otter?" Another few moments of silence. "Do you know how Mark died?"

The old man takes another spoonful to his mouth. He looks back to me. "Are you Mark?"

I think about telling him that I am Mark, my good friend Otter. But I don't. For some reason that seems like a cruel trick to play. I'm not here to play cruel tricks. "Do you remember Mark, Mr. Otter?"

He stops eating and his brow furrows. He seems to be thinking, trying to pull a memory out of his mind. Then his face relaxes and he scrapes the bottom of the bowl that contains the rest of the applesauce. "No. I don't think I do." He spoons more into his mouth. "They have good apple-sauce here."

He picks the bowl up and eyes it, then puts it back down and scrapes the spoon along the sides. "What do you remember about Mark?" I ask.

He stops scraping for a minute. "Mark's dead," he says without emotion.

"Yes I know Mark's dead. I was wondering what you remember about him." Another moment of silence. "Do you remember he is your son?"

We sit in silence for awhile as he continues to scrape the now empty bowl, trying to get more applesauce on his spoon. He is unsuccessful for there is no more left in the bowl. "Mr. Otter," I say quietly. "Would you like some more applesauce?"

He looks me in the eye and then smiles that same smile. "I could eat some more applesauce," he says, pushing his bowl towards me.

I pick up the bowl and head back out to the front desk where Kathy is going through some papers. "Is it possible that I can get Mr. Otter a little more applesauce?"

Kathy looks up. "Well, we don't like to feed the residents this close to dinner time." She gets up from her desk and takes the bowl from me. "But seeing how this is Willie's first visitor in I don't know how long, I think we can make an exception." She gives me a warm smile. "Isn't he just the sweetest old man?"

I appreciate her obvious caring for the elderly here at Haven of Rest. I smile. "I suppose he is. I haven't seen him in a long time."

Kathy goes through a door into the kitchen area, and then stops and pokes her head back out. "I forgot to ask if you would like some applesauce also?"

"No thank you. That's very kind of you to ask."

Kathy leaves and then comes back a few seconds later with a refilled bowl. I thank her and return to the old man who is in the same position as when I left him. "Here you go, Mr. Otter."

The old man pulls the bowl closer and plunges his spoon into the applesauce. "They have good applesauce here," he says, to no one in particular.

We sit in silence for a bit. We are now the only people in the dining area and the only noise is Mr. Otter's spoon hitting the bowl as he continues to feed himself applesauce. He stops for just a minute, "Don't you want no applesauce?"

"No. I'm fine, thank you."

"They have good applesauce here," and he finishes, setting the spoon down inside the now empty bowl. He leans back in his chair and slides it back, sliding it along the carpeted floor. Then he stops and pushes the chair under the table, grabs his spoon and looks at the empty bowl. He sees that there is no applesauce remaining and he pushes his chair back again. He seems confused.

Tom Smyly

"Are you okay, Mr. Otter?" I ask.

He looks at me, then at the bowl. "I was thinking about having some applesauce." He peers at the empty bowl. "But it looks like they don't have none." More silence. "They have good applesauce here."

I look at this old man, his rumpled clothes, his grizzled face, his empty smile, and I realize - there is going to be no confrontation here. If I thought there would be a reckoning, an accounting for years past, I was mistaken. There would be none of that. There would be no recognition of past deeds. There would be no confronting on past conduct. There would be no acknowledgement for transgressions of long forgotten times. There was only this old shell of a man, finishing his applesauce.

The old man looked at me and gave me that same empty smile that I saw over forty years before. There was as much to it now as there was to it then. "Who are you?" he asks me.

I look him in the eyes. "I'm Jake, a friend of your son, Mark."

He simply stares at me for a few more moments. "Are you Mark?" he asks again.

"No. I'm not Mark," I say softly. "I'm his friend Jake."

"Oh," he says. "You look like Mark."

"Do I?" I ask. "How do I look like Mark?"

There is no response, just him continuing to look at me. Then he turns his attention to the empty bowl. I ask again, "Mr. Otter, how do I look like Mark?"

I wait in silence for an answer and I can feel the anger growing inside my chest and starting to come out in my voice. "Do I have the short hair, the humiliating haircut that you made him wear to school? Only done to embarrass him? To humiliate him? To make him feel worthless?"

I notice my voice rising but I don't try and control the emotion that I am feeling. "Do I have bruises on my arms where you would hit him if he did or didn't do something? How about cuts on my lips and face where you slapped him? Do I have any of these things that make me look like Mark?" I know that I am starting to lose control of my emotions, but I ignore the inner voice telling me to calm down. "Do I look afraid every time I see you? Do I have the fear on my face from hearing your footsteps in the hallway, wondering if you're coming for me? Is that what makes me look like Mark?"

I realize that my voice is getting louder as I am sitting in this empty dining room. I try and talk through clenched teeth as if that might soften the volume. I'm starting to breathe more heavily, even to hyperventilate some. I am staring at this old man, anger welling up in me, and he continues to smile the same empty, meaningless, no feeling smile. The smile of Otter's youth. My jaw is clenched, my muscles are tense. And I stare at this old man.

"Maybe my arm is broken. Do you recognize the cast? The broken arm he got because he had to keep you from hitting his mother. Maybe you recognize him from the times he had to stand in the way of you hitting her. Do you remember that?"

"How about when you kicked him out of the house, his house, and he had nowhere to go? Do I look like that?"

The same look stays on the face of this old man that I am yelling at, almost spitting on, as my words tumble out of my anger. His expression doesn't change. "You look like Mark," he says again.

Then I realize that this is not why I came here. I was unsure of the reason, but this couldn't be it. I look into the face of this old man. This pathetic, dementia-ridden old man. My face softens. My breathing comes back to normal. I feel my jaw unclench. "No, Mr. Otter," I say, my voice barely over a whisper. "I'm his friend, Jake."

The old man looks at me, the same vacant smile on his face. "They have good applesauce here."

Then it hit me. No matter how much you revisit the past, there is nothing new to see.

I sigh as I stand up, a long exhale from deep inside me. I put my hand on his shoulder. "I'm sure they do. Goodbye Mr. Otter." And I take my hand off his shoulder, turn and walk towards the reception area.

Kathy and Amber are still behind the counter. "Thank you for your help," I told them. "This is a nice place." Not entirely the truth, but the staff seemed nice. They seemed caring.

"I'm so glad you were able to visit," Kathy said with a smile. "Willie is such a sweet old man. I don't think he has had a visitor since his wife died."

I took a step closer to the counter. "When did his wife pass away?"

Kathy wrinkled her brow. "Hmmm. Maybe four years ago." She turned to Amber. "When did Willie's wife die, do you remember?"

Amber took a couple of steps closer to where I was standing. "I don't think that I knew her. Maybe it was before I started working here."

"Probably was," Kathy replied. "Anyway. They were the sweetest couple. They would sit next to each other for hours. She would rub his neck and stroke his face. They were quite the lovebirds." She smiled again at the memory. "Did you know his wife? What was her name?"

I was quiet for a second, processing what I just heard. "Linda."

"Yes. That's it. Linda. They were so sweet together." Kathy looked at me. "Did you know them?"

"Yes. It was a long time ago." I turn to walk outside. I stop. "Thank you again for your help," I tell them once more.

"Please come back and see us," Kathy says, once again with the warm smile. "I'm sure Willie would be glad to see you."

I resisted the urge to tell them I would not be returning, but I smile and give a little wave.

I walk back outside and notice that the breeze has picked up. The tree limbs are moving, swaying with the wind. The Adirondack chairs are vacant and I sit down in one of them. I want to cry, to weep, to feel anguish, to mourn. But I can't. There should be enough sadness for me to cry tears that have been held on to for so many years. But I can't. I just feel.....nothing.

I thought about my friend, Mark Otter. And I thought about why I had come to this place, this assisted living center in the hopes of confronting this old man. But mostly I thought about how there, but for the grace of fate, go I. I wondered how different my life might look with this old, abusive man as my father. And how Mark's may have been different with a decent, caring parent. And I thought about who makes those decisions, how the fates work out.

Then it dawned on me....there are no heroes in Mark Otter's story.

I sit there for a while and I lose track of the time. Occasionally, residents and staff wander by me, but no one says a word. I continue to feel nothing, and I sit in a sort of haze.

Eventually I remember that I need to pick up Orson from his doggy daycare. I get out of the chair and turn back and look inside the large windows of Haven of Rest. It is obviously meal time and I can see a number of residents sitting down at the tables, crowding the area where I had just been. I look to see if I can find Otter's dad, but I can't pick him out. Just as well.

There is a Buddhist teaching that says when you get hurt, maybe struck by someone else, that is pain. The strike across your face, it hurts. It aches. That is what pain is. However, there is a second agony. This is your reaction to the strike, your reaction to the pain. The getting angry, the plotting of revenge. Maybe even the traveling hundreds of miles hoping to confront someone over conduct from long ago. This is suffering.

I decide, sitting in an Adirondack chair in front of Haven of Rest Convalescent Center, to suffer no longer.

I walk across the parking lot and settle into the pickup. Then it's back onto the freeway, back to the Valley. I know Orson is waiting for me.

. . .

There was an elderly woman who each day would go down to the stream and collect water. She carried two pots, each hung on ends of a pole stretched across her neck.

One pot was in pristine condition and would easily carry a full load of water. But the other pot had a crack in it and would lose half of its water during the trip back to the elderly woman's home.

This went on for some time until the elderly

woman's daughter confronted her mother for bringing back the half full pot.

"Mother. Why do you waste your energy in filling one of the pots only to lose half of its water on the return trip? You should replace the cracked pot with one without cracks, of which we have plenty."

The elderly woman merely smiled at her daughter. "Have you not noticed the side of the path where the cracked pot leaks its water, that it is full of flowers? I planted them there, knowing that the leaky pot would water them on the return trip home. Then I pick the flowers and decorate my home with them. Without the flaw in the pot, I would not be able to grace my home with such beauty."

The daughter smiled in understanding.

OCTOBER 22

M Y BACK STARTS TO ACHE FROM LEANING AGAINST the same tree for so long. I guess I have been sitting in this position for quite a while, and I can see the sun settling below the trees that are scattered around me at Sunset Hills Cemetery. Orson has been sleeping and he doesn't raise his head as I begin to stir, just opens his eyes to take in what is happening. I notice that the breeze has calmed as the evening is taking hold. I look off in the distance and see that the kids are no longer playing soccer. I must have dozed off.

I get to my feet and start walking about the gravestones once again. Orson rises and follows me and I continue to mentally read off the name of each deceased person from the headstones. Eventually I wind my way to an area that is sectioned off from the rest of the cemetery. This is a rock garden, with beautiful stones arranged in lovely patterns among about a dozen trees, and there are flowers and shrubs in lovely arrangements all around the grounds.

This is a section of the cemetery reserved for the placing of ashes of those who have chosen to be cremated. There is a paved path that narrows its way through the area and it is ringed by a railing with the names of those whose remains are scattered here. I read each one, looking for the plaque with the name Mark Otter. About five years ago, I paid the cemetery to put his name on one of the small plaques on the railing that circled this garden. Though I have never been to this particular cemetery, they were the ones willing to do this over the phone, place the name on a plaque of someone whose remains have yet to be placed.

I eventually find the small plaque, really just a nameplate, along the railing towards the back of the walkway. Mark Floyd Otter. That was all it said, no date of birth, no date of death. Looking at some of the other nameplates I see that some have dates but others don't.

I like the area where this small token of Otter's life is located. It is away from the entrance to the cemetery, and noticeably quiet. The only noise I can hear is the rustling that the trees make when the breeze passes through them.

Next to the Mark Floyd Otter nameplate is another. Leila Louise Hennessy is engraved upon it. It is the name of Otter's birth mother, Linda Otter's sister. I discovered the birth and death dates of Leila many years earlier. Through a family history research website, I found her death notice in a Charlotte, North Carolina newspaper from December 1958.

"Leila Louise Hennessy, 18, died in a motor vehicle accident on December 2. She is survived by her parents, Floyd and May Linda Hennessy, a sister, Linda Lynn Hennessy, and a son, Mark Floyd Hennessy. No services are planned."

Like her son Mark's nameplate, I decided against putting any dates on it. Even though there were no ashes scattered in the memorial for her, I thought it good to have her name said once more.

Orson comes up alongside me, and he senses the change in my mood. It has become more reverent, more solemn, and he sits for a second, then settles down on the path, facing the area where ashes are scattered. He lays his ears back, feeling the seriousness of the moment. It's as if he knows why we are here.

Cemeteries are for those still living. The dead are elsewhere.

I open the backpack I carried into the cemetery and pull out the purple hydrangea that had been placed on the windshield of my pickup a couple of days ago. It has wilted a bit, but still has its color. I place it on Otter's nameplate. "Here. I'm giving this back to you," I say to no one in particular.

I reach into my backpack again and pull out The Repository. It has only about 1/4 the ashes as when I started, and I reflected on the many places of the last two weeks where I had left pieces of my friend. "I hope you like where you've been placed," I say over the edge of the railing, touching the nameplate. Then I sprinkle some of the dust into the garden, tossing it away from the path and over the railing, over the nameplate bearing his name.

I save about 1/2 of what is left and I close up The Repository and put it back into my backpack. I then pull out a copy of the LA Times, dated about two years ago and I flip through the pages until I find the page I'm looking for. I had called the LA Times and asked them to run this obituary. They gave me some push back, saying it was too far in the past, but I finally was able to persuade them that everyone needs an obituary, everyone needs their life recognized, and that it was merely an oversight that Otter didn't have one. That explanation plus $350 apparently sealed the deal.

I read to the souls that have been scattered here.

"Mark Floyd Otter. Born November 12, 1958. Died May 3, 1981. Mark, who went by his last name Otter to his friends, died suddenly, leaving a void to those that knew him. He was a kind and gentle soul, always concerned about others who were less fortunate than he. He was funny, always with a joke, making his friends laugh. He was smart, especially in Mathematics. He was especially skilled in the martial arts, having obtained the rank of black belt in Tae Kwon Do.

Mark grew up in a physically and emotionally abusive home. He carried these scars quietly. He had family members who knew this. He had teachers who knew this. He had friends who knew this. He had friend's parents who knew this. Still, nothing was done. And that is the tragedy with his death.

Mark Otter liked to write poetry. He said that it helped him process life. This is one of the last poems he wrote:

THE SOURCE
by Mark Otter

I see my body in the mirror.
Skin stretched over bones.
The house of a heart.
Heart and bones.
This body limits me.
Keeps me from being me.
This body isn't me.

Me is a me without the boundaries
Of skin and bones.
Me has never been born
And will never die.
Before this time on earth, I was free.
Birth was just a door I walked through.
It will be the same with death.

Did you get out of life what you put into it?
Did you spend your life avoiding
Barren relationships and
Empty graves?

Truth gets harder to find, maybe
I don't have the truth in me.
Or me in the truth.
Searching for a place to fit in.

So sing with me
And hold my hand.
Like a river beginning its journey to the sea
We will meet again
At the source.

If you witness or suspect abuse, please call someone in authority, like the police. You can usually do it anonymously. You can also call the domestic abuse hotline at 1-800-799-SAFE (7233).

Mark is survived by his friends."

I let these words settle over this sacred ground. I could feel the sanctity of this place, the place with dozens of names on dozens of nameplates, perhaps hearing their names that last time. I know there are the spirits of many in and about the rocks and trees and flowers and shrubs.

I touch Otter's name plate one last time, then turn away and Orson and I finish the walk around the loop circling this area of the cemetery. I read some of the nameplates that are on the railing, saying them aloud to Orson as he walks slowly behind me. A few times he pauses to take in some of the many smells that must have been wafting on the breeze. I noticed that flowers have been thrown over the railing into the garden, and I knew that I wasn't the only visitor that this area had seen lately. I was glad for that.

I reflected on the Mexican holiday Dia de Los Muertos, celebrated as a time for friends and relatives of the deceased to gather together to celebrate and pray for friends and family members who have passed on. The tradition is set with the belief that one never really dies until their name is spoken for the last time. I worry about what happens when I am no longer on this earth. Will I be the last person to speak my friend's name?

I stop and say his name aloud, aloud to all of the souls who are at rest here. "Mark Otter." I let that settle in the wind and then I say it again. "Mark Otter." I stand, letting the utter silence engulf me, the only sound the wind passing through leaves, seeming to have a message for me. The wind whispers a message of tranquility and I feel at peace. It's as if all my ghosts up and died. Right here at Sunset Hills Cemetery.

I look down at Orson who is now sitting, listening to all of the sounds that move around us. He looks up at me and as he catches my eye, he wags his tail. I reach down and scratch his ears. I think he is telling me that it is time to go.

We walk slowly out of this sacred area into the rest of the cemetery, and then straight down the path to the parking lot. I open the tailgate and get Orson's food and sprinkle it into his dinner dish, and while he is eating, I pour him a bowlful of water. I sit on the tailgate as he finishes. I know this will be my last time in this place, or Southern California for that matter. I have no reason to come back.

When Orson finishes, I lift him into the back seat, just as I had when we started this trip together. He settles into the seat and stretches out, preparing to nap. He is tired from his busy day making friends at the doggy daycare.

I'm tired too. It has been a long day. So I gather up what I need.

Peace of mind for this battered soul.

A hopeful heart for times to come.

A lullaby to quiet my mind at night.

A light to guide my footsteps in the darkness.

I start the engine and sit quietly for a few minutes in the parking lot, watching a gentle breeze move the tree limbs back and forth. I hear Orson breathing heavily, already asleep. I put the truck in gear and pull out of the parking lot. It was time to go home.

EPILOGUE

AUTUMN HAS RETURNED AGAIN TO MY MOUNTAIN home in Montana. It's my favorite time of year, the leaves turning beautiful colors of red and orange. The temperature begins to drop quickly as night comes wandering in at the end of each day. I love the sunlight on the mountains as it exits, leaving the dark to settle in. I revel in the quiet of the evenings.

A year has passed since I left and returned on my quest to find some meaning in the death of my friend, Mark Otter. I am at peace with my journey.

During the past year, Jenna had Matt build a small studio home in their backyard and they moved Mom into it, giving her a place to peacefully live out her remaining years. Susan and I have already driven to Corvallis twice for a visit and I have gone once on my own. Mom is happy there and I'm glad that she is safe and well cared for.

I officially retired from my research position at Montana State and I have started trying to publish some of my research, then stopped, then started again, papers detailing some of my projects. I'm not sure if and when I will finish writing them, but I enjoy the process of putting ideas onto paper. It wiles away my time.

Susan says she is retired, but she wanders into the physical therapy clinic on occasion and helps out. She continues to be my amazing companion and confidant, keeper of my soul. She is my best friend. She grounds me.

I planted several hydrangea bushes along the property line that borders the back edge of my home. I used the rest of the contents of The Repository in planting them. They flower beautifully, an array of blues and purples and pinks. I can see them from my back deck. I think of Otter whenever I sit out on the deck. Wherever he is, I hope he is at peace. I think he is. He no longer visits me in my dreams.

I started building a writing/art studio in the back yard, a log cabin of sorts where I can write and read and meditate. This is also a place where Susan can work on her pottery, a passion of hers. I enjoy the physical labor of the work and it is a practice of mindfulness to live in the present moment as I construct the small building. Jenna and Matt and Mom came out and visited over the summer and Matt gave me some of his expertise. I'm about three quarters done. I'm not sure when I'll be finished, but the roof is on and the walls are up so I don't have to worry about the upcoming snows getting inside.

Orson is aging gracefully, more gracefully than I am. He is certainly feeling his age and his walks are getting shorter and shorter. He will be breaking my heart soon, when he heads for his next stage of being. Sitting alone with Orson by my side during my travels was a step towards heaven. He would sit without jealousy or ego, sensing the solemnity of the moment, always at peace with himself. If I could be half the person Orson is I would be twice the human I am.

I try and reflect on what I learned from my travels of a year ago. My Buddhist teachings tell me that the source of most unhappiness is in the having of expectations. This belief was cemented on the trip. Still, I feel at peace. At the very least, my friend Otter needed to have his name spoken one more time.

It is a truth of life that one needs to forgive oneself to find peace. I'm still trying to figure out this whole forgiveness thing. Sometimes it's hard to keep track of all of one's sins.

I often reflect back to a book written by the Benedictine nun and theologian Joan Chittister, *The Gift of Years: Growing Older Gracefully.* She talks about the compulsion to look back, to explain yourself to others about why you did or didn't do something, that this compulsion is one of the most direct roads to depression. These thoughts threaten the quality of the time that we bring to the present.

I understand these words now.

Susan often tells me this story and I will leave it here.

There are two friends who are farmers that live next door to each other. One day they read about the Lost City of Gold. This excites them greatly, so they sell all of their possessions and set off in search for this lost city. They go on a quest to find this fabled city of wealth and prosperity. They spend one year in a fruitless search. Soon two years pass, and then two become five and they continue to search. Soon ten years have passed with no finding of the Lost City of Gold.

One day, they climb over a large mountain and looking down the other side, they see this beautiful city, nestled in a lovely valley, one that is glowing in the sunlight. They have found it! The Lost City of Gold!

One friend spurs his donkey forward and he begins to gallop toward the beautiful city. He can hardly believe his good fortune. His mind is full of possibilities as he contemplates his soon found wealth. As he travels down the mountain, he turns and sees that his friend is far behind. He stops and waves at his friend and encourages him to hurry. But the friend continues on his donkey at a leisurely pace.

Frustrated, the first friend turns his donkey around and gallops back towards his slow-paced companion. When he reaches him he says, "Hurry! We are almost there! The Lost City of Gold is within our reach! Let's go!"

The slow-moving friend pauses. He looks at his good friend and says, "It's good here too."

Yes. It's good here too.

Tom Smyly

ACKNOWLEDGEMENTS

Writing a novel is certainly a labor of love, and while it requires many hours of solitude, it is not written alone.

I would like to thank the wonderful and patient people at Luminare Press. Their help and guidance is appreciated and they have a wealth of knowledge that can be tapped into.

I also thank so many family and friends who motivated me and helped me shape characters, most of the time unknowingly so.

Most of all, I would like to acknowledge my editor, my wife, and my best friend, Janet Green. Without her lovingly going over every page, every word, gently making corrections and suggestions where needed, this work would not have come about. She grounded me when needed and urged me onward during the difficult times. I thank her for her love and guidance.

Made in the USA
Coppell, TX
26 March 2022

75587700R00260